Gamma Ten

Disclaimer

The events and characters described in this story are fictitious. Any resemblance to actual persons, living or dead, is unintentional and entirely coincidental. Any representation of any government or private organisations or businesses portrayed in this story is purely fictional. This story is not meant to cast aspersion upon any current or past branch of any government. Many of the locations and facilities described in this story do exist, however.

Gamma Ten

Acknowledgments

Jacket design courtesy of David Smith at 49th Floor Graphic Design, United Kingdom (david@49thfloor.co.uk)

Also by L. Robert Jones

The Starlight Murders

Assault on L

The Perfect Solution

Creating Eric

Newton & Einstein, More Stuff They Didn't Tell You

Chance – A Moment Too Far

Skrog

The Deer Hunt Conspiracy

Tales of Buckwood Mansions

Gamma Ten

Prologue

"How many?" "194 sir, including you and your lot. We're only able to confirm 40,000 worldwide. No one knows for sure anymore." The wind howled outside. It was forty below. "Food, water?" "Maybe enough for sixteen months, if we're careful. That includes the stuff you dropped, when we can get to it." "Hunting party?" "Came back empty handed again. Just nothing out there…" "How 'bout heating, ventilation?" "No worries. It'll all still be running long after we've starved to death." "Radios?" "Both radios died last month. Just got one of them working an hour ago. Lucky you got through. Last message from back home was five weeks ago, sir." "Pearce?" "Yes sir. They weren't exactly sure how many were still there." A long broad tunnel in front of them disappeared into the mountain. "We heard from Alaska every two weeks until mid-September. Most everyone else has gone silent."

The Group Captain tugged at the outside glove on his left hand. Moisture had gotten between the outer and inner gloves when he fell in the snow and had already started to freeze. "How's the visibility out there?" "About three meters if you can keep the blowing snow off your goggles. I could see the main antenna was still up – it may not be for long in this wind. Probably doesn't matter now."

Flight Lieutenant Gibbs stared at the rough hardwood planks that had been pushed into place as a makeshift floor. "Your radio message was a surprise, sir. Last we heard you wouldn't be joining us until summer. Weren't sure you would make it, sir." Group Captain Christopher shook his head. "That was the plan. Plan changed. If anyone had lost their grip on the stainless-steel cable you rigged up around the perimeter, they would be dead by now." "So how will you get back?" "We won't."

The Svalbard Global Seed Vault was completed in 2008 on the Norwegian island of Spitsbergen in the remote Arctic Svalbard archipelago at a cost of 45 million kr (US$8.8 million). It was intended as a secure backup facility for the world's crop diversity.

Gamma Ten

For decades the seed vault provided long-term storage of duplicates of seeds conserved in gene banks around the world to ensure security of the world's food supply against the loss of seeds due to mismanagement, accident, equipment failures, funding cuts, war, sabotage, disease, and natural disasters. By January 2056 it had become one of the last refuges for human survivors on Planet Earth. A few ancillary structures had been built in the preceding decade. There simply wasn't time to put up permanent buildings given the extremely hostile weather conditions ten months out of the year. Atmospheric oxygen levels at Svalbard had dropped to what was typical at the summit of Mont Blanc, the tallest mountain in the Alps.

The Svalbard Global Seed Vault was not designed for human occupancy. It was designed as a vault. As such the contents were intended to remain isolated from the rest of the planet, whether it be viable or catastrophically hostile. Human habitation was never considered. All that changed once the world's population realised it was experiencing a global extinction event. "Evolution can be very cruel sometimes!" Group Captain Christopher could still hear his Queensland University Professor's words even though she had been dead for eighteen years. Her students believed the Professor was referring to the demise of the dinosaurs when a rock the size of a city struck the earth and created the Chicxulub crater just off the coast of the Yucatan peninsula in Mexico. No one could conceive of a rock only centimetres in diameter causing a similar event sixty-six million years later. Indeed, the Professor's words were more prophetic than she could have ever imagined….

Gamma Ten

Chapter 1

"Welcome to the K Area Spent Fuel Storage Basin here at the Savannah River Site. When the Cold War ended and we shutdown the last of the nuclear production reactors at Savannah River in July 1992, the U. S. Department of Energy took avantage of the large unused storage capacity to relocate and house commercial power reactor spent fuel until a more permanent nuclear waste storage strategy could be implemented. That was almost exactly thirty-eight years ago. Unfortunately all this nuclear waste material is still here." Bill motioned the group of twelve citizens from "Leadership Aiken" to follow him into a very large room lit from below by an erie blue glow coming from the crystal clear water beneath them.

"Thanks for arranging a tour for us, Bill. Since you're the boss out here I figured you could get us in to see it." "No problem, Harold. Actually, I only manage the K Area Spent Fuel Storage area. It's a small part of the work that goes on at the site these days." "Yeah, well a lot of us have lived in Aiken for decades without knowing what went on at 'The Bomb Plant'. I guess you don't make bombs out here any more." "We never made bombs here, Harold. We just made the stuff that goes in them." Bill and Harold were on the same committee at church. Harold was one of several people Bill couldn't wait to get away from. At 188 centimetres, Bill was five centimetres taller. Harold was at least 20 kilograms heavier as well. He served as a City Councilman for the city of Aiken, South Carolina. That made his head about twice the size it should be. His favourite topics were himself and politics, in that order. Bill had little patience for political opinions, especially Harold's.

Gamma Ten

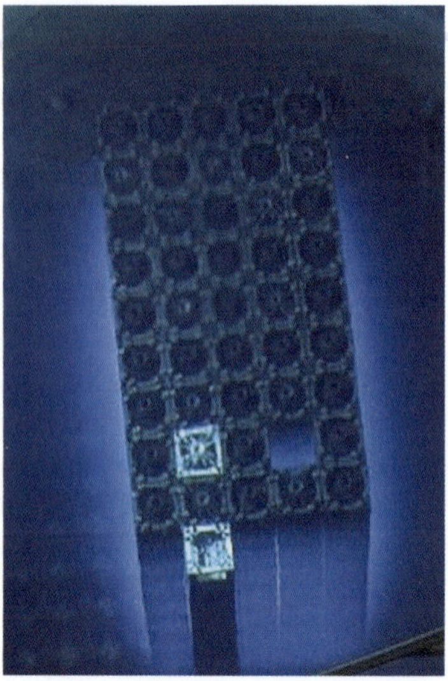

"I brought you something", said Harold in a muffled voice so others couldn't hear. "I know it's small, but you said you wanted to see a piece of meteorite from my collection. The guys at the astronomy club swear it's the real thing – magnetic even." Harold held out a small piece of rock about the size of a 10 cent coin. One side looked like it had gotten very hot. It was heavy as well. "You keep it as long as you like." Bill wondered if that meant it was just a loan, but reached out to take it anyway. Just as he lifted it from Harold's hand, it slipped and fell onto the metal grating, then bounced into the water filled basin below. Both Bill and Harold watched as the meteorite twisted and turned like a flat pebble in a swimming pool until it settled to the bottom next to one of the spent fuel containers thirty-three feet below.

"Oh, sorry", said Bill, as they both leaned forward looking down into the crystal clear water. "How do we get it back", Harold asked with his mouth still hanging open?" "Sorry, we don't", said Bill. "I'm afraid we don't have any tools that can retrieve something that small." Harold stood up abruptly, clearly perturbed that his precious gift was gone forever. "It's OK. I think I can get another one." Bill nodded. He didn't really want a meteorite in the first place. He had only mentioned it during a conversation at church the previous week when Harold wouldn't shut up about his favourite candidate for President. Bill did make note of where the meteorite landed, however. There was no 'procedurally allowed' way of retrieving something that small from the basin floor, but that didn't mean it couldn't be done.

In the water below there were rows and rows of cylindrical shapes in square containers glowing in the most beautiful shade of blue.

Bill explained. “This phenomenon is called Cherenkov radiation, which is essentially a shockwave of light. Radiation slows down as it travels from the spent fuel into water. Water molecules have to absorb the exess energy. The excited electrons in the water molecules then release that energy as light, which we see as a blue glow. It gives the entire spent fuel basin an almost supernatural feeling.” One lady in the tour group whispered to her friend, “The next car I buy’s going to be that colour!”.

Bill spent most of his time managing and scheduling a crew of fifteen operators, covering three 8-hour shifts. He still managed a free hour on occasion to spend some ‘hands on’ time with the tools of the trade. For the spent fuel storage basin the tool of choice was something called “Peter’s Tongs”. Anyone on his crew would readily admit Bill was as skilled at using Peter’s Tongs as any of them, save one. Picking up something next to one of the spent fuel containers as small as a 10 cent piece would be quite difficult. He couldn’t resist the challenge. A few ‘unathorized attachments’ did exist that made the job possible. Bill kept one pair of these in the tall metal cabinet in his office. They were throughly checked for radioative contamination after every use of course.

The best time to try was just after shift change as the evening shift was coming on. Everyone would be busy for half an hour getting turnover from the day crew that was just finishing. Bill carried the special nibs for the Peter’s Tongs in a canvass bag as he entered the basin area for the fourth time that day. The area where he dropped the meteorite was easily seen by anyone passing by. Not that it mattered. No one was going to ask him what he was doing. He could just say he was ‘practicing’. They all worked for him so no one was likely to pursue the matter. Still, it might be embarrassing if he was seen.

Peters Tongs were named after a small local metal shop owner in the Aiken area who saw a business opportunity when the Savannah River Plant was first built in the early 1950’s. He remained the only supplier of this indepensible tool for forty years. It was a simple thing – a 10.7 meter long aluminum pole with gripper jaws on the bottom end and a pistol grip at the top end that actuated the jaws via a long cable inside the pole. Bill carefully lifted the lower end of the tongs onto the work bench so he could attach the special nibs. The permanent jaws were too large to grasp something as small as the meteorite. Smaller nibs attached to the jaws using two small bolts with lock washers on each jaw.

Bill's struggle to get the nut started on each of the bolts was an unwanted reminder of the early onset of arthritus in several fingers on each hand. Such things were to be expected as a man grew older, but suffering arthritis while still several months from his fortieth birthday seemed rudely unfair. Shouldn't he be allowed a few more years with full faculties? Bill had other things to worry about. His twin daughters would be starting college in the fall, putting a strain on the household budget. Bill's dark brown hair, matching oversized eyebrows and mustache made him appear at least five years younger. There were those who believed his position as manager of the K Basin should have gone to someone older with more experience. A slender frame and above aveage height added to his youthful appearance. It was all a deception in his mind. He often felt ten years older than his age. Cross country running was always Bill's favourite physical activity, although he had to admit it was getting more difficult with each passing year. Having spent sixteen years at Savannah River Site, Bill had no other frame of reference in his professional life. He wondered on occasion if he had made the right career choice.

The hardest part physically for anyone working in the K Basin was dragging a 10 meter long aluminum pole over to the edge of the pool, then through an opening in the floor grating before sliding the length of the pole down into the water. All that had to be done without touching any of the clusters of spent fuel elements arranged in carefully ordered rows below. It was normally a two-man job, but Bill was confident he could manage it on his own. He had done so before on several occasions. It took a few more minutes to move the gripper over the location of the meteorite. Most of the spent fuel in that area of the basin had been out of the reactor for less than a year. That meant the blue glow was bright enough to clearly see the meteorite lying at the bottom next to the square container.

His first attempt missed the meteorite entirely. "'Swing and a miss' as they say in baseball'", he heard himself say out loud to no one. His words echoed off the one meter thick reinforced concrete walls and ceiling that enclosed the storage basin. Another attempt grasped the meteorite loosely but failed to hold on. The small piece of rock gently fell ten centimeters back to the bottom of the basin. The third attempt was more successful. Raising the Peters Tongs slowly upward, Bill held his breath while watching the radiation monitors located around the room. There was no reason to suspect the meteorite was contaminated, as the 300,000 liters of continuously filtered water in the basin was pure enough to drink. Half the length of the Peter's tongs was now out of the water when the meteorite suddenly jarred loose and fell again. Worse, it found its way among two of the spent fuel elements and lodged itself between them.

With the object to be retrieved wedged between fuel elements and under ten meters of water, Bill immediately realized the futility of continuing. It took another ten minutes to raise the Peter's Tongs completely out of the water. His failiure had no witnesses, but it was a failure nonetheless. Perhaps when that cluster of spent fuel elements was moved to another part of the basin the meteorite would be dislodged and fall onto the floor again. Then he could make another attempt. Such things happened on a frequency of years or longer. Bill's last thought about the matter was to simply dimiss the entire incident. Only he and Harold knew about the meteorite being down there, and Harold wouldn't remember any of it in a day or two.

Three months passed without Bill giving the lost meteorite another thought. Both daughters had just started college, each wanting to go to a different school, of course. The oldest daughter, by four minutes, insisted on going to University of Tennessee in Knoxville. She had done quite well on her entrance exams and was considering joining a sorority. Arlene thought Claire should wait until her sophomore year for such things. Diane decided to go to Auburn University in Alabama. Being an 'out of state' school, the cost was considerably higher. There was no talking her out of it, however. Her best friend was going to Auburn. That settled the matter.

Gamma Ten

Both parents found twin daughters quite a challenge. At the ripe old age of 19 they were full of confidence they could handle anything the world, and their parents, could throw at them. Brunette and 183 centimetres tall, both had trouble finding young men who wanted to dance with them. "Your height gives you an advantage in many things", Arlene kept reminding them. Neither of them saw it that way. Clothes were another problem. The choices for tall young women were limited. Arlene made some of their dresses for them. She was brunette as well, although nearly five centimetres shorter. Arlene was considered by most of her friends an over achiever. She was an excellent cook. She was also very active in the church, often baking cakes for their social gatherings. Both Bill and Arlene were active members of the church bridge club. Bill had little patience for most games, but found bridge an exception. Perhaps it was the social aspect of it that intreged him. Neither Bill nor Arlene ever missed their bridge night at the church every other Tuesday evening.

Something odd was happening in the K Area storage basin. Several of the crew had reported a grey film on the outside of several spent fuel elements. Bill finally found a few minutes to have a look for himself. The area of concern brought the lost meteorite to mind. He was fairly certain the two fuel elements in question were where the meteorite was last seen. Surely it was only a coinidence. No one else was aware of the meteorite's location in any event. "Let's get some samples of this film on the side of these elements, just in case it's some sort of corrosion we haven't seen before." Carl and Paulette nodded.

The K Basin crew included fifteen experienced spent fuel handlers, some with experience at other locations prior to coming to Savannah River Site. All had demonstrated their expertise at manuvering highly radioactive items of various shapes located under a mimimum of three meters of water, which provided both radiaton shielding and natural convection cooling. Zircoloy cladding on elements that had been out of a reactor for less than a year could melt from fission product heating if not cooled by the surrounding water.

Gamma Ten

Most operations in the K Basin were conducted during the 7:45 am to 4:15 pm day shift, but there was a crew of three on the 4:00 pm to midnight shift and another crew of three on the midnight to 8:00 am shift to monitor the conditions in the storage basin and deal with any unexpected occurrences. That might include failure of a pump or other piece of equipment, response to alarms, collecting daily water samples, etc. Members of the basin crew rotated in a counter circadian order, i.e., from day shift to night shift to evening shift, with several days off in between.

The sort of sample Bill had requested wasn't easily obtained. Scraping the surface of a spent fuel assembly had to be done with care. If the cladding happened to be thin in that area, any sort of scraping tool could penetrate and release fission products into the basin water. Very small amounts of radioactive contamination in the basin water were tolerable and constantly being filtered out. A large release of fission products could result in radiation levels that would greatly complicate operations in the area. If radiation levels were high enough the entire storage basin area could become off limits to all personnel until the levels were reduced.

Mary Anne's prowess with underwater tools was nothing less than extraordinary. It was said she could thread a needle under 9.1 meters of water if the job called for it. Such comments made her laugh, but she didn't deny it might be possible. Spent fuel elements were suspended about 40 centimetres above the basin floor. Only two of them had the dark grey coating of interest. The cylindrical shape added an extra layer of difficulty. Bill watched as Mary Anne carefully positioned the special scraping tool closer and closer to the cladding on one of the elements. Another technician had already positioned a catch pan beneath the assembly and 30 cm off the basin floor to collect any sample material scraped off the surface. Once contact was made only a slight up and down motion was enough to dislodge a sufficient sample which then fell onto the collection pan. The second technician immediately closed the lid on the collection pan securing the sample.

"Well done Mary Anne!" She acknowledged Bill's compliment with a slight bow. "Any other easy jobs you need done, sir?"

"Can't think of any at the moment." A Health Protection (HP) technician arrived just as Mary Anne was moving toward the doorway. Bill pointed toward the area where the sample collection pan would be raised to the surface. As it emerged from the water the HP technician signalled with a 'thumbs up'. The sample was free of radioactive contamination and could be safely packaged and sent off to the Savannah River National Laboratory for analysis.

"It's inorganic, although the crystalline structure is quite unusual. Not like anything I've seen before. Silicon and carbon are the only two chemical elements that can bond with themselves to make long chains. All life on this planet is based on carbon for that reason. In theory silicon can do the same thing, but only at very high temperatures. Silicon carbide, like this sample, is commonly used in industry. It makes a very good abrasive and is practically indestructible. Carbon makes up less than 0.1% of the earth's crust, while silicon makes up more than 27%, second only to oxygen in abundance. Think of all the sand on all the beaches in the world. It's literally everywhere. Now it appears they've got some SiC on their spent fuel elements in K Basin. Doesn't sound like anything to worry about." Aaron's boss nodded. It didn't necessarily mean he agreed with everything Aaron just said.

Bryan couldn't argue with the chemistry. Aaron had three degrees in chemistry, one from MIT and two from Caltech. Bryan's degree was in mechanical engineering. His disagreement was with the premise that silicon, like carbon, could form some sort of 'life form'. The idea was clearly preposterous! "Why do you think they sent us this sample, Aaron?" "Beats me, Bryan. Other than an odd crystalline structure, it's quite ordinary. I wouldn't have even looked at the structure but for the colour. It should be brown, not grey." "OK, but we must put something in the report. Stick some of this stuff in a beaker of water with a strip of Zircoloy cladding and leave it for a few months, like in the K Basin." Aaron frowned. "Humour me, OK?" Aaron shrugged. "What a pointless exercise", he mumbled as his boss left the room.

Gamma Ten

It was two weeks before Aaron found time to do anything at all with the SiC sample from K Basin. As he held the sample

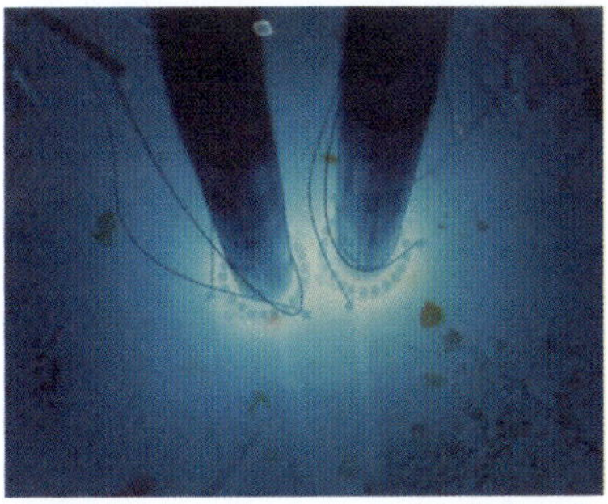

container in his hand, he suddenly had a better idea. A beaker of water wouldn't simulate all the conditions in the K Basin. However, there was an old facility in a sheet metal building at the rear of the Savannah River National Laboratory (SRNL) complex. It was built in 1970 and used to expose equipment to high levels of gamma radiation [1]. This facility contained highly radioactive cobalt with a half-life of about five years. The cobalt source was at the bottom of a water filled pit about eight meters deep. A quick calculation proved that even after six decades this source could still provide sufficient gamma radiation to simulate conditions near the spent fuel elements in the K Basin. Aaron obtained permission to use this ^{60}Co facility, found a suitable container for the sample, and lowered it into the intense gamma radiation field along with a strip of zircoloy cladding like that used on reactor fuel elements. He made a note on his calendar to remove the sample and re-examine it in one month's time.

Two months passed before Bill called to ask about the sample he had sent in for analysis. There were now several more spent fuel elements in K Basin with the strange dark grey film on them. The request made its way to Aaron's desk, which reminded him he had forgotten to take the sample out of the radiation facility in that old metal shed behind the main laboratory building.

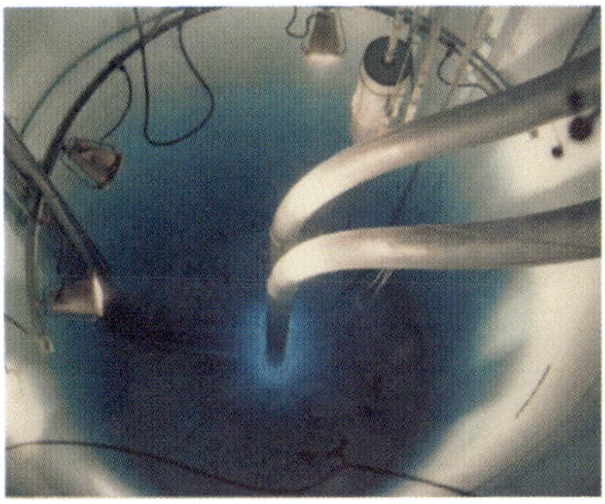

As the sample container was being raised in the tube that led up from the cluster of ^{60} Co slugs it became stuck in the S-bend and would not budge. "I don't understand how it could be stuck", remarked Aaron. "It went down through the tube easily two months ago." A bit of additional force was applied, and the container finally appeared at the top of the tube.

Health Protection had been summoned to check the container for contamination but there was none. The container was intact but noticeably swollen beyond its original size. "No wonder it got stuck. It's gone egg shaped", replied the same technician who had assisted Aaron two months earlier. "It can't be under pressure", Aaron remarked. "It's thoroughly vented. I can smell the nitrous oxide created by the gamma radiation field down there." After being surveyed and cleared by Health Protection, the container was removed to Aaron's lab. It had to be cut open because of the deformation. Aaron gasped when he first viewed the contents. The piece of zircoloy was partially encased in a porous material resembling a dark grey fungus. The original sample from the K Basis had expanded to fill the entire container.

Aaron was quickly on the phone with his boss. "It's inorganic…. No, no. I'm telling you it is not organic but still able to incorporate zirconium and other elements into its structure… It's not impossible. Come see for yourself. The crystalline structure is completely symmetrical, like I've never seen before…" "I'm on my way", Bryan replied, still quite sceptical of Aaron's observations.

Aaron's results attracted other chemists interested in this material's strange behaviour. "It could incorporate other chemical elements into its structure, yes?" "Yes, Hans. I think it could", Aaron replied. "What if it could incorporate additional carbon and silicon molecules. Could it self-replicate?" "We are looking at that", Bryan replied, suddenly siding with his chief chemist instead of opposing him. Aaron gave Bryan a concerned look. "How could something that is clearly inorganic grow", asked another? "It can't 'grow' in the biological sense. But if it can self-replicate it would increase its size." "How big could it get?" "Impossible to guess at the moment. But it doesn't replicate in the absence of a strong radiation environment." "But it does in the environment around the spent fuel elements in the K Basin…" "Well, yes."

Aaron realized it would be weeks before he could publish his report, and probably another week before it would reach Bill in K Basin through the plant mail. He and Bryan decided to give Bill a call. "You say it isn't growing?" "Not in a biological sense, no." "OK, well it has spread to six more spent fuel elements. All six of them have that gray film on them and it seems to be getting thicker. It sure looks like it's growing to me", Bill replied in a less than polite tone. "Could we agree that it's spreading?" "It sounds like it, yes", said Bryan. "So what can I do to stop it from 'spreading' then?" Aaron could sense Bill's frustration. "We're working on it", he replied. "Well you better work on it a bit faster before the whole damn basin is covered in it." Bill hung up abruptly.

What Bill hadn't told them was that radioactivity in the basin had been increasing slowly for the past three weeks. Fission products were leaking out of at least one fuel element, maybe several. He suspected the ones with the grey fungus on them were responsible. He might soon be forced to move these elements into a separate container so that they could be isolated from the basin water system. "Suppose that doesn't contain the problem", he asked himself out loud? "What then??"

----

[1] Richland, WA - Proceedings of the Eleventh AEC Air Cleaning Conference (CONF 700816), Richland, WA, August 1970, Vol. 2, pages 526-538

Oak Ridge, TN - Proceedings of the Twelfth AEC Air Cleaning Conference (CONF 720823), Oak Ridge, TN, August 1972, Vol. 2, pages 655-676

San Francisco, CA. - Proceedings of the Thirteenth AEC Air Cleaning Conference (CONF 740807), San Francisco, CA, August 1974, Vol. 1, pages 565-583.

Chapter 2

The Savannah River Site consisted of 803 square kilometres of federally owned property in southwestern South Carolina, bordering the Savannah River for about 27 kilometres. On the opposite side of the river were several communities in the state of Georgia. Augusta was the largest of these, with a population well over 100,000, about thirty-two kilometres to the northwest of the site. The United States Department of Energy (DOE) was responsible for five decommissioned nuclear production reactors, two chemical separations areas, waste processing, storage and disposal facilities, and several other support facilities on the property. Access to the property and the facilities on it was strictly controlled. A majority of the employees had to maintain a government security clearance in order to work there.

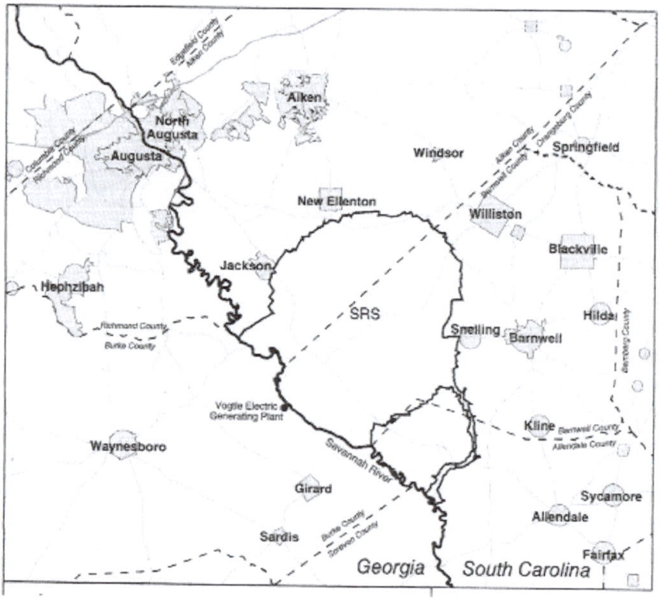

Most of the property outside the boundary of the site was privately owned farmland. There were several small communities surrounding the site as well. K Area Spent Fuel Storage Basin was one of two production reactor facilities that had been converted into nuclear waste storage sites after all the reactors were shut down in the 1990's.

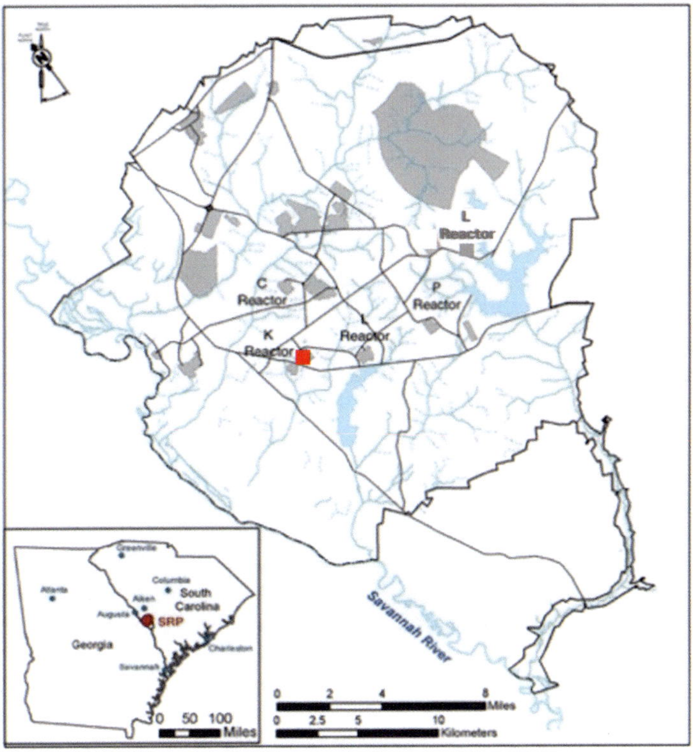

Gamma Ten

Bryan and Aaron were among the "elite", as those who worked at other facilities across the Savannah River Site liked to refer to them. On some occassions they were simply referred to as "the lab people". Either way, questions posed to the Savannah River National Laboratory (SRNL) were seldom answered quickly.

SRNL was originally a support organization charged with providing technical solutions to the myriad of problems associated with producing plutonium and tritium in heavy water moderated nuclear reactors. This was 'cutting edge' science in the 1950's and 1960's. When the Savannah River Laboratory became a "National Laboratory" in May 2004 it was charged with serving the entire Department of Energy Nuclear Complex. Local requests for assistance had to compete with national priorities. Bill's impatience was justified. He had learned bureaucracy makes the wheels of science turn slowly.

Aaron and Bryan often disagreed. Bryan was a firm believer in 'appearance based research'. That meant giving your superiors data that would support their prefered conclusions. Aaron believed you had to go where the data took you. If that data disagreed with what your superiors – Bryan in this case – wanted, then so be it. Bryan liked to give the appearance of being knowledgible about what went on in Aaron's laboratory, while having very little interest in any of it. Not as tall as any of the researchers he managed, each of them realized Bryan's behavior was influenced by a need to compensate for a lack of physical stature.

At 175 centimetres, Aaron was also below average height. Even so he was still 5 centimetres taller than his boss. Most thought Aaron resembled a once famous actor named Clark Gable. At 44 he was already beginning to grey a bit around the temples. His wife Geraldine thought it gave him 'character'. Aaron could boast one degree in chemistry from Massichuttites Institute of

Technology (MIT) and two more from Caltech in Los Angeles. He had also served as head of the Parish Council at the Catholic Church for the past two years.

Aaron's area of expertise was organic chemistry associated with nuclear waste. With nearly sixteen years of experience in analysing materials and solving problems unique to operations at the Savannah River Site, he felt he needed help with this one. The sample from K Basin was initially thought to be some sort of organic material that thrived in a high radiation environment, hence it was sent to Aaron's attention. Although it contained carbon, there was nothing organic about the sample he had examined. The collective opinion of half a dozen of Aaron's coworkers was that the time had come to call in experts in the inorganic field, especially any with unique knowledge of silicon and carbon compounds.

Geraldine turned and crossed the spacious living room to reach the land line phone on the small walnut drum table in the far corner. A large blonde upholstered couch and chair to match impeded her progress. Once past the couch the double bookcase was the next to get in her way. She was reminded of the reason that phone stayed in the hallway for so many years. She had insisted on keeping it, even though everyone in their social group had gotten rid of theirs decades ago. "Put it in the corner out of the way if you must keep it", Aaron had conceded. Geraldine was trying to think who could possibly have their land line phone number. She recalled her parents once had a paper phone book about five centimetres thick containing phone numbers for every household in the town. Surely no one still had anything like that.

"Who could be calling at this hour", she asked to an empty room. Aaron was already upstairs getting ready for bed. Geraldine had been right behind him at the bottom of the stairs. "Hello…. Yes, just a moment." Geraldine yelled up the staircase. "It's for you, dear. Someone from Caltech…". Geraldine had put up with Aaron's ways for 24 years. They had married while both were still in college. Their son Leonard was born soon after. Aaron's professional life had taken its toll on all of them. It took nearly five years in Los Angeles for Aaron to finish two additional degrees. Geraldine practically raised Leonard by herself during that time. Apparently, the people they met in Pasadena had decided to pursue him even to the opposite side of the country.

Geraldine's passion was gardening. The Catholic Church in Aiken had a very active gardening group, which Geraldine had selfishly chaired for nearly three years. There were those who felt she should let someone else take over. Being a redhead with a fiery temper, Geraldine forcefully disagreed. She did accept that it was someone else's turn to lead. She just wasn't quite ready to take a back seat. Her fair complexion did restrict her time in her own garden. Two skin cancers had been surgically removed in the past year. Perhaps a climate where the sun wasn't so bright would have suited her better. Geraldine saw little chance of that with Aaron's career at the Savannah River National Laboratory going so well.

Aaron had ignored the call. He really couldn't be bothered to go back downstairs at this late hour. He hurried out of the bathroom in only the bottom half of his pyjamas. Halfway down the stairs he realized he still had a toothbrush in his mouth. Running down the stairs with a toothbrush in your mouth wasn't a good idea. "Good afternoon, Aaron. It's Dr Schareshiem at the California Institute of Technology in Pasadena. I got your number off the Internet. Just read your message. I understand you've got some silicon carbide that's misbehaving?" Aaron cleared his throat, swallowing a bit of toothpaste in the process. "Yes sir. I… I had no idea someone with your reputation would be at all interested." "Actually, I'm more than interested. I'll be on the first flight into Augusta tomorrow if you'll have me." Aaron couldn't believe what he was hearing. "Yes sir, we'll get everything ready for you. You'll probably want to visit the K Basin and see for yourself." "I will indeed. See you tomorrow." "Yes sir. Good night, sir." Geraldine was standing in the bedroom doorway. "You look like a five-year-old on Christmas morning." "I am and it is", Aaron replied!

Bill was quite unaccustomed to having any of the 'lab people' visit his facility. "Was it something I said", he asked with a wry smile? Aaron and Bryan both frowned, missing the joke. Bryan wasn't going to miss the chance to rub elbows with one of the world's experts in the field of silicon compounds and structures. Aaron was more interested in learning some new chemistry. Bill, Aaron and Dr. Schareshiem walked around the basin to get several views of the area where the dark grey material had formed on the outside of the spent fuel elements. There were signs of it on nine fuel elements. Aaron invited Bill to accompany them back to the lab to examine the crystalline structure of the sample that had been irradiated in the ^{60}Co facility.

Dr Schareshiem stepped back from the microscope, frozen in thought and speechless for nearly a minute. "I theorized this reaction with zirconium almost four years ago. I never expected to see it! What exposure?" Aaron looked embarrassed. "I forgot it was in the ^{60}Co facility. I meant to take it out after a month but left it in for two. Total exposure was 150,000 sieverts." Dr Schareshiem shook his head. "Incredible! This reaction should have required a temperature of at least 2,000 degrees Celsius [2]."

"There is a lower temperature process for creating complex silicon carbide (SiC) architectures used in optical, electronic, and mechanical applications. This process allows three-dimensional SiC nanoscale architectures to self-assemble into a DNA-like structure, followed by subsequent conversion into silicon carbide using a lower temperature pathway (<700 degrees Celsius) via magnesium reduction [3]." Aaron smiled, pretending to agree.

"Obviously, it didn't get up to 700 degrees Celsius or it would have boiled the water in proximity to the cobalt source. The intense gamma radiation must have provided the energy necessary to catalyse the reaction without the high temperature. That must be what is happening in the storage basin." Bill was suddenly concerned. "It's chemically bonding to the cladding on the spent fuel elements, isn't it?" Dr. Schareshiem frowned. "Probably." Bill sat down on one of the old wooden lab stools and stared at the floor. He was looking for something soft to lean against as the lab stools had no backs on them. The solid granite bench tops were hard and cold. Bill wondered what sort of 'things' might have been sitting on them. The thin cotton lab coats they were all wearing seemed little protection against whatever might be on those countertops. He finally decided it would be better if he didn't lean on or even touch anything in the room.

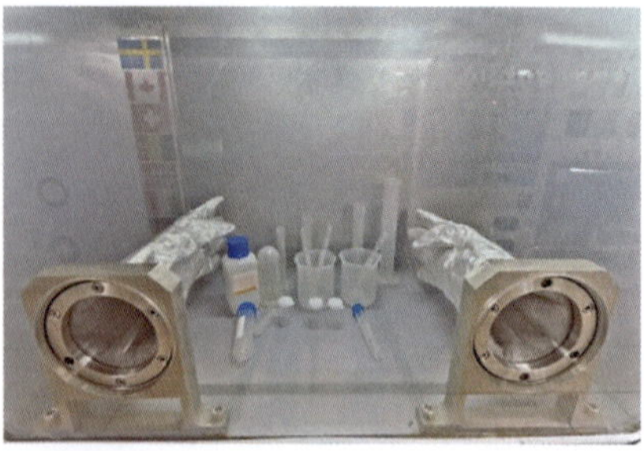

Aaron's lab was the third large room of five on C-Wing of the main Savannah River National Laboratory building. Each room could be entered from either of two parallel hallways, ensuring safe egress in the event of problem. Glove boxes and laboratory hoods, kept under negative pressure ensured that any release of airborne radioactive contamination would be captured on the building's filtration system and not released into the room. Lab coats were worn by anyone entering the room as a precaution. Aaron failed to mention that all the granite lab benches were cleaned daily.

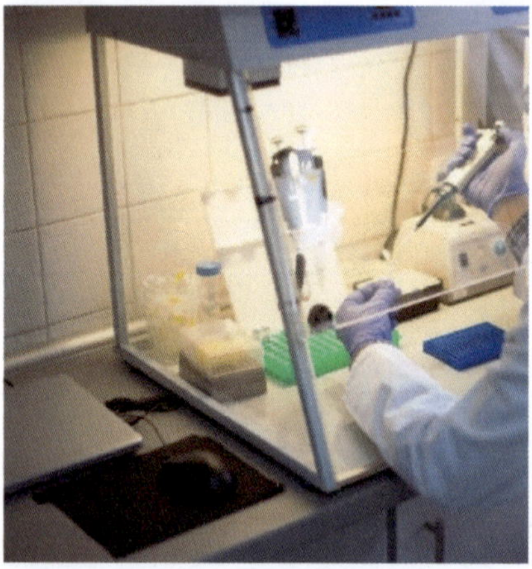

"What kind of engineer", asked Schareshiem? "Electrical", Bill replied, wondering if the good doctor would take that as an admission of mental deficiency. "Hmmm… OK, some basic chemistry. Carbon and silicon both have a primary valence of four. That means they can form compounds with themselves – chains of atoms. In the case of carbon those chains can be very long indeed. Think DNA. That's the stuff of life. Silicon can do the same thing, but it takes very high temperatures, far too high for any form of life to exist based on silicon. It's very stable at lower temperatures like your storage basin. Silicon has other problems too, but we won't go into that. Silicon and carbon can form a compound called silicon carbide. Silicon carbide is almost indestructible."

Gamma Ten

Dr Schareshiem began drawing shapes on the white board in Aaron's office. "Silicon carbide can form various crystalline structures, including cubic, hexagonal, and rhombohedral [4]

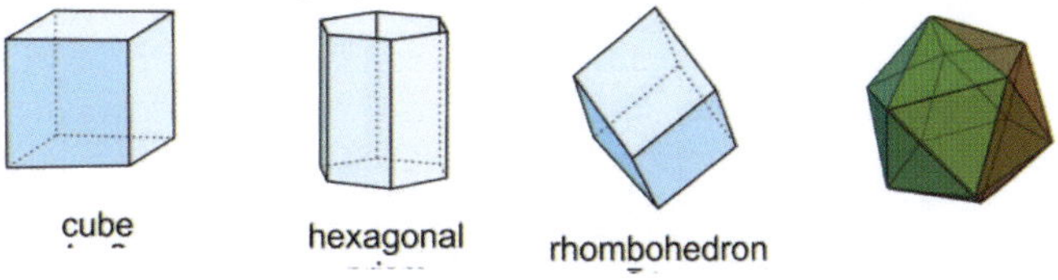

I've just been looking at a structure I thought was only theoretically possible. Until now no one has reported seeing silicon carbide in an icosahedron crystal arrangement. This structure is so geometrically perfect it could hypothetically extend itself indefinitely."

Bill nodded, but still looked concerned. "You mean it could make itself into a one-dimensional chain, like DNA." "No, this structure could support expansion in three dimensions", replied Schareshiem. "What I don't understand is where the silicon carbide came from in K Basin. There should be nothing but trace amounts of silicon and carbon in the water. There shouldn't be any at all in the zircoloy cladding on the spent fuel elements."

"Maybe it was in the meteorite", Bill mumbled. "What meteorite", asked Aaron? "The one I dropped into the basin several months ago." Bill looked up at each of them and shrugged. "You said nobody's ever seen this before. Maybe it came from the meteorite." Schareshiem was only half listening. He seemed lost in thought, then suddenly started expressing those thoughts out loud.

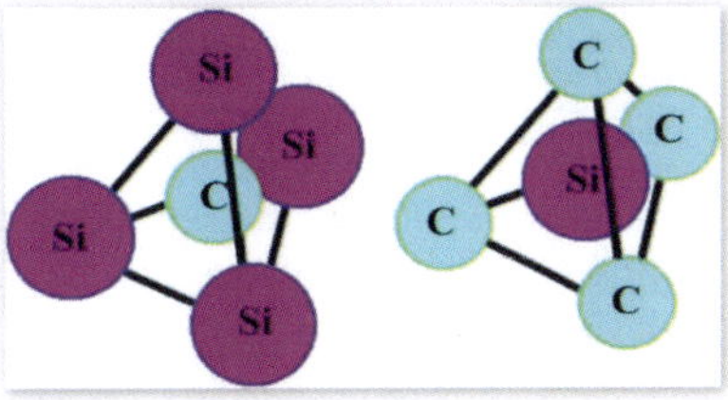

"Carbon and silicon combine in a tetrahedral bonding configuration. That results in a layered crystal structure which occurs in many different forms or polymorphs. More than 250 polymorphs of silicon carbide have been identified." [6, 7, 8]

"There are three possible arrangements of atoms in a layer of SiC crystal. A given layer may be stacked on top of another in a variety of orientations (with both lateral translations and rotations being feasible energetically). Silicon carbide may occur in a wide variety of stacking sequences—each unique stacking sequence generating a different polymorph (e.g., cubic, hexagonal and rhombohedral structures can all occur). You following me?" Bill shook his head. Bryan and Aaron offered no response. Schareshiem realized Bill was the only honest person in the room. He continued anyway.

"The hexagonal and rhombohedral structures, designated as the α-form (noncubic), may crystallize in a large number of polymorphs whilst, to date, only one form of cubic structure (designated as the β-form) has been recorded. Carbon by itself can form a tetrahedral structure, given high enough temperature and pressure. Those are called diamonds. Until now we've never seen an icosahedron structure in silicon or silicon carbide. "

"Silicon carbide has been found in certain types of meteorites. It's called moissanite and it's usually in minute quantities. Again, it's never been found with an icosahedron structure like this. If it's like other silicon carbide crystals it is soluble in molten alkalis, such as sodium hydroxide or potassium hydroxide, and even in molten iron."

Bill nodded this time. "There must be some moissanite in that meteorite I dropped in the basin."

"There must be", Schareshiem answered. "Natural moissanite was first found in 1893 as a small component of the Canyon Diablo meteorite in Arizona by Ferdinand Henri Moissan after whom the material was named in 1905 [9]. While rare on Earth, silicon carbide is remarkably common in space. It is a common form of stardust found around carbon rich stars. Examples of this stardust have been found in pristine condition in primitive (unaltered) meteorites. Isotopic ratios of carbon and silicon in the silicon carbide found in space indicate this material originated outside our solar system."

"We make hundreds of thousands of metric tons of silicon carbide every year, usually for sale as an abrasive called carborundum. It has excellent properties, including impressive resistance to wear and corrosion. Because of these properties, it has been used in many fields, including metallurgy, automotive manufacture, semiconductors, and electronic industries. Specific examples include melting of glass and non-ferrous metals, float glass production, heat treatment of metals, production of ceramics and electronic components. Silicon carbide is used to make igniters for gas heaters."

"There are several methods used to produce commercially available SiC [2]. The Acheson process is the most commonly used and was invented by Edward Goodrich Acheson to make SiC and graphite in 1893. This process is cost effective and can produce complex shapes. Others include the modified Lely process and the chemical vapor deposition process (CVD). The Lely process synthesizes bulk silicon carbide crystals through sublimation. SiC sublimes and is deposited on a graphite rod at the center of the crucible. The modified Lely process provides SiC single crystals with high purity and high crystalline quality. CVD is a method of producing SiC using a gas-phase reaction. The CVD process is beneficial because it can produce SiC with high purity and uniform composition. This process deposits SiC onto substrates, making it useful for producing related coatings. However, each of these processes requires temperatures of 2000 degrees Celsius or higher."

Bill held up his hand as if to surrender. "You've convinced me doctor. This stuff in my basin is going to be tough to get rid of, right?" "Almost impossible I would say", Schareshiem replied. Professor Schareshiem often found his small stature and soft-spoken manner caused some people to ignore what he had to say. He had been forced during his 66 years to overcompensate, giving him a reputation for being arrogant and demanding. "When one acquires a beard of white, they should be listened to", he was prone to say. His secretary insisted it was impossible not to.

"There is another concern with the moissanite in your spent nuclear fuel basin. As it incorporates the zircoloy cladding on the spent fuel into its molecular structure in the presence of a strong radiation field it undergoes expansion, forming a porous material that becomes a good thermal insulator [10]. Your spent fuel contains high concentrations of fission products that are generating a great deal of heat through radioactive decay. That heat must be efficiently transferred to the water in the basin. Anything that insulates the cladding surface from the water will allow the temperature on that surface to increase dramatically, possibly to the point of melting the cladding. Have you noticed any blisters forming on the fuel elements that have the grey coating?"

"No", Bill replied. But we have seen an increase in radioactivity in the basin water samples in the past few weeks." Schareshiem nodded. "That could indicate fission products are leaking out of the fuel and into the water. Suggest you take measurements and water samples as close as possible to the fuel elements in question." Bill nodded. "Obviously we need additional samples of this material from your basin for analysis", Aaron added. "I'd like to repeat the ^{60}Co irradiation with several additional samples."

"When were you planning to return to Pasadena", Bryan asked? Schareshiem was writing some figures in his notebook. He looked up somewhat startled by the question. "I'm not going anywhere until we've sorted this out. I trust you can provide me with a bit of office space…, maybe a desk and a connection for my laptop." Now it was Bryan's turn to look startled. "Of course", he replied, with no idea how such a feat was to be accomplished in a building that was seriously overcrowded already. "I'm not sure we can tie your personal laptop into our system, however. That system handles lots of classified information, you understand?" Schareshiem frowned at Bryan over the top of his glasses, clearly insulted by his comment. “I’m sure we can work something out”, Bryan quickly added.

Site Security promptly denied Bryan’s request to connect Schareshiem’s laptop into the Laboratory’s system. That was until the SRNL Director received a phone call from Washington. “Good morning, sir. I’m here to connect you to the SRNL computer system”, chirped a rather attractive young women who was young enough to be Schareshiem’s granddaughter. Schareshiem stood up from the large walnut desk and raised his hand for her to stop just inside the doorway. “No need. Just give me the protocols. I’ll do it myself.” The women looked puzzled for a moment, then handed him a slip of orange paper marked “Classified, Top Secret”, before turning to leave the room. Schareshiem followed and closed the door behind her. He then began searching for his glasses. He had three pair, one for reading another for the computer, and a third for distance. He found the computer ones on top of his head.

Nearly a dozen water samples were taken as near the affected fuel elements as possible. All confirmed small amounts of fission products were leaking out of the fuel elements at that location. This explained the slight increase in radioactivity in the water samples from the basin at large. There was no cause for immediate alarm and no additional precautions were warranted, but Bill was already considering what to do if levels began to increase. Isolating the affected fuel elements might be necessary.

“If we use both ^{60} Co sources, we can irradiate samples two at a time. How much exposure would you recommend”, Aaron asked? Dr Schareshiem scratched the tattered grey beard on his chin. He could see no reason to give it a trim, possibly because there was considerably more there to scratch than on his head. “I’d say three weeks. That will give each sample about 50,000 sieverts. The growth won’t be as dramatic, of course. But it should be enough. We can extrapolate from there”, Schareshiem replied. “Let’s put samples in one source with some chemical elements that simulate long-lived fission products. With the sample in the other source we need a bit of sand and a piece of charcoal.” Aaron looked confused. “Sand and charcoal?” “Trust me. I’ve been carrying this theory around with me for over four years. Can't wait to see if it works!"

A month had passed, and Bill had heard nothing from the 'lab people'. Meanwhile, radioactivity in the K Basin had been slowly increasing. The increase in background radiation around the basin wasn't significant, but Bill was worried, nonetheless. He called Aaron's number. "Schareshiem." "Sorry, I was expected Aaron to answer", Bill replied. "He's out back pulling the samples out of the irradiation facility. I'll get him to call you when he returns." The line went dead. Bill held the phone at arm's length and looked at it like a family member had just died in his arms. "What the .....", he muttered. Since he didn't have unescorted access to the part of SRNL where Aaron worked, Bill couldn't just get in a car and drive the 22.5 kilometres to the main administration area and confront Aaron and Schareshiem in person. "Patience is virtue." He repeated the phrase three times.

The first samples withdrawn were the ones containing simulated fission products. Like the Zircoloy, each of these materials had been partially consumed and the sample from K Basin had almost doubled in size. Examination showed the sample had incorporated these chemical elements into its crystalline structure at a molecular level. Because atoms of these other chemical elements are much larger than silicon or carbon the silicon carbide molecule had to expand. Of more concern was the measurement of thermal conductivity. This expanded form of silicon carbide was an order of magnitude less conductive than manufactured silicon carbide. The thermal conductivity resembled that of some of the ceramic insulators used decades earlier on spacecraft to protect them from being incinerated during re-entry into the earth's atmosphere.

"That's not good", replied Schareshiem. "It get's worse", Aaron remarked. "Look at the solubility." Schareshiem swiped at Aaron's tablet as several tables of numbers flew across the screen. "Hmm... Aqueous solubility is up eightfold as well. It must be the other chemical elements in the crystalline structure latching onto the water molecules." "That's why the radioactivity in K Basis in increasing", Aaron added. "No, no... That's not the problem", Schareshiem replied, looking even more concerned. "It can travel…" "What?" "The damn stuff can travel in aqueous solution", repeated Schareshiem! "I don't understand", said Aaron. "That's right. You don't. Where is the sample from the other irradiation source… the stuff in the other tube?" "We put it in four days after the other one. We haven't taken it out yet. " "Pull it out. Pull it out now", said Schareshiem wringing his hands. "NOW", he shouted!

Schareshiem waited impatiently as the other sample from K Basin was removed from the tube that led to the ^{60} Co source. "Be careful when you open it", he said in a nervous tone. "Only about half of the sand and charcoal are left", remarked the technician who opened the container. Both Aaron and Schareshiem leaned in to get a closer look. "It looks like it's expanded, like the other sample", Aaron observed. "Not like the other sample", Schareshiem corrected him. "I think you'll find it's not porous like the other sample. Its density hasn't changed. It's thermal conductivity and aqueous solubility are unchanged as well."

"How could it be larger then", asked Aaron? "It's the same as before but there's more of it. It's added more SiC crystals using the sand and charcoal…silicon and carbon as raw materials. It was just a theory, but now…." "What theory?" "Spontaneous self-replication!" "You mean it can reproduce like a living creature?" "No, no. It's not alive. It doesn't need any form of metabolism to generate the energy it needs. It gets its energy from radioactive decay of fission products incorporated within its molecular structure. There's no organic chemistry involved. It can only do one thing like a living organism. It can spontaneously make copies of itself in the presence of intense radiation." "So we just have to keep it away from radiation", Aaron remarked with a frown?

"Where is it now", Schareshiem asked with a wry smile? "On a bunch of spent fuel elements where there's lots of radiation." Schareshiem nodded. "And it's incorporating fission products that emit that radiation into its crystalline structure as we speak. The only thing it doesn't have is a plentiful supply of silicon and carbon, except for trace amounts in the water in K Basin." "We need to tell Bill he's got a bigger problem in his spent fuel basin", said Aaron. "Yes, and by the way he called to speak to you last week. Sorry, I forgot to tell you..."

Bill didn't take Aaron's news calmly. "So glad you finally got around to telling me! This stuff is spreading. I've got it on 15 fuel elements now! I don't have room to isolate that many." "Yes, very sorry. We need you to come up to the lab so we can talk about this ... plan what we can do." Bill accepted Aaron's invitation as an act of contrition. He took a deep breath and held it for almost a minute. "I'll be up there in an hour. All our government cars are out right now. I'll have come in my personal car. "Get here as soon as you can", said Aaron as he hung up the phone. "You knew about this, didn't you", he said turning toward Schareshiem. "I suspected", Schareshiem replied with a smile. "It was just a theory, really. I'll explain when Bill gets here. Better get Bryan in on it as well. Don't want him to feel left out." "Right", said Aaron, glancing up at the ceiling. Aaron had never understood what Bryan did exactly.

Bill arrived at the security portal and had to wait ten minutes for Aaron to arrive and escort him through. "We couldn't locate Bryan", Aaron replied to the annoyed look on Bill's face. "What does Bryan have to do with this", Bill had to ask? Aaron just shook his head. Once all were present in the lab Dr Schareshiem began scribbling diagrams on the white board.

"It was just a theory until now", said Schareshiem [11]. "Silicon carbide is hard to find here on earth. Almost all of it is manufactured as I explained several weeks ago. "Almost two months ago, actually", Bill mumbled. Schareshiem stopped and looked at him. "Whatever...", he mumbled. "You'll recall manufactured SiC has one of three crystalline structures assembled in layers. Unless it is only one layer thick this structure presents essentially only one reactive face for interaction with other chemical elements. In a rare instance some of the SiC might present two reactive faces if the layers are very thin or become separated in a porous configuration."

Gamma Ten

"The crystalline structure of the moissanite in your meteorite, and now in your K Basin, is icosahedral. That means it presents twenty reactive faces for chemical interaction. Those interactions can involve free silicon and carbon, if available. You will recall that one of the processes for manufacturing SiC is the modified Lely process where SiC sublimes and is deposited on the graphite rod. That process requires temperatures exceeding 2000 degrees Celsius. Apparently, the intense radiation can provide the energy required to catalyze the sublimation of silicon and carbon onto itself at temperatures below the boiling point of water. In the case of the sample we irradiated in the ^{60} Co facility, the intense radiation knocks silicon and carbon atoms off their parent structures, i.e., sand and charcoal, making them available for incorporation into the moissanite."

Bryan had finally arrived and was shaking his head. "You lost me somewhere after the bit about icosa… whatever structure, Dr Schareshiem." Schareshiem looked at Aaron for reassurance. Aaron looked puzzled as well. "What does all this mean", Bill finally asked? Schareshiem looked at the floor with an exaggerated sigh. "It means your moissanite is self-replicating using the radiation energy from the fission products in your spent fuel and free silicon and carbon in the basin water. It isn't 'growing' very fast because your basin water has very few silicon and carbon atoms for it to grab onto. But it is also incorporating molecules of zircoloy cladding into its structure. Once through the cladding it will be incorporating fission products as well."

"Those long-lived fission products will continue to give it a supply of energy from internal radiation. About two-thirds of these fission product isotopes will have essentially disappeared fifty years from now. Cesium and strontium are the most energetic and will be the biggest energy contributors for decades to come."

Gamma Ten

Radionuclide	Half Life	% After 1 Year	% After 5 Years	% After 10 Years	% After 30 Years	% After 50 Years	Type Radiation	keV
^{155}Eu	4.76 yrs	86.45%	48.28%	23.31%	1.27%	0.07%	Beta, Gamma	252
^{240}Pu	6.56 yrs	89.97%	58.96%	34.76%	4.20%	0.51%	Gamma	20
^{85}Kr	10.76 yrs	93.76%	72.46%	52.51%	14.48%	3.99%	Beta, Gamma	687
^{241}Pu	14 yrs	95.17%	78.07%	60.95%	22.64%	8.41%	Alpha	-----
^{90}Sr	28.79 yrs	97.62%	88.66%	78.60%	48.56%	30.01%	Beta	2826
^{137}Cs	30.17 yrs	97.73%	89.15%	79.47%	50.20%	31.70%	Beta, Gamma	1176
^{121}Sn	43.9 yrs	98.43%	92.41%	85.39%	62.27%	45.41%	Beta, Gamma	390
^{238}Pu	87.7 yrs	99.21%	96.13%	92.40%	78.89%	67.36%	Alpha	-----
^{151}Sm	88.8 yrs	99.22%	96.17%	92.49%	79.12%	67.69%	Beta	77

"Radiation dose is inversely proportional to the square of the distance from the source. Having radioactive atoms embedded in the structure of the SiC means the distance from the source is exceptionally small. At these distances beta and gamma rays can ionize even the most stubbornly stable molecules. The radiation dose can be high even from a small amount of these isotopes. I'm afraid your moissanite can keep on growing even if you could somehow separate it from the spent fuel. It carries its own supply of energy within it."

"So, we need to contain it in the K Basin", said Bill, stating the obvious. "Yes, but that may not be easy either. So long as it remains attached to the spent fuel elements it isn't going anywhere. However, this material is much more soluble in water than other forms of SiC because of the larger metal and fission product atoms it has absorbed. At some point it may start dissolving in the basin water." "Our sand filters and deionizers will take it out of the water in that case", Bill was quick to reply. "Sand filters…? How do you dispose of your filter media", Aaron asked? Bill began to see his point. "You claim silicon carbide is practically indestructible. How do we ever get rid of something indestructible that carries its own energy source and self-replicates using sand, one of the most common materials on earth?" "But it also needs carbon, right", Bryan suddenly declared? Schareshiem looked at him with a smile. "Yes, and you're full of it, sir!"

----

[2] Methods to Produce Silicon Carbide and Their Advantages – Acheson Process, Lisa K. Ross, (https://www.preciseceramic.com/blog/methods-to-produce-silicon-carbide-and-their-advantages.html)

[3] Brookhaven National Laboratory, Engineered Silicon Carbide Three-Dimensional Frameworks through DNA- Prescribed Assembly, A. Michelson, O. Gang, February 2021, BNL-221252-2021-JAAM (https://www.osti.gov/servlets/purl/1777428)

[4] Wikipedia, Silicon Carbide, en.wikipedia.org

[5] NASA Technology Transfer Program, Materials And Coatings, Silicon Carbide (SiC) Fiber-Reinforced SiC Matrix Composites (LEW-TOPS-25) (technology.NASA.gov.)

[6] Wikipedia, Polymorphs of Silicon Carbide

[7] Journal of Applied Crystallography, ISSN:1600-5767, Volume 46, Part 1, January 2013, pages 242-247 (https://doi.org/10.1107/S0021889812049151)

[8] Silicon Carbide, Comprehensive Semiconductor Science and Technology, 2001, sciencedirect.com (https://www.sciencedirect.com/topics/chemistry/silicon-carbide)

[9] Wikipedia, Canyon Diablo (meteorite)

[10] Science Direct article, Ceramics International, Volume 9, Issue 5, 1 March 2023, pages 8331-8338, Shenghao Li, Fang Ye, Laifei Cheng, Zhaochen Li, Junheng Wang, Jianyong Tu, "Porous Silicon Carbide Ceramics with Directional Pore Structures by CVI Combined with Sacrificial Template Method", (https://www.sciencedirect.com/science/article/abs/pii/S0272884222039736)

[11] New Scientist article, Matthew Sparks, 6 December 2023, "DNA nanobots can exponentially self-replicate" (https://www.newscientist.com/article/2406181-dna-nanobots-can-exponentially-self-replicate/)

[12] Stimson Center, Spent Nuclear Fuel Storage and Disposal, Trinh Lee, 17 June 2020 (https://www.stimson.org/2020/spent-nuclear-fuel-storage-and-disposal/)

[13] Spent Nuclear Pools in the U.S. – Reducing the Deadly Risks of Storage, Robert Alvarez, May 2011 (Institute for Policy Studies) (https://www.nrc.gov/docs/ML1209/ML120970249.pdf)

Gamma Ten

Chapter 3

Situated in the heart of Pasadena, California at the foot of the San Gabriel Mountains, Caltech's campus covered half a square kilometre, 16 kilometres northeast of downtown Los Angeles and approximately 48 kilometres from the ocean. The Caltech-managed Jet Propulsion Laboratory was about 11 kilometres away. Professor Schareshiem's secretary was beginning to wonder if he was ever coming back from South Carolina. "You have three grad students each wanting to present their doctoral thesis to the Board so they can get their PhD diplomas and professional credentials", she explained.

"Yes, yes. I know. That will all have to wait. There's something happening here that I can't let go of just yet. Maybe another three weeks… I'll get back to you as soon as I know more." The line went dead. Schareshiem's secretary looked up at several hopeful individuals standing patiently on the other side of her desk and simply raised her palms toward the ceiling. "This is intolerable", shouted one young lady. "I'm going straight to the Dean's office." All three abruptly stormed out into the hallway. Lydia got up from her desk and opened the door to the Professor's office. It was just as he left it almost two months ago. California sunshine was streaming through the windows. She sat down hard in the

Professor's leather chair, slipped off her shoes, and propped her feet up on the only vacant space on one corner of his enormous walnut desk. Obviously, he wouldn't approve. But then he never seemed to approve of anything, even when he was there. "Cantankerous old goat", she yelled! The room was practically soundproof. Lydia didn't care if it wasn't.

Professor Schareshiem's office was off limits to everyone except Lydia and the lady who came in to clean one evening each week. This was especially true in his absence. Nearly every square centimetre of his desk was covered by his collection of memorabilia from 40 years of academic success. Lydia cautioned all visitors. "The word 'collection' is an expletive if used in the Professor's presence." Every item on his desk had been carefully placed. Each represented a pivotal achievement in the Professor's career. He had a photographic memory in this regard. Anything out of place would be immediately questioned. "Where is it? Why was it moved? Why wasn't it put back where it belonged?" God forbid, anything should actually go missing, even for a day!

There were two Persian rugs on the floor, one in front of the desk and one to the side. Both were cherished gifts. He would never say who from. One entire wall was dedicated to the Professor's collection of books. J. R. R. Tolken's "Lord of the Rings" was there. Aldous Huxley's "Brave New World" and George Orwell's "1984" and "Animal Farm" were there as well. He liked to boast that every book of relevance to human progress was on that wall. Half were on chemistry, of course. Schareshiem insisted the two-meter burgundy drapes be changed to match the rugs. The new ones were a deep blue with gold embroidery. Two large windows looked to the east to catch the morning sun. That was Schareshiem's favorite part of the day. Lydia always found the Professor's absence a welcome relief, except when he didn't come back as scheduled. Her life was hell when that happened.

Artificially blonde, hazel eyed and 180 cm tall in three-inch heals, Lydia towered over the Professor at 168 cm. She was the only child in her family, the only women in Schareshiem's life as far as anyone knew, and the only one who could tell him where to go. She managed his lecture schedule and his travel schedule, both of which had been non-existent for almost three months now. Most men of fifty years or fewer found Lydia quite attractive and seemingly available. The problem was between her ears. She had a documented IQ of 137. Fulfilling the requirements for a degree from Stanford University in Social Sciences took less than three years. With an education certificate as well, Lydia was still denied the only job she wanted. That was teaching primary and secondary students. Working in the higher education system of southern California was her second choice. Most of her peers considered her quite unlucky to be working for a man twice her age. She preferred working for an older man who wouldn't hit on her constantly. Relationships, particularly marriage, did nothing but create stress in one's life, stress she could happily do without.

At the Professor's request Lydia had sent him copies of three doctoral student's materials to be presented to the board. To his credit he promptly reviewed all three and returned his judgement in favor of awarding two of them. He remained undecided on the third. "Hasn't worked hard enough", was his verdict. In truth it was the student's conclusions he didn't agree with.

Schareshiem (no one seemed to know his first name) had never married, although he had come close when he was in his early fifties. Sadly, she died in a car accident a week before the wedding. The Professor dedicated himself to his work and nothing else from that moment on. Now nearly 68, he was internationally regarded as one of the world's experts on silicon-based chemistry. "The Dean has given you two weeks to return to the university and resume teaching", said Lydia on her third attempt to reach him on his mobile phone. "Your students have rightfully complained that they paid for a syllabus featuring you and your reputation as a vital part of the curriculum. One of those students is the grandson of one of the university's largest donors. He is threatening to withhold over four million dollars in donations next year."

"Yes, yes. I know", replied the Professor. "Damn contracts and their restrictions." He had considered giving up his tenure at the university, but he needed the money, according to his accountant. Schareshiem had no idea how much money he had in the bank, nor did he care. He trusted Lorenz, Lowrey and Company to worry about such things. "I'll be back by end of next week." The line went dead as usual without giving Lydia a chance to pass on another vital message. All she could do was make a note of it on the Professor's calendar six months hence.

"I'm being forced to return to California", said Schareshiem. "I trust you can carry on without me. Please let me know the results of the samples in the ^{60}Co facility." "Will do, sir", was Aaron's reply. "And let me know how fast it's spreading in the K Basin, as well." Aaron nodded. Schareshiem found Aaron's methods and discipline impressive. Twenty years ago if he had needed an apprentice, he would have certainly considered Aaron on a short list of candidates. If only he could turn back the clock, there was much he could have done differently.

Aaron had been a chemist at SRNL for nearly 16 years. His list of accomplishments would impress any prospective employer, although he never contemplated leaving. He wouldn't be 70 for another 26 years. He expected to retire with a full pension when the time came. Aaron and Geraldine never planned to be rich. He had tried investing but it just wasn't 'his thing'. This was despite his son's success as a stockbroker in New York. "I can help you, Dad", said Leonard on many occasions. "Too risky", Aaron insisted.

Leonard looked more like his mother according to most who knew the family. He was much too tall, however. The men on Aaron's side of the family had never been known for their height. Geraldine found just the opposite in her family. Her father was 187 centimetres tall. His father, Leonard's grandfather, was about the same. That solved the mystery of why Leonard measured 190 centimetres in his stocking feet. That had nothing to do with his success as a stockbroker at the age of only 24. Not everyone who graduated from Columbia University with a degree in banking and finance got a job offer on graduation day. Leonard had a unique ability for picking winners. He couldn't explain it, insisting it was a gift.

Lydia looked at her watch. It was 4:35 pm Pacific Time when the Professor casually walked through the outer office door. "You just made it, sir." Schareshiem smiled as he walked straight to his office door, then stopped suddenly and turned to face her. "Today's Friday, right?" "Yes sir. It is", she replied. "My class on Monday?" "Yes sir, 1:30 to 3:00." "Very good." He opened the door, walked straight to his chair, and sat down as if he had never left. Lydia's desk phone rang. "Is he back", asked the Dean? "Yes, sir. I'm not sure he knows he left." "Good! Make sure he doesn't find out."

Aaron continued to irradiate samples of the moissanite that was spreading amongst the spent fuel elements in K Basin. Bill was becoming more concerned as the radioactivity in the basin water continued to slowly increase. There were thickening grey deposits on thirty-seven fuel elements by the time Aaron had completed irradiation of the third set of samples in the ^{60}Co facility at SRNL. Bill reported that the grey moissanite had bridged between some of the separate fuel elements, filling in the spaces between them. In this way it was able to affect an ever-growing number of them. "Perhaps we can slow it down by putting the affected fuel elements as far away from the others as possible", Aaron suggested. "We've already done that", Bill replied. "It may buy us some time, but I still don't see how we're going to stop it growing."

Aaron's wife Geraldine was keenly aware something was bothering her husband more than usual. He just wasn't himself. He never worried about problems at work in the past. He even seemed to have lost a bit of weight in the past few months. There were subtle changes in his appearance that only a wife of 24 years would notice. Greying temples and moustache gave him an air of authority, although he had no desire to become a manager at SRNL. He had turned down several such opportunities over the years. In his opinion managers, like Bryan, were a complete waste of space. All they did was push paper around and go to meetings. He didn't intend to give up his 'hands on' access to the chemistry he had enjoyed for many years.

Indeed, Professor Schareshiem appeared to have forgotten all about his visit to South Carolina and the moissanite in the K Area spent fuel storage basin. He couldn't afford to lose his tenure at

Caltech. A small envelope in his briefcase containing a tiny amount of the moissanite that had been irradiated in the ^{60} Co facility at SRNL would indicate otherwise. It was only about 10 grams and wasn't radioactive, so it didn't set off any alarms when he exited the SRNL building. Likewise, no one at the university could possibly know he had it. Schareshiem respected Aaron's abilities but he knew the authorities at SRNL would never consent to the types of tests he wanted to perform. He had to find out how the moissanite would react to real fission product isotopes, specifically the most energetic and persistent of them all – ^{137} Cs and ^{90} Sr.

Four weeks passed slowly until the Christmas season finally arrived. Schareshiem knew almost everyone at the Caltech laboratories would be off for the holidays. It wasn't likely anyone would be around to observe his activities. The local inventory of ^{137} Cs was kept in a shielded and locked laboratory hood at the far end of a long room. A somewhat larger amount of ^{90} Sr was kept in a similar configuration in another lab further down the hallway. Schareshiem had keys to both storage locations. The problem was moving one or the other of these materials so they could be placed in direct contact with his moissanite sample. Radiation alarms would surely go off if he tried to move either material.

The solution was a hollow lead cylinder, used first to move the ^{137} Cs sample to the other lab, then to act as a water-filled container for all three materials during the two-week holiday period. Schareshiem estimated that would be sufficient to see if the moissanite assimilated a measurable quantity of the ^{137} Cs and/or ^{90}Sr. He expected to open the lead cylinder on New Year's Day and put everything back before any lab personnel returned to work on January 2nd. The likelihood that anyone would notice a tiny difference in the ^{137}Cs or ^{90}Sr inventory was remote. That was a convenient assumption, at least. The Professor hadn't anticipated that the moissanite would physically bond with these coupons so that it couldn't be completely removed. Aaron hadn't seen this problem in any of his tests in the ^{60}Co facility at SRNL. It took a few moments for the Professor to recognize the difference. The metal samples in Aaron's tests weren't radioactive. The radiation all came from the ^{60}Co source. In Schareshiem's experiment the

Gamma Ten

^{137}Cs and ^{90}Sr were the source of the radiation. The moissanite resisted being separated from its energy source.

It was 11 am on January 1st when the Professor realized the difficulty. The best he could do with the tools available in the shielded laboratory hood was to use a wire brush to remove as much of the moissanite adhering to the ^{137}Cs and ^{90}Sr coupons as possible. He then placed his moissanite sample in a second lead cylinder and used the first cylinder to transfer the ^{137}Cs and ^{90}Sr coupons back to their original storage locations. Neither of these coupons would have access to any silicon or carbon. The minute film of moissanite adhering to them would likely go unnoticed.

By mid-January Bill began to notice locations in K Basin where the moissanite was extending upward along the walls of the basin near the affected spent fuel elements. There was only one location at first but a second appeared a week later. By February 1st there were four such 'columns', as he decided to call them. They were using the silicon and carbon in the concrete as raw materials. The danger was obvious. As these columns extended upwards, they came closer to the surface of the water which provided shielding from any radioisotopes incorporated within them.

There were several 'blisters' growing on the fuel elements as well. Some showed tiny bubbles forming and collapsing, indicating localized nucleate boiling. Basin water samples confirmed that fission products were being released into the water at all these locations, raising the background radiation around the edges of the basin to worrisome levels. Bill had already cautioned members of his crew not to spend any more time in the area than necessary to perform routine tasks. So far there was no indication of moissanite in samples taken from the sand filters but radiation levels in their vicinity were about ten times higher than normal.

Bill found himself in Aaron's lab once again in late February. "We've done another round of irradiations in the ^{60}Co facility just to confirm previous results." "I don't need any further confirmation that we have a problem", Bill barked. "What I need is an action plan to stop it." "I'm sorry I can't offer you one", Aaron replied. "We may be forced to simply isolate it in K

Basin." "You mean abandon the facility? Do you know how many metric tons of spent fuel we have in there?" Aaron seemed unmoved. "As long as we can keep water in the basin the fuel won't melt. The fission products are in a stable form, not airborne. We need to contain the water so that contamination can't get outside the basin itself." "What about the sand filters?" "Don't change them. Don't dispose of the sand as usual. That will give us time to work out what to do with it."

Aaron wasn't taking this matter seriously enough in Bill's opinion. "Look. My boss and his boss are asking me what I'm going to do. Right now all I can tell them is that we are keeping personnel radiation exposure to a minimum. Soon we won't be able to access the basin perimeter at all. We'll need to send in robots to perform the routine tasks that keep the basin water at the right level, etc. If we hurry, we may be able to have those robots ready in time." "Right", Aaron replied dispassionately. "Hell, in a few months we won't be able to get close enough to the sand filter to even get samples", Bill continued! Aaron nodded. "All I can recommend is 'containment'. Silicon carbide is practically indestructible." "Practically?" "OK, it IS indestructible using any chemistry I'm aware of."

"These days almost all nuclear waste is stabilized by encasing in glass, then buried in places where ground water can't get to it. That won't work in this case. My guess is this moissanite will 'eat' its way right through any glass containment, using the silicon in the glass as raw material and the radiation energy to replicate itself without limit. Is that what you wanted to hear?" Bill sat down on one of the old wooden lab stools again, refusing to believe there wasn't some other action he could take. "We must contain it, Bill. That's all we can do until we have a better answer."

"What about Schareshiem? What does he think", Bill responded? "Haven't talked to him since October. He seemed preoccupied with his own theories but wouldn't share them. It almost sounded like he was performing his own experiments. That's impossible without a sample of the moissanite, of course. Anyway, the university isn't giving him any more time to work with us." Bill nodded. "OK, containment it is! We'll keep it in the basin, keep the water topped up, and wait…"

Sending operations personnel into the basin area became prohibitive after the Easter holidays. Radiation exceeded safe levels, even for short excursions into the building. Twin robots arrived two weeks later from a company located in Atlanta, Georgia. Their capabilities were limited to making sure the water level was maintained in the K Basin, taking water samples, and offering video views of selected locations around the basin perimeter and the sand filters. Samples from the sand filters indicated high levels of radioactivity and colonies of moissanite inside the sand filter buildings. The ground around the sand filters was sprayed with a waterproof mastic material in an effort to contain the moissanite if it should emerge from either of the sand filter buildings. Procurement had managed to find a mastic material that didn't contain either silicone or carbon.

For obvious reasons, Professor Schareshiem couldn't share any information with Aaron about his work on the moissanite sample in the lab at Caltech. Since it wasn't sanctioned by anyone at the university, there was no one he could confide in. No one noticed the almost invisible film of moissanite on the ^{137}Cs and ^{90}Sr coupons, just as he had hoped. Like a child that had gotten away with something, his curiosity finally got the better of him on the last day of April. He found a quiet moment in the lab and looked to see if the ^{137}Cs coupon was still there. It wasn't. He also checked on the ^{90}Sr and found it missing as well.

"What happened to that ^{90}Sr sample we used to have", he casually asked one of the lab technicians? "It hadn't been used in years and we needed the space. We got rid of all of them." "Where did you get rid of them", asked the Professor, feeling his blood pressure rising? "They were bundled with a lot of other waste into a glass container and sent to the San Onofre Nuclear Generating Station (SONGS)[16]. They had some space in their spent fuel basin." Schareshiem felt a sudden rush of adrenaline. His heart felt like it was about to leap out of his chest. Should he notify the university and almost certainly be booted off the faculty? What would his accountant think of that idea? Did he dare to keep quiet and hope nothing would ever be traced back to him? How could it be? Aaron didn't know anything…

The Professor lay sleepless several nights a week for over a month, wondering what to do. He appeared more tired each day until Lydia had to ask. "You look terrible, sir. Not sleeping?" "So kind of you to notice, my dear", he finally responded. "I have… WE have a serious problem." He found himself standing in the Dean's office waiting for a much younger man to get off the phone. Finally he hung up and was startled to see Professor Schareshiem standing in the middle of his office. "Sorry, didn't hear you come in Professor. What's this urgent business you need to discuss?" "Bless me Father for I have sinned…", he began.

A phone call to the San Onofre Nuclear Generating Station confirmed the waste package sent to them had been placed in their spent fuel storage basin. "Where", asked Schareshiem? "They said its right in between two spent fuel containers, all safe and sound", the Dean repeated with the phone receiver still in his hand. "We must get that package back out of the spent fuel basin", pleaded Schareshiem. "Before it's too late".

Another week passed before the authorities at San Onofre allowed an aging Professor to visit their spent fuel basin. "See, it's right there", said the young lady assigned as his escort. Schareshiem could just see the location. "Can we get it out", he asked, trying to remain calm. "Get it out", she asked in disbelief? "No sir. We can't get it out. We won't be moving any of this material for several years." "Binoculars? Do you have binoculars?" The young lady retrieved a pair from the cabinet behind them. "It's broken open. Look." He handed her the binoculars. "Oh, I think you're right. Looks like a bit of dark grey stuff on one side. We'll have to get a sample." "Never mind", said Schareshiem. "I can tell you all about it."

Aaron turned off the bedroom light and was just about to slide his feet under the blanket when his mobile phone rang. Geraldine emerged from the bathroom with a look of disgust and a toothbrush hanging out of one side of her mouth. "Why can't anyone call at a decent hour", she mumbled, as if eating the toothbrush? "I've got it here as well", announced Schareshiem without even a 'good afternoon' this time. "So you took some of it back with you to California", Aaron questioned? "It's at San Onofre Nuclear Generating Station", Schareshiem replied, ignoring the question. "How did it get there?" "Abject stupidity", said Schareshiem. "When are you coming back to SRNL?" "Can't leave. They've decided not to terminate my tenure at the university because they need my help at San Onofre. If I leave California, my tenure will be terminated immediately."

"Do you still have a sample that hasn't been irradiated in the ^{60}Co facility", Schareshiem continued? "Yes, of course." "OK. See if you can destroy it with some sort of chemical attack. It won't dissolve in acids or in bases, but it will dissolve in alkaline melts and in most metal and metal oxide melts [15]. You'll need to get the temperature up to 1.500 Celsius in an inert gas or reducing atmosphere." "We don't have a furnace that will go that high in our lab", Aaron explained. "I don't need to hear about your problems. We just need the results, and quickly", Schareshiem barked. "We don't have much time to stop it!" The line went dead. Aaron's face was blank.

"You look like you've just seen a ghost", Geraldine replied, with the toothbrush still in her mouth. Her husband could only shake his head. "Where in hell am I supposed to find a furnace, certified for use in a laboratory hood, that will go up to 1,500 degrees Celsius", he asked his bedroom ceiling?

Aaron arrived at his office a few minutes before 7:00 am to find the SRNL Director sitting in his office. "Good morning, sir", Aaron said with a start. "What can I do for you?" "Tell me what I can do for you", the Director replied. "The Department of Energy (DOE) insists we give this stuff in K Basin top priority. Whatever you need we'll get it. Aaron leaned against the door frame to steady himself. He hadn't even come up with a plan yet.

[15] Washington Mills, SiC Properties, Meeting Tough Standards, Washingtonmills.com, (https://www.washingtonmills.com/silicon-carbide/sic-properties)

Chapter 4

Once the Department of Energy (DOE) at the Savannah River Site designated Aaron's work as top priority, tasks that normally took months got done in days. Aaron had only a few hours to develop the specifications for the furnace. Procurement Department was told to order it and have it shipped via air freight, regardless of the cost. It arrived in two days. Building maintenance had to install wiring capable of supplying the power the furnace would require. The lab hood also had to be modified to ensure any airborne particles and volatiles were captured on high efficiency air filters and activated charcoal beds. Aaron had no idea what might be released into the hood during the tests he was about to perform. The last thing they needed was to have any of the moissanite escape from the hood in particulate form.

Professor Schareshiem had no illusions about what Aaron might find. It was a long shot at best. As long as the moissanite was underwater it would be impossible to raise the temperature enough for any sort of chemical attack to be successful. Once out of the water the zircoloy cladding would overheat and melt due to radioactive decay of the fission products in the spent fuel. The release of those fission products, either airborne or into groundwater, would render the area uninhabitable to humans. Still, the Professor had to know if there was any possibility of destroying the moissanite directly. If not, there was no other option but to continue their efforts to contain it. Then the question was 'for how long'?

The San Onofre Nuclear Generating Station (SONGS) was a permanently closed nuclear power station located south of San Clemente, California, on the Pacific coast, in Nuclear Regulatory Commission Region IV. The reactors there had been shut down after defects were found in the site's steam generators. The plant was decommissioned in 2013 following over a decade of investigations and litigation in an effort to restart the reactors. The spent fuel storage basins were eventually emptied, and all radioactive waste was put into dry storage. As the need for radioactive storage facilities increased over subsequent years, the basins at San Onofre were refurbished and reopened in 2026. By August 2031 these basins were nearly full, with only a few incidental vacancies remaining.

It was late summer when Professor Schareshiem found himself leaning over the metal railing at San Onofre, once again peering into the crystal-clear water and admiring the shimmering blue glow down below. There were several colonies of the moissanite clearly visible. Nineteen spent fuel elements were involved. They had been segregated from the others in so far as practicable. They all shared a common water supply and sand filter configuration unfortunately. Two basin walls also had 'columns' growing on them, like those in K Basin in South Carolina.

Operations personnel reported that two fuel elements had been shipped from San Onofre to the Sellafield Spent Fuel Storage Site in the United Kingdom about three weeks after the container from Caltech was received. "Did anyone notice any sort of grey film on the items that went to Sellafield", asked a nervous Professor? "Nobody remembers seeing anything, but then we weren't asked to inspect the stuff we sent to the UK. We'll ask them to have a look when they get it." Schareshiem knew it would be too late by then. "Can they isolate those items rather than put them with everything else?" It was two days before they received an answer from Sellafield. The items from San Onofre had been placed in a basin immediately upon arrival. They needed the cask for another job. "Where", asked Schareshiem? "Fukushima, Japan."

Aaron's efforts to destroy the moissanite had confirmed it could be dissolved in several alkaline metal melts, including NaOH and KOH, and molten iron. The moissanite remained stubbornly inert at temperatures below 1,450 degrees Celsius, however. It would be possible to attack any moissanite colonies found outside the water filled basin, but radiation from the imbedded fission products would likely prevent direct approach by humans. The

Equipment Engineering Department at the Savannah River Site had considerable experience with robotics. They were designing, building, and testing robots that could carry blow torches and other heating devices for the task. Other robotics would be needed to deliver the alkaline metals. How the moissanite would react in the absence of an inert gas environment was anyone's guess. There might not be time for testing under controlled conditions. Aaron considered it likely they would have to put all of it straight into service if the moissanite escaped from the K Basin and/or the sand filters.

The Professor and others at Caltech had come up with another approach. Aaron decided to fly out to Pasadena to join them. "It's only for a week". Geraldine was less than thrilled, suspecting it would be more like a month. "Don't lay on the beach too long. The November sun in California can still give you a burn. Hope you enjoy the Thanksgiving holidays without your family. Don't forget over half the garden still needs digging over as well." "I'll be back before then", Aaron replied, nodding vigorously as he joined the security queue at the Augusta Airport. Bryan had to distribute Aaron's remaining projects at SRNL to others in the group. It wasn't an easy task since Bryan had no idea what Aaron had been working on before 'this silicon carbide thing' happened. He wasn't aware Aaron had given several others some turnover before he left.

Schareshiem's idea was to stop the moissanite from self-replicating, or at least slow it down. His peers had judged that impossible given the enormous radiation energy available from the spent nuclear fuel. "But if it expands outside the basin, we have a chance. It's simple geometry", he explained. "The moissanite crystals are replicating at the surface of the overall structure whenever they can find free silicon and carbon atoms. In the worst case, if we assume the overall colony is in the form of a sphere, then the surface area of that sphere will be 4 times Pi (3.1.4159) times the radius squared. As the colony grows, its surface area, and therefore its rate of self-replication, will quadruple for each doubling of the radius."

"Once the colony becomes separated from the spent fuel elements, it will only have radiation energy from the fission products contained within it. If these fission products are disbursed uniformly in the overall structure, then we can expect the fission product inventory of the colony to be diluted in its total volume. The volume of a sphere is 4/3 times Pi times the radius cubed. That means the fission product inventory, and therefore the radiation intensity, should decrease by a factor of eight for each doubling of the radius. If it grows large enough the radiation dose at the active surface will become small enough so that self-replication will cease." "Do we know the minimum dose rate needed for self-replication to occur", asked one of Schareshiem's grad students? "Yes", Aaron replied. "Unfortunately it seems to be quite low. We saw self-replication in samples that were only left in the facility at SRNL for 100 seconds. That amounts to a dose of 2.75 sieverts."

Schareshiem frowned. He immediately starting scribbling figures on the white board in his office, then stood back shaking his head. "I had to make a few assumptions about the uniform distribution of radioactive isotopes in the colony and the average distance between the radioactive atoms and those of silicon and carbon." He paused to look at the white board again. "A moissanite colony saturated with the fission product mix in a single spent fuel element could continue to self-replicate until it reached a spherical radius of 1.3 kilometres. That's 9.2 cubic kilometres! That's if it didn't find another source of radioisotopes before it reached that size." "My God!", exclaimed the grad student!

"What if the moissanite was able to redistribute the radioisotopes from the center of the colony to a thickness of less than a meter from the active outer surface", Aaron asked? Schareshiem erased some of his figures and scribbled new ones. "Worst case? Multiply by 96", he replied. "We'll have to create some computer models for all of this, of course. A viable radius of 125 kilometres and a volume of 883 cubic kilometres would be theoretically possible if it could do what you said." Schareshiem paused, then suddenly turned to look at Aaron. "Please don't tell me you've seen that kind of behavior in the samples you irradiated at

SRNL…" Aaron's face was blank. Then he turned and nodded slowly. "On three occasions." No one could speak for almost a full minute. The grad student bolted from the room. "He won't tell anyone, will he", Aaron asked with a panicked look? Schareshiem shook his head. "We will have to tell someone soon though."

Caltech's best computer modelers worked in shifts for the next three days. Several models were developed, then run over and over again with different variables. None of the results were as startling as Schareshiem's whiteboard estimate. All were alarming. After almost two weeks consensus formed around one set of figures. A maximum viable radius of a single colony could likely exceed 100 kilometres. "We have to stop it before it gets anywhere close to that size", Schareshiem proclaimed, without any notion of how that was to be done. "Surely the total fission product inventory in all the spent fuel storage basins in the world wouldn't be enough to keep a colony of this stuff going for very long, would it?" Schareshiem frowned at his grad student's remark. "I'm revising your PhD project. Find out the answer to that question if you still want your diploma."

Aaron stepped away from the others to take a call on his mobile phone. "It's out", said the voice on the other end. "Bill? What??" "It's out of the K Basin." "I thought the walls were reinforced concrete over a meter thick." "They are. But concrete has tiny cracks in it. This stuff has gotten into those cracks where some spent fuel elements are located very close to the wall. It must have expanded the cracks and allowed water to leak through to the ground outside. Look at the photo." Aaron opened the photo Bill had sent a few minutes earlier. There was grey material in several places on the ground outside the basin wall. It was some distance away from the sand filters where they had sprayed the mastic covering. "It's hot, too", Bill added. "What temperature?" "No, no. It's reading 22 millisieverts/hour. That exceeds our personnel safety limit of 20 millisieverts/hour. We can't get close to it. Groundwater samples are showing increased radioactive contamination as well, up to ten metres away from the basin outside wall. That means some of this stuff is water soluble. You guys need to hurry up out there."

Aaron handed his phone to Schareshiem. "It's on the ground?" "Yes." "Good. Now you can attack it with those robots of yours. See if you can dissolve some of it", Schareshiem shouted. Aaron's reaction was immediate. "This isn't your personal high school science project, sir", he shouted as he grabbed the phone from the Professor's hand and walked out of the room. Three thousand seven hundred and forty kilometres away Bill threw his phone against his office wall, startling his secretary sitting only a few meters away. Schareshiem closed the door to his office and didn't come out for the rest of the day. The next day Aaron booked the next available flight back to Augusta.

Finding out how much spent nuclear fuel there was in the world didn't take very long. "I've got the information you asked for", Schareshiem's grad student announced, unaware of the events of the previous day. "Very good, Brent", the Professor replied. "No it isn't, sir. It's not good at all. Look at the numbers...."

		US SNF Radioactive Inventory (Ci)		World SNF Radioactive Inventory (Ci)	
Isotope	Half-Life (Yrs)	2011	2031	2011	2031
Cesium 137	30.0	4,500,000,000	13,500,000,000	11,250,000,000	33,750,000,000
Strontium 90	29.0	3,000,000,000	9,000,000,000	7,500,000,000	22,500,000,000
Europium 155	4.8	22,000,000	18,000,000	55,000,000	45,000,000
Plutonium 240	6500.0	36,000,000	108,000,000	90,000,000	270,000,000
Krypton 85	10.7	150,000,000	225,000,000	375,000,000	562,500,000
Plutonium 241	14.0	3,200,000,000	4,800,000,000	8,000,000,000	12,000,000,000
Plutonium 238	88.0	240,000	720,000	600,000	1,800,000
Samarium 151	90.0	25,000,000	75,000,000	62,500,000	187,500,000
	SNF Total Curies	10,933,240,000	27,726,720,000	27,333,100,000	69,316,800,000

"I've also compared the numbers from twenty years ago with the latest inventory by converting the current figures back to the old unit of curies, used before we converted to metric in 2027 [13]. With three fusion plants under construction more than one-third of the commercial fission power reactors have been shut down. There isn't enough storage space for all the spent fuel elements. Some of it will have to stay in the reactor vessels for years, delaying their decommissioning." The Professor was shuffling his feet, clearly impatient to get to the one bit of information he wanted. "Total curies in the worldwide spent fuel inventory - over 69 billion. In today's units that's 2,553,000 million giga-becquerels (GBq)."

"Our computer models indicate 159,000 million GBq will be enough to sustain moissanite growth almost indefinitely, assuming continuous migration of the radioactivity to the surface of the colony where the moissanite crystalline structure is growing. Even if the radioactivity is distributed poorly and differs from optimum by a factor of ten there will theoretically be more than enough for the moissanite colonies to cover the entire planet. Fortunately the moissanite does not have access to all that radioactivity. It's spread all over the world in 30 countries, either in fission reactor spent fuel basins or still in the fission reactor vessels. At its peak way back in 2023 there were 449 fission reactors in operation worldwide [17]. In all the years since, no international agreement has ever been reached about how and where to permanently store all this spent fuel. It's just sitting in hundreds of places all over the globe."

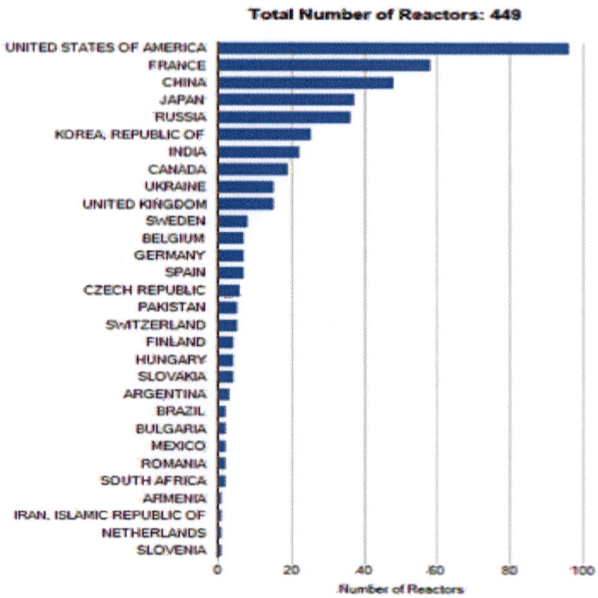

Gamma Ten

"Computer models for moissanite growth predict colony movement at an average speed of 0.40 kilometres per hour or 11 cm/second if there is sufficient radiation to make it grow. Something moving at that speed could possibly encircle the earth in eleven years if growing only in one direction. It could even cover the earth's surface in twenty-seven years, theoretically."

The Professor sat down in his leather upholstered chair, placing one foot up on the only vacant corner of his desk. Brent was afraid to leave until told to do so. For several minutes it appeared Schareshiem was no longer aware his grad student was still in the room. Finally he looked up.

"Excellent work, son. I'm approving your doctoral thesis today." "What about my orals before the board", Brent replied cautiously? "No need. We will probably be dispensing with a lot of things in the near future. Would you like to stay on at the university for a while as my assistant? Generously paid, of course." "Uh.. Yes, of course. When do I start, sir?" "Immediately!" As his new assistant closed the door behind him, Schareshiem was thinking about that future. In his late 60's, it was quite possible he would still be alive in eleven years. He doubted he would be alive in twenty-seven. He had no children to worry about. Brent was only twenty-four. The Professor didn't envy Brent and those of his generation. He considered the likelihood their future would be quite challenging indeed.

Brent's past was a bit of a mystery, even for him. Both his parents were killed when their private plane crashed off the California coast. He was only four. Raised by his Uncle Harry, Brent learned his strong work ethic and keen interest in science from his uncle's associates at the University of Southern California in Los Angeles. At the age of 13 it was obvious Brent was going to be quite tall. Uncle Harry managed to get Brent admitted as a grad student at Caltech at the early age of 21, before losing his battle with cancer a few months later. Brent's age and aptitude for computer science quickly gained him a bit of notoriety with the faculty. At 193 centimetres, Brent's only problems were finding young ladies tall enough to dance with and getting in and out of cars, especially those sporty two-seaters.

Aaron gave Bill a call the moment he was back in his office. “Can I see it”, he asked? “Yes, of course. You just can’t get closer than 10 meters. Radiation levels are too high. Be sure you’re wearing your dosimeter.” Geraldine was expecting her husband home by 6 pm to finish decorating the family Christmas tree. There were some special ornaments that required his personal attention when being placed on the tree each year. Their son, Leonard, had flown down from New York on the 18th. Aaron had barely spent a quarter of an hour with his son since arriving home from California. “I’m going to be a bit late”, Aaron announced when Geraldine answered the phone. “How late?” “Not sure. I have to work tomorrow as well.” “Tomorrow’s Christmas Eve, Aaron!” “Uh.. Oh yes. So it is. Can’t be helped. Talk to you when I get home.”

“It’s worse than I expected”, Aaron remarked. Both he and Bill were outside K Basin the next morning as soon as it was light. “I promised Geraldine I would be home by noon.” “I had to make the same promise”, said Bill. “It’s still growing, isn’t it?” “Yes, but not as fast as when we first found it. It seems to be slowing down as it gets larger.” “There’s hope, then…” “Yes. We’ll be trying various methods to destroy it the first week in January.” “You haven’t spoken to Schareshiem”, Bill had to ask? Aaron looked out across the field toward a stand of pine trees. “Nope. The man can go straight to hell!” Both men stared in silence at the grey blob in front of them, stretching two meters by four meters. “We may still need his help”, Bill remarked. “Yes, I’m quite sure we will....”

“The background radiation levels are increasing all around it as well”, Bill continued. “Some of it is water soluble, seeping into the ground over a much larger area. We’re still able to take soil samples by hand. Not sure how we’ll keep it from getting into the groundwater and aquafers that feed Pen Branch Creek, Four Mile Creek, and ultimately the Savannah River.” Aaron frowned.

Gamma Ten

"You need the University of Georgia Ecology Lab people for that one." "Talked to them last night", Bill nodded.

It was a warm Christmas Eve in California at 17 degrees Celsius. Brent and his fiancée were lying on a less crowded area of Venice Beach. Four hours for $20 seemed a reasonable fee, considering you couldn't walk across the free public beach without stepping on someone. It was quite comfortable in the mid-afternoon sun. "So the old man just gave you a PhD and a job all in one breath?" "Yeah, I couldn't believe it. Not like him at all." "Are you sure he wasn't drunk?" "Nope. Sober as a judge." "Most of them have a bottle behind the bench these days." "We just need one to marry us", said Brent. "Remind me when that is", she replied with a grin, her blue eyes full of mischief. "Two weeks from Sunday. Don't you be late. And find something suitable to wear, OK?" "Better call me the night before and remind me", she continued. "Will do", Brent replied, looking at a point where the surf met the clear blue sky. It was every man's dream to lay next to classic California blonde on a classic California beach. She punched him in the ribs. "Swim?"

"Who should we invite", Brent continued as they walked knee deep in the surf? "That'll be up to my father I expect. You'll be inviting Schareshiem, right?" "Of course, but he won't come. Doesn't go in for that sort of thing. Does your father know anyone at Caltech?" "He must know a few people there. He sends the University a cheque every September." "A cheque? Didn't know they even existed anymore." "Dad's stuck in the past. Likes to do things the 'old fashioned way'. He hasn't mentioned doing it this year, though. Anyone besides Schareshiem to add to the list?" Brent shook his head. "No one in particular."

The east coast was busy preparing for a nor'easter. Aaron made it home from K Area just ahead of it. Twenty-six centimetres of snow was expected in Augusta. Snowplows had been positioned along the major roadways. The Christmas Tree was in its usual place in front of the large window in the front room. Leonard had built a fire in the stone fireplace. He gave his dad a hug, then handed him a glass of Glenlivet, before sitting down on the black leather sofa. "It's a bit early isn't it", Aaron asked in a rhetorical voice? "It's Christmas Eve, Dad." He motioned for his father to sit in the matching recliner. Arlene was in the kitchen, clanging dishes together, pretending she couldn't hear what they were saying. "We've got a lot to talk about. I've barely seen you since I got here. What's so important at work that you can't take some time off for Christmas?"

"Nothing for you to worry about", Aaron replied. Leonard let his father's comment hang in the air for a few moments. "OK Dad. Have it your way. You know you could be making a lot of money in the market." "Yeah, so you keep telling me." "I could help you, you know. I can't invest directly, but there's nothing to stop you from taking my advice. My clients pay me well for my help with their portfolios. I won't charge you a penny." "Well, that's kind of you", Geraldine remarked with a crooked smile as she entered the room. "Why won't you let me help you", Leonard pressed? "I'll think about it", said Aaron. Truth was Aaron didn't have any excess income to invest. The mortgage interest rate kept going up every year. He could barely afford the monthly payments.

Aaron and Geraldine were more concerned about their son's future than their own. In his mid-twenties and still single, Leonard insisted he just never found the right girl. Being 190 cm tall might put some women off, but with Geraldine's good looks plenty of women should find him quite attractive. The problem was Leonard's work habits. Sixty-hour work weeks were commonplace in his business. He simply didn't have time to date anyone. That was his story and he seemed to be sticking to it. Geraldine had been expecting grandchildren for nearly two years. She had to accept the fact that it might never happen.

The conversation that evening was quite different at Bill's house. He couldn't wait to hear about his daughters' experiences at their respective universities. Claire had to admit the University of Tennessee wasn't everything she had hoped for. She was thinking of changing her major from Business to Marketing. "What's the difference", Arlene had to ask? "The men in Marketing seem a lot smarter – and better looking", she replied. "Surely you can't make a decision on that basis, and after only four months", Bill offered.

Arlene gave Claire a knowing smile. Diane pretended to be eating, but the grin on her face gave her away.

"And you", asked Bill, shifting his gaze to the other twin? "What have you been up to at Auburn?" "Classes are hard", Diane replied, determined not to follow her sister's lead. "You said Engineering was easy, Dad." "I never said that", Bill responded with a frown. "Yes, you did", Arlene interrupted. "You did say it was easy." Bill's face went blank. He didn't remember anything of the sort. Unfortunately he was outnumbered. With three women in the family he was always outnumbered. It was something he accepted a long time ago.

"I'm pledging Pi Beta Phi, however", Claire interrupted. "Do you have time for a sorority in your freshman year", cautioned Arlene? "Yes, mother", Claire responded with a defiant look. "I'll fit it in. No problem!" There were times when Bill wondered if the sacrifices he and Arlene were making for the sake of their daughters' education were worth it. 'Of course every parent probably wonders the same thing', he thought to himself. They could live in a more affluent neighborhood, drive a better car, and put more money in retirement savings if ….

Claire and Diane looked so much alike even their parents couldn't tell them apart sometimes. Besides being tall and brunette like Arlene, both had Bill's dark brown eyes. On the topic of clothing, they almost always disagreed, except when it came to their mother making a dress for each of them, of course. Otherwise, Claire preferred a more formal 'dressy' look. Diane was the 'blue jeans and t-shirt type. Sometimes they switched outfits just to confuse their parents. Neither Bill nor Arlene was in any hurry for them to get married. The cost of a wedding wasn't in their budget at the moment. The possibility that either or both of them might meet someone and leave college before graduating couldn't be ignored, however.

Bill's mobile phone rang just as Arlene was bringing in the pumpkin pie, still hot from the oven. It was a Christmas Eve tradition. She looked at her husband and shook her head. "Don't answer that", she said without really thinking. Bill got up from the table and went into the front room. He knew how much Arlene disliked someone taking a call at the dinner table. “Yes”, Bill replied as he took a seat on the sofa. “We’re picking up activity in Indian Grave Branch Creek just south of Four Mile Branch. It’s not much but it’s significantly above normal background.” Bill didn’t respond. He knew that meant there would eventually be radioactivity in the Savannah River. It was just a matter of time. Should they notify the press? What could they tell them? Was there a way to stop it? There wasn’t.

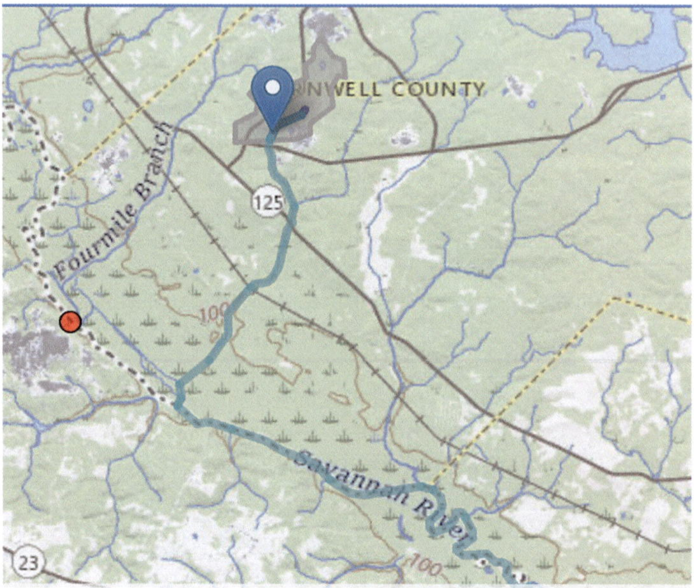

“OK, thanks for the call”, Bill replied in a business-like manner. A feeling of helplessness came over him as he put his phone down on the coffee table. All the managers had been required to attend a media training course just a year earlier. The hardest sessions were what they called thc ‘gang bang’. That’s when reporters are shoving microphones at you in front of a half dozen cameras, trying to get a picture or a quote to go with the news report they wrote several hours before. For the victim the feeling was exactly like being buried alive. "Your pie is getting cold", Arlene called from the dining room.

[15] Washington Mills, SiC Properties, Meeting Tough Standards, Washingtonmills.com, (https://www.washingtonmills.com/silicon-carbide/sic-properties)

[16] Wikipedia, San Onofre Nuclear Generating Station, (https://www.google.com/search?q=san+onofre+nuclear+power+plant&ie=UTF-8&oe=UTF-8&hl=en-gb&client=safari)

[17] Number of Nuclear Power Plants in the World – Statista, Statista.com.

Chapter 5

Lydia was busy scheduling the Professor's visits to nuclear sites in several countries. He'd already advised those at San Onofre Nuclear Generating Station to isolate the problem as much as possible. There wasn't much else they could do. Unfortunately a potentially contaminated cask had been sent to the United Kingdom and then on to Japan. Operations at Fukushima were still being hampered by radioactivity in some locations and in the sea where contaminated wastewater had been dumped decades earlier.

The Sellafield Site in the United Kingdom had been alerted to inspect their basins at least once a week. Schareshiem decided to go to the UK first, then to the La Hague site in northern France. His purpose was to make the largest spent fuel storage locations aware of the problem and that it needed to be taken seriously. Japan was closer to California, but a special courier had alerted authorities at Fukushima to isolate the empty cask from Sellafield and not put anything in it. Schareshiem asked Brent to accompany him. Having never travelled outside the United States, it was an opportunity he couldn't pass up. "You'll need a passport", the Professor reminded him three days before they were to leave. "Already have one", Brent replied. It was his fiancé's idea several months earlier. Something about spending their honeymoon in Europe. The trip with Schareshiem meant putting his wedding on hold for a few weeks. His fiancé wasn't pleased – unless there was the possibility of moving the honeymoon to Marseille.

In years past Schareshiem would have simply sent an email to other spent fuel storage sites around the world alerting them to possible moissanite contamination. Nowadays, with environmental activist groups monitoring text messages and email traffic between National Laboratories, universities, and other locations conducting scientific research it was impossible to know who might read a sensitive email or message. It might even be printed and used as evidence during litigation. Phone calls were secure as long as both parties knew each other well so they were confident the call wasn't being recorded. Schareshiem would have to talk to unknown individuals at other sites. That was too great a risk. Both Aaron and Bill were reluctant to discuss their work even in the privacy of their own homes. Voice activated systems in the home recorded everything that was said. No one was ever sure if these systems might be hacked, with the recordings being sold to the highest bidder.

The only option was to visit the nuclear waste sites and hold face to face discussions in secure locations. Brent had compiled information the Professor would need in his efforts to persuade those in authority. "I've gathered enough data to make a convincing argument", Brent announced, standing in the doorway to Schareshiem's office. "There is a lot more out there than what I'm showing on this chart, but this should be enough to convince them the entire planet may be at risk. The computer models indicate in the worst case that just the ^{137}Cs and ^{90}Sr inventory at these ten locations would support a super colony that could link up to cover 123% of the earth's surface, or 424% of the earth's land mass."

"There's no such thing as 424%", Schareshiem replied with a grin. Brent dismissed the Professor's attempt at humor with a slight sweep of his hand. "Even in the best case just these two isotopes at ten sites could result in 12 % of the earth's surface or over 42% of the earth's land mass being overrun." Schareshiem leaned back in his burgundy leather chair, shook his head, then just stared at the hundreds of books on the rows of shelves across the room. "God help us if this stuff gets out in the world at large."

Location	137Cs Inventory (GBq) *	90Sr Inventory (GBq) *	Colony Size (Sq Km) Worst Case	%	Best Case	%
K Basin (USA)	19,000,000,000		60.4	3.7	6	0.37
Sellafield (United Kingdom)	125,000,000,000		397	24.5	40	2.45
Irish Sea & Artic Ocean (UK)	11,700,000,000		37.2	2.3	3.7	0.23
Fukushima (Sea of Japan)	4,000,000,000		12.7	0.8	1.3	0.08
Chernobyl Site (Ukrane)	29,600,000,000		94	5.8	9.4	0.58
La Hague (France)	106,000,000,000		337	20.8	33	2.08
San Onofre Power Station (USA)	6,450,000,000		20.6	1.3	2	0.13
Brown's Ferry Power Station (USA)	5,900,000,000		18.7	1.2	1.9	0.12
Sequoyah Power Station(USA)	5,400,000,000		17.1	1.1	1.7	0.11
Watts Bar Power Station (USA)	5,800,000,000		18.4	1.1	1.8	0.11
K Basin (USA)		18,430,000,000	58.6	3.6	6	0.36
Sellafield (United Kingdom)		121,250,000,000	385.1	23.8	38	2.38
Irish Sea & Artic Ocean (UK)		11,349,000,000	36.1	2.2	3	0.22
Fukushima (Sea of Japan)		3,880,000,000	12.3	0.8	1.2	0.08
Chernobyl Site (Ukrane)		28,712,000,000	91.2	5.6	9	0.56
La Hague (France)		102,820,000,000	326.9	20.2	32	2.02
San Onofre Power Station (USA)		6,256,500,000	20.0	1.2	2	0.12
Brown's Ferry Power Station (USA)		5,723,000,000	18.1	1.1	1.6	0.11
Sequoyah Power Station(USA)		5,238,000,000	16.6	1.0	1.7	0.10
Watts Bar Power Station (USA)		5,626,000,000	17.8	1.1	1.8	0.11
	318,850,000,000	309,284,500,000	1,996	123.1	197	12.3

* All values as of January 1, 2032 (137Cs half life - 30 years)
* All values as of January 1, 2032 (90Sr half life - 29 years)

The fight from Los Angeles over the north pole to Heathrow Airport in London took less than 4 hours. Brent got up at one point to stretch his legs and looked out the window. The sky was black. The planet's curvature was unmistakable. The illuminated sign over the doorway between business class and first-class seating wasn't all that comforting. Neither was the fact that some people still insisted the earth was flat.

Sellafield, originally known as Windscale, was a large multi-function nuclear site close to Seascale on the coast of Cumbia, England. Sellafield covered an area of 2.7 square kilometres and comprised more than 200 nuclear facilities and more than 1,000 buildings. It was Europe's largest nuclear site and had the most diverse range of nuclear facilities in the world with a workforce that often exceeded 10,000 employees. The United Kingdom's Central Laboratory was located on the site. There had been numerous attempts to decommission portions of the site in 2025 and 2028. However the need for nuclear waste storage made decommissioning impossible.

Gamma Ten

Professor Schareshiem had little patience for pleasantries. British customs and sense of politeness were lost on him. He had been warned the British often think Americans are 'too direct'. He considered that a compliment. Nevertheless he attempted to be on his best behavior. "Ladies and gentlemen, my reason for being here today is quite serious. We have identified a substance in several of our spent nuclear fuel storage facilities that is of grave concern. It is possible that a recent shipment into your facilities here at Sellafield may have contained some of this material."

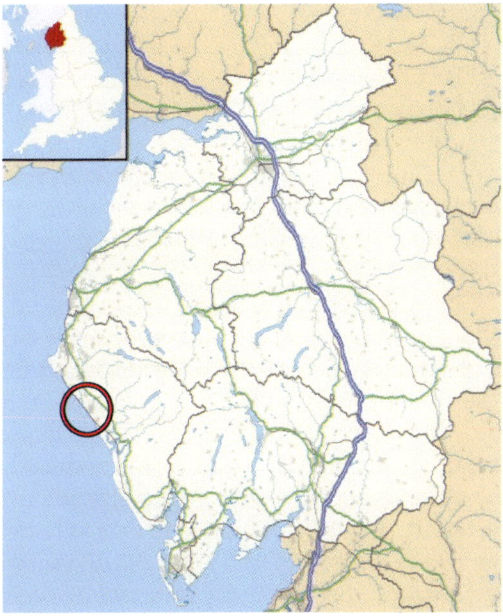

"Our experience with this material has shown it to be difficult if not impossible to control. At the moment our only effective strategy is to contain the problem in so far as possible. I wish to reassure you that work is being conducted at several locations in the United States in an effort to control the spread of this material and possibly eliminate it completely. However, failure to do so could potentially result in widespread release of fission product inventories into the environment on a scale never experienced before."

"Dr Schareshiem, while we respect your concern about this problem, it is quite difficult for us to believe that some small amount of alien material in your spent fuel storage basin could possibly pose so great a threat. If we should find some of this material in one of our facilities here at Sellafield, I'm sure it will be a simple matter to remove it." Schareshiem looked down at the podium directly in front of him for a moment, then shook his head slowly. "I can assure you, sir. Controlling its growth will be much more difficult that you imagine." "Growth", asked another member of the Sellafield staff? "How could any organism 'grow' in the presence of the intense radiation found in our spent fuel basins?"

"It's not organic", Schareshiem replied. "It's inorganic – silicon carbide, to be exact. Your characterization of it as 'alien' is quite appropriate. It is exactly that – a form of silicon carbide, or moissanite, no one has ever seen before. And it makes copies of itself using the radiation from our spent fuel. It self-replicates, expanding its unique crystalline structure in the process. It also attacks the cladding on our spent fuel, resulting in release of radioactive isotopes into basin water." There were looks of disbelief around the room. "Perhaps I could talk with some of the chemists on your staff?" The room went silent. A tall well-dressed man in the back of the room cleared his throat rather loudly. "Please continue Professor." Everyone immediately turned their attention back to Schareshiem.

"Silicon carbide comes in a great many forms because silicon and carbon combine with themselves as well as each other through a natural affinity to form strong symmetrical bonds. All silicon carbide forms are essentially indestructible at temperatures found in our spent fuel storage basins. This new 'alien' form of moissanite has a crystalline structure quite different from anything we've seen before."

"There are four distinct differences. First, it has an icosahedral crystalline arrangement that provides a greatly increased number of active faces for bonding with itself and with other elements, including the cladding and fission products in spent fuel. Second, it can make copies of itself using the radiation in fission products and any free silicon and carbon that is available. Silicon is a common element in concrete, like the walls of our spent fuel basins. Carbon is found in the soil, in plants, and in all living creatures on earth."

"Third, it can incorporate radioactive elements into its crystalline structure, thereby ensuring a steady supply of radiation energy. That means it has energy to make copies of itself even without an external source, like highly radioactive spent fuel elements, nearby. Because the incorporated radioactivity is internal the radiation dose at molecular distances is very high, even from minute quantities of fission product isotopes. Fourth, our tests have shown that this form of moissanite is more soluble in water than ordinary silicon carbide by almost an order of magnitude. That means it can leak from our basins and travel through groundwater, streams, and rivers – carrying fission products within it."

"When you say it can 'grow', you mean it can increase in size simply by using radiation energy to add on more silicon carbide to its crystalline structure using some sort of intelligence or instruction?" "No. No intelligence is required. Think of it like the rock garden some of us had as a child. We started with a brick. After a while crystals began to grow on the brick. After a few weeks the entire brick was covered with crystals. The crystals weren't 'alive'. They had no intelligence or instruction within them. They just 'grew' by simple chemical bonding. This 'moissanite rock garden' can potentially grow to cover very large areas." "How large?" Schareshiem motioned for Brent to put his chart up on the screen. "In theory, it could cover the entire planet in your lifetime!"

The room went silent again. "Surely this is impossible. There must be a way to stop it", exclaimed one Sellafield staff member. "How", asked the well-dressed man in the back of the room? "We don't know yet. We're still working on it", Schareshiem replied. "We've constructed walls or dams in front of it. Groundwater simply carries the crystals through the ground under it. It just continues again on the other side. We've tried to construct roadways on it but in a majority of locations it wouldn't support the weight of the vehicle, leaving the vehicle immobilized. We've built bridges over it, but the concrete foundations and pylons disintegrate after only a few months. The moissanite crystals seep into the interstitial spaces in the concrete and then expand, causing cracks that cause the structure to fail. Our experience in the K

Basin in South Carolina is a good example. Bridges would have to be built on steel foundations and pylons. There isn't enough steel in the world to build bridges over the entire country. Moissanite isn't strong in compression – it won't support a building. Steel pylons would have to be driven through it into the ground underneath."

"We've tried ploughing it off the roadways to clear them for normal traffic. It doesn't always grow back, but what is left on the roadway is still enough to destroy the wheel bearings and undercarriage on the vehicles. The cost to wash a major highway completely free of it would be prohibitive. We do have miliary vehicles that run on metal tracks. They can drive over these colonies, often sinking into the 'grey sand' as they call it. The tracks fail once the moissanite gets into the metal linkages. Our experience is similar to that in the Gulf Wars of 1991 and 2003, with ordinary sand that got into the tracks of the tanks and other track vehicles. The most serious problem is loss of farmland and contamination of rivers, making the water unusable for domestic or industrial purposes."

"We've even tried using explosives to clear the moissanite from the roadways. That was a disaster. We couldn't use explosives where there was a lot of radioactivity because we would have dispersed it into the air and contaminated a huge area. Where the radioactivity was low, we thought it might succeed. We were wrong. The explosion filled the air with what looked and tasted like volcanic ash. The air was unbreathable for several days. This airborne material slowly settled out over a much larger area than before. Nobody dared try that again! All we can do is contain it for now." "Thank goodness there's none of this stuff here at Sellafield", remarked one of the principals near the front of the table. A young lady standing near the rear door of the conference room raised her hand slowly. "Excuse me, sir." Everyone looked around. "That may no longer be true."

It took nearly an hour to get clearance and proper clothing for the Professor and Brent to view the area of the basin where the fuel element from San Onofre had been placed. Each took turns with the binoculars. "There it is", Brent announced. It was difficult to spot but there was a dark grey film on one small area of the fuel element. "Also on the concrete wall", the young lady remarked. "Yes", Brent replied. "Young eyes!", mumbled Schareshiem to the radiation control technician standing nearby. He nodded. He couldn't see it either.

Several more discussions were held over the next three days. Sellafield management agreed to follow the Professor's advice, including moving other fuel elements as far away from the affected one as possible. "I'm sorry we are unable to stay", said Brent. We have another location to visit, and then we really must return to California to continue our research on ways to interrupt the replication mechanism." "Please keep us informed", the Site Manager replied. Schareshiem was already in the car. Their train to Manchester was scheduled to depart in thirty minutes. It would take them longer to reach Manchester airport by train than it took to fly from Los Angeles to London. The flight from Manchester to La Hague, France only took 95 minutes, after spending almost two hours in the security queue at Manchester Airport.

The La Hague Site was a nuclear fuel reprocessing facility on the Cotentin Peninsula in northern France, with the Manche Storage Centre bordering on it. La Hague had provided nearly half of the world's spent nuclear fuel reprocessing capacity since beginning operation in 1976. Their inventory included spent nuclear fuel from France (70%), Japan (9%), Germany (17%), Belgium, Switzerland, Italy, Spain, and the Netherlands. The non-recyclable part of the radioactive waste was eventually sent back to the user nation.

As far as anyone knew, nothing contaminated with the moissanite had been received at La Hague. Since it contained one of the largest inventories of spent nuclear fuel and other radioactive waste in the world, Schareshiem felt it necessary to brief them on the moissanite problem. The French reception was more confrontational than what they experienced at Sellafield. French authorities had a lower opinion of Americans in general. Management at La Hague was quite sceptical of the Professor's message.

Gamma Ten

Since they had no reason to suspect moissanite was in any of their facilities, Brent's predictions were treated as pure fantasy. Neither of them was even offered a tour of the facilities there. "I suppose the French spent fuel basins probably look a lot like those at Sellafield", Brent commented, as they were escorted out of the facility. "Might as well look for a good French restaurant with some nice fish and a good bottle of Pouilly Fuisse", Schareshiem replied. "Just so the trip won't be a total waste." Brent gave a thumbs up.

The last nuclear waste storage facility on Professor Schareshiem's itinerary was the Fukushima Site on the east coast of Japan. The site had been alerted by courier to put the empty cask they received from San Onofre in isolation. Under no circumstances were they to introduce anything radioactive into this cask. Air France provided a smooth flight across the European and Asian Continents in just under four hours. Tokyo was quite different from what Brent was expecting. With a population of over 44 million people, he was happy to let the Professor navigate the public transportation system until they reached their hotel. A bullet train took them north to the Fukushima Site the next morning.

Fukushima Site management had arranged a cordial greeting for Schareshiem and his 'staff'. With typical Japanese efficiency their guests were escorted to a small conference room at the facility. "We have done as you requested", their escort announced. "Would you like to see the location?" "Not at the moment", Schareshiem replied. "Perhaps later." Once everyone had arrived Schareshiem delivered essentially the same information as at the Sellafield and La Hague Sites. "As long as no radioactive material is introduced into the cask then the moissanite will remain dormant." "We will be reimbursed for the loss of this cask", one staff member asked? "Yes", said Schareshiem, with no idea who would be paying the Japanese over $180,000 to ensure the cask was never used again.

During the three weeks Schareshiem and Brent were travelling Brent and his fiancée exchanged text messages almost daily. Two days before returning to Los Angeles she stopped replying. "Perhaps she's misplaced her phone", Schareshiem suggested. "Or they've lost Internet service temporarily." Brent shook his head. "Not likely." He would sort it out when he arrived home. He had barely put his luggage down in the flat when there was a knock on the door. "This came for you Special Delivery while you were gone. Since I live next door, the postman asked me to sign for it." "Thanks very much." Brent closed the door. He had a mailbox downstairs like everyone else. He never checked it. No one ever sent things by post anymore. It was a plain square envelope with no official markings.

Dearest Brent,

I would have sent you a text but didn't want to be a distraction from your work with the Professor. I'm afraid I have some bad news. My parents and younger sister are moving to Saint-Tropez on the southern coast of France. They've sold the house here on Catalina Island for $9.8 million. Dad said it was a good price. He seemed to be in a hurry to sell although he won't say why. I will have to go with them of course. We will be leaving before your return. Please come visit us in Saint-Tropez as soon as you can. Shall we put the wedding plans on hold? I'll keep the dress and the engagement ring and hope for a better time. Call me when you can...

All my love,
Liza

Brent had visited Liza's family home on the island several times. It was one of the most beautiful locations on Catalina. He couldn't image why her family had decided to sell so quickly. A bit of research revealed three other estates on Catalina Island were up for sale as well. All three were listed at bargain prices. Perhaps

Liza's father could have gotten more if he hadn't been in such a hurry to leave. Then he had one more thought. He checked the list of Caltech's largest financial patrons. Liza's family was 14th on the list. The owners of the other three properties up for sale were also on the list of Caltech patrons. Was that just a coincidence? Or had someone with knowledge of the moissanite problem advised these people to sell? Only a handful of people at Caltech knew about the projections of moissanite growth. It was much too early to warn the public in any case. Brent chose not to mention his predictions to anyone. He had no idea who he could trust. He also had no idea how to contact Liza now, or if his marriage would ever take place. He couldn't afford to chase her around the world. If his calculations were accurate, he might never catch up with her.

During the weeks while Brent and the Professor were traveling, the situation at K Basin deteriorated rapidly. Radiation levels inside the building had risen to the point that neither Bill nor any of his staff could enter for more than a few minutes. Robotics provided by Equipment Engineering Department were sent in with video cameras, allowing the situation to be assessed hour by hour. Water makeup to the basin was not in jeopardy, but remote actuators had been hastily installed to allow remote operation of valves and pumps if necessary. There was significant moissanite on the ground around the building and around the sand filters. Moissanite covered about 30% of the sand filter building. Radiation levels around the sand filters were prohibitive. All Bill and his crew could do most days was watch the moissanite colonies grow.

By late August, video of the K Basin showed moissanite completely filling the spaces between a growing number of spent fuel elements. That meant those areas were insulated from the water around them. Layers of small bubbles on exposed surfaces in those locations indicated widespread nucleate boiling. That explained the increasing radiation levels in the building and sand filters. "Zircaloy cladding undergoes a crystallographic transition from the α phase to a β phase at temperatures exceeding about 800 degrees Celsius, although the transition temperature is affected by the amount of hydrogen contained in the metal cladding as well as the heating rate. The zircaloy doesn't actually melt until it reaches

1850 Celsius", Aaron explained. "Of course that doesn't account for how much zircoloy is being incorporated into the moissanite structure itself." Bill had no idea what Aaron was going on about. He just nodded politely and changed the subject.

Aaron had developed some theories about attacking the moissanite with molten iron and other metals in an effort to 'decompose' the crystalline structure. Tests in SRNL had shown the moissanite crystals would decompose at molten iron temperatures. The problem was how to attain those temperatures outdoors. A possible solution was to place a metal hood over the moissanite in a single location, then use blow torches to melt the iron and the moissanite inside the hood. Trials in the field were hampered by high radiation levels, of course. Robots were only partially successful at maintaining the required temperature. After several weeks it was clear that local areas of a colony the size of Bill's kitchen could be 'decomposed' over a period of a few days. Scaling up such operations to attack colonies covering hundreds of square meters would be practically impossible. The colony outside the K Basin and sand filter building was already much too large to be 'decomposed' by any method devised so far.

Bill and his crew now had only one job. That was to keep the K Basin full of water. The makeup rate was almost six times what it had been during previous years. Cracks created in the concrete basin walls by the expanding moissanite was the only possible explanation. That meant water and soluble fission products were leaking into the soil and groundwater outside. Those fission products were continuing to supply the moissanite outside the basin with energy for self-replication.

Bill recalled reading about the accident at Chernobyl in 1986 when helicopters were brought in to dump sand onto the exposed molten reactor core. Of course sand was the last thing Bill needed. Using helicopters to dump water into K Basin wouldn't work because of the concrete roof over the basin. It seemed ridiculous to have to consider such extraordinary methods to keep the spent fuel in the basin covered with water. Nevertheless, if such methods were ever needed it wasn't too early to begin planning for them. If a large number of fuel elements became covered in moissanite and melted, radiation levels even thirty meters away would be prohibitive. How would they prevent the entire inventory of spent fuel from melting, with volatile fission products, such as ^{85}Krypton, becoming airborne over hundreds of square kilometres of the South Carolina countryside?

Gamma Ten

Chapter 6

Professor Schareshiem couldn't afford any more time away from the university. He still hoped to find some way to retard or even stop the self-replication process. Altering the basic icosahedral crystalline structure would be impossible. It was incredibly stable, even more stable than diamond. The only possibility was to saturate the moissanite crystalline structure with non-radioactive atoms so that it no longer had interstitial space left for radioactive ones.

"So how do we trick the moissanite into preferring non-radioactive molecules over radioactive ones", Brent had to ask? "Simple", replied the Professor. "We find some molecules that have greater chemical affinity for bonding with silicon and carbon than any of the fission products in the spent fuel." The Professor's simple solution proved quite elusive. It was early August before he saw any progress whatsoever. In the absence of intense radiation the moissanite molecule proved to be quite 'antisocial'. Temperatures approaching 2000 degrees Celsius were necessary for any chemical bonding to occur in the laboratory.

"It simply doesn't work in the absence of radiation", said Schareshiem. Aaron held the phone tightly to his ear. Geraldine was snoring loudly on the pillow next to his. He got up slowly, took the phone into the bathroom and shut the door. He turned on the shower to cover the sound of the conversation. "We need to do it in your ^{60}Co facility at SRNL. How soon can we do that?" Aaron was still waking up. "I'll have to get additional approvals. No one's ever placed anything highly radioactive inside the irradiation containers in that facility. Putting actual fission products inside the container would risk contaminating the access tube. We wouldn't be able to clean it properly, making the entire facility unusable in the future." Aaron was obviously not in favor of what the Professor was suggesting. "If we don't find a way to stop this moissanite spreading, it won't matter if your facility is contaminated. Make sure you don't get any moissanite in the water around the ^{60}Co source. We don't want this stuff growing on the ^{60}Co slugs as well." The line went dead.

Aaron came out of the bathroom to find Geraldine sitting up in bed staring at him. "Why are you taking a shower at 3 am", she asked? Aaron just shrugged as he climbed back into bed and went back to sleep. He realized later than morning he had to give the Professor's demand serious consideration. He wasn't given the chance to tell Schareshiem the original sample of moissanite was essentially gone. Earlier tests had rendered the tiny amount that remained unusable. Any sample Bill might be able to get now from K Basin would already have significant fission products in it. "Is there any part of the colony on the ground where the radiation levels would permit you to get a sample?" "There might be", Bill replied. He handed the phone to a radiation control technician who happened to be in his office. "There is one area that looks like a long arm sticking out from the sand filter. We can get you some of that." "Great. About a hundred grams will be enough." "Will do", replied the technician.

A small sample weighing 94 grams arrived in a small lead cask the size of an oversized thermos bottle and weighing nearly 24 kg. Outside the cask the sample read 5.3 millisieverts/hour at three centimetres. Direct handling wasn't an option. Inside a shielded cell Aaron split the sample into four parts of roughly equal weight. The first sample would be irradiated while in contact with equal parts of ^{137}Cs and ^{90}Sr. A second sample would be placed in the other tube with equal parts of iron, copper, ^{137}Cs and ^{90}Sr. It was Professor Schareshiem's hope that the iron and copper in the second container would compete with the caesium and strontium for sites in the moissanite crystalline structure. This should result in the second sample increasing in radioactivity only half as much as the first sample. The remaining two samples were kept in reserve so the test could be repeated if necessary.

"Three weeks in the ^{60}Co facility should be enough to give us measurable results. It will also give us a benchmark to compare against your computer models. Obviously, we're all hoping the computer models are grossly overestimating the rate of colony growth", said Aaron. "Agreed", replied Schareshiem, although he had a great deal of confidence in Brent and others at Caltech. It was a clear case of mixed emotions. Waiting was always the hardest part of any test. It was early October when both containers were removed from the irradiation facility. Aaron could hardly wait for the radiological analysis.

"You were almost right, Professor", said Aaron. "What do you mean almost?" "Radioactivity in the second sample increased only 65% compared to the first sample. Apparently the moissanite has a 15% preference for materials that are radioactive over materials that aren't." "No, no. It should be the other way around. Silicon has a greater affinity for iron and copper than for caesium or strontium", Schareshiem protested. "You must have done something wrong." "I'm sure you are right, sir. But only in the absence of intense radiation. I have two samples remaining. We can run the test again if you insist", Aaron offered. "Yes, yes. I do insist", replied he Professor. "I do indeed. Try it again with zinc and magnesium."

This time Aaron intentionally withheld information. He was surprised Schareshiem didn't ask about growth rate. Unfortunately the moissanite growth during this latest three-week irradiation was 79% of Caltech's computer model predictions, taking into account the differences in sample temperature and radiation dose rate. Aaron had hoped to argue Brent's extreme predictions were pure fantasy by several powers of ten. Unfortunately they were in reasonable agreement. Bill didn't take Aaron's news cheerfully. "Run everything again? That will take another three weeks at least. Meanwhile I'm up to my neck in this stuff. We're losing valuable time. Isn't there anything else we can do?" "I suggest you plan to abandon K Basin in another month or so", said Aaron, as calmly as he could manage. "Don't think it will be that long", Bill replied.

There were three entrances into the K Area spent fuel storage building. By the time Aaron had completed irradiating the second pair of moissanite samples in the SRNL ^{60}Co facility all three K Basin entrances were blocked by moissanite colonies. Two robots had been moved into the only open floor areas remaining inside the building. Unable to reach their charging stations, each robot's battery would be exhausted in another week. That would put an end to any video surveillance of what was happening in the water filled basin. The operating assumption was that practically all spent fuel in the basin was encased in moissanite, resulting in significant release of fission products into the water due to nucleate boiling and melting of zircoloy cladding. Water level in the basin was unknown. Judging by radiation levels near the building and radioactivity in air samples, it was likely a significant fraction of the spent fuel was no longer under water and had melted completely.

Aaron's estimate of when the K Basin would have to be abandoned was fairly accurate. No one could get closer than forty meters to the building. Bill's focus now shifted to monitoring groundwater and attempting to prevent fission products from reaching local streams and eventually the Savannah River. Airborne radioactivity monitoring, particularly for ^{85}Kr showed no unusual radioactivity in areas outside the Savannah River Site. There was no need to inconvenience the public just yet. Radioactive inventories in the basin were far less than those in a reactor meltdown, like at Chernobyl. After months, or in some cases years, in storage all the short-lived fission products had decayed to stable isotopes. Only the radioactive isotopes with half-lives of several years or more remained. The probability of significant airborne radioactivity reaching any location off site was remote.

In an effort to appease Professor Schareshiem, nonradioactive metal salts were introduced into the soil around the moissanite colonies growing outside the building. Aaron's tests had shown this might slow the growth of the colony by up to 35%. Pumping solutions of metal salts into the soil had one undesirable effect, however. Adding all this water accelerated the movement of moissanite and radioactivity toward local streams, like Indian Grave Branch Creek, then Pen Branch Creek and Four Mile Creek, and ultimately the Savannah River. The experts at the University of Georgia Ecology Laboratory at the Savannah River Site predicted radioactivity from K Basin would reach Pen Branch before Christmas. Water samples taken from Indian Grave Branch on Thanksgiving Day showed significant amounts of ^{137}Cs and ^{90}Sr. The moissanite colony was on the move.

“Of course”, the Professor replied. Aaron struggled to think of a polite response. “It will follow that which supports its continued growth.” “I fear we’ve just made it move faster”, Aaron finally answered. “Yes. Anything you do to slow the growth will accelerate its spread. I thought that was obvious”, Schareshiem continued. Aaron terminated the call. For a second time his initial admiration for Schareshiem had turned to contempt. It was quite clear the Professor was more interested in conducting a gigantic chemistry experiment than in slowing the radioactive contamination of a significant portion of South Carolina countryside, and possibly part of Georgia as well.

Brent’s office at Caltech was tiny compared to Schareshiem’s luxurious accommodations. He had a light grey metal desk and an old chair discarded by the clerk at the end of the hallway, all in a room the size of a closet. At least he was on the same floor, and only thirty meters down the hall. Brent had begun factoring the growth results from Aaron’s tests in the ^{60}Co facility at SRNL into the computer models. “Thc revised models, when averaged, estimate the moissanite could cover the entire planet in eleven years, worst case. That’s of course if the colonies had immediate access to all the fission product inventories in all the nuclear sites in the world.” Schareshiem showed no reaction. “In the best case it would take twenty-seven years.” There was still no response. “If we’re talking about just the total land mass, it might take as little as seven years.” “How would it know to just stay on land and avoid growing in the sea”, asked the Professor? “I suppose it wouldn’t.” “OK, we’ve got at least eleven years to study it, then?” Brent returned a blank expression.

Schareshiem hadn’t given up on his idea of interrupting self-replication in this unique icosahedral silicon carbide structure. This form of moissanite had many unusual properties. Nevertheless it was a simple combination of silicon and carbon, two of the most studied elements in the periodic table. An entire field of organic chemistry had been devoted to the study of carbon and its compounds for well over one hundred years. Silicon was one of the most abundant elements on earth. It had combined with oxygen over billions of years to cover the beaches of the world.

Diluting the supply of radioactive isotopes with non-radioactive metals was only partially affective. The silicon carbide crystals clearly preferred the radioactive isotopes. That wasn't a sign of some inherit intelligence. The silicon carbide crystals simply had a stronger chemical affinity for the more energetic radioactive atoms. The key was to find a way to stop the colony's crystalline structure from transporting fission products to the active outer surfaces. The moissanite crystals couldn't make copies of themselves without energy from radioactive decay. Once separated from an external radiation source, like spent nuclear fuel, it would stop growing. The fact that the cask at Fukushima showed no moissanite growth proved the Professor's point. Schareshiem hoped to starve the moissanite colonies of the energy they required for growth, like the moissanite in the Fukushima cask.

The Professor's latest idea was to limit crystalline growth to a parabolic function rather than an exponential one. If he could stop the migration of radioisotopes to the active surfaces of the silicon carbide molecules, growth would be parabolic at best, possibly even linear and self-limiting, i.e., it couldn't grow beyond a certain size. If growth was parabolic, Brent's models showed it would take twice as long to spread across the planet. That would be enough time to find ways to contain it. If growth was linear, a small portion of the planet might remain uninhabitable for billions of years, but the rest would be unaffected. Nine and a half billion people would have to crowd into a slightly smaller space but at least homo sapiens would survive.

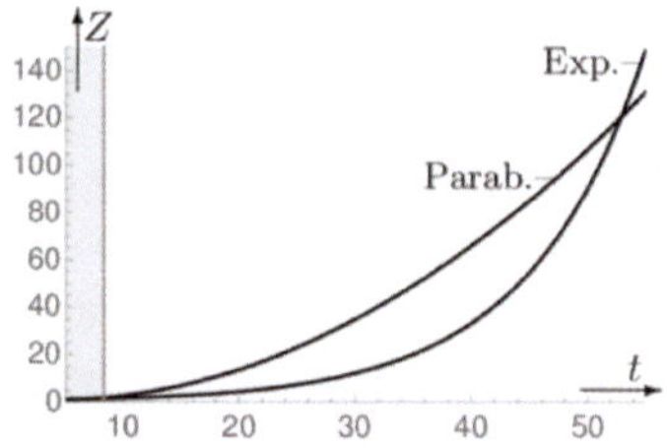

Brent was a bit more optimistic about keeping the moissanite colonies from reaching the numerous sources of radioactive isotopes scattered all over the globe. He didn't accept his boss's premise that the moissanite would eventually reach every nuclear facility on the planet. Surely there were ways to prevent that from happening. So far, the problem was confined to K Basin in South Carolina, San Onofre in California, and Sellafield in the United Kingdom. "Not exactly", Schareshiem replied. "Someone at Fukushima decided to flush that cask Sellafield sent them with seawater." Brent looked puzzled. "Seawater, son! Like discharging the flush water back into the sea…" Brent had to consult his tablet. Then his expression changed. "There's 4,000 million GBq of ^{137}Cs and 3,880 million GBq of ^{90}Sr in the sea water and in the fish off the coast of Fukushima." Schareshiem nodded slowly. "So now we may also have a moissanite colony growing in the sea off the east coast of Japan." Schareshiem nodded again.

"Can you explain how large molecules absorbed by the silicon carbide crystals migrate to the chemically active sites on the crystalline surface", asked the Professor? "We all thought you were the expert", Aaron replied. He had grown tired of chasing every rabbit the Professor could dream up. Time in the ^{60}Co irradiation facility wasn't free. Others at SRNL had booked time in it as well. Irradiations could last for weeks or months at a time. "I can't explain it, but your tests proved it happens", Schareshiem replied in a terse manner. "We need to find some way to stop it." Aaron took a deep breath. His disdain for Schareshiem's arrogance was counterproductive and unprofessional.

"Our tests here at SRNL don't prove anything. We only observed the behavior in two very small samples. That doesn't mean it will behave the same way on a scale of meters or tens of meters, much less thousands of meters. How can we stop a process we can't even describe, Professor? Attacking this problem with trial-and-error tests in the ^{60}Co facility would take years. If your calculations are correct, it will be too large to control in less than a year. If you want to know how fast it grows on a macro scale, why not just watch as it covers several hundred square kilometres of South Carolina farmland along the streams that flow into the Savannah River." The call ended in the usual manner.

Aaron had developed a plan to monitor the colony's growth along the banks of Indian Grave Branch Creek, Pen Branch Creek and Four Mile Creek all the way to the river. The University of Georgia Ecology Lab suspended all their other work on the Savannah River Site and devoted their entire staff to the effort. They were particularly interested in how the fish in these streams would respond to a moissanite invasion of their habitat. It only took a month to find out. Newts and other amphibians along the banks were the first to disappear. Fish lasted a few months longer. The upper tributaries of both streams were completely free of fish by mid-December. The prognosis for 2033 appeared grim. "So where did the fish go then", Brent asked in late January? He had taken to calling Aaron himself as his boss seemed reluctant to do so. "Ecology Lab people can only guess, but since there are no dead fish anywhere, they believe they've all been consumed.

"How about the 'fish's growth rate'", Brent continued, carefully avoiding any mention of radioactivity or nuclear waste. That was why he called. "It's only early data, but it looks to be about halfway between the worst- and best-case numbers your computer came up with." "That gives us nineteen years", said Brent. "Nineteen years for what", asked Aaron? Brent suddenly remembered the growth rate predictions had only been shared with those on Caltech staff. No one was allowed to mention anything about the entire planet theoretically being consumed by moissanite. That information would have caused worldwide panic. The less the news media knew, the better. "Sorry, something the Professor is working on. How about inside your facility?" Aaron paused for a moment. "No one can get in at the moment", he replied. The entire K Basin building was surrounded by dark grey regolith. No one could get near it in any case. It had been declared off limits to all personnel. All the roads into K Area were closed.

Professor Schareshiem knew Aaron was correct. It was impossible to stop the migration of energetic radioisotopes to the chemically active faces of the icosahedral crystals without first understanding why this phenomenon was occurring. Surely there was no intelligence involved. There was no cognitive process. How could there be? Yet the moissanite was able to sustain it self-replication. As radioactive atoms were added to the silicon carbide molecules these energetic atoms were able to remain at the active faces and not get buried within the crystalline structure. It appeared each crystal was able to turn itself 'inside out' to keep the radioactive molecules on the active face, much like a tree grows. Only the outer skin or bark of a tree makes new cells. The rest of the tree is just a wooden structure supporting the cells in the outer layer as they carry water and nutrients to the leaves that are absorbing energy from the sun.

Schareshiem was forced to accept the phenomenon in this moissanite as perhaps a 'learned chemical behavior'. Was such a thing possible? No one had ever seen it before. A learned survival technique, perhaps the result of millions or billions of years of existence in the cold vacuum of space. Astronomers had discovered a great many exoplanets covered in grey regolith and showing no evidence of organic life. Why was silicon carbide rare on earth but common in space outside our solar system? 'Has our atmosphere shielded the silicon carbide on earth from the solar radiation it required to self-replicate', he wondered?

Bill was forced to make a decision. Did they keep adding water to the K Basin after it was obvious some of the spent fuel had already melted? Water was leaking into the soil at numerous locations carrying fission products. The moissanite colony was following as the water and fission products reached local streams. Should they stop adding water and let the rest of the fuel melt, releasing a greater fraction of the fission product inventory in the spent fuel into the environment? "Your call", replied his management. They needed plausible deniability when the environmental lawsuits began piling up. By the time the makeup water supply was turned off roughly half the fission product inventory in the K Basin had found its way into the environment extending several miles. Most of it was in groundwater and some in nearby streams.

Radiation levels along the banks of Indian Grave Branch Creek and Pen Branch Creek had increased to the point that direct access to the water was no longer permitted. Four Mile Creek was still accessible, but radiation levels were rising. Background readings averaged between 15 to 30 millisieverts/hour at one meter in many locations. Moissanite on the ground made the footing hazardous as well. The ground was covered in it for hundreds of meters around the streams. It gave the appearance of being solid but broke into dark grey regolith when stepped on. It could be quite slippery when wet as well.

Samples of this regolith were delivered to the shielded cells at SRNL weekly for Aaron's attention. Aaron had no idea what he was supposed to do with them. Space inside the shielded cells was at a premium. Moissanite samples were accumulating and they were growing. Any sample growing outside its container could infect the shielded cells. After a month the Lab decided to stop collecting samples and return all the existing ones in the shielded cells back to the field. They were dumped unceremoniously onto the ground near the edge of the colony using the same robots that collected them. Two other robots were entombed inside the K Basin building. The other two robots were returned to Oak Ridge Y-12 site in Tennessee. The University of Georgia Ecology Lab had to resort to using airborne drones to collect water samples. This was difficult in areas where trees and brambles had grown over the streams.

Gamma Ten

By late December the moissanite colony had covered 17 square kilometres along the shores of the Indian Grave Branch Creek and Four Mile Creek.

By the end of January 2033 it had covered an additional 96 square kilometres. A significant portion of the Savannah River Site had to be declared off limits to all but Radiation Control Technicians and University of Georgia Ecology Lab personnel. The only public highway passing through the SRS was still open, but the colony was moving ever closer. It was only a matter of weeks before it would have to be closed. The Department of Energy (DOE) had already drafted a statement for the news media explaining the closure as a security precaution. The closure would be advertised as 'temporary', with apologies to the public for the inconvenience of having to drive over forty miles out of their way to get to communities in the southern portion of South Carolina near the river.

This would attract the attention of the news media, who had failed to notice that almost one-sixth of the Savannah River Site was covered in a strange looking 'grey soil'. Local reporters were only casually interested in stories about 'problems at the K Area spent fuel storage basin'. The endless controversy over who actually won the election in November had captured everyone's attention to the exclusion of everything else.

Gamma Ten

In late February the DOE was forced to admit there was a problem across the Savannah River Site, with nearly 260 square kilometres covered in moissanite. The closure of SC highway 125 caused a public outcry as expected. The "security" explanation was quickly dismissed as several private pilots had taken photographs of the area. It was clear that over a third of the entire Savannah River Site had been abandoned. Fortunately very few facilities were impacted, but the entire site was on alert that they might have to shut down operations and evacuate with less than a week's notice. Trees and other foliage showed obvious signs of radiation damage. There were signs of moissanite on tree bark in some instances, due to the radioactivity in the groundwater being taken up into the trees. Wherever the ^{137}Cs and ^{90}Sr went the moissanite followed.

University of Georgia Ecology Lab personnel were analysing samples of soil and foliage. Radioactivity levels varied. Drones flew over and dipped down to take water samples of L Lake, which was now inaccessible. There was no evidence of fish in L

Lake, but that was not too surprising since it had never been stocked since being built in 1982. Samples taken from various locations at the edges of the colony were visually consistent. Technicians reported the edges of the colony resembled lava flows, but at ambient temperatures. The edges did not move fast enough to be observed without watching for several minutes. Background radiation levels were too high to allow direct observation for more than a minute or two. Most samples were taken using robots.

The Department of Energy held meetings in the main administration building at SRS, in their offices in Aiken, South Carolina, and in the Forrestal Building in Washington, D.C. throughout the month of February. The month ended as it began, with no progress toward a solution. Aaron was the featured speaker of course, which left him little time to do anything else. Bill had described to Aaron how the meteorite fell into the K Basin. Aaron had further described the incident to so many audiences he kept visualizing the event in his sleep. Of course that was the explanation to why this was happening at SRS and not happening anywhere else in the world. Truth was it was happening elsewhere in the world, specifically at San Onofre Nuclear Generating Station in California. No one in the DOE would have been even slightly interested in anything happening there.

Chapter 7

By mid-March 2033 Georgia Ecology Laboratory personnel detected higher than normal levels of radioactivity in the Savannah River. The Vogtle Nuclear Power Station on the Georgia side of the Savannah River began to notice increasing radioactivity in the river as well. Even though the reactors at Vogtle had been shut down since 2029, the Savannah River still supplied makeup water for the Vogtle spent fuel storage basin.

It was Aaron's turn to call Brent the first week in April. He was calling from home, so he had to watch what he said. "I've got some more data on how fast those fish are growing." They agreed on some assumptions before Aaron hung up. Brent called back two days later. "Based on half the fish in your inventory being released into the streams, you could theoretically have fish in 60% of all the streams, rivers, and lakes in the continental United States in four years. If you added the fish from a location on the other side of the river, it could be more than 75%." Nobody watching the K Basin problem had yet considered the spent fuel inventory at the Vogtle Nuclear Site in Georgia, directly across the river from the Savannah River Site. If the moissanite found its way into the spent fuel basin there, matters would escalate even faster. It was time to consider all the communities downstream, especially the port city of Savannah, Georgia.

Aaron convinced the DOE that getting Professor Schareshiem to the Savannah River Site was imperative. If there was anything that could be done it would have to be done soon. Caltech refused the DOE's request but sent his assistant instead, much to Aaron's relief. It was Brent's help Aaron needed. Aaron met him at the Augusta Airport on a Monday evening. "Flying east is never easy", Aaron commented. "I can never remember if jetlag is supposed to be worse flying east or west, but flying east has always been worse for me." "Same for me", Brent replied with a smile. "Daylight disappears too quickly."

"I think we have enough data on the colony here at SRS to calibrate your computer models", said Aaron once they were in the car on the way to the Augusta Hilton. It's not growing that fast yet, but that may be due to the slow movement of ^{137}Cs and ^{90}Sr through the soil. There's not as much moissanite in the water as we predicted but some of it has reached the river. We've alerted the folks at the Vogtle Site. It may be too late. If they've topped up their spent fuel basin with river water in the past few weeks we may have a problem there as well." Brent nodded. "It will take a few days to update our models. Time on the computers at Caltech is allocated to many users. Even though this has high priority, I can't guarantee we'll get the time we need immediately." "Understood", Aaron replied.

It was a week before Brent had what he needed. "I can access the machines at Caltech through my laptop for mundane things, but I have to use a portable secure terminal for the information we need in this case." "Looks like an ordinary laptop", Aaron observed. "That's intentional. If it's stolen at the airport or somewhere else, the thief will find it's inoperable. Just a string of binomial gibberish. The electrical impulse patterns in your hand are unique, like a fingerprint, only better. Someone could cut off your finger to get your fingerprint. Electrical impulse patterns are impossible to steal or copy. I am the only creature on this planet who can make this secure terminal connect to the machines at Caltech. All information is encrypted with two private keys, one on each end." "Sixty-four-bit encryption", asked Aaron? "Two-hundred and fifty-six-bit. The fastest computer on earth would need longer than the age of the universe to crack it. Neither the news media nor any environmentalist groups are going to know anything about this until we're ready to tell them."

"So it's downloading the computer's predictions now", Aaron asked? "Yes, we'll have it in a few seconds. Your data confirms we are dealing with a parabolic expansion, not an exponential one." Tables of numbers were displaying in sequence. "Can you print a hard copy?" "Yes", but only to a hardwired printer. We can't risk any of this getting on one of your networks." Aaron nodded. "I've got an old ink jet printer in a cabinet in my office. Should have thrown it away twenty years ago. It's got a cable connection." Brent smiled as he looked over the relic now sitting on Aaron's desk. "So that's what they looked like. I always wondered where they put the socket to plug in the cable. I've never seen anything like that." "Now I just have to find a compatible cable…", Aaron mumbled, as he looked further back in the cabinet. There was an old box containing nearly two dozen of them. "That's quite a collection", Brent remarked. "Found it. It's a USB-C." "I've got an adapter to the USB-E socket on your machine." It took almost three minutes to print the first table of numbers. "Sorry it's so slow", said Aaron. Brent nodded. He was accustomed to seeing a page printed ever three seconds.

Months	United States (Sq Km)	South Carolina (Sq Km)	Georgia (Sq Km)	California (Sq Km)
1	17	17		
2	103	103		
3	256	256		
4	552	547	5	
5	870	855	16	
6	3,466	3,419	47	
7	13,029	5,983	251	12
8	26,803	7,692	470	39
9	38,529	11,110	705	93
10	50,255	17,093	940	155
15	111,678	25,639	5,485	580
20	223,357	34,186	7,835	1,623
25	465,327	42,732	10,186	2,435
30	1,675,177	68,372	19,588	3,092
35	2,605,831	85,465	39,175	10,435
40	3,722,616	85,465	62,680	27,053
45	5,863,120	85,465	78,350	61,836
50	7,445,232	85,465		88,889
55	7,910,559	85,465		154,590
60	8,375,886	85,465		231,885
65	8,841,213	85,465		309,179
70	9,306,540	85,465		386,474

"Our best estimate, based on parabolic growth as your observations indicate, is that it will take seventy months for the colony that began in your K Basin to completely cover the continental United States. That's assuming it stops at the Mexican and Canadian borders, which it won't of course. Still that gives you an idea of how long we have." Aaron was shaking his head is disbelief. "Seventy months? To do what, exactly?" Brent raised his hands with palms pointed at the ceiling. "Your colony will cover all of South Carolina in three years. Assuming the spent fuel basin at the Vogtle Power Station across the river is now infected, four months after the start of the K Basin colony, it will cover the State of Georgia by the forty-fifth month. Even if the Vogtle basin is not infected yet, it will be eventually, as your colony will be growing on the Georgia side of the Savannah River in a month or so anyway. Georgia might have an extra a month or two."

"I really wish you would stop calling it 'MY colony'", Aaron replied. "Sorry", said Brent. "You're predicting it won't start growing in California until this summer. Why is that?" "They think they have it contained at San Onofre Nuclear Generating Station. No one at Caltech thinks their containment will last. We're just being pessimistic, I suppose. It may spread into Mexico and Canada which might slow its progress across the U.S. On the other hand it might spring up in new locations. If that happens it will spread faster, especially if separate colonies link up. Some scenarios are just too hard to model." "We may have less time than we think", Aaron replied with a sigh of resignation. "Right".

"So…, when do we tell the population of the world how much time it has left", Aaron asked? "Not for a while yet. That decision won't be ours to make." "So who do we tell, then?" "That will be up to the authorities at Caltech." "Like Schareshiem?" "No, much higher on the food chain than that. I suspect the Chairman of the Board of Regents is calling the President of the United States about now. It's quite likely no one in the government will believe anything the Chairman tells them. You're going to be spending a lot of time away from your family and friends."

"Perhaps they won't believe us either", said Aaron. "They will, as soon as 20% of South Carolina is evacuated because of 'cold radioactive grey lava' moving at nearly half a kilometre per hour", Brent replied. "We haven't seen it move anywhere near that fast here at SRS." "You will, once it consumes the radioactive inventories of all the nuclear reactors and spent fuel basins in South Carolina, Georgia, Alabama, Tennessee, and Florida. The Tennessee Valley Authority has three nuclear sites, two on the Tennessee River." Aaron looked worried. "Browns Ferry, Watt's Bar, and Sequoyah. They'll have to shut down and move all their spent fuel." "Where are they going to move it to", asked Aaron? Brent shrugged. "There is ^{137}Cs and ^{90}Sr in the sea near Fukushima as well. We also may have a problem at Sellafield in the United Kingdom. How long will it be before it gets to La Hague in France? And there's all that radioactivity around Chernobyl in the part of Russia that used to be Ukraine?"

Aaron was speechless, until his phone rang. "I think you better come up here, Bill.... No, not tomorrow – today. Brent has some bad news... I'm willing to bet his is worse than yours.... OK, see you in two hours." "He's forced to drive around the perimeter of the SRS, now that most of the roads on site are blocked off", said Aaron, after putting the phone back in his pocket. Brent shook his head.

Bill assumed he would be fired if the K Basin had to be abandoned. To his surprise, his management assigned him the dubious responsibility of directing all efforts to stop the spread of the moissanite. None of the management above Bill wanted to be involved with any of it. Nor did they want to stand in front of the TV cameras on the front lawn of the main administration building. They needed a scapegoat for this sort of disaster. Bill was clearly the best man for that job! At least they gave him additional staff. In fact, he could have as many people as he wanted, as hundreds had been forced to evacuate their facilities and had nothing else to do. What their new job entailed wasn't exactly clear. Bill was hoping Aaron and Brent had found the answer.

Bill studied the numbers Brent had printed. "I've got several hundred people wanting to know what they are supposed to do, and you show me this", Bill asked, with a look of incredulity? "Sorry", Brent replied. "I've got another set ready to print as well. It's not just your problem." The old ink jet printer suddenly came to life again. "This is what the rest of the world needs to worry about", Brent continued.

Months	UK & Europe	Japan	Ukraine	Russia
1				
2				
3				
4				
5				
6				
7				
8				
9				
10	57	18	46	74
15	190	73	277	245
20	569	438	692	736
25	1,517	876	1,476	1,964
30	3,791	1,460	2,306	4,909
35	7,962	2,627	8,301	10,309
40	13,269	7,663	12,912	17,181
45	27,297	17,516	18,446	35,344
50	39,240	29,558	24,902	50,807
55	51,182	43,789	36,892	66,270
60	113,738	54,736	69,172	110,449
65	227,475	87,578	138,344	196,355
70	473,907	131,367	207,515	306,804
75	1,706,066	182,454	345,859	441,798
80	2,653,880	291,926	553,374	601,336
85	3,791,257	364,908	691,718	785,419
90	5,971,229			994,045
95	7,582,514			1,227,216
100	8,862,063			2,699,876
105	9,383,361			4,417,979
110	9,904,658			6,381,526
115	10,425,956			8,590,515
120				10,308,619
125				12,026,722
130				13,744,825
135				15,462,928
140				17,181,031

"Our computer models indicate other locations around the world could begin to be impacted as early as ten months after the initial release at K Basin, assuming uncontrolled spread of moissanite colonies. That inadvertent transfer of a cask from San Onofre Nuclear Generating Station to Sellafield, then to Fukushima, was most unfortunate. The Japanese had the moissanite contained with no growth until they accidentally flushed the cask with sea water. It's difficult to know how the moissanite will react with the radioactivity in the sea off the Japanese coast. There may be a colony growing in the seawater near Fukushima already. We won't know until it shows up on the beaches there. Another colony is already growing in the spent fuel basin at Sellafield. That colony has covered more than half the spent fuel in that basin as of a week ago. It's just a matter of months before it gets out of the basin, based on your experience in K Basin, Bill." Bill was staring at the floor rather than Brent's numbers.

"We had to assume something about these other locations. For simplicity we assumed they will all experience colonies beginning to grow about nine or ten months after your colony started growing outside K Basin. Your facility is time equal zero. Everything else is predicted from that starting point." "Why", Bill asked, without raising his head? "Because you are the beginning", said Aaron. Bill shook his head violently. "Will someone please pinch me so I can wake up from this nightmare? You're telling me that if we don't find a way to stop this stuff it's going to cover the world." "Yes, in three decades – maybe a few years more or less", Brent replied.

"We can't destroy this stuff. We've already tried every method possible", Bill observed, waving his hands in the air. "We can't move all the spent nuclear fuel and other radioactive waste out of the path where the colony is growing. We've nowhere to move it to. If we remove the water from the spent fuel basins all the fuel will melt giving us airborne releases that will make large areas of the country uninhabitable for decades. If we keep supplying water to cover the fuel so it doesn't melt, the water will carry the moissanite and fission products into the soil outside. Either way it's going to get out of the basin. We can shut down all the reactors in the colony's path, but we've nowhere to put the spent fuel. You're telling me it won't stop growing because there is enough ^{137}Cs and ^{90}Sr in the world to keep it growing for 30 years." "Maybe well past the lifetimes of even our grandchildren", Brent added.

"So what does Schareshiem say about all these computer predictions", Aaron asked, just out of curiosity? Brent smiled. The last time I saw the Professor he seemed overjoyed with the 'prospect of studying such an interesting phenomenon'. He doesn't believe the numbers. He thinks it will stop growing before it finds enough radioactivity to sustain its self-replication." "Let's all hope he's right", said Bill. "There's always hope, of course. What do we do if he's wrong." Aaron remarked? "Who else knows", Bill asked? "Just the three of us plus four or five people at Caltech." "What do I tell the news media?" "As little as possible", Brent replied.

Local DOE representatives at the Savannah River Site promised a weekly press briefing every Friday at 3 pm, beginning in early February. It was no problem for them since no government employees were expected to attend, much less speak. This was Bill's eighth briefing. By this time he had all the talking points memorized. No need for notes or a teleprompter. As far as he knew the Site Contractor didn't own such a thing. The DOE had already issued a statement claiming the problem with radioactivity releases from K Basin was due to errors by the Site Contractor. New Site Contractor candidates were already being interviewed, they teased. Bill had no illusions that the new Site Contractor, whoever it turned out to be, would be keeping him on. Perhaps losing his job would be a blessing at this point.

"Yes, I have seen this 'grey stuff' covering the ground in several large areas of the Site. We've been analysing samples of it for some time." Bill didn't mention that he had only seen the edges of the colony through binoculars. He took another reporter's question. "Yes, it does contain some amounts of radioactivity. Some of that has reached the Savannah River, but there's no reason to be concerned at this point." "We've been told it is growing." "It has spread out over a wide area of the Site. That will make it more difficult to clean up, but we have a large staff assigned to the task." "Can you describe it – this grey material?" "Yes, it looks a bit like thick cakes of sand, but the material is a form of silicon carbide, rather than silicon dioxide or silica." "Can you walk on it, then?" "Yes, but it would crunch under your feet.

You would sink into it. I don't think you would get very far." Bill didn't mention how the radiation levels were too high to permit any physical contact.

"How thick is it..., on the ground, I mean?" "It is only able to support its own weight up to a thickness of a meter or so." There was no basis for that statement, but it sounded reassuring. "How fast is it spreading?" "I've not been able to see it moving. You would have to watch it for some time to see any movement." That was true. Bill hadn't seen it move faster than one tenth of a centimetre per second. Others had reported seeing movement of one centimetre per second. One only had to watch it briefly to see movement at that pace. No one had reported movement at eleven centimetres per second, as Brent's computer models predicted. Perhaps that was something akin to accelerating a spaceship to the speed of light - theoretically possible but not actually attainable.

Normally such press briefings would have provided Bill with some stressful moments. Perhaps at the beginning they did. He had become accustomed to them by now and found them quite boring. "You would think these people could think of some original questions, wouldn't you", he asked? Arlene looked up from her computer screen. She was preparing another article for the church bulletin on whether the Bible sanctioned same sex marriage. "Yes, Dear", she replied. Bill looked at her for a moment. Her long black hair draped luxuriously over one shoulder. Almost 40 and not a sign of grey. Perhaps she dyed it. Bill was never sure and chose not to ask. He simply paid the hairdresser when the bill arrived in the list each month. All he had to do was click the boxes he wanted to pay when he accessed his bank account online.

Everything was digital of course. He remembered his father talking about paper bills arriving in the mail and how he would gather them up and throw them at the staircase. The ones that landed on the top three stairs got paid. The rest would have to wait another month. He watched as his father wrote numbers on little pieces of colored paper he called 'cheques'. The cheques were placed in envelopes with clear plastic windows in them. The envelopes had to have 'stamps' glued onto them as well, before putting them in a metal box on the corner of the street where they lived.

Press briefings were typically held at the Department of Energy Offices in Aiken, South Carolina. This was for the convenience of the news reporters, it was said. It also kept them and their cameras away from the SRS property, except when an overzealous reporter decided to show up on the front lawn of the main administration building at the Site with only an hour's notice. Bill had to deal with those as well. Such events were completely unscripted and dangerous. With no others in attendance, a lone reporter often lacked the usual restraint of not wanting to embarrass himself in front of his peers. In those cases the reporter had already written his story. All he wanted was a salacious video clip or unguarded remark to add credibility.

The Department of Energy was much more concerned about the Savannah River problem than they let on. Press briefings at the Forrestal Building in Washington, DC maintained the same tone as in Aiken. However, those occupying the seventh floor of Forrestal seemed unable to talk about anything else. The office of the Secretary of Energy had been in discussions with Professor Schareshiem and others at Caltech for several months. No one could offer a definitive answer as to when they would gain control over the moissanite problem at the SRS. In fact, those at the university seemed rather cavalier about the problem. The DOE was focused on the releases of radioactivity, rather than the spread of some grey sand-like material. With radioactivity levels rising in the Savannah River the Secretary knew she couldn't stonewall the press much longer. If significant radioactivity reached the city of Savannah, Georgia a growing number of those in the opposing political party would be publicly calling for her resignation. What she needed was a way to deflect attention away from the DOE and find proof some other organisation was responsible.

One of her staff members found the solution. It was all the fault of the largest environmental protest group in the country. "GreyForest" had found a way to infest a large part of the Savannah River Site with an extremely resistant organism in their quest to force a shutdown of all operations at the site. Their guilt was obvious, from the name alone. GreyForest's actions had inadvertently caused the release of significant radioactive contamination when facilities had to be abandoned. "We'll need some of GreyForest's emails and other correspondence to prove this was all their idea." "Yes Ma'am. I'm sure our IT guys can put something together." "Make sure the correspondence goes back a couple of years. We need it to look like GreyForest has been planning this thing for some time." "Yes Ma'am."

"I have a statement to make before I take questions this morning", The Secretary of Energy announced. It was the usual Monday morning briefing, sparsely attended since no one was expecting the Secretary to say anything different. "This morning around 3 am seventy-five arrest warrants were executed at various locations around the country. Evidence now in our possession proves the environmentalist group called GreyForest is responsible for the situation at the Savannah River Site in South Carolina. This evidence shows they have been planning for over eighteen months to disrupt operations at the SRS. Those responsible will be prosecuted to the fullest extent of the law, I can assure you. Efforts are under way in South Carolina to clean up the mess they have created. We expect operations there will be back to normal in the very near future." The Secretary looked down at her notes to be sure she hadn't omitted anything. "Now, are there any questions?"

"We've been told you plan to replace the Site Contractor at the Savannah River Site. Is that correct?" "We have full confidence in the current Site Contractor and their ability to clean up the problem by the first of October. However, three other consortiums are interested in the contract at Savannah River. I'm sure any one of them can step in should the current Site Contractor fail to meet our deadline of October 1st."

Gamma Ten

Chapter 8

In March 2033, management at San Onofre Nuclear Generating Station (SONGS) found themselves forced to make the same decision Bill had made the previous November for K Basin. Several moissanite colonies were growing outside the spent fuel storage basin at San Onofre. The volume of makeup water required to keep the spent fuel covered had increased eight-fold. The local public was warned about airborne releases of radioactivity as the spent fuel basin had to be abandoned in the same manner as K Basin. San Onofre didn't have an exclusion area as large as the Savannah River Site in South Carolina. Even though the area near the Station was sparsely populated, the public was impacted to a greater extent. Some populations had to be evacuated. No one could say when they would be allowed to return to their homes and businesses.

The San Onofre Nuclear Generating Station located on the Pacific Coast Highway south of San Clemente, California had been shut down since 2013. However, like many other nuclear sites, decommissioning had been delayed because of a lack of funding. The spent fuel storage basin was still in use due to the shortage of such facilities worldwide.

By May there was a large moissanite colony around the Station. The Pacific Coast Highway was completely covered and had to be closed to all traffic. All decommissioning work at the Station was abandoned. The local news media became concerned with how fast this 'grey sand' was spreading and demanded to know when it would be cleaned up. Authorities at the Station referred the press to 'experts' at Caltech. Professor Schareshiem attempted to describe the technical nature of the moissanite growth, all of which fell on deaf ears. He then explained there was nothing they could do. That wasn't what the press wanted to hear, of course. The situation in California took the media's attention off the Secretary of Energy, but only temporarily. It was now obvious this wasn't just some sort of 'environmental terrorist' activity confined to one unfortunate facility in South Carolina. The Department of Energy's response to renewed demands for information was to stop holding press briefings.

When radioactive 'grey sand' began to show up on San Clemente Beach and other tourist spots along the California coast, the Governor demanded a federal response from Washington, D.C. The only response the President could offer was the miliary. Armed forces were mobilized in both South Carolina and California, with orders to 'do something'. That 'something' turned out be controlling the mass relocation of the populations around the Savannah River Site and the San Onofre Nuclear Generating Station as the moissanite colonies in both locations began to grow more quickly.

By August all populations and communities along both sides of the Savannah River had been displaced by the moving colonies of radioactive 'grey sand'. This included most of the communities in Barnwell, Allendale, Hampton, and Jasper Counties of South Carolina, as well as their counterparts on the Georgia side of the river. The Vogtle Nuclear Site had to be abandoned as well.

Army 'half-tracks' equipped with lead shielding bolted to the undercarriage were the only vehicles that could traverse the moissanite covering the ground. The colony varied from a half-meter to a meter in thickness. Only the leading edge of the colony was radioactive, proving Professor Schareshiem's theory about the moissanite being able to continuously push the radioactive isotopes to the active crystalline faces at the boundary where growth could occur. Radiation levels were only slightly above normal background forty meters past the leading edge. Unfortunately these vehicles traveling over the crystalline structure accelerating movement of the colony by fracturing the brittle material into tiny pieces, spreading them beyond the growth boundary. Helicopters had to be used in areas the army half-tracks couldn't reach.

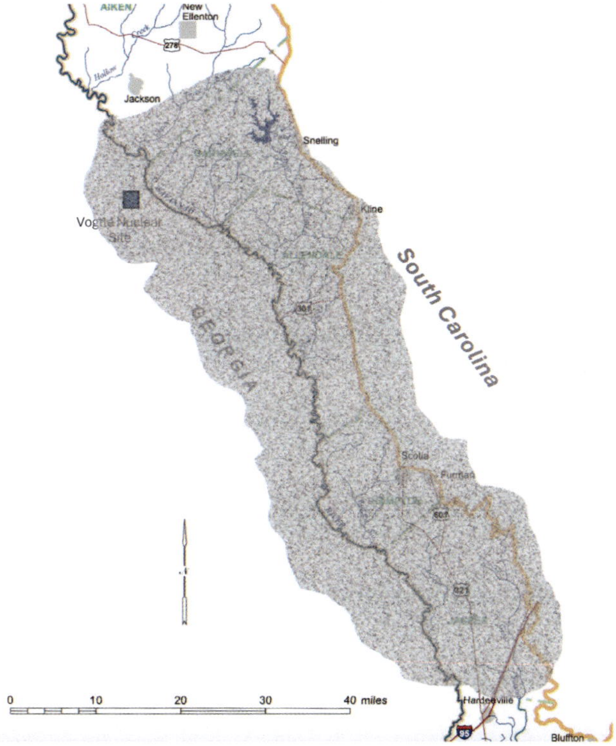

The military's emergency response plan for flood rescue proved to be quite effective. The only difference was the people rescued from roof tops and tree branches had no expectation the 'flood waters' would recede in a few weeks or even years. Only those who heeded the government's early warnings escaped with more than they could carry. Even those who left early often found roads covered and blocked by what appeared to be grey lava flows. Helicopters picked as many people off the car roofs as possible. Most were dehydrated and hungry.

SRS employees like Aaron, Bill, Bryan, and others living north of the site were fortunate that the radioactivity in the ground water flowed southwest into the river. Communities like Augusta, Georgia and those in Aiken County in South Carolina had a few months longer to plan their relocation. Neither Arlene nor Geraldine believed their husbands when they were told they 'may only have a few months to move somewhere'. Bill and Aaron had to prepare for the worst case. If this phenomenon couldn't be stopped, they would soon need all the money they could get their hands on. Cash was rarely seen in the past decade, but it could become the only form of payment accepted if online banking services collapsed when large populations were forced to relocate. Bill had planned to take out a small second mortgage on their house to cover his daughters' third and fourth years at university. "Why not borrow as much as we can", he asked Arlene? "If I'm wrong six months from now, we'll just pay it back plus a small amount of interest. It will be worth it for our piece of mind. If I'm right, we may not be able to sell the house for more than a fraction of what it's worth. We might not be able to sell it all."

Aaron and Bill were thinking alike. Aaron had already taken out the largest second mortgage he could get, while using their boat at the marina on Clark's Hill Lake as collateral for another loan as well. "Max out your credit cards and save your cash", he told Geraldine. "If the banks collapse, we'll never have to pay them off." "What if they don't collapse", asked Geraldine? "Then I'll happily pay them off with the money from the house." Geraldine looked worried. "It's time to get creative, Dear", he added. Of course he was just as worried as she was.

Both Bill and Aaron had been withdrawing cash from their current bank accounts and savings plans in modest amounts so as not to attract attention. Aaron was happy he didn't have the problem of liquidating a load of stocks and investments before they became worthless. Leonard might have been right at one point in time. That was in the past. Aaron and Bill each had places to keep large amounts of cash in the near term. The problem was how to take it with them when and if they moved. Bill was thinking the Midwest might be safe for a few years. Aaron was thinking Canada. Claire and Diane weren't pleased. Both wanted to finish at university and weren't planning on traveling to the Midwest to see their parents on weekends.

In California public evacuations were confined to the area east of the San Onofre Nuclear Generating Site. Beaches north of San Onofre were cordoned off, however, with signs warning the public that access was prohibited.

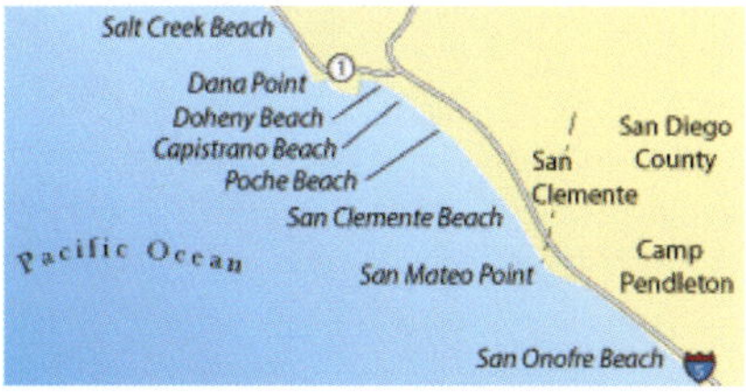

Traces of moissanite began appearing on San Clemente Beach, Poche Beach, Capistrano Beach, Doheny Beach, Strand Beach, Salt Creek Beach, Laguna Beach, and Crystal Cove Beach. Anyone who happened to have a Geiger Counter near any of these favorite tourist spots would immediately understand why. The State of California was losing an enormous amount of revenue. Businesses up and down the coast were forced to shut down. Coastal tourism in Southern California was essentially dead.

Professor Schareshiem and others at Caltech were besieged by the local and national press demanding answers. After several weeks it was decided that continued press briefings were a waste of everyone's time. Schareshiem had in fact left California to assist with operations at Sellafield in the United Kingdom. Spent fuel and nuclear waste storage basins there had not been abandoned. Every effort was being made to avoid that scenario if possible, using experience gained at the K Basin in South Carolina and at San Onofre in California.

In 2022 primary activities at the Sellafield Site had transitioned to nuclear waste processing and storage. The site's workforce size had included nearly 10,000 people in 2020. Staffing in 2033 was less than half that number. The local population around the Sellafield Site was sparce but there was no designated exclusion zone like the one at the Savannah River Site. The nearest population center was Seascale, with approximately 2200 permanent inhabitants. The population of Cumbria was less than 600,000.

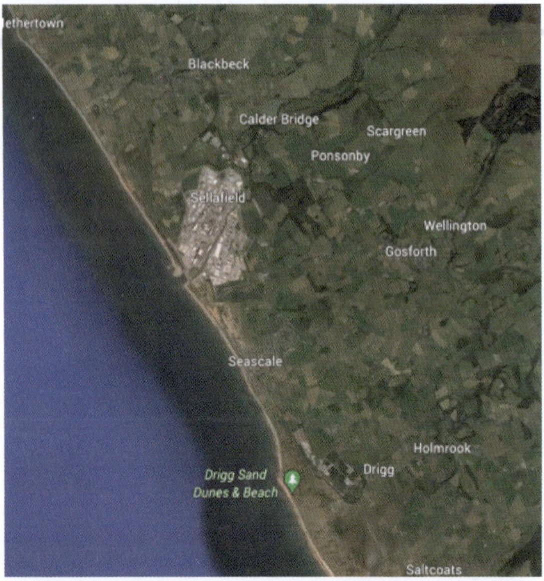
Nethertown
Blackbeck
Calder Bridge
Scargreen
Ponsonby
Sellafield
Wellington
Gosforth
Seascale
Holmrook
Drigg
Drigg Sand
Dunes & Beach
Saltcoats

Sellafield
Sellafield
Seascale

Moissanite growth at Sellafield had been contained by isolating those fuel assemblies affected into one basin with an isolated water supply. This basin was lined with stainless steel plate, preventing leakage through the concrete basin walls. The colony there was still growing but at a reduced rate. There was no evidence of nucleate boiling on the surface of the fuel elements and radiation levels were still manageable in the area. Professor Schareshiem had advised Sellafield to saturate the basin water with peroxides in so far as possible to promote the formation of silicon dioxide (silica) rather than silicon carbide. This had been partially effective at slowing the growth of the moissanite in the basin. Such treatment would be impossible once the moissanite escaped from the basin of course. It was simply a delaying tactic.

Residents and businesses along the banks of the Savannah River were alarmed at finding patches of 'grey sand' in many locations. The public had been warned to maintain a distance of at least ten meters from these deposits. There were those who ignored the warnings of course. Some collected their own samples and took them back to their living rooms to show to their friends and family. Radiation doses to these individuals weren't high enough to cause immediate illness, but several hospitals in Savannah, Georgia noticed an influx of patients with sores on their hands and feet. Radioactive contamination was found on their shoes and clothing. Within a week, federal healthcare agencies provided hundreds of additional staff who were trained to deal with contaminated patients. Brett Michael Sellars Hospital, St. Joseph's Hospital, and Georgia Regional Hospital in Savannah quickly set up separate wards to deal with an escalating problem.

By July 2033 all these facilities were overwhelmed. There were new reports of major 'grey sand' deposits on the popular beaches at Tybee Island. Nearly1000 tourists and 4200 permanent residents of the island had to be evacuated, each complaining about leaving their homes and belongings to be pilfered by looters. The military provided as much assistance as possible, but most of their resources were already tied up in other areas of South Carolina and Georgia. Snelling, Kline and Allendale, South Carolina had already been evacuated. The communities of Scotia, Furman and Hardeeville had to be evacuated less than a month later. Routine surveillance of these areas was from the air, with helicopters still finding people stranded on rooftops and other buildings even after several weeks. These people had survived by cutting holes in their roofs to allow them to access the upper floor where they had stockpiled food and water. Some had even erected tents or tarpaulins on the roof to provide shelter. One Army Colonel commented on the amazing resourcefulness and ingenuity some survivors had demonstrated. They were nevertheless more than happy to be rescued as they realized their situation wasn't transient.

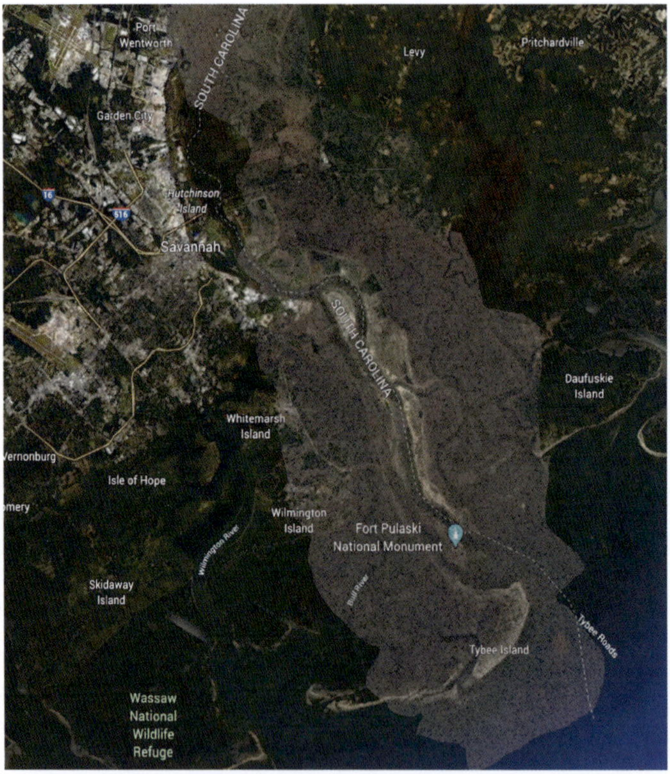

Gamma Ten

Within weeks this same scenario played out on other islands along the South Carolina coast. Many living on Hilton Head Island refused to leave their multimillion-dollar homes. When the miliary insisted, they reluctantly loaded their most prized possessions onto their twelve to thirty-meter yachts and sailed a few kilometres from the island, planning to return when the military had left. Permanent surveillance equipment alerted the military when they attempted to sail back into the various marinas. At that point they had no choice but to put to sea. Most sought havens up the coast as far as North Carolina. The residents there didn't exactly welcome them with open arms. All the marinas in North Carolina and Virginia were overcrowded and had no space for them. By August a few 'grey sand' deposits began to appear along the North Carolina coast as well

Professor Schareshiem left Sellafield for Japan after only a few weeks, satisfied his idea about peroxides had provided some delay at least. Privately, he had no doubt a major portion of the planet would be uninhabitable by the time of his death. Many were appalled at the Professor's lack of empathy. Schareshiem was content to leave nature to do what it must. Darwin's theory of evolution was oversimplified and not confined to organic chemistry as far as he was concerned. Why should the earth be the only planet that supports self-replicating chemistry? Maybe there were vast numbers of such planets. Maybe we had spent past decades following the water and looking for the wrong things. This moissanite didn't need water or oxygen. It just needed two chemical elements and a bit of energy. The universe was full of all three.

Fukushima power station was a disabled nuclear facility located on a 3.5-square-kilometre site near the towns of Okuma and Futaba in Fukushima Prefecture, Japan. The facility suffered major damage from a magnitude 9.1 earthquake and tsunami that hit Japan on March 11, 2011. The chain of events caused radiation leaks and permanently damaged several of its reactors, making them impossible to restart. Undamaged reactors were not restarted either.

First commissioned in 1971, the facility included six boiling water reactors, making Fukushima Daiichi one of the fifteen largest nuclear power stations in the world. A sister nuclear power station Fukushima Diani was located 12 kilometres south. It also suffered serious damage during the tsunami, at the seawater intakes of all four units, but was successfully shut down and brought to a safe state. The March 2011 disaster disabled the reactor cooling systems at Fukushima Daiichi, leading to releases of radioactivity into the air and substantial releases of contaminated water into the sea. A 20-kilometre exclusion zone was maintained around the facility.

The situation at the Fukushima Daiichi Nuclear Facility was quite different from Sellafield. The problem was offshore, not in their spent fuel or radioactive waste storage basins. The moissanite in the cask from Sellafield wasn't growing. It was well shielded from any radioactivity in the spent fuel basin where it had been placed. The problem was in the sea. As was common practice, the cask was flushed with seawater a week after it arrived. The moissanite was now growing in the sea off the east coast of Japan, where nearly 8 billion GBq of ^{137}Cs and ^{90}Sr had been spilled in March 2011. That radioactivity was largely taken up in the fish,

which Japanese fishermen could no longer harvest, for the first time in many millennia.

Adding peroxides to the sea east of Japan wasn't practical, of course. Professor Schareshiem wasn't sure he could provide any help to the Japanese. He was curious, however. The evidence wasn't on the beaches. It was almost a mile off shore, where fishing boats reported finding thousands of fish floating on the surface covered in 'grey sand'. Knowing about the accident at Fukushima Daiichi Nuclear Facility, the fishermen knew not to collect or even touch the dead fish. Schareshiem naturally had to see for himself.

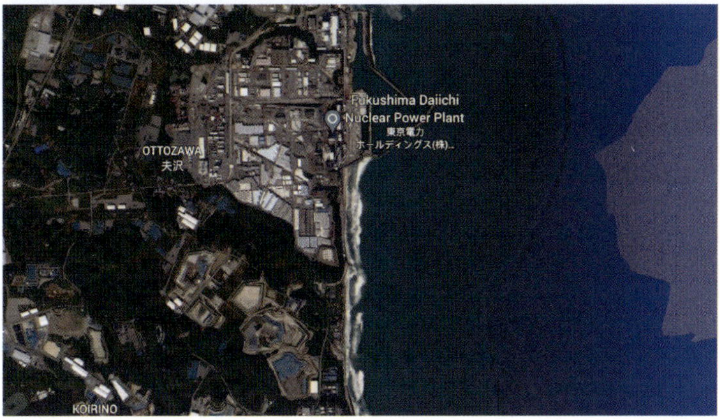

Gamma Ten

Several miles out from the coastal village of Tomioka there were dead fish as far as the eye could see. Over objections from the Japanese authorities, Schareshiem collected several fish and placed them in a lead container, refusing to let anyone else carry it. Management at the Nuclear Fuel Cycle Engineering Laboratories, part of the Japan Atomic Energy Agency, agreed to let the Professor analyse the fish samples in their facilities in Tokai. By November dead fish covered in 'grey sand' were turning up on Japanese beaches in alarming numbers.

It didn't take long to realize why there weren't thousands of dead fish off the coasts of South Carolina and California as well. The moissanite in Japan found the radioactivity it needed in the fish themselves, where it had concentrated through natural biological processes, known as the 'carbon cycle'. Recycling carbon from the atmosphere into living creatures, then into the soil and sea, then into the atmosphere again was essential to sustaining organic life on the earth. Fish kills on a global scale would disrupt the balance of carbon and jeopardize all life on the planet.

Much smaller amounts of radioactivity were dissolved in the sea off the coasts of South Carolina and California, and not concentrated in the fish – at least not yet. Unfortunately the fish samples at Fukushima couldn't indicate the extent of the colony off the coast of Japan. The colony there might be confined to a small area of a few hundred square kilometres, or it might be much larger. There was no way to tell. Aerial photographs and satellite images showed areas of dead fish but only in patches. The waters off the eastern coast of Japan were some of the deepest on the planet.

There were other satellite images that Professor Schareshiem and his colleagues at Caltech hadn't been shown. These images were of an area in Russia, previously known as Ukraine, surrounding what remained of the Chernobyl Nuclear Power Station.

Ever since the accident at Chernobyl in April 1986 satellites operated by several countries in the west had maintained close surveillance of the 4,143 square kilometre exclusion area around the sarcophagus that enclosed the remains of RBMK reactor number four. A quarter of the ^{137}Cs and ^{90}Sr released from the reactor was still present in the soil within the public exclusion area. These satellite images were classified secret because of what they revealed about the incredible resolution of cameras on the satellites in orbit.

After some debate, the United States National Security Administration (NSA) decided in January 2034 to invite Professor Schareshiem to view some of these images. He had to come to Washington, DC and be escorted into a Secret Compartmented Information Facility (SCIF). If he ever described the photographs in detail or revealed the location where he viewed them, he would immediately become a permanent guest at one the federal penal system's finest establishments, located in Leavenworth, Kansas.

"I've seen the photographs, Brent", the Professor insisted. "I'll be down to SRNL tomorrow, as soon as I can get a flight into Atlanta." "I didn't even know you were back from Japan", Brent replied, somewhat alarmed. "Can't talk about it now. See you tomorrow." The Professor terminated the call in the usual manner. Brent wondered why Schareshiem never ended a conversation politely. You realized the call was over when you heard it disconnect. 'The man has no social graces whatsoever', Brent mumbled. "What", Aaron had to ask? Brent looked puzzled. "My boss is coming to see us tomorrow." "Why…", Aaron replied? "He's keeping us in suspense." "Nothing new about that." "Yes, I think there is this time. I just can't imagine what…?"

Chapter 9

"It's there. I've seen the photographs", Schareshiem repeated the next afternoon, as he sat on one of the old wooden stools in Aaron's lab at SRNL. "In Russia", Aaron questioned? "How did it get there?" "The National Security Agency (NSA) has a theory. NSA believes the Russians misunderstood what they were reading about our problems at K Basin and in California. They may have concluded that we had found an 'organism' we could weaponize – a new biological or radiological weapon of some sort. One of their people must have obtained a sample and took it back to Russia with them." "How could they do that", Brent asked? "It would have set off the radiation detectors at the airport." "Don't know. Maybe they put a tiny sample in a small lead container. If they did get a sample, they would likely have taken it to a laboratory inside the Chernobyl exclusion zone. NSA has suspected for years that the Russians have a secret laboratory inside the exclusion zone where they conduct research on animals to see how they have responded to living in an elevated radiation environment for the past forty-eight years. What better place to investigate a sample of radioactive moissanite."

"Do you believe these guys at NSA", Brent asked? His generation was naturally sceptical of the government and their motives. Schareshiem shook his head. "I don't believe they told me everything. Of course not. But I did see the photographs. It's on the ground in nearly two dozen places about four miles from the sarcophagus. You could see the sarcophagus as well. The coordinates on the photographs were clearly inside the Chernobyl exclusion zone." "And they threatened to send you to prison, right", Brent pressed? "Yes", said Schareshiem. "Maybe just for talking to you two, so keep your mouths shut, OK?" Both nodded. "With at least 12 billion GBq of ^{137}Cs and ^{90}Sr still in the soil, we can expect a major moissanite colony to

develop there in the next year. The Russians will deny it, of course. The Russian government denies everything until forced to admit it. In this case they'll express surprise and claim the West has 'infected' their homeland in a scandalous and unprecedented act of radiological warfare. It will all be our fault – every mistake they make is always our fault. They play the propaganda game very well, always manipulating world opinion into whatever they want it to be."

Schareshiem had been forced to rent a car and drive from Atlanta because there were no flights into Augusta. The Augusta Airport had been overrun with moissanite several days earlier, due to its location close to the Savannah River on the Georgia side. The runways in Augusta were covered in 'grey sand' up to a half-meter thick. Fortunately the Professor had kept the rental car. There were none available in Augusta, Aiken or anywhere else within a 150-kilometre radius. Brent and Schareshiem returned to California on the only flight they could get out of Atlanta two days later.

Both Bill and Aaron were offered early retirement, as were all the employees at the Savannah River Site. Both had considerable retirement savings. Their retirement plans contained a clause prohibiting ‘early withdrawal of funds’, however. As Prime Contractor for the SRS their employer had requested and obtained a federal court order forcing those retirement investment firms to ‘waive that clause under the unprecedented circumstances’, and to release the funds while the matter was being challenged in several appellate courts. The retirement investment firms immediately filed for bankruptcy but were ordered to borrow money to fulfil their contractual obligations. Bill, Aaron, and many others in the area would be spending those funds in a manner no one could ever have expected.

Their monthly pensions fell far short of their salaries, especially after taxes were withheld. One of the first things Bill did was maximize the number of exemptions he claimed so that the federal and state tax withheld each month was a little as possible. That meant he would owe a healthy tax bill to the government when he filed his tax documents in April. That is, IF he filed his tax documents in April. Bill was betting he and many other residents of South Carolina wouldn’t be filing their tax documents this coming April or any other time. Could the Internal Revenue Service (IRS) really come after all of them? If the IRS tried to take the money from Bill’s bank account, they would find it practically empty. Aaron took Bill’s approach a bit further. He filed an exemption request with the IRS insisting he was exempt from tax withholding altogether. That meant he received his full pension with no tax withheld. Bill had to acknowledge Aaron’s creativity, while immediately doing the same. Their untaxed pension funds would be enough to let them live comfortably where the cost of living was much cheaper than in Aiken or Augusta.

Gamma Ten

It came as no surprise when neither Bill nor Aaron was able to find a real estate agency to list their house for sale. They simply abandoned their mortgages, 1st and 2nd, when they left the area. Real Estate agents were the first businesses to shut, followed closely by banks, who expected a run on any open branches. Fears were unfounded as no one complained. Those with any money in a bank account had already transferred it electronically to some other location and account number they felt was more secure. In truth, their money only existed as numbers in one of the bank's computers, which might be located anywhere in the world. Transfers of funds from one bank location to another was a façade to make the customer feel they had some control over their money. Fact was, they had almost none. All transactions and purchases were done with apps on mobile phones. There were some who still preferred using credit or debit cards when they could get them to work. The global economy now ran on the Internet. As long as it was still working no one seemed all that concerned.

It took nearly a month to arrange for a moving company to assist Bill and Aaron with their relocations. Aaron offered to share the cost with Bill and Arlene since both families were going in the same general direction. The moving company agreed if each of them paid 60% of the normal fee. Bill objected to being 'ripped off' until he found all the other companies were fully booked for the next six months. He and Aaron agreed to reduce their household furnishings by half so that both households would fit into the moving van. When their wives objected, they each rented the largest U-Haul vehicle available to carry whatever wouldn't fit into the moving van. The final arrangement was for the husbands to drive the U-Haul vehicles while Arlene and Geraldine each drove the one family car each family decided to keep. Selling the second car provided some additional cash for the trip.

Over Claire and Diane's objections, Bill and Arlene had decided to move to Rapid City, South Dakota. The cost of living was within their reduced income and there were a great many natural and man-made wonders to see in the area. Neither of them had visited Mount Rushmore nor any locations in that part of the United States. Now retired, they could afford the time to see as many as possible. Aaron and Geraldine had decided on Winnipeg in Canada. Neither planned to become Canadian citizens as there were lots of people living in Canada without giving up their United States citizenship. Aaron liked to fish although he hadn't had the time during the past few years. He looked forward to all the fishing opportunities he had read about in the Winnipeg area.

The moissanite colony had reached New Ellenton, South Carolina as Bill, Arlene, Aaron, and Geraldine departed Aiken, driving west to Atlanta, then north toward Nashville, Tennessee. They made Nashville be nightfall on the first day – quite a feat in Arlene's mind. Keeping four vehicles together on Interstate highways wasn't that difficult, although there were a few dirty looks from impatient drivers. It was expensive however, with hydrogen costing about $20 per kilogram, or about $18 per 100 kilometres for the cars and nearly $30 per 100 kilometres for the U-Haul vehicles. Keeping the group together would be more difficult once they got onto slower state highways and country roads. Arlene knew patience wasn't one of Bill's virtues. The moving van had left the day before. It would likely arrive in Rapid City several days ahead of them, depositing Bill and Arlene's property in a temporary storage unit just south of the city. Bill had arranged to view several rental properties in the area with a real estate agent he met online. With any luck they would find something suitable within a week.

The moving van would continue east to Sioux Falls, then north to Fargo and Grand Forks, before clearing customs at the Canadian border at Emerson. From there it was only 120 kilometres north to Winnipeg, Manitoba. Aaron and Geraldine parted company with Bill and Arlene at Sioux Falls and continued north to Fargo, Grand Forks, and the Canadian border. The moving company had arranged with border officials at Emerson to clear Aaron's U-Haul and contents through customs, as part of their service contract. The remaining contents in the moving van would be waiting for them in a temporary storage unit when they arrived in Winnipeg. The moving van would likely be back in St. Louis, Missouri by that time. They had the advantage of having two professional drivers who drove and slept in shifts. Time was money for these people, and they were getting busier by the day.

Aaron's only son, Leonard, wasn't pleased to hear his parents were moving to Winnipeg. "You're almost twice as far from New York as you were before. Why Canada? You could have found something here in the Adirondack mountains. It's absolutely gorgeous up there." "Too close to the sea", Aaron replied. 'And much too expensive', he was thinking. "Why don't you want to be close to the sea?" "I'll explain everything later, OK. Mom and I will let you know as soon as we're settled. You can come up and spend some time with us then. Do some fishing." "If I can get away from the job. Just let me know", said Leonard. Claire and Diane were convinced their parents had lost their minds. Surely, neither of them was old enough to have dementia. "What are they not telling us", said Diane? She had called her sister to see if Claire knew something. "I'm sure Dad will tell us when the time is right", Claire replied. She was 238 seconds older than her sister. That gave her the right to have the last word, or so she thought. "Can you imagine what plane tickets to Rapid City are going to cost", Diane continued? "Lots to see in South Dakota, I'm told", said Claire, ignoring Diane's question.

Claire finally managed to get through to her mother on her iPad. She then rang Diane and connected her into the video call. "We've been very busy here", said Arlene. "Your father has been moving furniture around trying to make everything fit. Not sure we're going to be able to keep everything we brought with us. Place just isn't that big, and it doesn't belong to us. Beautiful area though. So much to see in the time we have." Diane didn't miss her mother's slip. "Is Dad ill", she asked? "Is there something wrong with either of you?" Bill stepped into the video frame behind Arlene. "No, no. Nothing's wrong. It's just that we aren't getting any younger, you know. This is such a great place to spend our retirement years." "I don't know what to believe anymore. All that stuff in the news about where you used to work. Sounds like they really messed things up at that place. Is that why you had to move?" "Partly, yes", Bill answered. "Can't talk about it over the phone. We'll fly both of you up here during the semester break. We'll explain things then." "Don't know if I'm going to pass my economics class this semester", Claire announced. It seemed as good a time as any to deliver the bad news. Bill was looking away from the camera. He had a tear in his eye. He stepped away for a moment. Arlene continued the conversation. "The skills you learn at university may not be the ones you'll need to succeed in the world that is coming", She cautioned. "Survival may depend on a different skill set entirely." There was a lump in her throat. "We have to go. See you soon. Bye."

Most were not so fortunate as Bill and Aaron. Farmers in the western half of South Carolina and eastern half of Georgia watched helplessly as fertile land that had been in their families for generations was covered over in some sort of grey mineral they had never seen before. One farmer told the news media it reminded him of the stuff his grinding stone was made of, only it seemed to be everywhere. The farmhouses, barns, and other structures were still there. You just couldn't get to them. And the land couldn't be ploughed or planted. Nothing was growing on the land. Even the trees looked distressed. In the end everyone was forced to accept the military's offer to help them leave with as much as they could carry. "Where should we take you", asked one Army Sergeant? "As far away from this stuff as possible", was the answer. It was left to relatives and close friends to take them in, at least temporarily.

Virgil C. Summer Nuclear Generating Station was less than 130 kilometres northeast from Aiken, South Carolina. There were four other nuclear sites in South Carolina, including Catawba, H. B Robinson, McGuire and Oconee. None were more than 240 kilometres away. All contained sufficient inventories of ^{137}Cs and ^{90}Sr to accelerate growth of the moissanite colony moving through Aiken County. The V.C. Summer Station was watching the progress of the moissanite colony with interest, entertaining any and all suggestions as to how they might keep the colony from reaching the spent nuclear fuel stored there.

Gamma Ten

The oak lined streets in Aiken had never been particularly busy over the last half century. Now it was rare to see anyone not in military uniform in the town. Storefronts were boarded up to keep looters out. In fact, there was very little to steal in any of them. The miliary presence there was a waste of resources that could be better used somewhere else. The Colonel was asked if he would mind being quoted on that point. "Yes, I would", he replied. He was quoted anyway, and on the front page. He expected to receive a formal reprimand the next day. Instead he received orders to pull everyone out. They were needed further east near Columbia, the State Capital. The majestic tree lined streets of Aiken, South Carolina were to be abandoned to a pestilence no one seemed able to combat or even understand.

The situation on the west coast was only slightly better. The moissanite colonies had devastated the tourist season as half the beaches in California were closed. The military was helping people evacuate, applying lessons learned in South Carolina in real time. The colony on the ground around San Onofre Nuclear Generating Station wasn't as widespread as in South Carolina. It was threatening the historic Temecula wine growing regions of the state, however. The Governor was once again on the phone with those in Washington, demanding that something be done. The wine could be moved - the vineyards couldn't.

Unlike Bill and Aaron, Brent wouldn't be offered retirement. For one, he wouldn't reach the federal retirement age of 70 for more than 40 years. For another, the Caltech campus wasn't in immediate danger of being overrun by the moissanite colony. The San Onofre colony was moving up the California coast for some reason no one could explain. Brent's boss had been offered early retirement every December for the past six years. He refused. Schareshiem had a theory about the direction the San Onofre colony was moving but refused to talk about it. He didn't want the press hounding him again. Lydia buzzed with a phone call for the Professor. "Not in", he replied. "I'll take it", Brent interjected. If it was the press, they would simply make up something and attribute it to the University anyway.

"It's Oak Ridge National Laboratory in Tennessee. I've been trying to reach anyone at the Savannah River Site who knows something about this silicon carbide thing. Nobody seems to answer down there." Brent wondered if the caller ever listened to any of the major news networks. Most people simply read what showed up on their tablet or computer every morning under the CNN or MSN feeds. Artificial intelligence algorithms selected what showed up in your morning news feed based on your historical interest. If you very rarely clicked on news articles about South Carolina, you would never see anything about a third of the State being evacuated to avoid being covered in 'grey sand'. Confining each person's 'news bubble' to only those topics they had previously shown interest in was considered the best way to prevent overwhelming the population with information. News bubbles were also a convenient way to reinforce tribal identities that sustained political stability for the party in power. What you didn't know wouldn't hurt them.

"There's no one there to take your call. The Savannah River Site was abandoned some months ago, sir", Brent replied. "Perhaps I can help you. What is your question?" "We got some of that silicon carbide stuff here at Oak Ridge. There must have been some of it on the robots they sent back to us. We were doing some maintenance on our High Flux Isotope Reactor." "HFIR, yes I've heard of it", Brent interrupted. "Now we got this grey stuff growing on the concrete shielding about the reactor. We tried washing it off with a power washer. We got some of it off, but not all of it", the caller continued. How do we get rid of it", asked the caller? "Was it radioactive", Brent pressed? "Don't know. Background radiation around HFIR is hundreds of sieverts/hour.

That's why we use the robots." "What did you do with the wash water?" "Our floor drains go into the site low level wastewater system and the seepage basin." "How far away is the nearest stream or river?" "Melton Hill Lake is about two kilometres away." "Does Melton Hill Lake drain into the Tennessee River?" "Sure."

Professor Schareshiem had a three-meter by two-meter world map mounted on the wall in his office. There were red pins in the center of South Carolina and Georgia, lower California coast, upper west coast of the United Kingdom, east coast of Japan, the northern region of the Russian territory of Ukraine. He added a red pin to a spot in East Tennessee. There were plenty of red pins in the box waiting to be placed.

Brent added yellow pins at the locations of Brown's Ferry, Watt's Bar, and Sequoyah Nuclear Generating Stations, operated by the Tennessee Valley Authority. All three used water from the Tennessee River for cooling their reactors and for topping up their spent nuclear fuel storage basins.

Chapter 10

At 4 pm on December 12, 2033, the South Carolina State Capital became the first major population center to experience the spread of the moissanite across the legal boundaries of the city. Roughly half of the State's residents had been evacuated by then. One of the national news feeds featured photographs of grey patches here and there around Columbia city limits signs on Interstate Highway 20. Caltech's computer predictions were proving surprisingly accurate.

Professor Schareshiem was desperate to witness this phenomenon, but again the University would not allow him any more travel time. Brent's instructions were to call his boss at least once a day. "There's nothing to see", said Brent in response to his boss's incessant demands. "It's all over. I'm the only one here." Brent's rental car was parked on the side of the road. He had a small hand-held radiation monitor with him. It was reading about twice normal background levels. The streets were empty as far as he could see in every direction. Nothing was moving.

With more than a year's warning, the city and state governments had developed a detailed evacuation plan, relying on military support from the U.S. Army base at Fort Jackson, nearby U.S. Army Transportation Center, and the Army National Guard. By the time Brent and the moissanite arrived, the only people left in the city were those located in half a dozen high rise office buildings. Calculations indicated anyone on the fifth floor or higher would be sufficiently far from the colony on the ground that radiation doses would be negligible. If the colony showed signs of spreading upwards on the outside or inside of any of these structures, the occupants could be promptly evacuated.

City officials has spent the last six months converting the roofs of these buildings into helicopter landing pads. There were several companies along the gulf coast that specialized in transporting workers to and from offshore oil rigs. Doing the same for less than one hundred office workers in Columbia, South Carolina was welcome business. Those who volunteered to staff these offices agreed to set up living quarters in the buildings and work two weeks on and two weeks off to minimize the number of helicopter trips required. Brent contacted the air transport company and arranged a short flight over the city. A forty-minute flight cost him more than his roundtrip airline ticket from San Diego to Hartsfield-Jackson Atlanta International Airport. He hoped he could put the full amount on his expense account. When viewed from the ground or from the air, the city of Columbia, South Carolina was a ghost town. Even the animals in the popular Riverbank Zoo & Garden had been moved to other locations. "We missed the whole thing, sir. There's nobody here", Brent insisted.

Two months later only fifteen percent of Georgia's residents had been evacuated. The colony at the August Airport reached the Augusta city limits on February 18th. The evacuation in Augusta had not gone as smoothly as in Columbia. Military resources at Fort Gordon just west of Augusta had already been stretched to the limit. Their mission was accomplished, however. The only building in Augusta still occupied by February was the historic seventeen story Lamar building, which had been added to the National Register of Historic Places in 1979. Modifications to the Lamar Building were similar to those in Columbia. Constructing a helicopter pad on the roof meant the glass penthouse, added to the building in 1976, had to be demolished. One architectural critic had labelled the garish penthouse the "Eyesore of the Month", saying the addition was reminiscent of a 'Darth Vader helmet'. For decades a majority of Augusta residents considered the penthouse completely out of place atop such a historic building. Few were sorry to see it go.

Gamma Ten

"Why are these people in Columbia and Augusta still there", Schareshiem had to ask? "Their presence is essential to keep the Internet, online banking, and mobile phone systems operating. All the computer servers have been moved to the upper floors where they can be maintained and updated daily. Their greatest fear is that the Internet, including online banking and mobile phone service will fail. If that happens, they believe the global economy will collapse within weeks. Deliveries of food to grocery stores will cease. Pharmaceutical deliveries will stop. Hospitals will run out of supplies. Hydrogen refuelling stations will run empty so no one can travel. The airlines will all shut down. Electrical power grids will fail, not just in the United States but worldwide. The Internet runs everything. People used to worry about satellites getting knocked out by a solar flare or some other phenomenon in space. Now it's this stuff. They believe without the Internet the entire planet stops working."

Spring break gave Clare and Diane an opportunity to visit their parents in Rapid City. "This problem in South Carolina and Georgia is serious" their father began after they were settled comfortably on the sofa. He wasn't joking - they couldn't remember ever seeing their father in such a sombre mood. "I and a few other people were privy to information just prior to our leaving South Carolina and moving up here. If you believed anything I've ever told you, please try to understand what I am telling you now." Claire and Diane both nodded, but still didn't understand why everyone had been forced to leave their hometown of Aiken, or why their parents had to move so far away. Both listened quietly as their father recounted, for the fortieth time, everything from the moment he dropped the meteorite into the spent fuel basin in K Area, to growth of the colony outside the K Basin, to the evacuation of more than half the population of South Carolina and Georgia. He skipped over the technical bits, but insisted there was established science behind the predictions he cited.

"We have seen the news reports, of course", Diane replied. "Why so much fuss over some grey sand turning up everywhere?" "Radioactive grey sand, Diane. This grey sand is half a meter to a meter deep and the radiation doses at the leading edge are enough to make everyone ill or die of cancer." "But won't it just stop at some point", asked Claire? "It can't keep spreading forever. It will just run out of fuel, right?" "The people at Caltech in California say it won't", Bill replied. Neither Claire nor Diane was convinced. Both had no doubt their father was, however. Perhaps it was best to just play along. "So what are we supposed to do then. Just wait until this stuff gets to Alabama", Diane asked? "Or Knoxville", said Claire? "I'm told it's not far from Knoxville now", Bill added. Claire looked worried.

"A college education may have little value", Arlene interrupted. "I know that's a shock. It's hard to believe that privileges and infrastructure you've enjoyed since birth may not be there in the future. There have been times in the last two centuries when public services, processed food, and manufactured goods simply weren't available. We may all have to face another time like that in a few years. Everyone will have to relearn how to become self-sufficient, how to grow their own vegetables, hunt or catch fish, purify water, etc. to survive", Arlene urged. "I have some books for you to read. Please, please don't discard them. Keep them in a safe place where you can refer to them often." Arlene handed each of them a sturdy wooden box. Inside each was a well-worn copy of "The Complete Book of Self-Sufficiency" by John Seymour, copyright 1976, published by Faber and Faber Limited, 3 Queen Square, London. "I know you think your parents have lost their minds, but I can assure you we haven't. Your father has shown me enough information to know what he is telling you is true. This book may well become more valuable than any college textbook or university degree. You will need it after we're gone. Trust me on this."

The room fell silent for several minutes. Bill and Arlene were left to wonder about all the sons and daughters in the world who wouldn't or couldn't understand what was to come. They had done all they could to ensure their daughters were informed. It was up to them to prepare for an uncertain future. Bill finally broke the silence. "Now let's forget about all that and enjoy our dinner." Arlene disappeared into the kitchen and re-emerged with a huge roast turkey on a platter, surrounded by boiled potatoes. "Why not enjoy what we have now, rather than worry about tomorrow", Bill announced. Neither Claire nor Diane had ever been worried about much of anything. It would never be that way again. Bill had made several inquiries about properties in Alaska, if that time came.

Aaron and Geraldine found Canada a delightful place, with breath-taking scenery. Their first winter was brutal of course. They spent a fortune on clothes that no one would have ever needed in sunny South Carolina. Canadians seemed to have all the same concerns about cost of living, government meddling in their lives, and inflation as those who lived in the States south of the border. It took several calls before Leonard agreed to take time away from Goldman Sacs to visit his parents in Winnipeg. "I still don't understand why you had to move so far from Aiken. There must be some way to clean up all that stuff down there. The government just doesn't want to spend the money. And why leave the country? Is there something you aren't telling me? You're not in any legal trouble, are you Dad?"

"No, no. Of course not. We just didn't want to have to move again until we're forced", Aaron insisted. Leonard looked puzzled. "There is something you need to know", Aaron continued. Fortunately the house they were renting did not have voice activated devices. If you wanted something switched on or off you had the flip the switch yourself. It was quite inconvenient at times. "The future may not be as rosy as we'd hoped." Leonard smiled. "Goldman Sacs is doing just fine. I'm expecting a larger bonus than last year's. Financials are solid, Dad. Nothing to worry about." It was Aaron's turn to smile. "That's not the worry, son." It took about half an hour to explain the predictions regarding moissanite colonies growing around the world. "How do you know these guys at Caltech are right? Sounds like science fiction to me. How could some sort of carborundum grow without being alive? If Steven Spielberg was still around, he would probably want to make a movie about it. Sounds like rubbish to me."

"I've spent my entire professional career studying various chemical effects caused by radiation from nuclear materials. I can tell you this phenomenon couldn't be more real. I've handled bits of it in the laboratory. I've seen it grow when I put it in our ^{60}Co irradiation facility. There is no one on this planet who can tell you more about this stuff than I can." "Sorry Dad. Didn't mean to make you angry. It's just too bizarre to believe, that's all. I've seen the reports about all the evacuations in South Carolina. I'm sure you and mom wouldn't have left Aiken if you didn't have to. I'm just trying to get my head around this idea that it can keep spreading for years. Surely there is a way to stop it." "No one's found a way so far. We must accept the possibility that it can't be stopped – that it may cover the entire planet." "I haven't seen anything in the news about such an extreme prediction", Leonard scoffed. "That's because what I've just told you hasn't been released to the public. Such information on social media would cause widespread panic. People might believe financial institutions were about to fail."

Leonard laughed. "I'm quite sure Goldman Sacs is too big to fail, Dad. I've read the reports about extraordinary measures being taken in South Carolina and Georgia to keep the Internet, online banking, and mobile phone servers working. All that's completely unnecessary. Both the Internet and online banking systems are very robust and there is ample redundancy. There are so many safeguards against failure. As long as the major financial centres in New York, London, Singapore, Hong Kong, San Francisco, Chicago, Zurich, Tokyo, Frankfurt. Dallas, Seattle, Houston, and Atlanta are functioning it really doesn't matter if others around the world fail. We could lose Atlanta, Houston, and Frankfurt entirely without much effect."

"I understand the concern", Leonard continued. "Eighty-nine percent of all farm produce is delivered to supermarkets by carriers scheduled on the Internet. Sixty-nine percent of all manufactured merchandise is purchased through online shopping networks. One hundred percent of that is delivered to peoples' homes every day is scheduled on the Internet. Deliveries of hydrogen used in our cars and other vehicles is all scheduled on the Internet. Virtually all financial transactions are made and recorded via online banking. All airlines and public transportation are routed using the Internet. The Global Positioning Satellite (GPS) system used by all the planes and ships relies on the Internet. Trust me. The Internet is simply too big to fail, Dad!"

"As long as it has electricity", Aaron interrupted. "So far it appears the moissanite does not affect underground or overhead electrical transmission lines. It seems to ignore electrical currents entirely." "Most major locations have backup power in the form of batteries and hydrogen powered generators on site, in any case", said Leonard. "That's a temporary solution", Aaron added. "The problem will be maintenance of transmission and generating equipment, particularly the nuclear generating stations. They could be the first to go."

"Just the other day…", said Geraldine, feeling left out of the conversation. "I was in the supermarket. The machines wouldn't accept the app on my phone or any of my debit cards or credit cards. I was told it was 'cash only' because the Internet connection had been lost. I tried the cash machine outside the store. It was 'out of order' for the same reason. I had to leave my shopping in the store and go home without it. It was such a helpless feeling!" "It was only temporary though, right", her son declared? "What if lasted for a week, or a month", said Aaron? "What if the Internet was lost all over the planet?"

Leonard didn't enjoy arguing with his parents. He could see their concerns were genuine. "There have been several studies...", he replied with a more sombre tone. "According to all but one of them, nearly seventy percent of the world's population would be dead from starvation or disease within five months if the Internet was lost permanently." "What about the other study?" "Eighty-one percent."

When 'grey sand' was discovered on Santa Catalina Island and San Clemente Island in the summer of 2034, the Governor was immediately notified. San Clemente Island was inhabited by nearly 200 United States Navy personnel. The island was home to an auxiliary naval airfield and United States Navy SEALs training facilities. The southern end of the island was the Navy's only remaining ship-to-shore live firing range. Public access was not allowed. Naval personnel weren't allowed to complain about the grey sand or anything else.

Catalina Island nearby was home to Southern California's largest private land trust, established in the early 1970s by the son of William Wrigley Jr., and his family. They wanted to preserve the natural beauty of the island and set aside more than 88% of the land as 'forever wild'.

That included miles of unspoiled beaches, secluded coves, and the habitats of several unique plant, animal, and insect species. Fewer than 5,000 people were allowed to permanently inhabit Catalina Island. Most were wealthy donors to the Governor's political party, and to his re-election campaign. The Governor's staff was quickly overwhelmed with protest messages and requests for assistance from the State. There was a common theme in all these urgent communications – 'Get rid of this stuff polluting our beautiful island or we'll get rid of you'! The Governor made promises that were impossible to keep. To no one's surprise all the occupants of Catalina Island were forced to leave in furious protest. The Governor expected to be voted out of office in the same manner in November.

Professor Schareshiem, his secretary, and his assistant were among the last to leave the Caltech campus in Pasadena. Brent argued for San Diego to the south. Schareshiem insisted they go north. While everyone was trying to get away from the advancing menace, Professor Schareshiem wanted to stay as close as possible in an effort to predict where it would be going next. The warmer March weather should have been a time for celebration, not conceding defeat. They continued their work at Stanford University about 32 kilometres south of San Francisco. Brent had loaded the entire database of moissanite growth calculations onto his laptop. He no longer needed a connection to the computer models at Caltech. The Professor hoped to stay at Stanford for the rest of the year, possibly longer. There was a slowly evolving sense of inevitability, however.

Every new observation, whether from South Carolina, Georgia, or elsewhere proved worrisome. Difficulties at the HFIR reactor at Oak Ridge, Tennessee were reported in late March, causing great concern. The colony there was preventing access to some parts of the reactor building. The reactor was shut down as a precaution. If the colony reached the reactor vessel it might cover it entirely. That would greatly reduce heat transfer, causing the nuclear fuel inside to melt with a major release of fission products. 'Is that what we can expect when it reaches other much larger reactors, like V.C. Summer Station in South Carolina, or Watts Bar in Tennessee', Brent wondered while staring at the ceiling at 3:06 am?

On the 4th of April 2034 Los Angeles, California became the third and largest population center to be invaded by a moissanite colony. Several national news agencies carried the photographs. Los Angeles County, the largest single county in the United States, covered over 10,000 square kilometres. The Governor of California and the Mayor of Los Angeles were prominent members of opposing political parties. They disagreed publicly on almost everything. Still, neither could identify any political gain in obstructing the orderly evacuation of the city of Los Angeles. To everyone's surprise the two men found ways to work together for well over a year to accomplish the impossible. Military resources in the State were stretched to the limit, supporting the evacuation of more than fourteen million citizens. Many simply relocated to other western states, like Arizona, Utah, and Oregon. California lost 27% of its population and 68% of its tourist trade in just eleven months. Roughly half of those leaving Los Angeles moved further across the United States. Some went north into the Vancouver area in British Columbia, Alberta and Saskatchewan, Canada.

Gamma Ten

Without benefit of advice from Aaron's son Leonard, management of several financial institutions in the Los Angeles area made the decision to maintain a limited staff and vital equipment on the upper floors of several buildings in the city. A number of helicopter transport firms were eager to ferry employees and supplies from high-rise roof tops. Their primary customer had been Los Angeles International Airport. It was now a ten square kilometre expanse of bare concrete runways and empty buildings. As the moissanite colony continued to expand across the State, distances the helicopters had to travel became longer. Short hauls across the city became flights of an hour or more.

Financial firms in San Francisco were considering their options. They had an extra year to prepare. Unfortunately their most important assets were located in a building without a roof, the Transamerica Building. There was no place for a helicopter to land there. Moving all that equipment would mean a disruption of financial services for three months, possibly longer. Would the public tolerate such a life-changing event, even if they knew it was only temporary? Was it an expensive exercise in futility? Or was it an inexorable premonition?

Gamma Ten

State and local governments in South Carolina and Georgia had performed admirably but it was small self-organized groups of ordinary citizens who proved more innovative under pressure. A number of those living on upper floors of apartment complexes in Columbia and Augusta convinced officials they could sustain themselves if given sufficient funds to create makeshift landing pads on their roofs. Air taxi services, able to carry up to four passengers in a single trip, struggled to meet demand in these communities at first but expanded rapidly. Flying cars had been viewed as an expensive novelty for over a decade. Now they became a necessity, suddenly made affordable with government subsidies amounting to 80% of the purchase price. These vehicles could be self-driven with room for a single passenger. The market for flying cars grew rapidly in California as well.

Flying cars were good for the daily commute to the roof of another building less than five kilometres away, while air taxis were required for trips between affected cities, like Columbia, Savannah, and Augusta. One problem for those owning flying cars was where to park them. Roof top landing pads had to be expanded only months after they were built. A few citizens were old enough to remember a children's cartoon series on television, called "The Jetsons", featuring dome-shaped glass houses in the sky and flying cars. Hydrogen refuelling stations had to be provided as well and resupplied frequently. This led to development of another type of flying vehicle – a flying hydrogen tank. The principles of hydroponics were put to good use in many locations. Rainwater collection and purification equipment was provided in each occupied building at government expense. Balconies were used to grow vegetables of all varieties. Food that couldn't be grown had to be delivered – more business for commercial air delivery services.

Communities like Atlanta remained outside the moissanite colony. Land and roadways remained clear. Life there continued as it had in prior years. Helicopters were required for groups of ten or more into and out of cities inundated in 'grey sand'. The federal government expressed renewed interest in vertical take-off vehicles for short commercial markets. Several companies had offered to develop VTO aircraft that could carry up to 100 passengers. Only a small number of existing commercial buildings could handle the weight of such vehicles. It was thought one such elevated terminal in each major city would be sufficient. An airport terminal located thirty meters above the ground had never been envisioned before. Now it was a necessity. The problem was finding an existing structure in each major city that was tall enough, strong enough and large enough.

Gamma Ten

Chapter 11

Congress and the President had been briefed every two weeks during the past twenty-eight months about the moissanite problem. Professor Schareshiem had impolitely refused to attend any of those briefings, insisting it was a waste of his time. "I'm afraid you have no choice, sir", announced the Air Force Colonel standing in the ancient burgundy carpeted hallway outside the Professor's door. The Professor's apartment was on the third floor of one of San Francisco's most famous historical buildings. He had to call in some favours to acquire such a prestigious domicile. He had managed to bring some of his favorite pieces of antique furniture with him from Los Angeles. His weakness for anything ornate with Queen Ann legs was well known. Unfortunately the apartment was small, forcing him to leave half his collection behind. Schareshiem's only concern was that he might have to move again and lose his 17th Century sofa, upholstered in red velvet, with mother of pearl inlays in the armrests.

It was 6:45 am in San Francisco. Schareshiem called Brent who was still asleep. "You can sleep on the plane. You have 20 minutes." "Yes, sir. I'll be ready", Brent replied, still unsure what time it was. It seemed quite warm for April as he walked the short distance from his flat to the lot where a dark blue van with no windows was parked. It took less than an hour to reach Travis Air Force Base.

Brent looked around the small cabin. There were no windows here either. Did the U.S. Air Force have a problem with windows? He was searching for anything that looked familiar. There were no seatbelt signs or other clues as to what sort of aircraft they were on. The brief look at the outside while boarding hadn't helped. It didn't resemble any commercial aircraft he'd seen before. "How fast are we going", he asked the officer sitting across from them? "I'm sorry that information is classified, sir", was the reply. "Altitude?" The officer shook his head. "Will we be getting a meal", Schareshiem asked? "I'm afraid I missed breakfast this morning." "No sir. There is no food on board." The Professor looked particularly disappointed. "You won't have time to eat it in any case sir", the officer added. "We will be landing in fifteen minutes." Brent looked at his watch. They had only been in the air for an hour. Knowing the distance from San Francisco to Joint Base Andrews Naval Air Facility Washington, he could work out the average flight speed of the aircraft. It was Brent shaking his head this time. The officer smiled.

Brent and the Professor were escorted to a waiting area at Andrews. It was 6:30 am in Washington. "Relax gentlemen", said the Colonel. "You know I'm too old for this sort to thing, right", replied Schareshiem. "Yes, sir. You will deliver your briefing in the Senate Chamber at approximately 9:00 am. We will pick you up at 8:00 am and take you over by chopper. Until then please accept our hospitality. If there is anything you need there will be an officer right outside the door." "There is something I need", replied Schareshiem with a slight frown. "A little advance warning! But it's too late for that now, isn't it?" "Yes sir", replied the Colonel. "How about some breakfast instead?" "Yes, please", both 'guests' replied in unison.

"The following conclusions can be inferred from the data collected so far", declared the Professor to a huge room where half the seats were empty:

- Where groundwater is available to transport water soluble fission products through the soil, the moissanite colony moves faster than where groundwater is absent. The moissanite naturally follows the radioactive isotopes in solution and in the soil.
- The colony grows more quickly in areas where the gamma radiation levels are most intense. Colony growth rate is not directly proportional to radiation intensity, however.
- This extraordinary form of moissanite is ten times more soluble in water than any form of silicon carbide we can manufacture. That means it can be transported by streams, rivers, and ocean currents.

- So far, all our attempts to destroy this extraordinary form of moissanite have been unsuccessful. It does not react with acids or alkali. Temperatures exceeding 1200 degrees Celsius in the presence of molten alkaline metals will cause it to dissolve. Those conditions are not achievable outside a laboratory or foundry environment.

"Why can't we stop this stuff from spreading?" "The energy that makes it grow comes from radioisotopes contained inside its crystalline structure", Schareshiem replied. "How can you say it's growing but insist it isn't alive?" "I'm happy to use any words you wish, Senator. What words would you like me to use?" There was no reply. "You said your conclusions were based on 'data collected so far'. You've been collecting data for years now. How much more could you possibly need? Are you planning to wait until the entire State of South Carolina and half of Georgia have been evacuated before you do something?" Another Senator quickly rose to his feet. "Let's not forget the great State of California, gentlemen." The Senate floor quickly disintegrated into partisan bickering about who was to blame for this problem, which states and districts should be given priority, and who among them should never have been elected in the first place.

The Vice President's gavel pounded the podium for nearly three minutes before everyone took their seats again. Professor Schareshiem wanted to proclaim this was the reason he had refused to stand before the various Senate investigating committees in the past two years. He gave his assistant an angry look. Brent shook his head quite forcefully. Schareshiem reconsidered, choosing instead to stare at the furthest row of empty seats and remain silent.

Brent found it strange no one in the Senate asked for predictions. He had expected his boss to call on him for figures, times, and projections. He had grabbed his laptop on the way out the door that morning for that purpose. All these people seemed concerned about was how this would affect their prospects for re-election, even though the next election was two years away. Some things never seemed to change. Neither of the two Senators from

South Carolina was even present in the Chamber. The senior Senator from Georgia never said a word.

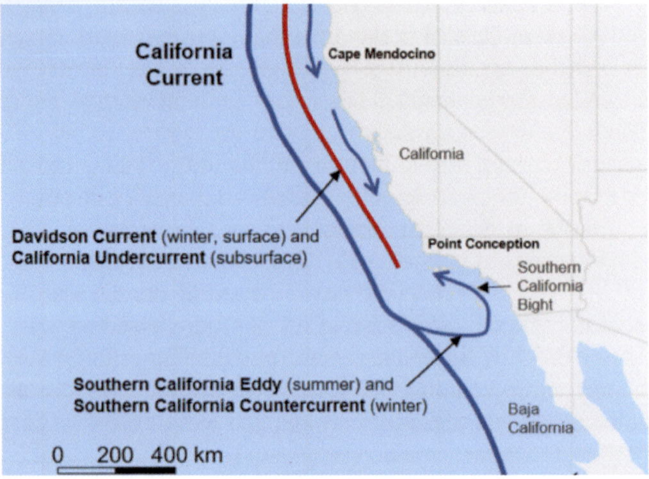

There was one conclusion the Professor hadn't mentioned. It was the reason moissanite hadn't progressed south along the California coast toward San Diego. The 'Southern California Countercurrent' was a phenomenon that caused the ocean currents to flow north between the Channel Islands of Catalina and San Clemente and up the coast past San Onofre Nuclear Generating Station to Point Conception. North of that location the ocean currents along the California shoreline flowed south.

The High Flux Isotope Reactor (HFIR) in Tennessee was constructed by the United States government to produce transuranic isotopes such as plutonium and curium at the Oak Ridge National Laboratory. The reactor operated at eighty-five megawatts thermal over most of its life. Since it first went critical in 1965, the in-core uses for HFIR broadened to include materials research, fuels research, and fusion energy research, in addition to isotope production and research for medical, nuclear, detector and security purposes.

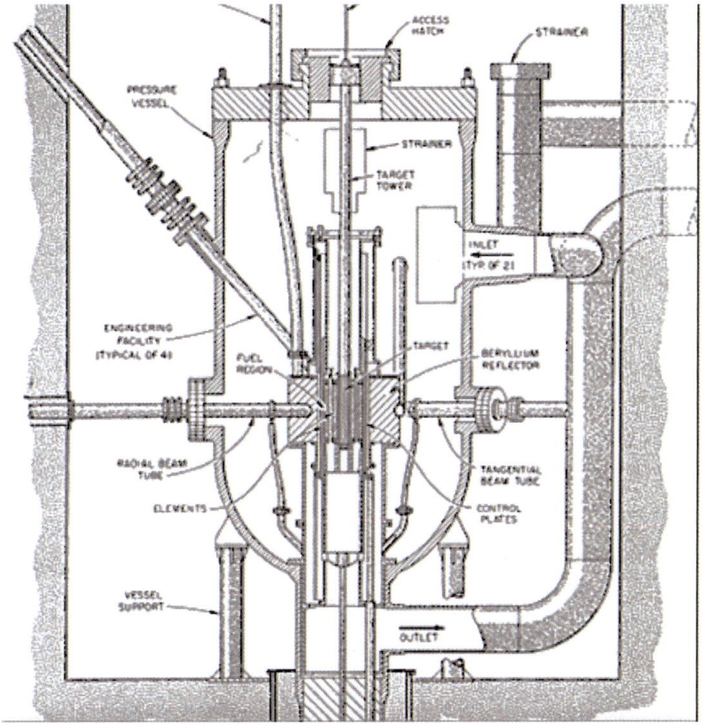

The reactor core assembly was contained in a 2.44-meter-diameter pressure vessel in a pool of water. The top of the pressure vessel was 5.2 meters below the pool surface. The reactor core was cylindrical, 0.61 meters high and 380 millimetres in diameter. Even though operating at less than one twentieth the power of commercial reactors, the short-lived fission product inventory in HFIR was higher than in commercial spent fuel elements, which had been sitting in storage basins for months or years. The high radiation levels near the water tank and reactor vessel accelerated moissanite growth, causing it to displace the water in the tank and completely fill the space around the reactor vessel in only six days.

Attempts to flush water through the tank and around the pressure vessel were unsuccessful. The primary cooling water system continued to operate but equipment was inaccessible due to high radiation levels in the absence of water shielding in the tank. When the primary cooling water system ultimately failed on June 3, 2034, temperatures inside the insulated pressure vessel reached the melting point of the fuel in less than twelve hours. The molten fuel penetrated through the pressure vessel, tank, and concrete beneath. Airborne release of fission products was minimal. Portions of the Y-12 area at Oak Ridge were evacuated as a precaution. Almost the entire fission product inventory was taken up by the moissanite and carried into the ground water underneath the reactor building, which leached into Melton Hill Lake and the Tennessee River. The city of Knoxville, Tennessee and the University of Tennessee campus were put on alert but were not immediately evacuated.

On June 10th, the moissanite colony in South Carolina forced abandonment of the Virgil C. Summer Nuclear Generating Station north of the Columbia. As everyone feared, a similar scenario to that seen at Oak Ridge played out at V.C. Summer, but over a longer time period. Operations personnel managed to prevent the moissanite from reaching the reactor vessel for nearly four months by erecting barriers of various types, first outside the reactor containment building, then inside the containment surrounding the reactor pressure vessel. Cross contamination of portable equipment eventually allowed the moissanite to breech the various barriers and establish a foothold around the reactor vessel.

The reactor had been shut down in April as a precaution. Consuming silicon and carbon in the concrete, the colony progressed outside the reactor building, preventing access to more and more of the equipment needed to maintain reactor cooling. By the time all forced cooling was lost, decay heat was low enough that natural convection cooling alone was enough to prevent fuel melting. The insulating properties of the moissanite eventually eliminated that means of heat transfer as well, just as it had done at Oak Ridge. Estimates of fuel melting ranged from 50% to 90%, depending on which set of airborne release data one chose to believe. Again most of the fission product radioactivity was consumed by the moissanite, greatly reducing the airborne releases inside the containment dome.

Airborne radioactive contamination outside the containment building was below levels that required evacuations of the public. The issue was mute in any case. The public had already evacuated months earlier due to the advancing moissanite colony. The prevailing winds carried traces of radioactivity toward Florence, Wilmington, and Myrtle Beach. Florence had been abandoned in March. Wilmington and Myrtle Beach were in the final stages of evacuation. Marinas at both locations were completely deserted. All anyone would hear was the sea birds calling and the peaceful sound of the ocean lapping against the abandoned wooden pylons. The best information Brent could get from the South Carolina State authorities was that 82% of the State's population had left the State. Still, there were many who insisted on staying in Columbia and a few other cities where high-rise accommodations were viable. Their precious Internet must not faulter - the 'grail' must not be lost.

Those staying in the major cities still needed electricity. Loss of the V.C. Summer Nuclear Generating Station was a major blow to the electrical grid supplying those still living in Columbia. The magnitude of the electrical supply problem was coming into focus. No one was offering any solutions. Three other nuclear generating stations in South Carolina were threatened, including Catawba, Robinson, and Oconee. Each of these reactors had time to remove all the fuel elements from the reactors before the moissanite arrived, but there was no place to send them. The original plan was to send the spent fuel to K Basin. Of course that was now impossible. In 2034 twenty-four percent of all electricity in the United States was produced by nuclear generating stations. That percentage was similar in Japan (22%) and the United Kingdom (28%), but much higher in France (68%).

Desperation allows the human mind to accomplish the impossible. Those achievements are often temporary, however. Individuals with means, often working with local governments, likened the moissanite invasion of their neighbourhoods to a slow-moving flood. Floodwaters always receded, however. Scientists warned this flood would not. Most of the affected population heard the predictions but didn't understand them. A man could easily walk fast enough to stay ahead of this flood. It never seemed to be more than a meter deep. It even looked solid enough to walk on, although everyone was warned to stay at least twenty meters away. Anyone ignoring the warning would have discovered a surface that was quite porous, too brittle to support their weight, and quite abrasive.

There were some in California who insisted this strange material would eventually distribute all the dangerous radioactivity on earth to every corner of the planet. Most scoffed at that idea. With almost all of South Carolina and half of Georgia 'flooded', those living comfortably in high rise apartments and office buildings couldn't say what they would do long term. Everyone assumed they could easily escape if problems arose. They would just go somewhere else to live. The analogy often cited was the Polynesian Islands, where for hundreds of years the natives canoed from one island to another as often as they liked. Only a few people in local and state governments were beginning to consider the impact of lost farmland in South Carolina and Georgia. The first casualty was the peach crop in South Carolina. The price of fresh peaches tripled in only a few months.

No one had seen the Governors of South Carolina or Georgia on television or other news broadcasts in months. Rumours had it that both were now living somewhere in the Midwest. There were public announcements from time-to-time detailing plans for cleaning up the moissanite flood so things could return to 'normal'. Nobody could define 'normal', however. Those who remained in affected states clung to the notion that the 'federal government' would deal with the problem in due course. The government's plan was to be announced in two weeks. The same announcement was broadcast two weeks later, etc. Congressional paralysis ensured that no appropriations were passed to deal with the problems in South Carolina or Georgia or California. State governments had been remarkably effective at solving local problems but struggled on a larger scale, believing their 'island communities could survive for many years. Federal agencies lacked consistent congressional leadership. They continued to flounder and bicker amongst themselves, each afraid to accomplish anything for fear the opposing political party might claim credit.

The first recorded death to be indirectly caused by the moissanite invasion was a young lady who fell from a high-rise balcony in Columbia, South Carolina. Her family's lawyers argued that she fell to her death because of the high cost of having her groceries delivered by air taxi, which forced her to grow her own vegetables on her apartment balcony. Tending her vegetable patch on the ninth-floor balcony would not have been necessary if not for the moissanite 'flood' which drove up the price of her food to the point she could no longer afford to eat. Robotics were used to retrieve the woman's body, which was intombed in nearly a meter of silicon carbide surrounding the base of the apartment building. It took almost a week to recover as many pieces of the body as possible. All had to be buried in a lead lined casket.

With the legal precedent set, more and more people filed lawsuits against the state and federal governments, claiming injuries and even deaths had been caused by the moissanite menace. The courts ruled that those who placed themselves in jeopardy, despite government warnings, could not sue the federal or state government. There were those who tried walking on it, driving a vehicle on it, setting fire to it, or washing it away with high pressure hoses, etc. Even those who survived such foolishness faced a substantially increased risk of latent cancer in future years. They would surely expect the government to pay for their medical care in that event.

All those who elected to live 'above the moissanite flood' depended upon delivery of food, water, and other essentials by air. Water no longer came out of the tap or the shower head in infinite supply. Technologies originally developed to manage the use of consumables on the International Space Station found many applications on the planet's surface. When all the water treatment plants were shut down and overrun, all water for washing, bathing, and drinking had to be delivered. Water for washing and bathing was filtered and reused until it no longer met safety criteria. It was then used to flush toilets. Sewage treatment plants had been overrun as well. The final act at each of these facilities was to divert all raw sewage into the nearest river untreated. It hardly mattered since no one would be drawing water from these rivers for domestic purposes. All cooking appliances were powered by electricity, the only commodity that didn't have to be delivered. So far, the buried electrical cables had not been affected. There was no longer any way to access them, however. Hands-on maintenance was impossible. Fortunately none was needed in the near term.

The escalating cost of supporting people living and working in buildings surrounded by moissanite caused many businesses in South Carolina and Georgia to reconsider their operations there. Most realized after less than a year their situation was untenable. The state governments were out of money and ideas. The federal government continued to bicker and boast about broad solutions, while it was painfully clear there weren't any. Worse still, they realized they would be blamed for many deaths as the support structure for those 'islands' amongst the moissanite ultimately failed. The only essential function that couldn't be lost was the Internet. The decision was made that the integrity of the Internet, especially online banking systems, was the United States highest priority, regardless of the cost. The United Kingdom and Japan were facing the same dilemma.

In 2032 California had been the largest sub-national economy in the world. If California were a sovereign nation, it would have ranked in terms of Gross Domestic Product (GDP) as the world's fifth largest economy, ahead of India and the United Kingdom. By 2035 California's economy had collapsed. Their GDP had shrunk by nearly $4 trillion in less than three years. All of this was due to growth of moissanite colonies along the California coast and expansion inland, making 80% of southern California essentially uninhabitable. Like slow moving forest fires, the colonies grew up and over the hills as well as in the valleys. Millions of homes in the hills above Los Angeles had to be abandoned along with their contents. Most were owned by very wealthy individuals who discovered all the money in the world wasn't enough to hire a moving truck. The demand for such vehicles was suddenly 100 times the supply. Helicopters were in short supply as well and not suited for moving household articles. Those lucky enough to afford such transportation were forced to take only a few family heirlooms. Paintings and other artwork collectively worth billions of dollars were entombed by the slowly advancing moissanite colonies.

It was much worse for those less wealthy. Many found themselves cut off when moissanite covered backroads leading out of the hills. Some attempted to drive their vehicles across the moissanite but found it wouldn't support the weight of the vehicle. Attempts to drive the stalled vehicle simply shredded the rubber tires. Forced to walk on it, they found themselves sinking into the abrasive material with their feet and legs being lacerated by the sharp edges of microscopic broken crystals. Unable to escape they soon collapsed and eventually bled to death. It was impossible for the government to determine how many had gone missing in this manner since the corpses were consumed by the moissanite for their carbon content. The material they were imbedded in needed only three things to keep growing – silicon from the sandy soil, carbon from the soil or living creatures, and gamma radiation. It found ample supplies of the first two and carried the third within the advancing edge of its crystalline structure.

California's rich green forests were slowly overrun, with native wildlife fleeing in front of the dark grey menace or being embedded in it. Interruption of the normal cycles of life in these wooded areas caused the trees to wither and die within months after the natural undergrowth was buried around them. Many square kilometres of dead trees became the perfect fuel for forest fires. With the moissanite covering the ground these fires could only be fought in some locations and only from the air. Supplies of pilots and of fire retardant were exhausted within a month. The price of fuel for the planes was rising rapidly. The Governor of California was forced to abandon the effort and let the dead forests burn. The Governor's advisors doubted even the Giant Sequoias northwest of San Francisco or the huge redwoods further up the coast could be saved. Smoke from these fires could be seen by satellites, spreading nearly 100 kilometres out into the Pacific Ocean.

Chapter 12

Professor Schareshiem and Brent were forced to leave San Francisco in January 2035. Their plan was to stay in Sacramento as long as possible, then move on to Reno, Nevada. Brent tried to convince Schareshiem that staying just ahead of the advancing colony was pointless. The Professor seemed to have an almost romantic fascination with the advancing colonies, however – something no one could understand. Salt Lake City, Utah was to be their "final' destination. Brent no longer believed there would be such a thing as a 'final destination', only constant relocation to stay far enough ahead.

Southern portions of the city of San Francisco began evacuations in March 2035. The evacuation did not go as well as it had in South Carolina or Georgia, partly because much of the city's population refused to take the warnings seriously, and partly because the California State Government had used up most of its resources trying to save the beaches and forests. The miliary assisted, taking advantage of lessons learned in the southeast, but the population simply wasn't cooperative. When the advancing colony blocked access to the Golden Gate Bridge people finally realized the seriousness of the situation. By then massive traffic jams were inevitable. The Golden Gate Bridge became a parking lot filled with abandoned cars. Those who were able to walk to safety survived. Those who couldn't didn't.

Hydrogen fuel supplies had all been depleted. A small percentage of cars and other vehicles in the United States were electric. Electrical charging stations were still operable but access to them was blocked by the overwhelming volume of vehicles needing to be charged. Many had to abandon their vehicles and strike out on foot with insufficient supplies of food and water. Tens of thousands perished from exposure to the weather, exhaustion, and starvation. Corpses left to rot along the sides of roadways resulted in widespread disease that spread through the air. Some national news agencies characterized the San Francisco experience as the first taste of what the entire planet might be facing over the next few decades. Governments and populations in states not yet threatened insisted the matter had been blown out of proportion to serve some political agenda. There was, however, a developing realization in Washington, D.C. that these 'alien colonies' might eventually threaten the entire country.

In the United Kingdom every member of Parliament had reached that conclusion a year earlier based on events in and around Sellafield. Since that time all of Britain's resources had been focused on keeping London habitable, at virtually any cost. As the busiest financial center in the world, London was also the country's population center with over 9 million people living on less than 1% of the land area.

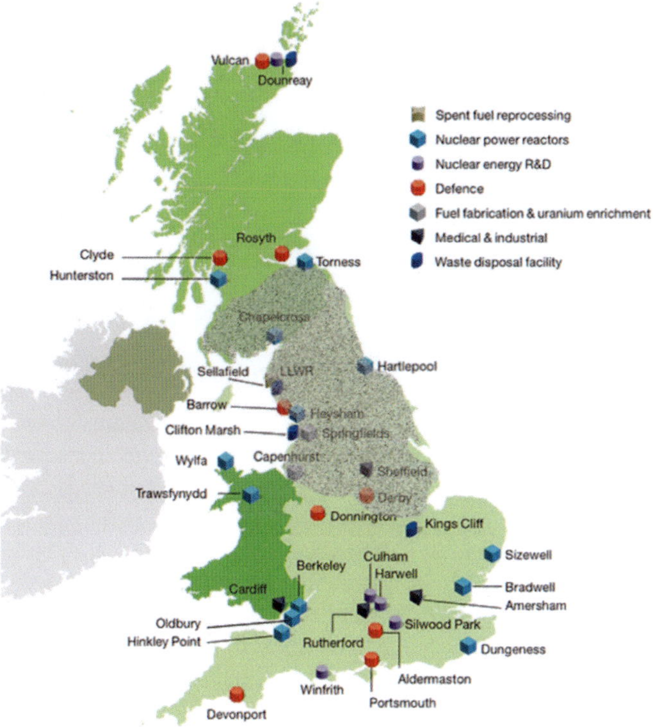

Gamma Ten

By late 2035 nearly 38% of England and half of Scotland had been abandoned to the moissanite colony that began at Sellafield. The United Kingdom had become three islands instead of only two, with a vast uninhabitable zone separating Scotland in the north from England in the south. Blackpool, Manchester, Liverpool, and the Isle of Man had been abandoned in similar fashion to cities in South Carolina, Georgia and southern California. The moissanite colony was expected to reach Birmingham, Glasgow, and Edinburgh in the next few months. Some residents elected to stay in high-rise apartments and office buildings but faced the same challenges as in the United States. All roads and railway lines to Scotland were completely cut off. Travel between Scotland and England was by sea or air.

Of the eight nuclear generating stations in the United Kingdom, four had been overrun by the colony. They included Hartlepool, Heysham 1, Heysham 2, and Torness. The colony would reach a fifth station, Hunterston B, in a few months. Although Hunterston B had not operated for over a decade, the site still contained a significant inventory of spent nuclear fuel. These facilities had been consumed by the moissanite, allowing the colony to grow essentially as Professor Schareshiem and Brent had predicted. Of the remaining nuclear generating stations only one, Sizewell B, continued to operate, suppling power to the south of England including London. The remaining two stations, Dungeness B and Hinkley Point B were in a similar condition to Hunterston B. Losing 15% of its electrical generating capacity caused problems across the United Kingdom. That impact was mitigated somewhat by the exodus of populations returning to the European Continent. Decades of rampant legal and illegal immigration into the United Kingdom had suddenly shifted into full reverse. People of middle and eastern European descent were returning to their countries of origin by the tens of thousands each month.

Authorities in France, alarmed by the growth of moissanite colonies across England, worried this strange material might find its way across the North Sea and appear on their shores. Armies of French volunteers combed beaches, once stormed by British and American soldiers nearly a century earlier, searching for something unusual. Any sign of 'grey sand' was to be reported immediately to the local police. Meanwhile a visitor from

Sellafield failed to change shoes as instructed before entering one of the spent fuel storage areas at La Hague. Minute particles of moissanite fell into the storage basin when the visitor walked across the floor grating over a storage pool. Sellafield issued a public apology, but the damage was done. A new moissanite colony was now growing on the European Continent. The colony could spread from La Hague in all directions – south into Spain and east into Germany and other countries.

Deliberations in Washington, D.C. began to take a more cooperative tone as Congressmen and Senators began to realize this 'grey flood' might reach voters in the western and midwestern states in the not-so-distant future. "Mr. Speaker, I fail to see how any of this is going to affect the Great State of Arizona. The southern third of my state is desert, with barely enough water to keep a few lizards, rattlesnakes, and cactus alive from one year to the next. I don't see how this stuff can grow under such conditions. As for the rest, my experts are telling me this organism, whatever it is, will never get that far. It will stop growing before it ever gets out of California." "Our experts from Caltech are saying it will", yelled back the Senior

Congressman from California. It doesn't need water to grow. All it needs is sand and spent nuclear fuel. Your Nuclear Generating Station at Palo Verde is the largest in the United States. What happens when it gets there?" The Palo Verde Generating Station, located near Tonopah in western Arizona was only 72 kilometres from downtown Phoenix, a community of 4.7 million people. It was the only nuclear generating station in the world not located near an above ground body of water.

The Senior Congressmen from Nevada, New Mexico and Utah had all planned to make the same argument. None of those States had any nuclear generating stations. One such facility was to be located in Utah but was never built. Nevada did contain a major inventory of spent nuclear fuel, however. The Yucca Mountain Nuclear Waste Storage Facility was located on federal land adjacent to the Nevada Test Site in Nye County, Nevada, about 130 km northwest of the Las Vegas Valley. By 2035 this facility contained an inventory of spent nuclear fuel that rivalled the largest storage sites in the world. This inventory was located thousands of meters underground where in theory it should remain isolated from groundwater and human excavation for centuries. The Congressman from Nevada, once strongly opposed to the construction of the Yucca Mountain Facility, now proudly argued it was perhaps the only location this 'moissanite thing' couldn't reach.

Congressmen from western and midwestern states each took the opportunity to proclaim their States were immune to this menace for various reasons. When it was finally Georgia's turn, the mood began to shift from denial to acceptance. The Congressman from Georgia described his State as mostly abandoned. Everyone had seen the news reports but hearing the descriptions in person was sobering. The Congressman from Georgia spoke for only twenty minutes. "I would yield the balance of my time to my honourable colleges who represent the Great State of South Carolina. Except they're not here today. They weren't here yesterday. They won't be here tomorrow, either, because they don't have a State left to represent."

A rare moment had come for those in the United States Congress to put politics aside and work together for the good of the country and its citizens. Several news reports noted similarities between the way the government used to work in the middle of the previous century compared to this newfound conscience in a crisis. Most had imagined such a thing to be impossible unless there was another world war. No one expected the next world war would last long enough for the government to do anything. In this instance there was time for government to do something. The question was what would it be?

Historians and academics were recruited to advise Congress and government agencies on lessons learned from the past crisis, as well as vintage skills prior to invention of the Internet and even the industrial revolution. Many remembered the pandemic of 2019-2021, especially governmental actions that were later found to be counterproductive. Methods for food production and transport to markets in the pre-industrial era might become essential to people's survival if remaining fuel supplies for tractors and other farming machines ran out. Books describing how people lived in the 1950's to 1980's were suddenly in great demand. Others recounting methods of farming in the Victorian and Edwardian eras quickly sold out online and in bookstores, not just in the United States but around the world. Many governments found themselves trying to lead from behind the populations they governed. It seemed people had already decided their elected representatives would be of little assistance. Ordinary citizens decided they were on their own.

Most of the libraries in the world had closed in the past decade. Since all the information in them was available through the Internet, books made of cloth and paper were considered a thing of the past. Private collections like the ones in Schareshiem's office were rare. About one person in twenty thought to take their favourite books with them each time they relocated. That became more of a burden over time. Most thought all the books in the libraries would still be there if they were able to access them again someday. That depended on whether the environment inside the abandoned buildings remained cool and dry. Paper books might survive for many decades under the best conditions.

Almost as an afterthought, Congress decided it needed to hear again from the experts who had been following this problem from the beginning. What was left of the faculty management from Caltech could hardly object to Professor Schareshiem's request for travel on this occasion. Most Congressmen still hoped a way would be found to stop, possibly even destroy, these moissanite colonies. The Professor's presentation was not what they were expecting.

"My apologies for your disappointment", Schareshiem began. "The only people currently working on those sorts of solutions are priests, charlatans and magicians." "But how can this material continue to spread if it isn't alive? And if it is alive, why can't we find a way to kill it", asked the Congressman from Missouri? As often happened in Congressional proceedings, the ensuring banter between the nation's elected representatives consumed another quarter of an hour of the Professor's time. "IF I MAY CONTINUE", Schareshiem shouted as loud as he could. The Speaker's gavel suddenly found its voice, reducing the din to a manageable level. "If I may continue", said the Professor. "Our estimates of how fast this material can spread are purely theoretical and have ignored the human element. That human element may well accelerate the problem." No one had a clue what the Professor was talking about. He smiled. Finally he had their attention.

"Some of our fellow citizens are helping to spread this material for their own reasons, defeating our efforts to contain it", Schareshiem continued. "We're aware of several extremist environmental groups who don't believe the scientists and the government. These groups are collecting moissanite samples and testing them on their own, inadvertently spreading the material to areas not yet affected. Several anti-nuclear groups have concluded these moissanite colonies are nature's revenge for our development of nuclear energy, especially nuclear weapons like those used on Hiroshima and Nagasaki nearly a century ago. They believe they are called to help nature spread this material. There are also private citizens who take samples of the material as souvenirs of some sort. They put them on their mantle pieces as conversation points, unaware some are radioactive if taken from the leading edge of a colony. Several groups we've seen most recently are anarchists who hope to find ways to weaponize this material to further their quest to overthrow their government."

Gamma Ten

Finally declaring a national emergency, the United States Congress demanded a list of actual and/or potential impacts of the advancing moissanite colonies. Those most crucial to the entire nation included:

- Reduced food production due to loss of farmland and livestock in South Carolina, Georgia, and California.
- Slow deliveries of pharmaceuticals, food, and other essential commodities due to blocked railways, roads, etc.
- Escalating costs for all commodities due to shortages, rising transportation costs, and fuel shortages.
- Potential for electric grid failures due to lack of maintenance.
- Interruption of Internet and online banking services in an increasing number of locations
- Shrinking job markets, leaving many unemployed and homeless.
- Pressure on city and state governments to cope with rising numbers of derelicts and unemployed.
- Lack of adequate housing for the growing number of evacuees.
- Overloading of welfare systems, food banks, and homeless shelters
- Growing demand for miliary support of evacuations as the moissanite colonies moved inland from California and expanded into Tennessee, Alabama, and North Carolina.

Congressional legislation to cope with the situation was urgently drafted, brought to the floor for a vote, and given bipartisan approval within two weeks. A few Representatives objected, arguing the impacts on the federal budget had not been thoroughly scrutinized. Their objections were duly noted, for the record. No one in Congress could say how many people or businesses in the country would be paying taxes in another twelve months. Budgetary concerns, once a major topic of leverage and persistent disagreement between Congressmen every three months, had suddenly become irrelevant.

The approved legislation included:

- Subsidies for farmers who could transport and sell their produce at local markets.
- Online tutorials for the general population describing techniques used before the industrial revolution to grow food and livestock.
- Subsidies for families who took in relatives or boarders.
- Subsidies for hotels willing to take in the homeless and those who had been evacuated.
- Urgent construction of shelters in schools and sports centers for evacuees.
- Alteration of designated highways to allow flow of traffic out of areas being evacuated on all lanes.
- Provision of temporary jobs for evacuees who could work to construct emergency shelters, transport goods, and provide other social services.
- Subsidies to expedite transport of pharmaceuticals and medical supplies to affected populations.
- Subsidies for companies producing solar panels and other electrical generating equipment that could be deployed locally and did not rely on the national electrical grid.
- Subsidies for development of methods to remove moissanite from railways and roads on a limited scale and where radiation levels would permit.
- Diversion of all available military resources to the construction of temporary housing for evacuees, temporary roadways, and bridges, etc.
- Declaration that owning or distributing samples of moissanite is a federal crime carrying severe penalties.
- Prioritization of federal funds to ensure continued operation and support for the Internet and online banking.

While those in the U.S. government were focused on emergency legislation, private industry was working to protect their most valuable assets. For large oil companies, those would be their refineries along the Texas and Louisiana gulf coast. Obviously, they couldn't be moved out of harm's way. Some might be duplicated overseas at substantial cost, however. Their second most valuable asset was the United States Strategic Oil Reserve. That could be moved to other locations around the world, given enough ships and enough time. International partnerships were proposed and approved in a matter of weeks. Activities at the ports of Houston, Corpus Christi, Beaumont, Lake Charles, New Orleans, and Mobile ramped up quickly. Oil tankers were staged just outside these ports waiting to be loaded for destinations in Australia, Venezuela, Saudi Arabia, Greenland, India, and the Philippines.

More than half the United States Strategic Oil Reserves went to Australia. Australia had agreed to provide humanitarian aid to countries with airfields large enough for the C-17 Globemaster III to land and refuel. The aim of the RAAF was to have the capability to reach any point in the world, not necessarily at Australia's expense. Several countries without adequate facilities managed to construct them. Given the Globemaster's maximum range of 10,000 kilometres fully loaded, flights leaving from Sydney could reach any point in the east by refuelling at Jakarta, Honolulu, Manila, Kolkata, and Shanghai. Flights leaving from Perth could reach any point in the west by refuelling at Johannesburg, Cairo, Rome, and even the United States Air Force Base at Thule, Greenland. In-flight refuelling was no longer practiced as the RAAF's mission had changed. Tankers now delivered to refuelling locations around the world instead.

In years past Australia had eight fossil fuel refineries that met all domestic fuel demand. Four of those facilities were still operating after over half a century. Reactivating some of the ones that had been retired was considered, with intent to convert almost all such operations to the production of diesel fuel for ships and aviation fuel for the military. Australia's extraction of its own crude oil and related petroleum products had declined over several decades, with a relatively small volume being exported to Asian refineries. Domestic oil production was not currently sufficient to meet Australia's total demand, even if all of it was refined domestically. A lot of production was condensate (a very light crude and by-product of national gas production). While it could be processed into fuel in an emergency, it was typically not considered commercially viable. As a result, much of Australia's refined fuel products had been either directly imported or refined from imported crude oil feedstock. Receipt of a major portion of the United States Strategic Oil Reserve changed everything. The new joint mission of oil refining companies in Australia was to convert as much of a huge new resource into diesel and aviation fuel as quickly as possible.

Concepts for the Internet originated with the 20th Century military, who needed a robust, diverse, and redundant system to guarantee uninterrupted communications despite a large number of single point failures (military strikes). The electrical supply grid in most countries also had some of these features but to a lesser degree. These design features helped both systems continue to function when normal maintenance became impossible. High voltage overhead power lines were unaffected by moissanite colonies on the ground below until adverse weather or other event required access to make repairs. Without such access gradual deterioration of these systems was slow but inevitable. The demand for solar panels and other means to generate power locally without reliance on the electrical power grid began to rise sharply. Companies producing such equipment enjoyed a boon in business, making huge profits until supplies of raw materials were interrupted and eventually ran out. Local generation of electric power extended the life of some systems by a few years at best.

In May 2035 the moissanite colony that began in K Basin entered Atlanta, Georgia. More than 85% of the state had been evacuated. There were many buildings in Atlanta that could remain occupied, as the 'grey sand' slowly filled the streets of the city. Air taxis had developed considerable experience at ferrying employees who volunteered to stay. By this time there was an ample supply of flying cars as well, for those wanting greater independence. Companies who insisted on maintaining critical operations in cities like Atlanta, Los Angeles, and San Francisco provided such vehicles to their employees at no cost. There were not enough parking spaces on roof tops, however, and travel distances were getting longer month by month. Supporting those living above the moissanite was becoming more and more expensive.

In Atlanta, as in Los Angeles and San Francisco, most resources went toward keeping the Internet and online banking systems operating smoothly. Almost all bank branch locations, where one could deposit or withdraw money with a teller, or meet face to face with a bank representative, had disappeared by 2027. All meetings with bank employees were conducted online. All cash withdrawals were from automated machines. Cash was hardly ever carried or used. Almost all debit cards and credit cards were phased out in 2025 and 2026. All financial transactions were conducted through online banking or using debit or credit apps on mobile phones. In the United States it was widely believed that the economy would simply collapse if more than 10% percent of the population lost access to the Internet for more than a week.

Operations personnel at Watts Bar, Sequoyah, and Browns Ferry nuclear generating stations had been warned about moissanite contamination in the Tennessee River. All three took precautions to avoid untreated river water entering their facilities. Engineering personnel believed the moissanite could be effectively filtered out by a series of sieves and absorbers at the reactor cooling water intakes. Such measures had been hastily added at great expense at all three facilities. The effectiveness of filtration was unproven, but the Tennessee Valley Authority (TVA) had promised the government it would do everything possible to keep these stations operating.

The Watts Bar Nuclear Station was located on a 7.2 square kilometre site in Rhea County, Tennessee between the cities of Chattanooga and Knoxville. In 2030 the population within 80 kilometres of Watts Bar was 1.4 million. The Sequoyah Station was located on 2.12 square kilometres 32 km north of Chattanooga, abutting Chickamauga Lake, on the Tennessee River. In 2030 the population within 80 km was 1.3 million. The Browns Ferry Station was located on the Tennessee River near Decatur and Athens, Alabama, on the north side of Wheeler Lake. In 2030, the population within 80 km of Browns Ferry was 1.7 million.

Filtration measures proved effective in delaying moissanite entering the reactor cooling systems at all three TVA nuclear generating stations. Engineering scale tests showed the apparent solubility of moissanite in water was due to its ability to form a colloidal suspension of very high transparency. Although the particles of moissanite in suspension were microscopic and practically invisible, they could be filtered out. This was considered a significant breakthrough. Unfortunately this discovery came too late to save the nuclear generating stations in South Carolina.

TVA's success was short lived, however, when grey deposits were found on spent fuel in the storge basin at Watts Bar Station. Investigation found a vehicle had been admitted to the spent fuel storage basin area at Watts Bar without being checked for contamination on its tires. Vehicles were always checked for radioactive contamination before being allowed to leave the building. Checking the tires before entry was a new requirement, often missed.

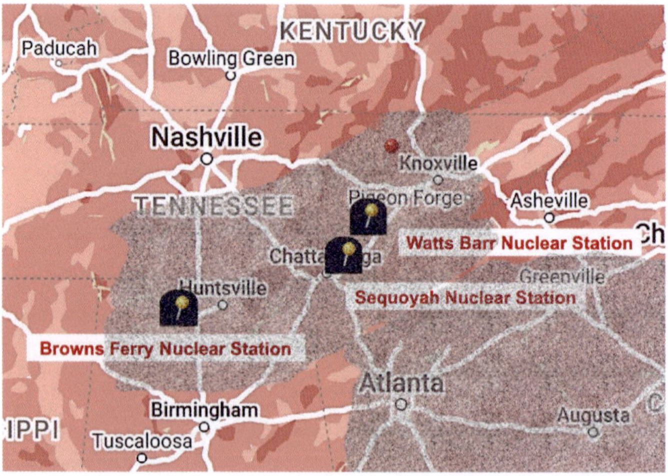

Ultimately all three TVA nuclear generating stations had to be shut down and abandoned as the moissanite colony spread first over Watts Bar and then over Sequoyah and Browns Ferry in less than a year. Moissanite colonies at these stations joined up with the one now covering 90% of Georgia and advancing northward from Atlanta. The impact on overall electrical generating capacity in the southeast

United States was significant even though demand in South Carolina and Georgia had dropped by 95%. Knoxville had been evacuated, along with the University of Tennessee campus. Nashville was watching developments to the south very closely. The colony was threatening Birmingham, Tuscaloosa, Montgomery, and the campuses of the University of Alabama and Auburn University.

The Congressional Representative from Arizona had been proven partially correct. The state border with California had not stopped the 'grey flood', however. The lack of groundwater and rivers in portions of Arizona bought residents of Flagstaff, Tucson, and Phoenix much needed time to relocate. The loss of the Palo Verde nuclear generating station was felt across the State. Further north the concern was over what to do with Las Vegas. Much of the real estate there was owned by wealthy patrons with considerable influence in Washington, D.C. They demanded something be done.

Anyone who lived near a major river or lake feared discovering grey sand on the riverbank. State and federal government agents monitored the shores of the Great Lakes and the Mississippi River all the way down to New Orleans. As the colony moved north up the California coast those in Oregon and Washington State began planning their next moves. The public had reluctantly accepted the fact that escape was the only choice available to them. The question was 'escape to where'?

Gamma Ten

Chapter 13

Loss of the fishing industry along their entire eastern coast left a significant portion of the Japanese population without income, and the world without an important food source. The impact on the Japanese economy was felt immediately. As in other countries threatened by moissanite colonies, the wealthiest citizens left their homeland without delay. Most lost a major portion of their wealth in doing so. That was still better than suffering the fate of those who could not leave. Beaches were closed as soon as the 'grey sand' began to appear. Tourist visits to Japan dropped dramatically.

Moissanite colonies on the beaches spread inland at an alarming pace, sustained by spent nuclear fuel inventories at five out of the eight nuclear power stations that were still operating in Japan in 2034. Spent nuclear fuel still existed at ten other Japanese nuclear power stations that had been shut down decades earlier. Twenty-five percent of the Japanese Islands was evacuated by May 2037. The northern half of the main island was cut off from the southern half, in much the same way as in the United Kingdom. Computer models predicted that 50% of Japan's land mass would be covered in moissanite by March 2038.

There was no immediate need to evacuate anyone in Ukraine, as the area surrounding the entombed Chernobyl nuclear power station was already a radioactive exclusion area. The not-so-secret Russian laboratory had to be abandoned, of course. When questioned, the Russian government denied there was anything unusual happening in the Chernobyl exclusion zone. Unclassified satellite photographs proved otherwise. The Russians blamed the United States and United Kingdom, just as Professor Schareshiem had predicted.

Gamma Ten

What remained of the once capital city of Kyiv was the first to be threatened by the expanding moissanite colony as it expanded outside the exclusion zone. Nuclear power stations at Rivne and Khmelnitskiy would be next. Fortunately the largest nuclear power station in Europe and the tenth largest in the world was some distance away to the southeast at Zaporizhzhe. It had suffered some damage during the Russian invasion of 2022-2025 but was returned to service in 2026.

By July 2036, nearly 80% of the Continental United States was uninhabitable. Elementary healthcare was difficult to find. Many had died from simple illnesses or injuries, much as they had in the Middle Ages. World history seemed to be repeating itself. Employees who had been living in high-rise islands in the major cities eventually had to abandon those locations. Supply routes and travel times had become untenable. Ninety percent of Internet servers in the United States had failed or shut down soon after they were abandoned. New York, Chicago, Minneapolis, Detroit, Baltimore, Philadelphia, Washington, and other cities that had not evacuated were struggling with the slow Internet speeds and lengthy interruptions. Some days there was no Internet service at all.

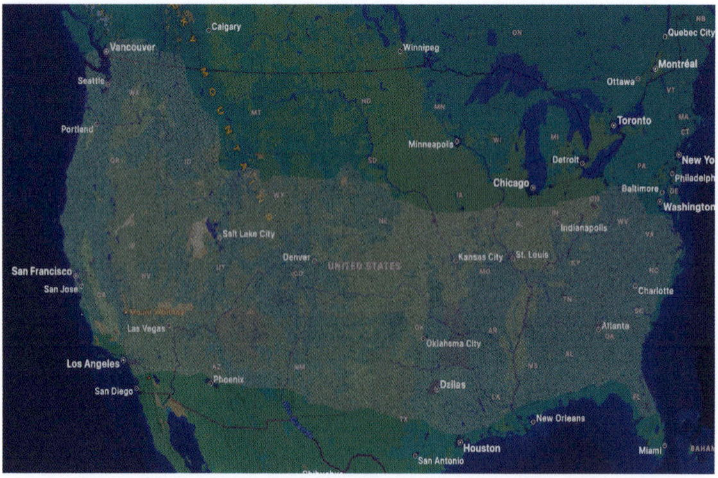

Medical and pharmaceutical supplies, especially antibiotics, were in short supply due to supply chain failures. The cost of life-saving drugs was prohibitive if they could be found. Those with means had already fled the country, most moving to Alaska or remote areas of northern Canada. The wealthiest 1% had relocated to remote or underdeveloped areas of Australia, Greenland, South America, and Africa, in the belief that locations with no nuclear reactors, spent nuclear fuel, or other sources of gamma radiation might escape the grey menace altogether. They seemed surprised to find their private jets could not land at these remote locations.

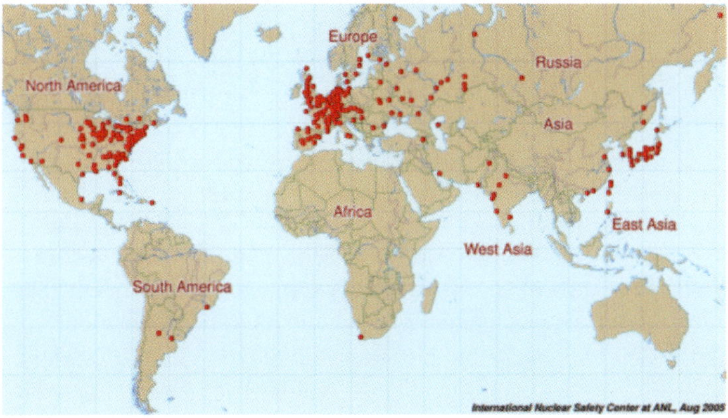

Forced to make overland journeys across arid, frozen, or untamed terrain, they complained constantly about the lack of heating, air conditioning, electricity, and other amenities they had always taken for granted. Many of them were deserted by their hired hosts mid-journey, left to perish despite their burgeoning bank accounts and investment portfolios.

The irony of the world's richest people wanting to live in the most underdeveloped areas on the planet wasn't lost on the news media. For the past 75 years the poorest people had risked their lives in a desperate effort to reach the richest nations. Lacking their own private aircraft, many had drowned as they attempted to cross stormy seas in inflatable boats too small to carry them.

Those without means to leave the Continental United States watched prices of food and electricity skyrocket as unemployment climbed to 10%, then 20%, then 40%. Families unable to simply fly away to another continent eventually became isolated without money or food and with no means of escape. Some recalled historical accounts of volcanic eruptions, like Vesuvius. "If only people had time to leave…", studies concluded. "But what if there was no place left to run to", questioned one report. "Like if Yellowstone erupted again? How would people escape an event that covered 60% of the United States in volcanic ash a meter deep?" The answers to those questions were more horrifying than anyone had imagined. As more and more farmland was lost food supplies fell far short of demand. People fought for what food was available, much as those in war torn countries had fought for food and water during repeated wars in the middle east and elsewhere during past decades. Many committed suicide. Some people simply froze when they couldn't pay their utility bills.

Bill and Arlene lost contact with Bill's parents and Arlene's father, who were living in Cincinnati and Detroit, respectively, when the Internet became unreliable. They had no idea if either of them had moved and if so, where. Bill, Arlene, Diane, and Claire moved from Rapid City to Fairbanks, Alaska in early summer of 2035, intent upon learning the survival techniques of the Inuit. Aaron and Geraldine moved from Winnipeg to Anchorage one month later. They had no idea where the other members of their families were either.

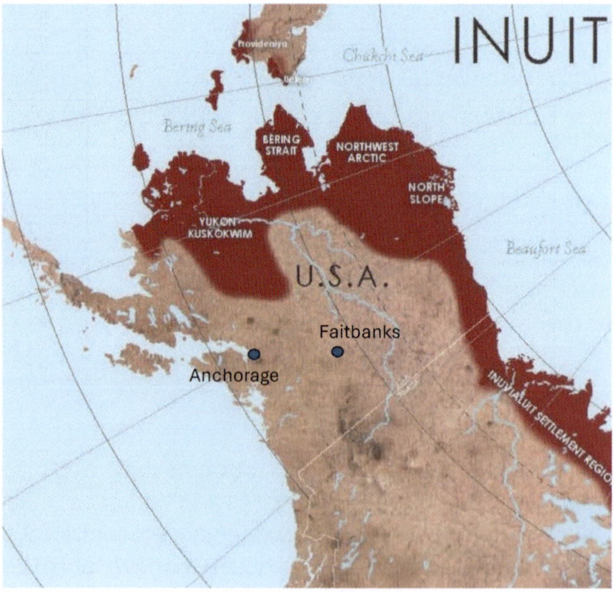

Gamma Ten

Both Fairbanks and Anchorage had experienced phenomenal growth, with populations doubling in the past ten months. Local governments were struggling to provide housing, sanitation, and other services on such short notice. Leonard complained again about his parents being so far away he wouldn't be able to see them very often. The shortest flight route from New York to Anchorage was over 7000 kilometres. Driving time was 85 hours. While weather in Alaska could sometimes be a bit unpredictable, the summer season (mid-June through mid-August) was usually the mildest and warmest time of the year, especially in the interior, where temperatures could reach well above 27°C. It was not uncommon to see temperatures reach 33° C in Fairbanks. Both families discovered summer evening temperatures in Alaska could still be quite cool.

Aaron did his best to persuade Leonard to leave New York and relocate somewhere closer to them. "You mean in Canada", Leonard asked? "Or Alaska. It's quite pleasant here", Geraldine replied. "I'm not eight years old, Mom", Leonard replied. "I can take care of myself." "So how are things there", Aaron interrupted, before an argument ensued? "Slow. All the markets are down, some more than 40%. Nobody's buying 'futures' these days. It's a buyer's market with so many cashing out, but nobody is buying. You could make a killing right now, Dad!" Aaron shook his head. "You still have a job then?" "Yes. People are wanting advice about the best time to sell rather than when to buy." "Can you still get everything you need", said Geraldine? "Pretty much. It's all imported now – nothing is grown or made in the USA anymore."

"None of the grocery stores have steak. No California wines either. Lamb and pork come from Australia or New Zealand, but the prices have tripled. It's great if you are a vegan. Lots of people upstate, where there's still some unspoiled land, are growing their own vegetables." "Can you still buy stuff on the Internet", said Aaron? "Yes, but it might not arrive for several months. There are ships sitting offshore waiting to enter the New York harbour. It's really something to see. If you go up about sixty floors and look out the window you can see over fifty ships on the eastern horizon. They're just sitting there, full of cargo they can't unload. All the docks in the city are working twenty-four/seven."

Gamma Ten

People were once told electricity generated by nuclear reactors would be so cheap it wouldn't have to be metered. Now people were fleeing from it to countries having no nuclear facilities at all. The Internet, designed to be the most reliable infrastructure in history, was found to be rather fragile. Dependence on the Internet and nuclear power had turned out to be a curse rather than the utopia people were promised. Generations had forgotten how to survive without these luxuries. Now they had to relearn forgotten skills that meant the difference between life and death.

Bill and Aaron had to accept their stay in Alaska might also be only temporary. In another few years, when the electrical grid began to fail and when supply chains began to breakdown across the North American Continent there would be few places left. They were determined to enjoy the time that remained. What better place to do that than in some of the most beautiful country nature had to offer. "Having a deadline is the best way to focus the mind", Bill remarked. There was still hope the moissanite might eventually stop growing for lack of radioactive materials to sustain the crystalline growth.

Things began to change quickly as the first snow arrived the last week in September. Diane insisted it would probably melt in a few days. Claire bet it wouldn't. Two weeks later it was 100 millimetres deep in Fairbanks. That was just the beginning.

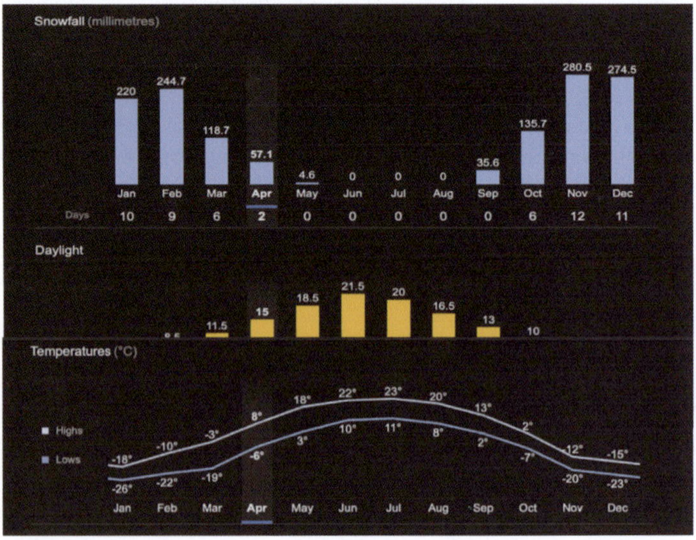

Anchorage didn't fare much better. A closer look at average weather for Alaska was revealing, and a bit late. They could hardly change their minds now.

The scenery in Alaska was breathtaking on the days when you could see it. 'Purple mountain majesties' adorned every horizon, just like the song promised. Those pristine photos on the Internet could be a bit deceiving, however. It did look that way one day out of ten. Two days out of ten nothing was visible for more than a few hundred meters. Those photographs didn't convey the cold and the wind. The air was clean and a bit thin. The altitude took some getting used to.

Fairbanks was about a six-hour drive from Anchorage, weather permitting. The two families agreed to meet at Denali National Park as often as they could. At the midpoint between Anchorage and Fairbanks, Denali provided a dramatic example of the stunning natural beauty of Alaska. Denali National Park and Preserve encompassed 19,186 square kilometres of Alaska's interior wilderness. Its most popular attraction was the 6,190-meter-high Denali, also known as Mount McKinley, North America's tallest peak.

The park's terrain included tundra, spruce forest, glaciers, and was home to wildlife including grizzly bears, wolves, moose, caribou, and Dall sheep. Diane and Claire wanted to climb Denali, of course. The local park ranger convinced them it was not a task for inexperienced climbers. They pretended to agree, at least for the moment. Denali National Park was an ideal place to takes one's mind off an uncertain future. Neither Arlene nor Geraldine knew how much time they had left. They weren't concerned about themselves. What kept them awake at night was the realization that their children had to learn to survive in a world so very different from the one they grew up in.

Although their stay in Alaska might be temporary, it was good practice for their next, and probably final, destination, either Iceland or Greenland. Neither Alaska nor Canada, with their vast resources, could keep pace with the numbers of people moving there to escape the moissanite colonies. Eventually the electrical grid would fail, first locally, then on a broader scale, leaving millions of people without heat. The local forests could provide firewood for a time, but soon the ability to transport it to those who needed it would be lost. Local generators and solar panels provided much needed backup power for the Internet, the only reliable connection most people had with the rest of the world except for a few short wave radios. Fuel for the generators had to be brought in overland at escalating cost. Supply chains were already stretched to the limit. Solar panels were effective for less than half the year. Winter months afforded very little sunlight when electricity for heating was needed most.

"Maybe we can meet in the spring when things thaw out again", said Arlene during their weekly Facetime call. Geraldine agreed. Aaron had been told the summer season could be extremely short in Alaska, usually lasting from late June until early August. Both couples had read as much as they could about how to survive in inhospitable surroundings. Neither had much experience with the type of adverse weather common to Alaska. None of them were prepared for the black flies that would eat you alive when you went outside in summer. Those idyllic paintings of the beautiful Alaskan mountains and pristine lakes were grossly misleading in that regard. There was no shortage of money for either Aaron or Bill. Government pension payments continued to show up in their bank accounts on the first day of each month. At least that system was still working. They withdrew cash often, leaving only small amounts in their bank accounts.

Claire and Diane were back in school again. So were their parents. Enterprising members of several Inuit groups had discovered there was a huge market for demonstrating survival skills and methods used by their ancestors. Such information had become extremely popular, not just with those living nearby in Canada and Alaska, but worldwide. The Inuit had learned to thrive in a difficult environment.

Their staple diet was the fat and meat of seals, rich in iron and vitamin A, which helped them withstand the cold. More importantly, they had adapted culturally: their clothes, footwear, dog sleds, kayaks, hunting strategies etc. were all purpose-designed for the Arctic.

Hunting and fishing were still vital to the Inuit civilisation. They treated Nature with great respect. The modern world provided many challenges to their way of life. To their credit the Inuit had taken advantage of modern tools, including the Internet, snow mobiles, and aircraft to protect their future. In Canada, the Inuit were able to manage their own autonomous territory, Nunavut, established in 1999.

Five thousand years in the past, several groups of people settled on each side of the Bering Strait. Hunters of several origins found this area to be a rich hunting ground for fauna both on land and in the sea. These were the first traces of the Eskimos' ancestors.
When the ice caps of the American continent melted a thousand years later the hunter communities along the Bering Strait migrated southwards into America and along the Arctic coast as far as Greenland. They evolved into two lines - Paleo-Eskimo and Neo-Eskimo. The latter branch spread out across the Arctic to become the ancestors of the Inuit.

Even in the 21th Century the Inuit depended on hunting, not just for their food but also for materials to make tools, build shelters and make clothes. They were able to draw a subsistence livelihood from their fragile natural environment without unbalancing it. In winter, the Inuit hunted marine mammals (seals, walruses, and cetaceans). In summer they moved inland from the coast hunting caribou, fishing in the rivers and lakes, snaring birds and taking their eggs, and gathering berries and herbs. The men hunted, made tools, and built kayaks while the women prepared animal pelts, sewed clothes, dried meat, looked after the children, fished, and gathered lichen, seaweed, etc. Seals were a favourite prey because their meat was so nourishing, but the Inuit also used the mammal's waterproof skin as well as its bones. Similarly, whenever the Inuit managed to kill a whale, they used practically every part of it: the blubber was used for food and for oil to heat and light their homes, the whalebone or baleen was used to make bows for hunting, and the bones themselves were used to make sleds.

The Inuit's contact with the modern world resulted in a number of changes. Their lifestyle in the 21st Century bore little resemblance to that of their grandparents. Their kayaks had been replaced by motorboats. Most lived in wooden houses instead of igloos made of snow or earth. Most also used guns instead of harpoons and travelled on snow mobiles instead of dog sleds. Some Inuit worked at paid jobs, while some lived off welfare. Nevertheless, many skills and traditions survived. Now the world had suddenly found a need for those skills. There were those within modern Inuit communities who saw an opportunity to teach those skills and enrich their communities in return. In 2030 there were approximately 125,000 Inuit belonging to about 40 different ethnic groups. A people once largely ignored, neglected, and misunderstood had become a vital resource to billions who needed to learn how to survive without modern infrastructure.

Igaluk greeted Bill's family in the traditional Inuit way. "I will teach you what I know. It will not always be a pleasant experience. Are you prepared for that?" All four nodded, although Claire was a bit apprehensive. This was not an online course where students simply listened and observed. This was 'hands on' training. Each had their own salmon to gut and clean. Bill and Arlene had cleaned fish before but never one this large. Bill hesitated as the arthritis in his hands had gotten steadily worse. Each salmon was almost a meter long. It was clearly a new experience for Claire and Diane. They made the best of it. "You have all done well", said Igaluk. Tomorrow we will do something bigger." The 'something bigger' was an adult seal. Each seal weighed over 100 kilograms. Aaron managed to move the carcass around as he stripped the seal skin away from the flesh underneath. "The knives are very sharp", Bill cautioned the others. Arlene needed Igaluk's help but eventually succeeded. "You must build your strength", said Igaluk. "You might not have someone to help next time." Claire and Diane preferred to just watch. "This will do you no good", said Igaluk. "I will start, and you must finish."

Igaluk was very patient. It took Claire over an hour and Diane nearly two hours to finish stripping the oily seal skin from their animal. No one cut themselves. "You must learn to do it faster", said Igaluk. "You won't always have so much time before the bears or wolves arrive and take your kill." Everyone nodded. "This is much harder than I thought", whispered Arlene when she felt sure Igaluk couldn't hear. "Igaluk turned to look at her and smiled. "You have all done well today. Tomorrow we will do something bigger." Claire looked at her father shaking her head. "How…" "Just do your best", he replied.

An adult male Cariboo can weight up to 180 kilograms. The five of them had to hike nearly two kilometres up to a shelter for their next training session. Claire and Diane took the smaller animals, each weighing about 140 kilograms. Arlene's was a bit larger. Bill's Cariboo was massive. It was impossible to move it on the huge wooden platform. He had to work around it from all sides. Igaluk demonstrated the proper way to field dress the Cariboo, beginning with slicing open the abdominal area and removing the stomach, intestines, heart, and other organs. "Do not throw these away", Igaluk cautioned. "We will use them later." Removing the hide took considerably longer. It was strenuous work. The temperature was -6 Celsius so the organs froze quickly. "We can thaw them when the time comes."

Diane was the last to finish. "We will not make it back to your lodge before dark. You will get a bonus lesson today", said Igaluk. "You must find your way back down the mountain in darkness." Igaluk handed each of them a battery powered light. "If you had worked more quickly you could be sitting by the fire now." Obviously Igaluk has anticipated their situation. Bill felt they had all worked as fast as they could, especially given his disability. He resented Igaluk's comment. Since they were completely dependent upon Igaluk's assistance to find their way back Bill chose to say nothing. Indeed it took almost an hour to reach the lodge again. The temperature had fallen to -14 Celsius as they entered the large atrium inside the lodge. The stone fireplace was roaring. "Tomorrow we will cook your Cariboo on an open fire", Igaluk announced. Arlene smiled, partly from exhaustion and partly from relief. "Finally something I know how to do…" Indeed, all three female members of Bill's family excelled at cooking. None were able to start the fire with flint and steel, however. They had to give Bill due credit for his contribution. "Working together we survive. Working alone is certain death", said Igaluk.

Their final lesson required all five to hike much further up the mountain. After two hours it was obvious they would not be making it back to the lodge that evening. "We will be building a shelter for tonight. There are five of us. We will keep each other warm", Igaluk announced. Bill realized his ability to start a fire was about to face the ultimate test. Igaluk began collecting small timbers, underbrush, and broad carpets of moss. Everyone followed his lead. By nightfall they had constructed a shelter just large enough for them to huddle together out of the lightly falling snow. Each took their turn staying awake for two hours, placing more wood on the fire to keep it going. Stacks of wood were placed around the fire to dry and to reflect heat back into the shelter. Morning finally arrived with the sunlight breaking through the aspen trees, their white bark reflecting the light so that it filled the mountainside. "We have been lucky", said Igaluk. The snow had stopped. "It could have been much worse." Bill looked at his thermometer. It read -9 Celsius. "I suppose none of you have eaten Cariboo intestines before", Igaluk asked? "Maybe, if they're cooked", Arlene replied, realising bacon, eggs, toast with jam, and coffee weren't available. "Please", Igaluk asked, as he reached into his backpack? "I believe there will be enough."

Gamma Ten

Chapter 14

Professor Schareshiem, Brent and other refugees from Caltech had relocated to Chicago in August 2035. Their focus had shifted from simply monitoring the moissanite's progress across the country to predicting its effects on the planet as a whole. Brent was becoming more concerned about their own survival. Just moving every time the moissanite colony appeared on the horizon wasn't a long-term strategy. Eventually they, and everyone else, would wake up one morning to find they were out of options. The Professor made it clear he expected to die of 'natural causes' long before that morning came. The opportunity to study and analyse a global phenomenon no one could have imagined was all consuming.

Average global temperatures seemed to be falling in recent years after rising for the past century. Melting of the polar icepacks and glaciers had ceased. "Moissanite reflects more solar radiation which may be counteracting the effect of increased carbon dioxide in the atmosphere", Schareshiem reasoned. "Perhaps global warming will no longer be of interest", said Brent. "Decreasing oxygen in the atmosphere due to deforestation may be the next step", said Schareshiem. "What about the death of plankton and other oxygen generating organisms in the sea", Brent added? Schareshiem nodded, then stared at the floor. "We may have less time to study this phenomenon than we thought…"

Brent's plan didn't include studying moissanite colonies for the rest of his life. He had already contacted officials in Australia about relocating there. As expected, the Australian government had been overwhelmed with requests for asylum. Australia was a continent of contradiction, having an enormous land mass, much of which was practically uninhabitable without government assistance. That government assistance was woefully inadequate to support millions of refugees fleeing the moissanite invasion of their own countries every month. Perth, Sydney, Brisbane,

Melbourne, Adelaide, and other major population centers along the Australian coastline had only one tenth of the housing needed. Temporary shelters reduced the numbers of refugees on the streets, but there still were many living at the mercy of the elements. Australian law enforcement could not prevent widespread violence and looting under these circumstances. Attempts were made to implement a 'dusk to dawn' curfew but they were largely ineffective.

Brent's contact in Australia was about his same age. They met at a student conference in the spring of 2030 in Los Angeles. By 2036 Group Captain Christopher had already established himself as an exemplary officer in the Australian Air Force (RAAF), currently stationed at Lavarack Barracks in Townsville on the northeast coast. Being of aboriginal descent, his first name was unpronounceable in English. His foster parents gave him that name as he never knew his biological parents. He was dark skinned and considered unusually tall at 185 centimetres. Chris, as Brent called him, had a Chemical Engineering Degree from the University of Queensland. It took several attempts to reach him on a video call. "You're probably wishing you had taken that job offer from DuPont about now, right", Brent remarked? "Nah. Too boring. I like a bit of excitement." "Have you ever seen anything like this in Queensland before?" "Never like this, mate. Everyone seems to think they can just take whatever they want. If it's food, we probably just let 'em get away with it. Maybe clothes as well. If it's jewellery or computers or stuff like that. Well, ya can't eat jewellery, can ya", said Chris? "So if I come to Brisbane, can you help me find a place?" Chris's face was blank. Brent took that as a sign he shouldn't have asked. "Sorry", said Brent. "I don't want to be a problem for you."

"No worries, mate, but ya don't wanna go to Brisbane", Chris replied after a few moments. "The further south ya go the worse it gets, 'specially on the east coast. Brisbane isn't safe. Too many boats coming in from Papua New Guinea with all sorts. Can't do anything for ya there. Ya fly into Melbourne, OK? That's ya best route. If ya can't get a commercial flight, I may be able to get ya on a miliary flight into RAAF Base Amberley, about 40 kilometres from Brisbane. I'll figure how to get ya up to Townsville. Nobody messing with Amberley or Townsville because of all us military. There's a place here in Townsville. Might not be what ya used to, but you'll be safe.

My sister's got a flat not far. Not very big." "I can't stay with your sister, Chris." "Ya won't. She was killed six months ago in Sidney. Some bloke ran over her trying to outrun a police car. Place is empty, 'cept when I go there sometimes to get some peace and quiet."

Brent was looking across the room at a blank wall. "Sorry to hear about your sister. I wasn't expecting you to put me up. I'm just worried about getting into the country. Immigration stuff and all that." "No worries, mate, like I said. Ya tell me when ya want to come. I'll make it work." "Probably not for another six months. We're still OK here in Chicago. I'll keep your offer in mind." "I can't guarantee how long I'll be here, but if I am ya're in", said Chris. "Thanks very much. I'll get back to you when I know." Brent's other option was Greenland. It was just too damn cold in Greenland!

Professor Schareshiem's focus had shifted again, this time from climate effects to tracking the movement of moissanite colonies across the planet. Brent was especially interested in how long it might be before it showed up in Australia. "The ocean currents are all wrong – or right, depending upon your point of view", Schareshiem observed. "That might buy the Australian, South American and African Continents some time. Who knows. Some of the colonies in Europe, North America and Asia might stop growing." This was the first and only time Brent had ever heard the Professor admit to such an outcome. Schareshiem had always insisted the colonies couldn't be stopped until they covered the earth. It was almost as if he was cheering them on! "Do you think that's possible", Brent had to ask? "No", his boss replied with a smile. "I was joking." Brent had to wonder about the Professor's sense of humour.

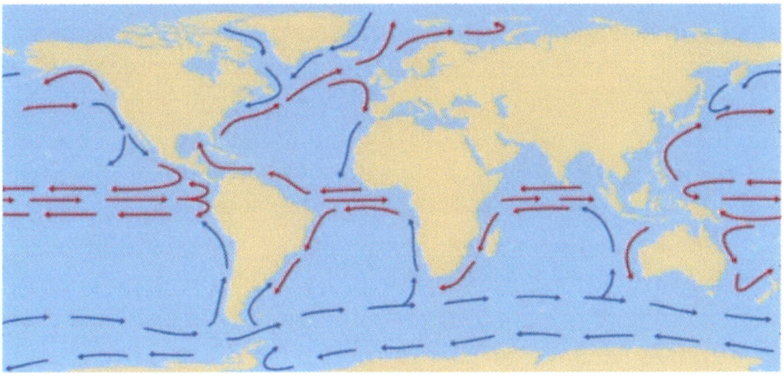

Cold Atlantic currents could carry moissanite down from the United Kingdom along the coast of Spain and onto the coasts of Morocco and Western Sahara. Pacific currents along the west coast of North America might carry moissanite south along the Mexican coast but no further. Pacific and Atlantic currents along South American coastlines all flowed north making it unlikely moissanite would be carried south to Ecuador and Peru on the east coast or Venezuela, French Giana, or Brazil on the west coast. Pacific currents off the coast of Japan all flowed north, away from the Philippines and Australia to the south.

Brent was no wiser than before about Australia. "If you really want to 'get away from it all' I'd recommend the Island of Spitsbergen, halfway between Greenland and the Norwegian Coast", said Schareshiem. "That will probably the last place on earth the moissanite will go." Schareshiem's remark caught Brent off guard. He had mentioned nothing about wanting to leave the Professor's employ or the University organization, what was left of it. "Is that where you plan to go, Professor", Brent asked? "No, no. I don't plan on going anywhere", Schareshiem replied rather quickly. "I'll be in the ground in another six months if you believe the medical staff at Rush University Medical Center. The doctors in San Francisco found it months ago. Doctors here in Chicago agree unfortunately. Stage 4 colon cancer, they say. You need to look out for yourself, young man." Brent was speechless, trying to process what he had just been told. "I'm so very sorry, sir. I had no idea…" "Don't tell anyone, OK? You go wherever you feel safe. I figure the planet has about 10 to 12 years left if this moissanite thing doesn't stop. Spitsbergen will likely be your last refuge."

"But why Spitsbergen", Brent pressed? "How much do you know about gyres?" "Never heard of them", said Brent. "A gyre is a circular flow of the ocean formed by Earth's wind patterns and the forces created by the rotation of the planet. Beneath surface currents of the gyre, the Coriolis effect results in what is called an Ekman spiral. Surface currents are deflected by about 45 degrees, but each deeper layer in the water column is deflected to a lesser degree. This results in a spiral column descending over 100 meters. Gyres interrupt oceanic currents, isolating the waters within and forcing contaminants to be carried around them. A subpolar gyre located between Greenland and Norway contains water that has been isolated from the Atlantic and Artic Oceans for centuries according to every sample taken. Moissanite crystals are not carried by the atmosphere. Ocean currents are the only way they can reach the most remote locations. Spitsbergen Island is in the center of the most unique gyre on earth. Its waters will be the very last to carry the moissanite crystals. It's possible moissanite won't enter those waters for a very long time. Spitsbergen might remain free of the moissanite for decades. Find out as much as you can about Spitsbergen. Start planning now. The next ten years may go rather quickly."

Several days passed before Brent could Google Spitsbergen Island.

> *"Spitsbergen is largest island of the Svalbardarchipelago, part of Norway, in the Arctic Ocean. Spitsbergen, with an area of 39,044 square kilometres, is approximately 450 kilometres long and ranges from 40 to 225 kilometres wide. The terrain is mountainous, and most of the island is covered with glaciers. The highest point on the island is Mount Newton (1,717 metres), in the northeast. Other notable peaks include Hornsundtind (1,431 metres) and Drygalski Crest (1,423 metres). Many other peaks on the mountainous west coast have elevations over 900 metres."*

Brent was thinking this would be the last place on earth he would go for a holiday. If he believed Schareshiem it might be the last place he would be able to go in ten years' time!

Numbers coming out of Washington, DC had become meaningless. No one was paying attention to them anymore. They were alarming in the beginning. Now everyone was numb. By August 2034 the number of people unaccounted for had reached 143 million. With so many people leaving the country it was impossible to get an accurate account. The death toll estimate had risen to 98 million. The vast majority of these were entombed in moissanite, making recovery of the bodies almost impossible. Only a few percent of the corpses were left exposed, which helped reduce the spread of insects and disease. Someone pointed out there was no valid way to measure any of it. Almost a year later the number unaccounted for in the continental United States had risen to 245 million persons. The death toll estimate was 183 million. Other countries attempted to estimate similar figures for their populations.

Gamma Ten

Various mathematical models had been developed in the previous century for estimating mass casualties in the event of a range of imagined catastrophes. These included such things as:

- Rupture of a dam on a major river (5,000)
- Meteor the size of a bus striking a major city (20,000)
- Yellowstone eruption (100,000 immediate)
- Eastern European-Russian (conventional) war (400,000)
- Asteroid (1 km diameter) striking a major city (20 million)
- Global nuclear war (200 million)
- Asteroid (10 km diameter) striking the Earth (5-9 billion)

There was no mathematical model for a slow-moving flood that covered the entire surface of the Earth over several decades. There were far too many variables for such a simulation. People's behavior was a major uncertainty. No one could possibly predict how affected populations would react. Secondary effects might greatly influence the outcome. Loss of farmland and livestock could be estimated but how the import supply chain would cope with huge losses in domestic produce and food supplies was very difficult to predict. Some thought it best to examine historical events instead:

- Great Flood of 1889 in Jamestown, Pennsylvania (2,200)
- Corona Virus pandemic in 2019-2021 (7 million)
- World War II - in battle (15 million)
- Spanish Flu -1918-1920 (28 million)
- Mongol conquests in the 13th Century (30 million)
- World War II - civilians (45 million)
- Black Death when it reached London in 1348 (200 million)
- Human predecessors in Africa were pushed the edge of extinction 900,000 years ago when unknown events drove the population down to only 1280 individuals. It took 117,000 years for that population to recover.

Even though no one put much faith in any government's accounting of human losses, there were those in the United States government who considered the official process of publishing the death toll each and every day quite a serious matter. To do otherwise, they argued, would make them seem incompetent. Congress decided it should hold public hearings to make sure the job was done properly. The Senior

Senator from Oklahoma was first to take the floor. "Everyone uses an app on their phone to buy things. If a person uses their banking app, they must still be alive, right? The online banking system can sort this out for us." The Junior Senator from Kansas objected. "Not necessarily. A family member may be using the phone, or it might have been stolen." The Senior Senator from Massachusetts had another idea. "Why don't we look at records of U.S. passports being used to enter other countries. That will tell us how many have left our country." "Wrong again", shouted the Junior Senator from South Dakota. "What if they use their passport to enter one country, then another country a few months later, and then another after that? Do we count that as three different people leaving the United States?"

"What about all the people who don't have passports? Lots of people have left the United States without a passport." "Really", replied another Senator with an alarmed look? "Let's not waste time looking at passport data", interrupted the Junior Senator from Maine. "Look who's talking here. Your state isn't even affected yet", another Senator smirked. "Neither is yours", shouted another. The spectacle was captured by all fourteen television networks. Videos went viral on the Internet within minutes. "What does it matter", one news reader commented? "It doesn't matter that almost 200 million people are dead", quipped another?? Sadly, to the vast majority of people left in the United States it didn't. Their thoughts were on their own survival. Some news reports considered 'this moissanite thing' the next logical step in evolution. It was the 'struggle for survival' and 'survival of the fittest', just as Charles Darwin had proposed. "What if the next step in evolution doesn't include humans, or any organic life forms for that matter", said one talking head? "So be it", said the other.

Leonard's situation in New York was becoming untenable. The moissanite colony was still some distance away but supplies of food and other goods were becoming harder to find, week by week. Local grocery markets in the city were closing, unable to get deliveries. That meant walking further and further each day to find an open market. Those that were open had fewer and fewer choices. "I'll probably have to leave the city next month." "Where will you go", Aaron asked? "Not sure yet. My firm will pay for the move, but just like everything these days, the choices are limited. There are no cabs in the city anymore. Subway service is only a fraction of what it used to be. Maybe Toronto or Montreal." "At least that's in the right direction", Aaron replied.

Life in New York was much worse than Leonard let on. Nearly 85% of the buildings on Manhattan Island had been abandoned, with no electricity or heat. Most of these had broken windows and doors allowing anyone to enter at their leisure. At least the homeless people in the city now had shelter, which meant the streets were free of them sleeping under cardboard boxes on public walkways or huddled in building entrance vestibules. Those buildings that did have electricity were paying a premium price. Of the various electrical power grids in North America, only three were still operating by July 2036. Most of that power was being generated in Canada and delivered to northern U.S. States via the Quebec Interconnection. Fifteen percent of that power was nuclear.

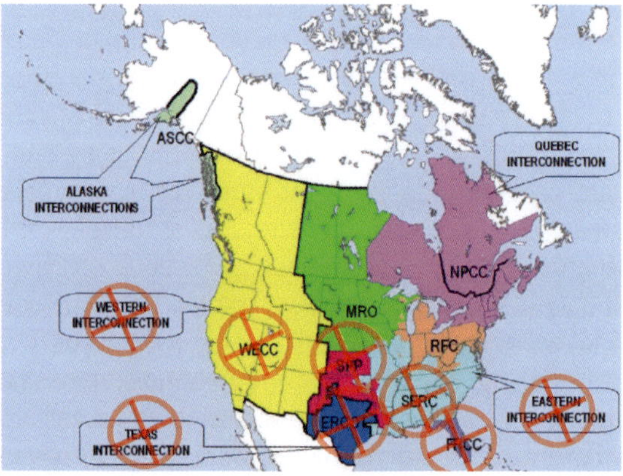

Personal safety was also an issue. Compared to five years earlier, only 1 in 20 New York residents still lived or worked in the city. For New York policemen that number was 1 in 30. Many New Yorkers who remained were destitute, lacking the means to leave or any place to go. Leonard rarely ventured out of his flat on the 14th floor after dark. Access to his building was controlled 24/7, so they said. Still, it seemed anyone could walk in and take the elevator to any floor. At least there were paid security guards in the lobby during daylight hours. Truth was Leonard had no idea when he would be relocating or if the firm would be paying for the move. He wasn't even sure how much longer he would be employed. The New York Stock Exchange was barely in business, with trading down to a few percent of what it was just a few years earlier.

Gamma Ten

Geraldine knew her son wasn't telling them everything. She read the online New York Times religiously. Street crime had doubled in the past year. Most companies with offices in New York had closed them. The city was no longer a major financial center. There weren't any major financial centers left in the United States, in fact. London markets had tripled in size, absorbing essentially all the U.S. financial business. Flights out of New York's Kennedy Airport now numbered just ten a day. There was one flight each evening to Heathrow in London. Geraldine prayed Leonard would make it onto one of those flights before they stopped entirely.

Chapter 15

By May 2037 Brent was forced to leave Chicago. O'Hare Airport had announced it would cease operations in sixty days. He no longer had any idea where Liza and her family might be. If he could get a flight to the south coast of France, there was no guarantee she would be there. He had only one option left. There were no commercial flights to Melbourne or any other location in Australia. "Sorry mate, no miliary flights into Townsville. There's one flight into Amberly next week. I can get ya on it at O'Hare next Saturday. Can ya make it?" Chris had been following the situation at O'Hare through the Australian news media. Facetime was still working. No one could be sure for how long.

"Yes. Schareshiem's funeral was three weeks ago. Lydia and I were the only one's there. The rest of what used to be the faculty at Caltech left Chicago months ago. The Professor would have preferred no funeral at all, but Lydia wanted to pay her respects to the man who drove her crazy for over a decade." "Understood. Just get on that flight, mate. It's only 1400 kilometres from Amberley up to Townsville. They'll want an access code to let ya on the plane. Flight number is RAAF15738. Access code is Christopher2981. Got it?" "Yes. What time?" "Not sure. Military flights don't operate to precise timetables like commercial flights. Don't expect too many comforts, either. Just be at O'Hare at 7 am. Ask at the miliary information counter. Ya might have to wait a bit." "No problem."

Gamma Ten

Brent had to wonder what sort of RAAF plane would be flying as far north as Chicago.

He had no problems boarding the C-17 Globemaster III at O'Hare. There were nineteen others already on the flight, all military. Brent was the only one in civilian clothes. He couldn't remember feeling quite so out of place before. Most of the huge plane was filled with cargo. "We'll be making some stops", warned the co-pilot. "One of them was to pick you up, mate. Hope you're not in a rush." Brent shook his head, while wondering how long it would be. Thirty-two hours was the answer. The journey reminded him of those city busses that stop every two blocks to drop off and pick up passengers. This one picked up fuel and a bit of food at each stop as well, landing briefly in Toronto, Ramstein, Khartoum, Istanbul, Quezon, and Port Moresby in Papua New Guinea. The toilet was a metal bucket behind the rear bulkhead.

"Can I leave the plane for few minutes", Brent asked at Ramstein? "No. Not enough time, mate", replied the co-pilot. Four hours seemed more than enough time to find a 'real' toilet. Apparently, the military had their own way of answering questions. Brent realized he had two choices: accept the miliary answer or don't ask. The enormous size of the C-17 Globemaster III meant a relatively smooth flight, even over the Pacific. The landing at Amberley in Queensland was a bit bumpy, however. Brent pretended not to notice.

There had been only twenty-one commercial flights showing on the 'Departures' display at O'Hare that morning. None were to any place in France. The 'Arrivals' display was switched off. O'Hare in Chicago, Kennedy in New York, Dulles in Virginia, and Boston-Logan in Boston were the only commercial airports still operating in the United States. Once the busiest airport in the world, Hartsfield-Jackson Atlanta International Airport was the first major airport to be abandoned. That shifted a great deal of traffic to the other airports around the country. It also caused serious disruption in international flights around the world. LAX in Los Angeles and San Francisco International Airport were the next to be shut down. Baltimore-Washington International (BWI), Dallas-Fort Worth International, George Bush Houston Intercontinental, and Louis Armstrong New Orleans International airports eventually had to close as well. Commercial flights into the United States decreased dramatically during the same period of time. The United States Government insisted that O'Hare, Dulles, Kennedy and Boston Logan airports remain open for official government travel purposes.

"I'm so glad you called. Your father and I were getting a bit worried. How are things in New York?" "I don't know", Leonard replied. "Quite frankly I don't really care anymore. I'm in London. Just arrived yesterday morning. Everything's still working here, except for cars all driving on the wrong side of the road. I've got to remember to look right instead of left before I step off the curb. The cabs are black, and the busses are red, with two levels sometimes. Looks like they would tip over going around a corner, but they don't. Aaron poked his head into the frame so Leonard could see him as well. "Your mom and I visited London the year before you were born. Still remember the busses. So glad you're safe." "People here have been told they might have to leave in less than a year if this mess comes further south. Everyone's hoping it will stop before then, of course. "Maybe it will", Aaron lied. "Enjoy the time you have there, son." "Will do, Dad".

"Maybe Leonard will meet someone in London. He was always too busy in New York", said Aaron. Geraldine have him a strange look. "What", he replied? "I know we said we wanted grandchildren, but that was a long time ago. I'm not sure I want them anymore." Aaron's smile faded. "Does anyone really want to bring a child into this world? What sort of future would they have", she continued? Aaron stared at the floor for a moment, then nodded slowly. Worldwide birth-rates had plummeted in the past five years while the sales of contraceptives quadrupled. Maternity wards in many hospitals had closed. Preschool enrolments were a small fraction of what they used to be. More than half of preschools and childcare locations had closed due to lack of children. If a miracle happened and portions of the planet remained habitable, would there be a 'next generation' of humans to live there? Perhaps this was nature's way of reducing the population to a number that could survive on a much-reduced land area and fewer natural resources.

By October 2037, the country known as the United States of America ceased to exist, for all practical purposes. All land areas except for Alaska, Hawaii and Puerto Rico were covered in moissanite and uninhabitable. The United States Congress continued to function, however, rehoused in the largest building they could find in Honolulu, known as the 'First Hawaiian Center'. First Hawaiian Bank and the Contemporary Art Museum were evicted from the building by federal legislation which allowed seizure of private property by 'right of immanent domain'. Both the bank and the museum sued, of course. The issue was decided by the U.S. Supreme Court, who had recently relocated to that same building.

Elsewhere in the world people began to realize they might be facing a global extinction event. The worldwide suicide rate had climbed to one person in twenty. Morgues were overwhelmed. Mortuaries were often forced to omit embalming procedures entirely. Countries where medically assisted suicide was legal were flooded with persons who just wanted to end their lives peacefully. Drugs for such 'medical procedures' were in short supply. Others escaped into virtual reality devices – most hoping never to return to reality. Half of those were found dead from starvation. Cruise ships had become more popular than ever. Those who could afford it lived on them permanently until they ran out of fuel. Passengers had to choose between starvation or drowning. Speculation about the last refuges was rampant. Consensus formed around Australia, Southern Africa, South America, Alaska, Greenland, Iceland, and the Antarctic. The richest 0.1% in the world had already gone to one of those locations. Brent had chosen Australia.

Chris couldn't get to Amberley in time to see the C-17 land. Brent was so happy to get off the plane he didn't really care. Just sitting on a bench that wasn't moving in a rather sparce looking building with a working toilet was good enough for the moment. "Sorry I couldn't get here quicker, mate. Normally a 15-hour drive. Took a bit longer this time", Chris confessed. "No problem. I've spent the last 90 minutes reading the RAAF bulletins on all the billboards." Chris laughed. "Necessary propaganda. Don't put too much faith in what ya read. Miliary life's not really like that. Come on. Way out's over here." A dusty green British Land Rover was parked in the lot just outside the gate. "Nice ride", Brent remarked. "Not mine. Could never afford it. Military property assigned to me. If it gets a dent, they court martial me." "Really?" "Nah." Chris smiled. "Get in. Ya're drivin' – I'm sleepin'." "I don't know how to get to Townsville", Brent protested. Chris pointed to the small screen on the dash as he folded his arms and closed his eyes. "Satnav, mate."

Chris was asleep before Brent was out of the car park. There were signs here and there. RAAF Base Amberley was proud to be the largest Royal Australian Air Force miliary airbase in Australia, with over five thousand uniformed and civilian personnel. Located 50 km southwest of Brisbane, it was headquarters to No. 95 Wing and covered approximately 16 square kilometres. Following the female voice on the satnav, Brent found his way off the base in 20 minutes. He'd been on the road for about four hours when Chris woke up and looked at the dash panel. "Almost out of petrol, mate, and I need a wee." He looked out the right window, then the left. "We can stop at Maryborough. It's just a bit further." "You know this road pretty well then", Brent asked? "Driven it almost every month for past three years. That's when I'm here. I get 'bout an hour's notice when they send me somewhere else in the world for a few months. Never know when that might happen. If ya can't find me, don't look too hard. Nobody's gonna tell you where I am, OK? Just wait for me to come back."

Maryborough boasted a population of about 20,000 residents. Onc of them came out of a small shop just off the side of the highway to ask if they wanted petrol. Brent remembered his grandfather telling stories about people who would come out to your car, fill up your petrol tank, even clean your windscreen, and take payment without you even getting out of the car. On this occasion both Chris and Brent were keen to find the toilet. "Key's on the hook just inside the door", yelled the attendant as he was putting 100 litres into the tank on the Land Rover. "You just made it", said the attendant. "Nah, could've made another ten miles at least", Chris replied. Back on the road Chris took over driving. "Get much sleep on the plane?" "Not much. Hard to get comfortable on a steel bench." "Yeah, Globemasters are built to carry cargo, not passengers. Ya can put enough food, water, and medical supplies on one of them things to keep 150 people alive for a year."

A few moments of silence were all Brent needed to drop off for some much-needed sleep. It was dark when he woke. "How long?" "Nearly six hours. Didn't have the heart to wake ya. Need a stop?" "Yes." Chris pulled off the side of the road. "How do you manage", Brent asked once they were back on the highway? "Manage what? Oh ya mean bladder control. When ya're in the military ya follow orders. Ya don't stop for a wee unless ya're ordered to do so." "And the same for…" "Yep. It's an acquired skill. Does take practice…"

Brent was shaking his head and smiling as he looked out the window. An occasional vehicle passed by, flashing its headlights in their eyes. "Not much traffic on this road", he observed. "Not now. I have seen it bumper to bumper. Depends what's goin' on." Brent nodded for some unknown reason. "Ya came at a good time", Chris continued. "We're in a lull. It can change quickly. Bit slow at Townsville right now. Should be able to slip ya in." "Slip me in?" "Ya're not here legally mate. Ya didn't clear immigration. The government has no record of ya being here. Just keep a low profile. Don't say too much. We don't have any of this grey sand stuff here, but if we find any ya might just be able to help, seeing as how ya know so much about it."

It was just before dawn when the Land Rover reached Townsville. RAAF Base Townsville was a Royal Australian Air Force Base located in Garbutt, 3.7 kilometres west of Townsville in Queensland. RAAF Townsville was the headquarters for No. 1 Wing Australian Air Force Cadets and, along with Lavarack Barracks, established Townsville as a key military centre in Australia. The base's airfield was shared with the Townsville Airport. Chris handed Brent the key to the flat in Garbutt. "Let yourself in and get some rest. It might be a few days before I can get back to ya. There's food and beer in the fridge." It took a few minutes to figure out how to turn on the television. Brent was never good at such things.

It was four days in fact. The fridge was almost empty. Brent was getting worried. He had no Australian money and no idea where to find the nearest market. "I've spoken to people at the base", Chris began. "They've agreed to listen to whatever ya have to say about that grey sand stuff, unofficially of course." "What does that mean 'unofficially'." "That means nothing ya say will be recorded or written down since legally speakin' ya not here, mate." Chris could be a bit abrasive sometimes. Brent thought for a minute. "Fair enough", he replied.

"Can you tell me what you're hearing from the Russians and the Chinese?" Chris shook his head. "They don't share intel with us. They don't even tell each other what's goin' on. Remember the Russians didn't tell us about Chernobyl until we rubbed their noses in the evidence. What we do get is lots of propaganda, about how the West has weaponized this 'grey sand' thing and somehow infected their homeland. They constantly boast about how they will make the West pay for using a chemical weapon against the Geneva Convention. "

"We have satellite photos", Brent replied. "We can see it's spreading over both countries. Not sure about how it got started in China. Russia's problem started in Ukraine. Most of Russia is still free of it. It will be many years before it reaches Siberia. There are nuclear plants on the far northern coast of Siberia. But so few people up

there." Chris looked away suddenly to take a call. "Got to go. Problem on the reef." "What sort of problem", said Brent? "Barge." "I need to see it", said Brent. "If I get ya on base, ya gotta keep ya mouth shut." "Agreed."

"There's room on the chopper", Brent insisted. "Absolutely not! No civilian personnel on a military flight", said Chris, with a stern look. "What about the plane I came in on", Brent replied? "Don't know nothin' 'bout that, mate. Nobody on that plane remembers ya being there." Chris turned and walked toward the chopper. Blades were already rotating. "Take a radiation monitor", Brent yelled. Chris held up a small yellow and black box without looking back, as he continued across the tarmac.

The helicopter was off the ground and over the horizon in another ten minutes. It was two hours before Brent's phone rang. "Damn barge is too hot to approach. Chinese markings but some aren't legible. Part of the barge is covered in grey sand. That your stuff?" "Yes, that's moissanite. Don't let it get onshore." "Too late", Chris replied. "Barge tipped on its side when it grounded on the reef. Some of the concrete containers fell onto the reef. That grey sand has washed onto the beach in at least three locations. Radiation monitors are pegging when we get near it. What should we do?" The line was silent. "Hey mate. Ya know all about this stuff. What should we do?" Brent sat down on the long wooden bench behind him and let out a long sigh. "It's too late. No point in towing the barge back out to sea. It won't make any difference now. There's nothing you can do."

Gamma Ten

There was no evidence the Chinese government or any of its agents had deliberately towed a barge carrying radioactive waste containers onto the Great Barrier Reef. Once the incident was reported, they claimed the barge had been lost at sea many months earlier. They had searched for it, of course, but were unable to locate it. They did not want it back and refused to take any further responsibility for it now that it had capsized on the reef. The Australian government was expected to clean up the mess at its own expense. The Chinese very politely declared themselves not responsible, as usual. The introduction of radioactive waste onto the Australian Continent was insult enough. Now it was no longer a safe haven for a dwindling human population.

"It had to happen eventually", Brent announced to a small group of military officers at Townsville. There was an air of resignation in the room even if most of them believed it might be possible to stop the moissanite colony from getting a foothold. Brent patiently described everything that had been tried in the United States without success. No one asked why he was at Townsville, much less if he was there legally.

The last thing Group Captain Christopher needed was a civilian to look after. "I'd like ya to meet Flight Lieutenant Gibbs. If ya need anything and I'm not available Gibbs here will help ya out. Brent instinctively reached out to shake Gibbs' hand. Gibbs seemed surprised at the gesture. He hesitated for a moment, then took Brent's hand firmly. "You can usually find me in Barracks No. 12", Gibbs replied. His hair was noticeably longer than others at Townsville. He looked older than most of the others and a bit over regulation weight as well. Standing next to each other, Group Captain Christopher and Flight Lieutenant Gibbs were about the same height, like bookends. That was where the resemblance ended, however. Gibbs' hair was a dusty brown with moustache to match. Both stood out against his fair skin. Chris had never married, joining the RAAF the month after his university graduation. He considered himself a career soldier. Chris also spent more time in the gym, being 14 years younger. Ether man looked like they could take care of themselves if it came to it.

At age 45, Gibbs was somewhat of a celebrity at Townsville. It wasn't because of his rank. Someone of his age could expect to be a Squadron Leader or even a Wing Commander. Gibbs had sacrificed his miliary career to keep a promise to his wife who died during the Covid pandemic in spring of 2020. Gibbs' daughter was three when she lost her mother. Gibbs promised his wife on her deathbed he would take care of their daughter no matter what happened. Both his parents were deceased. There was only Gibbs' sister to help raise the little girl until the age of 12. After his sister's death, Gibbs was forced to declare himself 'not deployable overseas'. That declaration was quite understandable with Gibbs being a single parent. Nevertheless, it disqualified him for promotions he would have acquired under normal circumstances.

Having watched his own country being overrun by this grey menace, Brent had no desire to see it do the same thing in another country almost as large, but with a much smaller population. Actually he had little choice in the matter. At the moment there was nowhere else for him to go. At the Townsville Base Commander's request Brent put a chart of land area (square kilometres) consumed month by month on the screen in the largest conference room on the Base.

"Gentlemen. My friend Group Captain Christopher just introduced me as an expert on the grey sand that has been spreading across the planet and has now found its way onto your shores here in Australia. I would have disagreed with that introduction in years past but the real expert, Professor Schareshiem, has sadly passed away. I and others studying this moissanite phenomenon at Caltech in Los Angeles have been forced to flee our homeland."

Gamma Ten

Months	UK & Europe	Japan	Ukraine	Russia	Australia
1					
2					
3					
4					
5					
6					
7					
8					
9					
10	57	18	46	74	
15	190	73	277	245	
20	569	438	692	736	
25	1,517	876	1,476	1,964	
30	3,791	1,460	2,306	4,909	
35	7,962	2,627	8,301	10,309	
40	13,269	7,663	12,912	17,181	
45	27,297	17,516	18,446	35,344	
50	39,240	29,558	24,902	50,807	
55	51,182	43,789	36,892	66,270	
60	113,738	54,736	69,172	110,449	
65	227,475	87,578	138,344	196,355	
70	473,907	131,367	207,515	306,804	2,306
75	1,706,066	182,454	345,859	441,798	3,844
80	2,653,880	291,926	553,374	601,336	7,688
85	3,791,257	364,908	691,718	785,419	38,440
90	5,971,229			994,045	76,880
95	7,582,514			1,227,216	153,760
100	8,862,063			2,699,876	384,400
105	9,383,361			4,417,979	768,800
110	9,904,658			6,381,526	1,537,600
115	10,425,956			8,590,515	3,075,200
120				10,308,619	4,612,800
125				12,026,722	6,150,400
130				13,744,825	7,688,000
135				15,462,928	
140				17,181,031	
145					

"All I can offer you is a series of computer model predictions about what this phenomenon will do next. As you know the Continental United States and nearly all the populated areas of Canada and northern Mexico are now uninhabitable. It's one thing to read about such things or see reports on the news. It's quite another to see it slowly flood the land, making it unfit for biological life. Now you are faced with this prospect.

Months	Australia	China	S. America	Africa	Greenland
1					
2					
3					
4					
5					
6					
7					
8					
9					
10					
15					
20		2,879			
25		4,799			
30		9,597			
35		47,985			
40		95,970			
45		191,940			
50		383,880			
55		767,760			
60		959,700			
65		1,919,400			
70	2,306	3,838,800			
75	3,844	4,798,500			
80	7,688	6,717,900	1,784		
85	38,440	8,157,450	3,568	304	
90	76,880	9,597,000	7,136	607	
95	153,760		14,272	911	2,166
100	384,400		17,840	1,518	108,300
105	768,800		26,760	2,126	216,600
110	1,537,600		35,680	3,006	649,800
115	3,075,200		53,520	3,644	1,516,200
120	4,612,800		71,360	4,251	2,166,000
125	6,150,400		89,200	5,162	
130	7,688,000		124,880	6,073	
135			160,560	7,288	
140			178,400	8,199	
145			356,800	9,717	
150			713,600	10,931	
155			1,070,400	12,146	
160			1,427,200	18,219	
165			1,784,000	22,774	
170			3,568,000	27,329	
175			5,352,000	30,365	
180			7,136,000	60,730	
185			8,920,000	91,095	
190			10,704,000	151,825	
195			12,488,000	212,555	
200			14,272,000	273,285	
205			16,056,000	364,380	
210			16,769,600	455,475	
215			17,304,800	516,205	
220			17,840,000	576,935	
225				637,665	
230				728,760	
235				819,855	
240				910,950	
245				1,032,410	
250				1,153,870	
255				1,396,790	
260				2,064,820	
265				3,036,500	
270				6,073,000	
275				9,109,500	
280				15,182,500	
285				21,255,500	
290				25,810,250	
295				30,365,000	

This chart shows the predicted land consumption in the other countries that haven't been severely affected to date. Again, the figures are square kilometres consumed month by month after it first broke out of K Basin in South Carolina in December 2031, nearly six years ago. These estimates correlate well with western satellite photographs of Russia and China, even though these countries officially deny our estimates.

"Unfortunately the mathematical models I developed at Caltech have proven remarkably accurate. These charts show how the moissanite colonies are expected to spread across the largest of the remaining countries. The nations in this table account for roughly 70% of the land area on the planet. There is little reason to believe that the remaining 30% will escape completely. We still hope that some remote locations might not be affected for quite some time. We had hoped Australia would not be affected this soon. Whether this Chinese barge on the Great Barrier Reef was placed there deliberately or simply drifted in on its own matters not. It's there now. We have to deal with it. We have been unable to predict the movement of this material in the oceans, but we know from our experience in the waters off the Japanese coast that it can move through the oceans and along shorelines. It consumes fish and other aquatic life in the process. More importantly it kills the plankton that generates oxygen that we breath. Professor Schareshiem was studying the decrease in oxygen levels in the atmosphere when he died. This decrease is slight and of no consequence at the moment."

"So you're saying Australia will be covered in this stuff in five years?" The question came from someone in the back of the room. Brent couldn't see his rank. "That's the worst-case estimate at this time, sir", Brent replied. "What's the best-case estimate", another officer asked? "Don't know until you can get me an assay of what's on that barge. Moissanite feeds off the gamma radiation from long lived isotopes, like strontium and caesium. I need to know how much strontium and caesium is on that barge." An officer in the front row laughed. "You are joking, right? We can't get within 60 meters of that barge. Radiation levels are too high." "You'll have to rig up something that you can hang from a chopper, maybe. It's time to be creative, gentlemen." Those in the room began to grumble amongst themselves, shaking their heads. Some stared at the ceiling while others had their heads bowed, examining the floor. "We'll find a way", shouted Group Captain Christopher. The room went quiet. He had no idea how.

An hour later Chris found Brent on the sidewalk outside one of the barracks. "Serious about needing an assay of what's on that barge, are ya?" "Yes I am." Chris shook his head. "Piece of advice, mate. Americans can be too direct sometimes." "You mean telling your superiors they need to be 'creative'." Chris nodded. "We don't do 'creative' in the military. We follow orders. If this is just a personal science project, they won't help ya." "I assure you it isn't personal. Professor Schareshiem had a theory that there must be an energy threshold below which the silicon carbide crystals would stop replicating. ^{90}Sr and ^{137}Cs are the primary radioactive isotopes that drive the self-replication of the moissanite crystals. If we can get a radioactive spectrum of what's on that barge, I'll be able to tell how long that material has been out of a reactor."

"Both ^{90}Sr and ^{137}Cs have half-lives of about 30 years. Much of the material on that barge may have been in storage for that length of time. That means the radiation energy from those isotopes is down to half. In another five years they may have decayed sufficiently to slow or even stop the growth of the moissanite. The amounts of ^{90}Sr and ^{137}Cs already in the moissanite are being diluted in two dimensions as it spreads out. Unlike most nations Australia has no nuclear power stations, or spent nuclear fuel, or other sources of ^{90}Sr and ^{137}Cs to resupply the moissanite with the gamma radiation it needs. It's possible it may slow down. We may have longer than five years." "How much longer?" "Impossible to make such a prediction with any level of confidence until I get an assay of what's on that barge." Chris nodded slowly. "What equipment would you need for this 'chopper over the barge' thing?" Brent smiled as he handed his friend a typed list.

Chapter 16

Townsville was home to Australia's CH-47F Chinook fleet. The wind buffeted the huge helicopter as it hovered over the Great Barrier Reef. Rain was spraying into the open doorway. Brent strained to look down at the capsized barge just below. "Can you get a little lower", he yelled over the noise of twin chopper blades. He was fighting back the urge to throw up that morning's breakfast of two scones and tea. The pilot lowered the chopper another three meters. "Can't get any closer. Radiation levels are over the limits now. Can't stay here much longer", yelled Group Captain Christopher. "I'm getting the data now", Brent yelled back. Just a few more minutes." Chris held up five fingers. "No more", he yelled. It was seven minutes before Chris ordered the pilot to abandon the location and head back to Townsville. "I hope ya got what ya wanted, 'cause we're not going back. Our radiation badges are probably over the limit already. I'll have to answer for that", Chris announced. Brent gave a thumbs up. "Thought you said no civilian personnel on military flights." "What military flight", Chris replied?

It only took a few hours to analyse the data. "This stuff hasn't been inside a reactor for 28 years. There's not as much ^{90}Sr and ^{137}Cs as I expected. The Chinese must have had this material lying around for some time. That's good. I need a few days to run the models on my laptop again, but Australia may have a lot longer than the five years I said earlier. If I overlay the results on a map I can tell where it's likely to go last." "Perth's the other side of the country", Chris volunteered. "Yes, but it's on the coast. Depends on how this stuff moves around in the ocean currents." "Somewhere out west, then?" "Yes. I'm afraid you'll have to move the Townsville Base in that direction." "How soon?" "Maybe a year. Maybe two", Brent replied. "Don't wait too long."

In London Leonard was wondering about where he was going next, along with 9.5 million Londoners. Zurich was rumoured as the next destination for those in financial markets. That move happened in March 2037, quite a bit sooner than expected. By June of that year the United Kingdom had suffered the same fate as the United States. There was simply no habitable land area left in either country. A majority of the nuclear power stations in Europe were south and west of Switzerland. European governments had been assured that, and the mountainous terrain, would buy them some time, although Zurich was only 38 kilometres from the nuclear power station at Beznau. Less than a year after moving to Zurich Leonard's firm declared bankruptcy and abandoned their operations in Europe. Leonard had not heard from his parents in Alaska for several years. He assumed they were still alive. He knew his father to be a very resourceful individual. If there was a way for them to survive, he was sure his father had found it.

By March 2037 failure of the electrical grid in Alaska and loss of the Internet forced Bill and his family to use their Inuit training sooner than expected. Electrical supply had been unreliable, with brown outs and black outs happening more frequently during the past year. Solar batteries only got enough sunlight to charge during June, July, and August. Bill kept in contact with Aaron by radio, but their communications were brief. "We need to get you to Fairbanks in June", Bill said. "Anchorage will be a ghost town soon. I've been working on something that might save both our families."

Paper wealth was now worthless. Nobody was buying stocks or futures anymore. Many wondered if they had a future at all. Real wealth was having the things one needed to survive. People were hoarding non-perishable food, bottled water, and other necessities, putting a greater strain on supply chains and transport systems. Bill remembered reading about people who built bomb shelters in the 1960's and '70's - stocking them with food and water in the event of a nuclear attack. That mentality seemed to have re-emerged in every society. Paper money was quickly losing its value. Even gold wasn't worth much anymore.

Leonard used the last bit of money he had to make his way by train to India. There he purchased passage on a ship to Anchorage. There was only one ship that delivered goods to Alaska, and only during the summer months. If his parents were still alive, they must still be in Alaska. If they were dead, they must have had good reason to go there. He hoped they were still in Anchorage or somewhere nearby.

Gamma Ten

It took six weeks for the ship to arrive in Anchorage. Leonard wasn't prepared for what he found there. "When will the next ship be arriving", he asked the first attendant he found on the dock? "Who knows", the man replied. "We always assume this will be the last one." Many of the shops in Anchorage were boarded up, as if the owners planned to return. It was late July. Maybe the owners all went on holiday during July. Other shops had broken windows and had obviously been looted of anything valuable. Leonard found the police station four blocks from the dock. There was a handwritten list posted on the wall with names of those still living in Anchorage. It went on for eleven pages. Leonard finally found Aaron and Geraldine's names on the list. Both had been scratched through with "Fairbanks" written beside them. "How can I get to Fairbanks", he asked the man in plain clothes sitting behind a desk? "There's a truck leaving in four hours", replied the man as he pointed to a paper sign pinned to the bulletin board next to the list of names. Apparently, there was only one truck, and it only went to Fairbanks on Tuesday. "Where would I go to find this truck", Leonard persisted? "Back to the dock, then south along the boardwalk to the end. Better hurry. Sometimes he leaves early." "Can you please give him a call and say that I am coming?" "Nope. Phones haven't worked for months. Just walk fast." The man turned back to his carving. It looked to be a small animal of some sort.

Leonard found the truck parked just where he had been told. It was an open bed truck, modified to hold two metal bench seats with a makeshift canvas roof overall. The rear end of the truck bed was left open. An elderly man was sitting inside an old wooden building about twenty metres away. "Is that your truck outside", Leonard asked? "Yep", the man replied without looking up. "I was told you are going to Fairbanks." "Yep." "I need to get to Fairbanks as soon as possible. Can I pay you to take me there?" "Yep." Leonard waited patiently. "How much then", Leonard asked? "How much you got", said the man, looking up? Leonard realized the man wanted to negotiate. As a hedge fund broker he considered himself pretty good at such things. "$30", he offered. The man laughed. "$200. $250, if you want food." Leonard only had $400. He thought for a minute. "How about $150?" "$200, or I leave in an hour without you", the man replied.

Gamma Ten

Having just paid $200 to ride 580 kilometres in the back of an old truck for six hours, Leonard was determined to be in it when it left Anchorage. He settled in the corner on the lefthand bench just behind the cab. His watch read 10 pm. The sky was still quite bright outside. Leonard was wondering if he was the only passenger this evening.

He woke with a start as the truck lurched forward. There were eight other passengers, four sitting on his bench and four on the bench across from him. "Didn't want to wake you", said the lady across from him. "Are all of you going to Fairbanks", Leonard asked, trying to piece together where he was?" "We better be. Don't think this guy's making any other stops along the way", the lady replied. "Ain't nothin' to stop for", said another passenger. "Do any of you know anyone who recently moved to Fairbanks", Leonard asked? "Aaron and Geraldine", replied the man sitting a bit further down. "They left Anchorage about three weeks ago. "My name's Leonard. I'm their son… I don't suppose this vehicle has seat belts." Another man handed Leonard an old piece of rope about two metres long.

Leonard looked at the rope and grinned. "How much?" "Free", said the man. "'bout the only thing that is anymore." "I heard the driver complaining to someone at the dock about the price of petrol for his truck", interrupted another passenger. "He gets enough to make one trip a week from Anchorage to Fairbanks and back. Has an extra tank on the truck. If the ship don't show up next month, he won't have no petrol and he's out of business. We might be the last ones to make this trip. After that it's dogsled or walkin'. Take about 12 days to walk it if you walked ten hours a day in summer. Never make it in winter, even on a dogsled.

Aaron and Geraldine couldn't believe their eyes next morning. It was 4:30 am when Leonard climbed out of the truck in Fairbanks. The sky was as bright as before. He found out where his parents were living by inquiring at the Fairbanks Police Station. Bill had talked to Igaluk who had negotiated an agreement with Inuksuk, the leader of one of the Inuit groups north of Fairbanks, to adopt both families. Now they needed to add Leonard to the deal as well. Inuksuk was reluctant to alter the agreement. If any one of them couldn't carry their weight and became a burden on the group, they would be cast out to starve or freeze when winter came in a few short weeks. Neither Aaron or Geraldine or Leonard had been through Igaluk's training. He could not speak for them the way he could for Bill and his family. Aaron, his wife and son would have to learn very quickly, or they would not be accepted into the Inuit group. Their survival depended upon their ability to meet several challenges determined by Inuksuk.

Aaron and Geraldine were in their mid-50's but both were avid runners and lifetime members of the fitness center at Odell Weeks in Aiken before moving north. Leonard was now in his mid-30's. Even though his job had kept him behind a desk most of the time, he had visited the gym regularly while in London. Inuksuk had no desire to embarrass anyone, but he had a responsibility to those in the Inuit group who elected him as leader. He could not be seen as lenient with outsiders. Everyone had to pull their weight. Even the elderly were expected to work to their capacity. The group would not and could not accept anyone who had not contributed or could not contribute to the overall needs of the group. That is how they had survived for centuries. That was how it must be. Inuksuk's challenges were physically and mentally taxing. It was a difficult 24 hours for all three. Everyone agreed they did their best. Inuksuk looked around the group that had assembled for the trials. Each of the elders had a vote. One by one each gave the sign of approval. Inuksuk turned to Aaron and smiled. "Welcome to our family. But you must hurry. Winter is just over the mountain. You must build shelters and collect as much as you can before it arrives. We will help you." That work was far more demanding than Inuksuk's challenges.

"The Inuit lifestyle is quite difficult but better than starving or freezing", Aaron admitted after the first week. They were lucky as the first snowfall was almost two weeks late. Bill and his family had a year to practice their survival skills, with help from Igaluk, before having to completely rely upon them. Aaron and family had a great deal of catching up to do. "They will learn quickly", said Inuksuk. Bill nodded.

Gamma Ten

Each family member had to become proficient in a growing number of tasks, including:

- Carrying water (or melting snow)
- Cutting and collecting firewood
- Building & tending fires
- Preparing food and cooking meals
- Building and maintaining shelters
- Catching fish in streams and lakes
- Hunting and butchering seals, deer, and other animals
- Preparing and curing animal hides
- Feeding and caring for sled dogs

"There is much to be done. The stream may look the same each day, but the waters that flow past today will never pass us again. If we waste a day, it will not be returned to us", said Inuksuk. Stomach upsets were common as Aaron, Bill and their families got used to a completely different diet. Aaron had tasted venison before, but seal meat was something quite different. "It must be an acquired taste", Bill suggested. Aaron shook his head. "Hope I live that long." Inuit living was hard work, but no one had problems falling asleep at night. Overcoming the mental and physical challenges was very rewarding. Arlene, Geraldine, and the twins found they could live without makeup. It no longer served any purpose. There were no beauty parlours either. Inuksuk's group owned two snowmobiles, but it was impossible to find fuel for them. They were left to rust in the snow. Communication with the outside world was by radio, but only in summer months when there was enough sunlight to charge the solar batteries.

Winter can arrive quite suddenly in Alaska. What Aaron and Bill had experienced since their arrival in Anchorage and Fairbanks hadn't prepared them for living outdoors. Larger Inuit shelters, intended for multiple families, were heated with open fires twenty-four hours a day. Some of these had been built long ago and maintained for decades. Smaller shelters, like the ones Aaron and Bill had hurriedly constructed out of seal skins, were not heated at night. They simply weren't large enough and there was no one to tend the fire. Constructing something more comfortable would have to wait until the following summer. Everyone began to realize this would be their worst winter. If they could survive until summer, life should become a bit easier. Basic hygiene had to be redefined. Everyone slept as close together as possible to share warmth. As snow accumulated around their shelters, both families realized the benefit of added insulation against the subfreezing temperatures, particularly at night. Bill recalled an old saying first attributed to Abraham Lincoln. "If you cut your own firewood, it warms you twice." First you had to dig your way out of the entrance if more snow had fallen overnight.

Conditions in northern areas of Canada were similar. Many in the United States had fled to Canada and were now being forced further north into the wilderness. Most thought the Great Lakes would act as a barrier to further moissanite expansion. The Lakes did delay expansion northward, buying locations like Thunder Bay and Sudbury an additional year. Much of the far northern Canadian wilderness had never been explored by humans. Even the Inuit were struggling, having to relocate further into that wilderness than they wanted.

Although Leonard's time in Zurich was short, he took in as much of the natural beauty of Switzerland as he could. Even as the moissanite colonies slowly progressed across the European Continent there were locations on the highest peaks where people could escape its advance. They would quickly run out of food, however.

Gamma Ten

By summer of 2038 twenty-five percent of Europe had become uninhabitable. For all human purposes the United Kingdom, France, Spain, Portugal, Germany, and the United States no longer existed. Ukraine was no longer part of Europe since the Russian occupation in 2028. It too had been abandoned along with nearly 4% of the land area in Russia.

Two-thirds of the Japanese Islands had been abandoned as well. Japan's economy was driven primarily by fishing and export. Fishing was no longer viable as the radioactivity released from Fukushima energised the growth of moissanite in the sea even before it made landfall. Exports depended upon transportation of Japanese products by ship and by air. As fossil fuel supplies began to run out the cost of shipments by sea and by air became prohibitive. Ships that could cross the oceans under sail were suddenly in high demand. Once owned only by the very rich, there simply weren't enough of them. Most were luxury yachts not suitable for carrying cargo.

A very small portion of humanity was located where the moissanite would never reach them. Orbiting the earth every 90 minutes at an altitude of 408 kilometres, these six individuals had perhaps the most frightening view of what was happening on the planet below. They reported what they saw twice daily. They also needed fresh supplies periodically. All the launch locations in the United States and in Europe were inaccessible. Two launch sites, one in India and one in French Guiana, remained in operation. The International Space Station had been in operation since November 2000. Now it seemed its mission would be terminated, with astronauts from the United States, United Kingdom, Japan, and India forced to return to a planet whose future was uncertain. Three of them had already made the decision to remain on the ISS. They would rather spend their final days in space. Those on the ground agreed to resupply them for as long as possible. Eventually the ISS would slip out of orbit and burn up, probably somewhere over the Pacific Ocean. The astronauts who remained aboard would be dead long before then.

In many remote locations around the world 'highly educated people' were having to toss their university degrees in the bin and learn an entirely new set of skills. There were locations in South America, Southern Africa, Philippines, Greenland, and Iceland where one could hope to live for another decade or more? Native populations freely shared their knowledge and customs to help those who had been displaced from their homelands. These included:

- Inuit in Greenland and Iceland
- Hawaiian and Polynesian natives
- African tribesmen
- Native groups in Brazil, Kenya, Peru, etc.
- Tibetans in China and India
- American Indians who had been forced further north into remote regions of Canada
- Wangkatja group of peoples living in the Kalgoorlie Boulder area east of Perth

Unfortunately those who were disabled or not physically fit found it impossible to maintain their new lifestyle. It seemed Darwin's theories about "struggle for survival" and "survival of the fittest" had become more than just empirical explanations of now life evolved over thousands or millions of years. There were now thousands of human casualties every day all over the planet as nature manifested these principles in modern times and with very real consequences. Those with great wealth had selfishly refused to share their good fortune over the past century, claiming that sharing that wealth would violate capitalistic doctrines and lead to a failed communistic or socialistic society. States and governments were left to support those at the bottom end of the financial system, no matter the reason.

Now all had to return to a communal lifestyle where everyone had equal status and equal opportunity. This was especially difficult for those who considered themselves among the elite in modern society. Modern society, as they knew it, no longer existed. Survival meant being part of a tribal existence where everyone's abilities were equally valuable. The most primitive cultures on the planet had no difficulty sharing their wealth of knowledge and customs with the many refugees now invading their homelands. Certainly none expected to become rich or powerful. There was no desire for personal gain. Newcomers who expected to be greeted with privilege were disappointed. Some refused to adapt, condemning this new lifestyle as communistic. In this new world they were left to die.

Chapter 17

Despite Brent's unspecified immigration status, his presence at the RAAF Base in Townsville was no longer under scrutiny. His initial predictions of how the moissanite on the Great Barrier Reef would spread along the north and eastern coasts proved to be exceptionally accurate. A few sceptics remained, particularly in the higher ranks of the RAAF. This didn't affect progress toward eventual relocation of the Base, its personnel, and its miliary assets. By January 2039 it was clear relocation had to happen in a matter of months, not years.

The logical choice was Amberley to the south. The problem was space. Amberley was already the largest RAAF Base in Australia. Amberley was home to No. 1 Squadron (operating the F/A-18F Super Hornet), No. 6 Squadron (operating the EA-18G Growler), No. 33 Squadron (operating the Airbus KC-30A), No. 35 Squadron (operating the C-27J Spartan) and No. 36 Squadron (operating the Boeing C-17 Globemaster III). Amberley was also home to Army units making up the 9th Force Support Battalion (9 FSB). Located on 1.6 square kilometres, RAAF Amberley already employed over 5,000 uniformed and civilian personnel. Accommodating an additional staff of 140 civilian and 132 RAAF personnel, aircraft and support equipment was a significant challenge. For the past four years a primary mission of both Townsville and Amberley was transport of food and supplies to displaced populations in remote areas around the world.

During the past year that mission had expanded to include support for evacuation of over 180,000 people in Cairns and surrounding area in their own country. Both missions were rapidly expanding. Townsville was also home to three infantry battalions 1, 2 and 3 RAR as well as Engineers, Artillery, Calvary, Signal and CSS Battalions, amounting to almost 7000 personnel. They would have to relocate as well. At the moment nobody had any idea where.

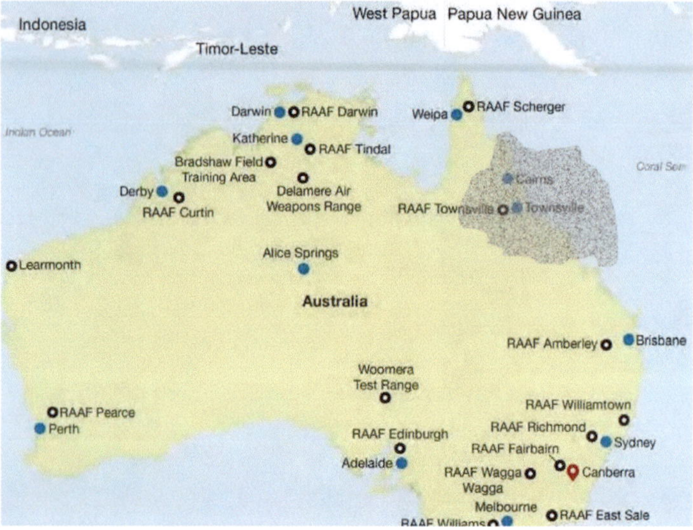

By summer of 2039 Group Captain Christopher was spending most of his time flying supply missions to points all over the globe. Officers of even higher rank with pilot's qualifications were being assigned to fly missions outside Australia if a plane was available. The C-17 Globemaster III was the aircraft of choice due to its cargo capacity and flight range. Maximum payload of the C-17 was 77,500 kilograms. With a payload of 73,000 kilograms and an initial cruise altitude of 8,500 meters, the C-17 had an unrefuelled range (round trip) of 5,200 kilometres. The C-17's cruise speed was 830 kilometres/hour (Mach 0.74). The Globemaster was designed to operate from runways as short as 1,067 meters. This gave it the capability to land and take off in remote areas where airfields were below normal standards. The problem of space at Amberley had been solved by keeping most of the C17's in the air. Any that were on the ground were being loaded by anyone who wasn't pilot rated. It seemed to Brent the massive planes where either taking off or landing continuously.

Every six months Brent persuaded Chris to take him on one of the supply missions overseas. He hadn't forgotten about his initial flight on a Globemaster from Chicago. He promised himself he would never board another C-17. Curiosity got the better of him, however.

Gamma Ten

The first three flights had been to Davao City in the Philippines. This one was a bit further. "We'll be stopping at Pearce near Perth to refuel, then on to Singapore. Ya won't be able to see very much there", Chris cautioned. "We may not even land, which means we can't refuel. They'll radio us about an hour before to let us know. That gives us time to rig the parachutes for a drop. Ya'll be expected to help with that." Brent nodded. "Somehow the crowds always know we're coming. If they're not under control, it won't be safe to land. They could storm the plane and we'd never get off the ground again. They'd likely hold us hostage until their demands are met." "What sort of demands", Brent asked? "Could be anything. Most likely they would demand other supply flights be redirected to this location." "Then what?" "Then they would kill us."

Brent sat back abruptly. "That bad?" "Yes, that bad. If we do land don't even think about leaving the plane. We'll be down and up again as fast as possible." Brent never imagined such conditions could exist in the 21st Century. Only the strongest would survive, and only if they were lucky enough to be in the right locations. Much of the world had regressed to a primal state, like existed tens of thousands of years in the past. Physical competition for food, water and the raw necessities of life determined one's survival. So it was again. That competition would eliminate the weak and infirm, strengthening the herd over time. If anyone did survive, would there be changes in their DNA as a result? Would there even be time for that? Evolution requires a great deal of time. Would humans simply go extinct in a geological blink of an eye? For decades people wondered if someday nuclear weapons would wipe out our species. We said we were too smart to let that happen. Perhaps our 'peaceful' use of nuclear energy had produced the same result. Perhaps we weren't so smart after all…

It took nearly a year to move all the personnel and assets at Townsville to Amberley. The last of it left Townsville in November 2039, a month before the moissanite arrived at the Base perimeter. The city of Townsville had been evacuated much earlier, with help from the resident military. Twenty percent of Australia's land mass was now covered in moissanite. Brent's predictions about the growth rate slowing down got a lot of attention. "It would slow down, you said", barked one of the senior officers at Amberley. "Not yet", Brent replied. "We can see that. We'll have to evacuate Amberley in another 14 months if it keeps coming. What does your computer model say about that?" "I'm afraid that's about right", Brent replied.

The officer shook his head. "So where do you suggest we go next?" "Further west to Woomera would be my advice", Brent replied. His calm 'matter of fact' manner denied the officer an opportunity to get angry with him. Brent was just the messenger who didn't want to be shot. He didn't want to be left behind either.

It was nearly 10 pm when Brent's computer made a dinging sound. The noise was familiar – he just couldn't remember what it meant. He popped it open and found an email in his inbox. He hadn't received an email in over two years. "Where are you?", it read. "You first.", he typed. "Perth", came the answer. "Amberley", he replied. There was no response. He was about to close the screen and retire when it dinged again. "This is Lydia. I had to leave Rome. Thought I might find you down here." "Did anyone else from Caltech come with you?" "No just me. They all went somewhere. Don't know where. I think we're all that's left." Now it was Brent's turn to stop and think for a minute. "Are you well", he asked? "Yes, and you?" "Yes. I didn't know the Internet was still working. I stopped being able to access Google or Instagram or Amazon or anything else years ago. All the servers and connections became unreliable. Outages lasted for days. Then online banking failed completely."

Gamma Ten

Brent paused to give Lydia a chance to respond. "I lost track of my parents fourteen months after I moved to Rome. They were in St. Louis. There's no database of missing persons anymore. It was all online. I have no idea where they are now. When all my financial apps stopped working in Rome, I had no way to pay for things. I had to find some way to live", she replied. "There was an elderly couple with a big house. Lots of rooms that needed cleaning. They took me in to do the cleaning and cooking and tending the garden. Gave me three meals a day and a room with a bed to sleep in. Everyone in Rome went back to trading goods and using the barter system. The banks here in Perth seem to still be working. It's cash only though. Looks like the email part of the Internet is still working here in Australia. No one knows how long the satellites will stay up though." "How did you get to Perth", Brent had to ask? "One flight a week. I had to use my last bit of money to get on it. Went to Kolkata, then on to Perth. Very long flight." Lydia couldn't see Brent's smile.

It was nearly two years before the RAAF was forced to leave Amberley. The advance of the moissanite colony had slowed somewhat.

The RAAF Base at Woomera had been a Defence-owned and operated facility since first established. The Base was located on the traditional lands of the Kokatha people in the outback desert area of South Australia, within the area designated as the 'Woomera Prohibited Area' (WPA).

Woomera was approximately 446 kilometres north of Adelaide. In common usage, "Woomera" referred to the wider complex involving a large Australian Defence Force aerospace and systems testing range covering approximately 122,000 square kilometres. Although the complex was closed to the public, four museum elements were open to the public all year round. There was also a long-established precious gems (mainly opal) field near the Coober Pedy end of the Stuart Highway which cut through the middle of the Range.

Brent found the terrain at Woomera quite different from Townsville or Amberley. If you could manage to stand on something more than a few metres high, you could see for about 50 kilometres in every direction. It reminded him of parts of west Texas he had visited once. Without a landmark of some sort one could get lost as surely as if they were in the middle of an ocean. Woomera was the very definition of the word "flat". It seemed the ideal place to test whatever the Australian military was testing. Brent admitted he hadn't a clue what that might be. Perhaps he was better off not knowing…

Gamma Ten

Moving RAAF personnel and military assets from Amberley nearly halfway across Australia to Woomera disrupted the schedule of humanitarian flights to displaced populations across the globe. Unfortunately the delays resulted in many deaths. It simply couldn't be helped. By January 2042 the RAAF was stretched to the limit. By 2043 the number of abandoned countries had grown substantially. These included the United States, Europe (including the United Kingdom), Japan, and China. In Russia 80% of the land area (far north) was still habitable. The demand for Australia's humanitarian relief flights to overseas locations began to decline. Brent was finally able to report some good news to the RAAF. "Moissanite continues to spread across Australia, but growth has slowed to half its previous rate." Just as in Arizona and New Mexico the arid climate in the center of the continent seemed to slow the spread of the moissanite colony. It was little consolation, however. By the end of 2045 they were forced to move again. This move was to Pearce near the city of Perth on the west coast.

Gamma Ten

Moissanite colonies had spread from northeast to southwest covering over 50% of the country, including almost all the northern coastline. Three of the country's petroleum refineries had been abandoned. The Kwinana refinery, owned by BP, was able to supply enough aviation fuel for RAAF humanitarian missions. Captain Christopher was flying missions to locations in Brazil, Peru, Kenya, and as far north as Greenland.

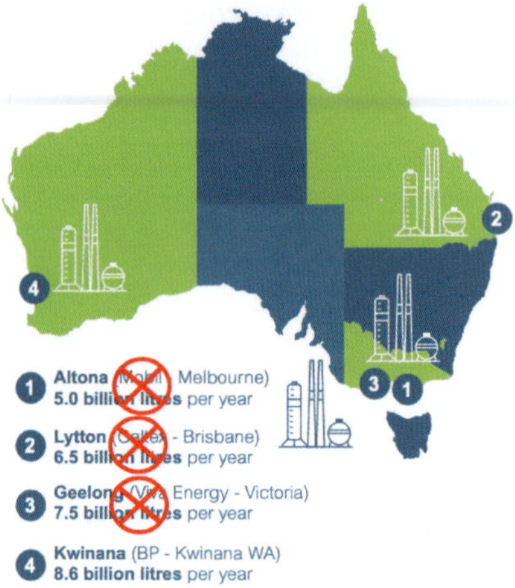

Brent continued to monitor the spread of the moissanite colonies by listening to radio messages on short wave frequencies. Unfortunately he didn't speak many of the languages he heard and had to ask for help from various interpreters at Pearce. He had no problem recognizing one voice, however. "Where in Perth. Over", he asked? "Wildflower, on top of the State Buildings.

Great views of the city and the Swan River. Food's excellent. 7:30? Over." "I can just make that", Brent replied. "If Chris will lend me his Jeep. Over." Brent hadn't seen Lydia since the Professor's funeral in Chicago. Being ten years younger, he had to wonder how much she had changed over the past decade.

"You haven't changed a bit." Lydia looked at him over the rim of her oversized tortoiseshell glasses. "Right", she replied. She took off her glasses and handed them to him. "You need these more than me, then." Brent smiled, holding up his hand to refuse the gesture. "So tell me about Rome." "Beautiful city when I got there. Not so nice when I left. Things went downhill quickly once Schareshiem's grey sand started shutting everything down across Europe." "You can't blame the Professor for all this." "I need to blame somebody, don't I", she replied? "People couldn't get their money when all the cash machines were switched off. Several dozen bank executives were killed in the streets. People were looting shops, burning overturned cars, barricading themselves in parts of the city. The police wouldn't even go there. Going out for dinner like this? No one could risk it. One shop in five was still open when I left. Markets were raided by street gangs. They just walked in, took everything they wanted, and walked out. Anyway I managed to get out before the real violence started. I wouldn't have left if Loren and Andrea hadn't passed away. They were in their 80's. Just couldn't cope with it. Left me enough money to get away and come down here. I'll be OK as long as enough women in Perth need their hair done twice a month. I was a hairdresser for two years before Caltech."

"You like it here, then", Brent asked? "Better than anywhere else from what I hear." Lydia stared at Brent for a moment. "Truth? How much time have we got?" Brent hesitated. He could lie. She would know. "Truth is, I don't know, Lydia. It seems to have slowed down here in Australia. The Professor thought it might but didn't want to give false hope. That was a lie. "If it keeps slowing down, we might have years yet. Maybe a few at least." Lydia nodded. A tear ran down her cheek. Her hands were shaking. "Just thought I'd ask. People here say we should all go to Kalgoorlie-Boulder. They don't think it can reach us there." "Why there?" "They won't say. Maybe superstition? Maybe some tribal legend? Nobody will say. They're just planning to go there when it gets close. That's where I'm going when the time comes. Nothing else for me to do." She forced a smile.

"You seem fit", said Lydia, changing the subject. "You helping the RAAF out at Pearce?" Brent smiled again. "That might be one description. I'm not sure they put much stock in what I tell them.

They keep me around anyway. Feed me, give me a place to sleep. Even take me on flights to places sometimes. Nothing else for me to do." He smiled, just as the food arrived. "Really good southwestern Australia cuisine here. Thought you might like something different from what you get at Pearce." Brent nodded. "It's very good." Lydia had always been difficult to read. He once considered asking her out in Los Angeles. Dating someone you worked with wasn't encouraged, however. There was the age difference as well. Ten years always seemed like a lot. Now that they were older the difference in their ages didn't seem to matter as much. Brent still found Lydia attractive. He just never was sure what she thought of him. Under current circumstances a romantic relationship would probably be the last thing she was interested in.

Brent needed to research the place Lydia mentioned. Kalgoorlie-Boulder was a unique community located in south-central Western Australia. It was formed by the administrative merger of the neighbouring towns of Boulder and Kalgoorlie in 1989 and was the principal settlement of the East Coolgardie goldfield, on the western fringe of the Nullarbor Plain and the Great Victoria Desert. Mining there began with a rush following the 1893 discovery of gold by a prospector named Paddy Hannan at a site 40 kilometres northeast of Coolgardie. The main deposit of deep rich ores came to be known as the Golden Mile reef. The area developed as Hannan's Find.

Gamma Ten

Kalgoorlie, the name given in 1894 to the town that grew there, was a corruption of the Aboriginal word *galgurli*, or *karlkurla*, meaning "silky pear," a local plant also called the bush banana. Boulder was gazetted as a municipality in 1897. Brent asked around on Base. Many at Pearce also believed Kalgoorlie Boulder was the last place the moissanite would reach. Maybe they were right.

Brent recalled Schareshiem's opinion on the matter. In case Lydia and the others were wrong about Kalgoorlie-Boulder, a great deal of work was needed to prepare the Global Seed Vault on Spitsbergen Island in the Arctic as humanity's last refuge. He would need Chris's help. In fact he would need to convince most of the officers at the Base at Pearce to support a major effort to stock the seed vault with as much food and other supplies as possible. "Will it be worth it", replied Lydia when they next spoke on the radio? "If all the women who survive are beyond childbearing age, humans will go extinct anyway. If there are newborns, they will grow up in a world that's so very different. They will listen to stories from their parents about the marvels of the 'modern world' and think it all sounds like a fairy-tale. Children will grow up never knowing about the life we've experienced." Lydia paused. "Except for the very long-lived radioactivity. That's our legacy. Over."

Brent nodded his head, even though Lydia couldn't see him. "When it comes to technology, it may take half a century to get back to where we were. Over." "Or not." Lydia paused. "We made many mistakes. We don't have to make all of them again. Over." Lydia's words caused Brent to reconsider his decision to include up to one-hundred books with the supplies being taken to Spitsbergen. Space for food in the seed vault was at a premium. Would a hundred books be worth sacrificing some of their food supply? He hadn't even decided which books to take. Now he was wondering if he should take any. Maybe humanity needed a reset button – a fresh start with minimal knowledge of the past. Perhaps ten books would be enough. But which ones?

Gamma Ten

By 2050 fewer RAAF flights out of Pearce were needed as the number of displaced population centers around the world continued to decline. No one could even guess at the number of dead by nation or worldwide. Australia's population had diminished to 10 million. That included refugees from other nations whose numbers could not be estimated. Planes and fuel were available for what Brent proposed. Was there anywhere to land on Spitsbergen Island? "Yes", Chris replied. "There is an airstrip there - an old airport no longer used for commercial flights. The runway's 2484 meters long, more than twice what the C-17 needs. Scheduling is a problem though. That runway is only accessible a few months of the year. We'll only be able to land there during their very short summer. It'll be winter here, of course, just to add to the fun."

Svalbard Airport was five kilometres northwest of Longyearbyen on the west coast of Spitsbergen Island. It used to be the northernmost commercial airport in the world with daily scheduled public flights. The airstrip was constructed by the Luftwaffe during World War II. It was refurbished in 1975 and made available for commercial traffic. Commercial flights ceased in 2032, however. "How far from the seed vault", Brent inquired? "Only three kilometres. The only way to get there is to walk. We'll need to drop our cargo from low altitude onto the ground near the seed vault, then come back and land. I'm told it's a half-hour walk in summer. We'll take a run up there in a few months when it's a bit warmer at Spitsbergen."

Brent wasn't looking forward to another boring flight on a Globemaster. "How long?" "Not long. We'll have to land at Johannesburg to refuel, then Cairo, then Thule Airbase, Greenland. From there we can make it to Svalbard and back to Thule Airbase without refuelling. The whole thing won't take more than 48 hours. Of course, ya have to come back again." Chris smiled. Brent nodded slowly. Why did this seed vault have to be on the opposite side of the planet from where he was? A considerable amount of logistics and planning would be required to get hundreds of metric tons of food and other supplies to Spitsbergen. Additional structures would have to be erected at the seed vault's location where it could all be stored. "That's what the RAAF is good at", Chris insisted. "Just a walk in the park!"

This 'walk in the park' turned out to be more than the Australian government was willing to pay for. Three billionaires, in undisclosed locations, provided over 10 billion dollars each to assist with converting the Global Seed Vault into a final refuge for the human species. They reasoned their money was worthless everywhere else in the world. In return they were guaranteed accommodations at the facility when there was no other place to go. It seemed privilege for the wealthy might possibly extend even to the moment of extinction. Scheduled flights from Pearce began as soon as the weather at Svalbard allowed. Neither Chris nor Brent made it on the first or the second flight. Chris drew the short straw for the fourth flight in early July. "Ya need to bring a book to read, mate. Ya can't just sit there for two days doin' nothin'." Brent wasn't much of a reader. The book he chose was "Brave New World" by Aldous Huxley. It was a poor choice. The main theme of the book was a warning that advanced technology could take over and humans could lose their humanity. It now seemed the opposite was much more likely. He put it down after the first two chapters.

Gamma Ten

Chapter 18

Deep inside an icy mountain on a remote island above the Arctic Circle between Norway and the North Pole a resource of vital importance for the future of human-kind was being protected. This resource wasn't coal, oil, uranium or precious minerals. It was seeds.

Millions of these tiny brown specks, from more than 930,000 varieties of food crops, were stored in the Global Seed Vault on Spitsbergen, part of Norway's Svalbard archipelago. It was essentially a huge safety deposit box, holding the world's largest collection of agricultural biodiversity. "Inside this building is 13,000 years of agricultural history," representatives for the Crop Trust, which managed the vault, used to say. Then they would open an enormous steel door leading inside the mountain. Summer tours of this remote facility were discontinued in 2030.

It would be difficult to find a place more remote than the icy wilderness of Svalbard. Apart from the nearby town of Longyearbyen, there was nothing there but a vast white expanse of frozen emptiness.

The Global Seed Vault had been dubbed the "doomsday" vault, which conjured up images of a storehouse of seeds for use in case of an apocalyptic event or a global catastrophe. Samples from India, Pakistan, Mexico, and Syria and other locations around the world were deposited there. Near the entrance to the facility a rectangular wedge of concrete stood out starkly against the snowy landscape, making the doomsday nickname seems appropriate.

Svalbard was chosen as the location of the vault for its remoteness. It was far away from wars, conflict between nations, and social upheavals created to benefit special interest groups.

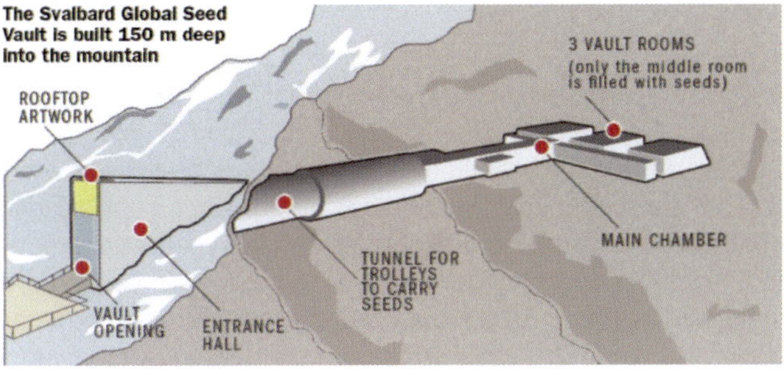

The entrance led to a small tunnel-like room filled with the noise of cooling systems required to maintain a constant temperature within the vault. A wide concrete tunnel illuminated by strip lighting led 150 meters into the mountain. At the end of this corridor was a chamber with an added layer of security to protect the vaults containing the seeds. There were three vaults leading off from the chamber. Each had a door covered in a thick layer of ice, hinting at the subzero temperatures inside. In each vault the seeds were stored in vacuum-packed silver packets and test tubes in large boxes that were neatly stacked on shelves from floor to ceiling. Each box had very little monetary value, but each held the keys to the future of global food security.

Over sixty years, agricultural practices had changed dramatically, with technological advances allowing large-scale crop production. But while crop yields had increased, biodiversity had decreased to the point that only about 30 crops provided 95% of human food-energy needs. Only 10% of the rice varieties that China used in the 1950s were still used in 2030. Over 90% of the fruit and vegetable varieties available in 1900's had been lost. This left food supplies more susceptible to threats such as disease and drought. The seeds lying in the deep freeze of the vault included wild and old varieties, many of which were not in general use anymore. The genetic diversity contained in the vault could provide the DNA traits needed to develop new strains for whatever challenged the world, or whatever a particular region might face in the future. One of the 200,000 varieties of rice within the vault could have the trait needed to adapt rice to higher temperatures, for example, or to find resistance to a new pest or disease. This was particularly important with the challenges of climate change.

The idea for the Global Seed Vault was conceived in the 1980s by Cary Fowler, a former executive director of the Crop Trust, but only started to become reality after an International Seed Treaty negotiated by the United Nations was signed in 2001. Construction was funded by the Norwegian government, which operated the vault in partnership with the Crop Trust. In an age of heightened geopolitical tensions and uncertainty, the Svalbard vault was an unusual and hopeful exercise in international cooperation for the good of humankind. Any organization or country could send seeds to it, and there are no restrictions because of politics or the requirements of diplomacy. Red wooden boxes from North Korea sit alongside black boxes from the United States. Boxes of seeds from Brazil sat atop seeds from Russia.

The Crop Trust and the RAAF were forced to make some difficult decisions by 2052. The Global Seed Vault contained over 1.2 million packets of seeds. The Crop Trust pointed with pride to the diversity of life being protected there. That diversity meant nothing, however, if no one survived to plant the seeds contained in the vault. Only one of the three vaults was full while the other two remained empty, reserved for future deposits. As much space as possible would be needed to store food and other supplies. This meant reducing the seed inventory to a minimum with priority given to the fifty crops that represented 95% of global food production.

The Global Seed Vault was not designed for human habitation. There were no living quarters, no plumbing, no communications equipment, insufficient lighting and no facilities for preparing and consuming meals. All three vaults were kept at -18 degrees Celsius by refrigeration equipment in summer. Permafrost and thick rock would ensure the seed samples remained frozen even without electrical power. Electrical power for the refrigeration equipment was provided by the public power plant at Longyearbyen, which burned diesel fuel to generate electricity for the area. Attempts had been made to convert to solar energy with only partial success due to the lack of sunlight in the winter months. Human habitation required temperatures considerably warmer than -18 degrees. After installation of thermal insulation in certain areas of the vault, existing refrigeration equipment could be converted to provide heating ten months of the year. This would require a robust electrical supply. Remaining staff at the Longyearbyen power plant expected they would have to shut down the station for lack of diesel fuel in less than a year. That left little time to find another source of electricity.

The RAAF erected an initial group of structures outside the seed vault for storing food and supplies that did not need a controlled environment. Time and cost dictated the choice of those structures. Canvas-covered geodesic domes were lightweight and easy to transport, yet strong and weather resistant when properly anchored into the rock surrounding the seed vault.

By summer of 2053 most of what remained of the human species had settled in the southern tip of Chile and Argentina and in larger numbers in Namibia, Botswana and South Africa in Africa. There were occasional radio communications with groups in Fairbanks and Honolulu as well. All but the largest island communities in both the Pacific and Atlantic had been abandoned due to lack of supplies. Those that remained were forced to survive on the food they could grow locally.

The recorded population of the Hawaiian Islands in 2030 was 1.3 million. Hawaii's population had been slowly declining during the decade ending in 2030 at an average rate of 12 people per day. The infrastructure to support over a million people on eight islands in the middle of the vast Pacific Ocean depended upon reliable air transport and shipping. Neither was available once commercial fuel supplies were depleted worldwide. There were a few 'ships under sail', but none had adequate cargo capacity. By summer of 2053 less than 2000 people remained on the 'Big Island'. The other islands had been abandoned. Those who remained had reverted to methods that existed before the islands were discovered by western civilizations. Traces of grey sand had been reported only on the Leeward Islands of Lisianski, Laysan, and Gardner.

Similar conditions existed in Puerto Rico, Cuba, the Virgin Islands, Jamaica, Haiti, the Bahamas, and the Dominican Republic. Further east it was the Azores, the Canary Islands, and Cape Verde. In the Pacific a significant number of the Polynesian Islands were still inhabited. Their proximity to Australia and the only surviving infrastructure on the planet gave them an advantage. Humanitarian aid to locations in Papua New Guinea, and communities like Jakarta, Makassar, Koto Kinabalu, and Manila were relatively simple compared to Greenland, for example. The difficulty for the RAAF was prioritizing ‘need’ vs. ‘proximity’. It was difficult to assess from radio communications alone where there was the greatest need. More food and supplies could be delivered to more people if the distances were short, i.e., a single flights. That meant leaving those further away to starve. The RAAF chose its missions carefully.

Brent had another concern. He wasn’t sure anything could be done about it. Measurements taken over the past five years indicated a significant drop in the oxygen content of the atmosphere. The effect wasn’t just in Australia. There was an environmental monitoring station in Johannesburg and another at Thule Airbase. They were reporting the same conditions. Measurements in the oceans found reduced amounts of plankton compared to a decade earlier. “Forget the Amazon rainforest”, Brent remarked. “Trees are amateurs compared to the microscopic powerhouses churning out oxygen beneath the waves. It's the phytoplankton, single-celled algae, that give us a breathable atmosphere. They’re the backbone of the marine food chain and the primary source of the oxygen we breathe. They’re like the lungs of the planet, inhaling carbon dioxide and exhaling life-giving oxygen through photosynthesis. These microscopic organisms are responsible for an estimated 80% of the oxygen in our atmosphere. That's more than all the rainforests on Earth combined.” Fish, whales, and other aquatic life had been decimated by the moissanite contamination as well. The seas had become toxic due to biological decay where the water temperature was well above freezing.

Brent recalled Aaron’s tests at SRNL showed the moissanite growth rate dropped by more than half at temperatures below 4 degrees Celsius. There was hope that aquatic life, including plankton, still survived in Arctic and Antarctic waters. That was one of the reasons Aaron had given for moving to Alaska. Of course humans had learned to thrive at higher altitudes in the Himalayan mountains in Tibet and at many other locations. It would take time to acclimate to lower oxygen content in the atmosphere as long as the reduction wasn't too great. The worst case prediction was that oxygen levels might drop to the equivalent of being at Vale, Colorado on a skiing holiday. Many people had not only survived such a thing but paid large sums of money for the privilege.

Weather had been a factor in setting the pace of the RAAF's efforts at the Global Seed Vault at Svalbard. Summers in Spitsbergen Island were short, sometimes only lasting five or six weeks. The RAAF used that time efficiently, but there was only so much that could be delivered, stored and constructed is so little time. A permanent staff of twenty miliary personnel had made substantial progress. Completion of additional storage structures outside the seed vault was running behind schedule by several months. Eleven of twenty-five had been completed. Flights from Pearce had to be adjusted accordingly. Chris and Brent decided to make another flight up there in July of 2054. After dropping their cargo over the site they landed easily at the Svalbard airstrip.

It was precisely half an hour's walk to the seed vault. Brent found the location quite sterile and uninviting. Everything was grey stone with jagged edges jutting out at oblique angles. It certainly fit the description of being "at the end of the world". Bare rock faces surrounded the vault entrance. Drilling holes through solid rock for water pipes had begun but showed little progress. Some remnants of snow and ice remained in crevices in the rocks. Inside the vault Brent was reminded of a tour he once took through Carlsbad Caverns in New Mexico. Every sound echoed so you couldn't tell where it came from. "It wasn't built for us", replied one of the officers stationed there. "My year is up. I'll be going back with you", he continued, with an air of excitement. Brent could sympathize. He wondered if he could last a year in this place, especially if there was a meter of snow on the ground outside. "It's not the snow or the cold. It's the wind", another officer replied. "The wind can be brutal." 'And the isolation', Brent was thinking. 'Indeed, it was not built for us…'

The vault containing the seeds was impressive. There were so many little silver packets all sealed and dormant. 'Would they ever be planted', Brent wondered. They were created to grow and flourish in the sunlight, not sit in a tomb waiting for eternity. Would humanity be forced to do the same? Was our time on the planet over? What would take our place? Surely not some crystals of carbon and silicon simply obeying the laws of chemistry.

A minimum staff of four RAAF personnel were on hand for the Globemaster's take off from Svalbard Airfield only four hours after their arrival. It would be a long 48 hours before they were back at Pearce. Brent's quarters there suddenly seemed quite luxurious. He had to radio Lydia to tell her about it. "Some have already left Perth for the Kalgoorlie-Boulder. Over." "How many? Over." "Few hundred, I think. I'm not ready to go with them just yet. Still thinking about it. Your grey sand seems to have slowed down a bit. Still plenty of time. Over." "Don't wait too long. Over." Brent was thinking Lydia and many like her could not survive at Svalbard.

The electrical supply problem at Svalbard had not been solved. Longyearbyen Power Station estimated six month's supply of diesel fuel that was left meant running out in mid-winter. RAAF made the decision to use two of their scheduled flights to Spitsbergen to deliver diesel fuel instead of supplies for the seed vault. If used carefully that would keep the power station operating for another two years at minimum output. It was a temporary solution at best. For the seed vault to remain habitable it must have its own power source that did not require non-renewable fuel. The solution was invented at a pub in Perth. "It's so windy in Spitsbergen. Why can't we put some windmills up there?" After some discussion the 'experts' in the pub decided it could be done quite easily. Just not by any of them, of course.

Gamma Ten

Even the Globemaster wasn't large enough to carry the huge rotor blades and mast of a wind turbine to Spitsbergen. Captain Christopher made an official request to the Emu Downs Wind Farm, about 200 kilometres north of Perth near Cervantes. Wind turbines

had been in operation there since 2007 at a cost of $180 million. "We're needing something smaller and not so expensive", Chris wrote. Design engineers at Emu Downs answered within the week. "We can do that", they replied. "It will take a couple of years."

"We don't have that long. Over", Chris replied on the radio. "How about six months. Over?" All he heard was static for nearly a minute. "We need to meet. Can you come up to Emu Downs? Over." "Yes. Over." "Tomorrow? Over." "Yes. What time? Over." "Whenever you get here. Over." "Thanks very much. Out." Brent insisted on going, of course. Chris unrolled a diagram of the Svalbard Seed Vault on a large conference table, showing where the wind turbine could be anchored into the mountainside. "What we need is a miniature wind turbine – like the ones you have at Emu Downs but about half the physical size." "One that size won't be cost effective. We did a quick 'return on investment' calculation. The ROI for a wind turbine that size remains negative for thirty years." Brent had to interrupt. "The return on investment may well be the survival of the human species. It doesn't need to make money. It just needs to keep us from freezing to death." Chris looked at Brent. "Us? You said 'us'." "I did", Brent replied.

The remainder of the meeting focused on how to reduce the size of the wind turbine blades and mast so they would fit into a Globemaster. All agreed the electrical output of the turbine would only be one-quarter of the 1.67 megawatts a full-size unit would generate. "My people tell me that will be sufficient", Chris confirmed. "Our thought was to install two of them for redundancy. We can switch between them for maintenance outages and charge our batteries when both are running." The engineers at Emu Downs nodded. "Yes, good idea. It will take two weeks to move the blades, mast and other components to Pearce. That leaves us two months to design and three and one-half months to build."

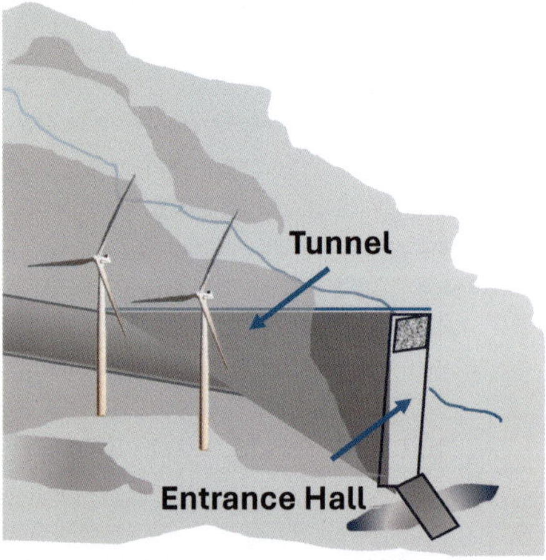

"That's just for one", Brent asked? "Yes, but we only need to do the design work once. We can have the second unit to Pearce two months after the first. Will that be satisfactory?"

Chris had to think a minute. Two more Globemaster flights would have to fit in with the existing schedule for humanitarian relief and the one flight to Spitsbergen each month already scheduled. "Cost", said Chis? "We'll do the job at our cost for materials and labour. $2.1 million, each." Chris sat back in the plush conference room chair and stared at the floor for a minute. "Sorry mates. I'm not authorized to go over $1 million for both." "Deal", said a man in a three-piece suit standing quietly in the back of the room. Everyone looked at him in disbelief. The man smiled and raised both hands with palms pointed upward. "Every one of my favourite holiday spots in the world is closed. What am I going to do with the money?" No one dared to reply.

There was also the problem of how to erect the wind turbines at the seed vault when they arrived. A crane would be needed to lift the blades into place once the mast was raised and anchored in a vertical position. "'Give me a lever long enough and a fulcrum on which to place it and I shall move the world', said Archimedes", Brent replied. Chris laughed. "Brave words mate. Can ya be more specific?" Brent sketched out an extension that would bolt to the top of the wind turbine mast. The extension would act as lifting point so that each of the blades could be hoisted into place once the mast was vertical. When all three blades were in place cables from this extension would raise the tips of all three blades into a horizontal position where they could then be bolted onto the hub of the turbine. When the cables were removed the mast extension could remain without interfering with the rotation of the blades. "There's your crane", he replied. "Can Emu Downs build that as well?" "Yes", was the answer.

The first delivery from Emu Downs was a week late. Group Captain Christopher had expected it to be two weeks late. The size of the 'beast' was the number one topic of conversation at Pearce during the entire week before it was loaded onto the C-17. The cargo compartment of a Globemaster was 27 meters long by 5.5 meters wide by 3.76 meters high. Brent was afraid the blades wouldn't fit. They did, with almost a half-meter to spare. The Globemaster would have to make four separate drops over the seed vault's location. Parachutes on each of the four packages worked as designed. The meagre staff at the seed vault secured each package where it landed and marked its location with a fiberglass pole and red flag extending three meters in the air. That would ensure they could find it during adverse weather and several meters of snowfall if necessary. Actual construction of the wind turbines would have to wait for summer and for additional personnel to arrive. With a contingent of less than a dozen people able to work outside only during summer months, the entire project would take years to complete. Weather became more of a limiting factor than the number of C-17 flights from Australia.

Chapter 19

By late 2054 small groups of 'refuges' in Western Australia had already begun relocating to the Kalgoorlie-Boulder area east of Pearce RAAF Base. Moissanite colonies around the world were still growing but at a significantly reduced pace where no nuclear isotopes were present in Australia, South America, Southern Africa, Greenland, and Alaska. This significantly extended the timetables for these locations beyond Brent's predictions. With little information coming out of these areas he still had to assume the worst. He did have observations from Western Australia. That gave him hope.

Farmland was being preserved where possible but it would only be enough to feed local populations, like at Kalgoorlie-Boulder. There was no means to transport food or supplies outside local communities with all commercially available fossil fuel supplies exhausted. What little fuel remained was controlled by the military. Each refuge area was forced to become a self-sufficient island. Communication between these islands was by radio only. The one thing Kalgoorlie-Boulder had in abundance was electrical power. With many of their customers to the east no longer there, the wind turbines at Emu Downs Wind Farm could supply almost limitless power to those in Kalgoorlie-Boulder and the surrounding area.

A substantial portion of Western Australia remained free of moissanite, but most of that land was too arid to grow food. Agriculture had not developed on a commercial scale in the Kalgoorlie-Boulder area either due to the arid climate. There were many theories about how much food the land might be able to produce with sufficient irrigation. There was electric power to pump water for irrigation if wells could be drilled deep enough. Most estimates of how many people could survive there were quite modest. Even though the moissanite growth in Western Australia had slowed to a fraction of its original pace, a few groups were impatient, actively planning to be the first to establish themselves in what might eventually be their last refuge. Lydia was a vocal member of one of those groups. "Late comers might find themselves without a place", she insisted.

By August 2055 the rush to move to Kalgoorlie-Boulder still hadn't started, at least not like during 1893 when gold was discovered. That's when prospector Paddy Hannan found gold near Mount

Charlotte in Kalgoorlie. The story goes that Hannan found gold in a gully. What originally consisted of a large number of underground mines was eventually consolidated into a single open pit mine. The Fimiston Open Pit was created in 1989 by Kalgoorlie Consolidated Gold Mines. It was Australia's largest open cut gold mine until 2016 when it was surpassed by the Newmont Boddington gold mine also in Western Australia. The Super Pit was located off the Goldfields Highway on the south-east edge of Kalgoorlie, Western Australia. The pit was oblong, approximately 3.5 kilometers long, 1.5 kilometers wide and over 600 meters deep.

Lydia's past association with Professor Schareshiem allowed her to claim some level of expertise about the moissanite colonies approaching Kalgoorlie-Boulder. She patiently explained to those who were interested how the crystalline growth depended upon gamma radiation from long-lived isotopes in spent nuclear fuel. Since there were no artificial sources of gamma radiation in Australia, it was possible the moissanite colonies would advance more slowly or even stop completely. Lydia's administrative skills were another asset. After all she had managed to organize the affairs of the most disorganized Professor Caltech had ever seen. "Let's not be too hasty. The devil's in the details. What do we take? What do we leave behind? How do we transport everything we might need since there's no fuel for any of the vehicles? We need to get this right the first time. We might not be able to come back." Lydia's voice was one of authority. It was also quite loud – even a bit irritating.

Many from Perth, Pearce and other communities decided not to wait. Lydia's advice was causing some concern. "We might not have a place, like you said", was a recurring comment. Lydia delayed her departure from Perth for nine months, then surrendered to the majority opinion. The Commanding Officer at Pearce ignored many voices on the Base for a year. He saw no reason to believe that Kalgoorlie-Boulder would be any safer than staying in Perth or Pearce. For that reason, the military did not provide fuel or vehicles to assist with the initial refugee movement. When grey sand began to appear on the beaches at Carnarvon, Geraldton, Perth and Bunbury the situation changed. Remaining personnel at Pearce began doing what they could, although their efforts fell far short of the demand. Anyone with a farm wagon and a horse or mule to pull it could name their price for a month's hire. Feeding the mule for that month was the responsibility of the lessee, of course. It was nearly 600 kilometers from Perth to Kalgoorlie-Boulder. That amounted to seven hours by truck or nearly a month by horse-drawn wagon.

It was January 2057 when changes were first noticed in the moissanite colony 27 kilometers north of Kalgoorlie-Boulder. The moissanite advance had slowed to about 50 meters per day. At that pace it would reach Kalgoorlie-Boulder in about 18 months. Visual observation of the leading edge showed it to be no more than twenty centimeters thick. Kalgoorlie-Boulder had three radios. All of them needed parts to get them working again. In the old days someone could have hopped on the Internet, found the radio parts on Amazon, and had them delivered within two days. What a luxury that was!

Leaders of the various indigenous groups insisted that for reasons they couldn't explain the moissanite would never reach them. Some claimed to have supernatural abilities to foresee the future. Others thought the Kalgoorlie-Boulder area to be protected by ancient and unseen spirits for whom the land was sacred. 'People believe what they want to believe', Lydia observed. Regardless, she felt more secure with people she had known for several years. With no working radios those at Kalgoorlie-Boulder had no information about conditions in Perth or Pearce. They could only guess that all the banks had closed. The crime rate had gone up as shops and businesses had been abandoned. Looting was probably

commonplace. It was 'survival of the fittest' again. Lydia had seen enough of that in Rome.

Fuel supplies for the military vehicles at Kalgoorlie-Boulder eventually ran out. They were left to rust after salvaging parts that might be useful. Those who had hired a wagon expected to keep it, and the horse or mule that came with it. It was highly unlikely the owner would travel 600 kilometers on foot or horseback to reclaim their property. Approximately 26,000 people who lived in the Kalgoorlie region prior to the influx of refugees made them welcome to a point. That point was when the leaders of the various refugee groups announced a rather communistic form of management for the food and other resources available. Those native to the area strenuously objected. They didn't mind sharing some of what they had but dividing up their personal property and belongings 'for the good of all' was not acceptable. The indigenous population still outnumbered the refugees two to one. The refugee leaders backed down in the end. Even so it was obvious the fundamental principles of democracy were perishable. Some of those principles might never been seen again. Relations remained tense between groups of refugees, and between refugees and the original population.

Lydia's certificate in education was of some benefit. She finally was able to teach as she originally wanted. She talked with those who would listen about what the children should be taught under these circumstances. Most thought they should first learn how to survive in a very different world. There was no need for lessons about computer programming or nuclear physics or even higher mathematics. If humanity survived another decade there would be time to teach those subjects again. Lydia's minor at Stanford University was in history. How much of that should the children be taught in this new world? Did they need to know about World War II for example? Perhaps there would be a need to study such events in years to come, if there were any 'years to come'. Only a portion of what Lydia had learned in school was useful now. Was the rest a waste of her time, then? There were many discussions about what was worth knowing these days and what wasn't. Nobody had the answers. Very few even seemed to care. What if it turned out there was a future? What then?

There were those in Lydia's group who found something exciting in this new world, or perhaps off it. The night sky was darker now than anyone could remember. Those with knowledge of the constellations and movements of the planets found themselves in demand. There were only a few things to do at night. One of them was to look up and marvel at how many stars there were. In many ways views of the night sky in the southern hemisphere were more spectacular than in the north. With space being a premium, no one thought to bring a telescope on their trek to Kalgoorlie-Boulder. Only a few of the native residents had one. Of those, only a fraction knew how to use it. There was an exception. One farmer owned nine of them of various sizes. Crowd control became a problem as word got around. There were too many people all wanting to 'have a look'. He and his family did their best on nights that were clear. Fortunately, most people lost interest after a few months. Those who became regulars made sure this man and his family were well supplied with whatever they needed. He was heard to remark, "I never dreamed my interest in astronomy would pay off."

Books were another luxury when space on a miliary truck or horse drawn wagon was restricted. Lydia brought only three. One of them was a bible. No matter how much she lost she refused to give up her faith. Another was an almanac of photographs from around the world. If they survived, she believed children had the right to see what the world used to look like. The third was a cookbook, even though many of the recipes called for ingredients that were no longer obtainable. If they only had a year or two left, she intended to eat well until the end even if she had to fight for it.

There were moments when Lydia's thoughts drifted back to Perth and dinner with Brent at the Wildflower Restaurant. She had to wonder if she would ever see him again. Without a working radio no one at Kalgoorlie had any information about Pearce RAAF Base. Brent was likely somewhere on the other side of the planet. She had always considered him too young and a bit naïve. He was smart but too trusting. She was convinced that would get him into trouble someday. Everyone had their own agendas. In the end they would do what was best for them. Maybe that's why she never married. There was never a man she was sure she could trust. "They all go astray", she remarked to two other women who were washing clothes at the wooden trough by one of the deep wells. One of them nodded. "Yep. Sooner or later. We let them think they are superior. The world works better that way." "Does it", replied the other lady? "Look where we are now."

"You can't blame the opposite sex for this moissanite thing", Lydia replied. "Why not? From what I've heard it was some man in the United States that started it." Lydia nodded. "It wasn't intentional." "Nothing is ever intentional", the lady continued. "I think we could do without them. I've been told there's enough frozen sperm in some vault somewhere in Norway to repopulate the whole world. Men are no longer necessary. We could do quite well without them." Lydia had to smile. 'What would happen to all the male babies', she wondered. 'What if this sort of person was put in charge of reconstructing society?'

There was a degree of irony in what many of the refugees believed. Many considered themselves survivalists. Yet none would admit to spending decades preparing for the wrong catastrophe. For decades self-proclaimed survivalists had argued against a world dominated by technology, where AI and autonomous drones and out of control weapons would wage a war against humanity. Some intended to offer passive resistance only. They refused to use appliances with artificial intelligence features or purchase self-driving cars, for example. Others were actively planning ways to sabotage operations and businesses that promoted artificial intelligence in government and private enterprise. Movies like `The Terminator' had become required viewing, even though it was out of date by three quarters of a century. Instead, it was the failure of that technology to cope with a simple chemical reaction between carbon and silicon that threatened to extinguish not just the human species but all organic life on the planet. Lydia found the irony compelling. She also learned that expressing her opinions on the subject could be dangerous.

There were survivors at locations other than Kalgoorlie-Boulder. Those in Alaska and northern Canada had learned to adapt to the lifestyle of the native Inuit. Bill, Aaron and their families found this way of life quite difficult but had learned to function as members of a unique community with customs that hadn't changed significantly in thousands of years. The Inuit were believed to be northeastern Siberian migrants from Asia and were descendants of what anthropologists called the Thule people who emerged from the Bering Strait and western Alaska around 1000 CE. Inuksuk spoke of a people before the Inuit who were taller and stronger. He believed the Inuit society had advantages by having adapted to using dogs as transport animals and developing larger weapons and other technologies superior to those of the previous culture. He had read about Inuit migrants who settled in Greenland during the 12th century. Much of what Inuksuk could tell them was from legend, but some of it had been recorded. Inuksuk was once a student of Inuit history and took pride in his knowledge on the subject.

Inuksuk told stories passed down from his ancestors about competition with other groups, such as the Algonquian and Siouan peoples to the south. Some populations were nearly wiped out by new infectious diseases brought by contact with Europeans. The history of the Inuits and Native American Indians seemed to be intertwined to a degree. Their philosophies and beliefs about use of the land, animals and other resources on it were quite similar. Bill had studied Native American Indian culture as a hobby. He was fascinated by their creativity and ingenuity at using every part of an animal they killed. Nothing went to waste.

Those who knew Bill, Arlene, Aaron, Geraldine and their children would have found them unrecognizable. Bill and Arlene were in their early sixties. Bill no longer suffered from arthritis in his hands, however. Aaron had just turned 70 with Geraldine only two years younger. Life with the Inuit had taken its toll. At their ages their abilities were limited. The rest of the group understood. Everyone, including Claire, Diane, and Leonard, had gained weight from the fat-rich diet of seal and other wildlife indigenous to that part of the world. Their clothes had been discarded as inadequate to protect them against the cold and the wind of Alaska. Each had spent roughly half their lives as a member of their Inuit community. All were grateful to have been accepted. In return all took part in teaching the Inuit children about the world that used to exist. No one could be certain if that world would ever be seen again. If somehow it was, Inuksuk wanted the children to be prepared to deal with it.

Reading lessons were held daily. Claire and Diane discovered they had teaching skills. The Inuit children were polite, respectful and attentive. Both young ladies found the teaching experience quite rewarding. Leonard struggled to adapt to his new circumstances even though he knew he had no choice. Eventually he found his niche with Inuits his age. At age 50 he discovered he had a talent for carving. Both wood and ivory were plentiful. “They are beautiful”, said Inuksuk, while looking over Leonard’s carvings. Everyone accepted him from that moment on. The Inuit had an ancient appreciation for art. Leonard worked alongside the other men of his age of course, but his carving abilities gave him a unique status among them. That was important in the Inuit culture.

Neither Inuksuk nor anyone else had ever established with any certainty exactly how the Siberian migrants managed to get to Alaska and the Aleutian Islands. Some theories suggested the Bering Strait was frozen over for centuries allowing Siberians to walk across from one continent to another. The lack of food and supplies for such long and difficult journey made that premise extremely unlikely. Other theories insisted they travelled by sea, following the Bering Strait in small boats, catching fish and killing seals to sustain themselves. There was some evidence to support that idea, but it wasn't conclusive. Regardless, the Siberian migrants' ability to make such a journey and their determination to survive in one of the most hostile environments on earth was impressive. Bill, Aaron and their families learned new skills every day.

Inuksuk had a habit of asking difficult questions, especially in summer when more than fifty sat around a large fire under a cloudless sky. "Are you happy here", he asked? Bill raised his hand indicating he would answer. He took a few minutes to consider what he would say. He had learned the Inuit were very patient. He was under no pressure to answer quickly. "Yes", he said finally. "It's a different kind of happiness. I do not say we are happy so that you will let us stay." Inuksuk nodded. He knew that to be the truth. "This life was very strange to us when we first joined you. You were very patient with us. You pushed us to the limits of our endurance. That was necessary. Rewards of this lifestyle were unknown to us then. But now we see the wisdom in your ways and your culture."

No one spoke for several minutes. The fire crackled in the silence. Inuksuk spoke again. "Would you leave us if you could go back to your world?" No one raised their hand to answer for several minutes. These was a glow from the horizon where the sun had perched itself before ascending again. Claire raised her hand. "No. That world offered many promises. Most were illusions, without value or substance. The life we have now offers a great deal more." She looked around at her parents, her sister, and the others. They all nodded. "We wish to stay." Inuksuk smiled, then nodded slowly. "Then you shall stay until all the stars above us have left the sky."

Over the past millennium every continent had managed to sustain an indigenous population, however small, that had not surrendered to the promises of technology. The knowledge and generosity of these indigenous populations was now the salvation of humanity. The indigenous peoples of South Africa were the three San peoples (Xan, Khwe and Khomani) and the Khoekhoe, including Nama and Griqua. In South America the surviving populations were mainly in Peru and Argentina. Peru's population included more than 4 million indigenous persons, of whom 83% were Quechua, 11% were Aymara, less than 2% were Ashaninka. More than 4% belonged to other Amazonian Indigenous Peoples. In total there were 55 Indigenous Peoples who spoke 47 languages. Of those in Peru, 96% were Andean and 3 % were from the Amazon. Indigenous people comprised 31% of the total population. The most populous indigenous groups were the Aonikenk, Kolla, Qom, Wichí, Diaguita, Mocoví, Huarpe peoples, Mapuche and Guarani.

Nearly all these indigenous populations accepted refugees with the understanding that they would do their share of the work to sustain the community. Those who refused were left to fend for themselves. Very few were capable of surviving on their own in hostile environments in Peru, Argentina, Namibia, Botswana, Eswatini, Lesotho, and the country of South Africa. The only functioning airport was at Johannesburg, but no commercial flights had landed there for several years. Cape Town was the only port, with an occasional sailing vessel arriving or departing. Local resources of food and water were limited across the region. Refugees found themselves subject to tribal judgements that were often quite harsh. Genocide was the last resort. It was the only practical solution in some situations.

Chapter 20

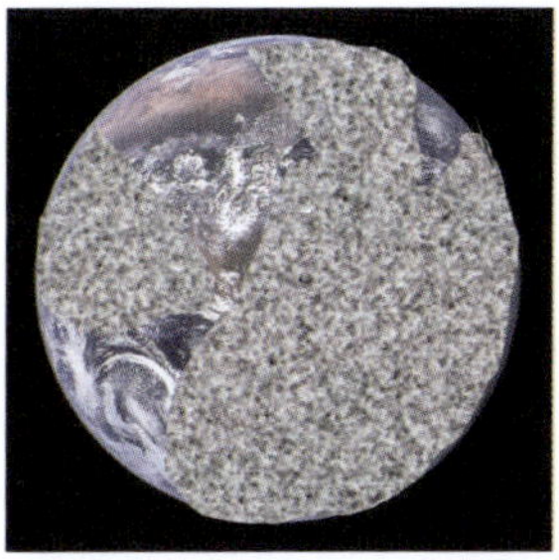

Group Captain Christopher looked out the window of Barracks No. 16 at Pearce RAAF Base. The calendar on the wall read February 2057. His 51st birthday was just last week. Few were there to celebrate. If anyone survived to document the events of the first half of the 21st Century, the period from 2045 to 2056 would surely be regarded as a lost decade. During that time fewer than a dozen locations on earth had any way to know what was happening outside a radius of three days walk. With the moissanite approaching the perimeter of the Base from the west, most of the personnel at Pearce had left. All but a few had gone to Kalgoorlie-Boulder. "Just three more flights", he said out loud to no one. "Almost there…" February was always quite warm in Australia. In three days he would be making another drop at Svalbard, where the weather couldn't be more different.

Brent had spent the decade learning to be a proper Aircraftsman in the RAAF. Forced to live with military personnel at Pearce, there was really no alternative but to enlist. Under normal circumstances that would have been impossible. For one, he was too old. For another, he wasn't an Australian citizen. He didn't even have authorization from the Australian Government to be in the country. No one seemed to object. By 2052 no one was even sure if there was a national Australian Government. As he was well known by everyone at Pearce, he was readily accepted into the ranks. He was the oldest Aircraftsman on the base, outranked by all the men his age. It was a humbling experience. "No worries, mate. Ya be catchin' up with 'em in ten years", Chris remarked. Brent had to smile. 'Did any of them have another ten years?' The computer models on his laptop didn't think so. He was allowed to keep that one piece of personal property against military regulations. Amazingly, it still worked if he could find somewhere to recharge. By 2057 charging points were getting hard to find.

Previous radio contacts in South America had all gone silent over the years. It was impossible to know if anyone survived there. All RAAF flights for humanitarian relief had been discontinued. Stockpiles of supplies at Pearce were almost exhausted. Was there enough aviation fuel at waypoints between Pearce and Spitsbergen to support the last three flights? Airfields at Johannesburg and Cairo had inexplicably remained free of moissanite according to the lone radio operator at each location. A man from the local population had volunteered to stay and protect the aviation fuel supply in return for food and supplies from the RAAF. He would have no reason to lie about conditions at the airfield. If planes couldn't land or there was no fuel reserve to protect, he would have no reason to stay. The fuel could easily be stolen by anyone with the right equipment, of course. They would probably kill the radio operator if he objected. Either way the fact that Chris was able to make radio contact at both waypoints meant the fuel was still there and it would be safe to land. Chris knew he couldn't count on the radio operator to help with refuelling, however. For that reason there were six extra crewmen on the flight to transfer fuel out of the underground tanks at those locations.

At this time of year the Svalbard airport would be iced over with as much as two meters of snow covering the ice. Anyone trying to land would end up in the sea at the end of the airstrip. This flight and the next would be drops on parachutes. The last flight was scheduled for July. That flight would land at Svalbard. They would leave the plane at the Svalbard airport, but off the runway just in case a miracle happened. It was possible someone somewhere might survive and come to their rescue before they ran out of food. Chris believed the chance of that happening was 1 in 5.

Planes carrying aviation fuel to Johannesburg, Cairo, Singapore and Thule had nearly run out of fuel themselves. The only operating refinery at Kwinana was processing the lowest quality crude oil feedstock. Chris contacted each of these airfields by radio again to verify there was enough fuel at each one to ensure the flight could reach Spitsbergen and return to Pearce. Recalculations for the remaining two flights confirmed there was just enough to support those missions as well. No more flights would be possible for more than a year until Kwinana could produce more aviation fuel. Group Captain Christopher was an experienced airman who had piloted many different RAAF aircraft. He had experienced serious difficulties in flight on numerous occasions in the past. His greatest fear was running out of fuel. There was no way to salvage the plane in that event.

Gamma Ten

The flight left Pearce on the 16th of February without incident. After a while Brent began to wonder again why he agreed to spend another 48 hours on a plane with no toilet. His laptop was fully charged and still working, even if there was no Internet to connect to. The battery would last four days if used sparingly. What puzzled him was why they had heard nothing from South America. His models indicated there should still be large land areas on that continent that were free of moissanite. That was especially true if the growth rate had slowed in the same manner as seen in Australia. Perhaps there were many survivors but no working radios. How would someone repair a radio without access to inventories of spare parts? Or maybe there was no electrical power. Components for electronics were sitting in warehouses around the world. There was just no way to transport them to where they were needed.

In fact, no matter what Brent's models predicted no one could say with any certainty how many people were still alive. It might be 100 million. It might be 10 million. Or it might be only 100,000. How many would need to survive to rebuild a modern society like he remembered? Lydia believed it would be better if we started over, however painful. Humans survived for centuries without modern medical procedures, without antibiotics, without global communications. Many would die unnecessarily as they did hundreds of years before. Was that somehow better? He shut his laptop. There were too many questions with no answers.

Thule Air Base, or Thule Air Base/Pituffik Airport, was the United States Air Force's (USAF) northernmost base, located 1,207 km north

of the Arctic Circle and 1,524 km from the North Pole on the northwest side of the island of Greenland. By 2057 there were only five members of the USAF remaining on the world's largest island. They had been ordered to maintain the airstrip at Thule Airbase until they were no longer needed there. It was a difficult mission for all. Group Captain Christopher was expecting to notify all five that their mission at Thule Airbase would be completed in another four months and they would all be transported to Australia, or wherever was safe. All modern communities in Greenland, including the capitol Nuuk, had been abandoned for more than a year. Only the Inuit remained. One could only hazard a guess as to how many of them there were. Some believed there might be as many as a thousand.

The C-17 Globemaster III made it to Johannesburg in record time. Weather in the southern hemisphere was quite good for most of the flight. There were no other planes in the air, so the plane's radar system wasn't really needed. The flight crew of three had an easy time of it. From time to time one of them came back to check on Brent and the six extra crewmen needed to refuel the plane in Johannesburg and Cairo. Refuelling a C-17 required special training. Solitary radio operators had a habit of falling asleep at their post. The one in Johannesburg was drunk when they arrived. He had nothing else to do. He was in no condition to help refuel the C-17 even if trained for the task.

The weather between Johannesburg and Cairo was much less pleasant. Turbulence was rarely felt on a plane as large as the Globemaster. Brent had his seatbelt on as usual when his laptop suddenly left his lap and slammed against the ceiling of the plane. "Sorry 'bout that, mates", yelled one of the flight crew from the cockpit. The plane had dropped 100 meters in a few seconds when it hit a downdraft. Brent reached down to retrieve his laptop from the floor. It was undamaged due to the hardened shockproof case around it. Until that moment he had always considered that purchase a waste of money.

The situation in Cairo was much the same as in Johannesburg. The radio operator there was drunk as well. He did manage to come out and greet the refuelling crew. They were the only people he had seen in four days, he claimed. Chris physically confirmed the fuel supplies remaining at both Johannesburg and Cairo. There was in fact enough for two more supply flights to Spitsbergen. The plane was quickly in the air again headed for Greenland. Brent kept his forearm over his laptop for the first hour. He couldn't risk it hitting the ceiling again. When his forearm got tired, he decided to lock it in one of the compartments on the other side of the plane. Like the toilets, the miliary rations available on the Globemaster left a lot to be desired. He wasn't expecting a gourmet dinner from the Wildflower Restaurant in Perth. Forty-eight hours with nothing but 'spam', pork and beans and warm beer would have been declared 'cruel and unusual punishment' in the United States. Inmates in the Federal Prison at Leavenworth, Kansas were eating better. At least they would have been if anyone was still there.

As soon as the Globemaster was within range Group Captain Christopher began trying to contact the Swalbard seed vault by radio. He was unable to get a response after multiple attempts. "Perhaps their radio isn't working", said one of the flight crew. "They have two. Could be something else – maybe atmospheric interference", Chris replied. "We'll try 'em again when we get closer." The radio at Thule Airbase in Greenland was working perfectly. "You are cleared to land", the USAF officer in charge replied. Chris acknowledged as required by protocol. Once on the ground the huge plane made a 180 degree turn to point upwind for take-off. There was no plan to stay at Thule Airbase any longer than necessary. When the copilot opened the door, he was immediately greeted by all five members of the USAF crew stationed at Thule Airbase. "Gentlemen", he replied. Then he noticed one of the men held his sidearm by his side.

"We're coming aboard, sir", said a second man. The co-pilot was in no position to argue. He turned to climb back up the ladder and into the plane with the five of them right behind him. Once inside they found themselves covered from the rear by six RAAF aircraftsmen with weapons of their own. Counting the flight crew they were outnumbered two to one. "If you do not drop your weapons, you will be shot", barked the co-pilot. All five complied. Group Captain Christopher emerged from the cockpit to take charge of the situation. "Why", he asked? No one answered. "That action may get you court marshalled. Surely, ya have some explanation." The senior officer in the group finally spoke up. "We thought there would only be three of you. There isn't enough fuel, sir. What is left will get you to Spitsbergen and no further. If we had told you this, you wouldn't have come. We are nearly out of food. We had to lie, or we would starve, sir."

Group Captain Christopher frowned. “We could shoot all five of ya right here and now. Save the USAF the trouble of a Court Marshal. No one would ever know anythin’.” He looked around the plane. Every crewman nodded. “We prefer to be shot rather than starve, sir.” There was complete silence for several minutes. The wind outside roared like death itself had taken flight. “No one will be shot, and no one will starve. At least not today. Get every bit of fuel ya can outta those tanks. I want ‘em bone dry.” “Yes sir”, barked the senior officer. What little food was left in the warehouse at Thule Airbase was carried onto the plane as well. “Let’s hope we make it”, Brent remarked as Chris turned sideways to pass through the narrow opening back into the cockpit. “Depends on the wind, mate. We get a tail wind, no worries. We get a strong headwind we’ll end up in the sea.” Brent took his seat again. He had either three hours to live or perhaps a year if they made it to Svalbard. Actually, it wouldn’t be much of a life even if they made it. He unfastened his seatbelt and crossed to the other side of the plane to get his laptop. Perhaps he could finally win a game off the laptop’s chess program.

Nearly three hours had passed. Brent managed a knight fork on black’s queen and rook. The black queen moved to B1 and called check. “Damn”, said Brent! The copilot came to the back of the plane to let everyone know the prospects for making Spitsbergen looked better than earlier. “Slight headwind, but not enough to put us off. Better get ready.” “Ready”, Brent replied? “Get your chute on, mate.” “What chute?” One of the other crew members threw a parachute onto the floor at Brent’s feet. “You’ll need three layers of ECWCS.” Brent looked puzzled. “Extended Cold Weather Clothing System. Somebody will help you on with the last bit and then your chute.” It was then that Brent remembered what Chris had said about not being able to land at Svalbard airport except in summer. It was summer at Pearce, but February was winter at Spitsbergen. “Where do I start”, Brent asked, once he realized what was happening. “What do I do with my laptop?” The copilot motioned for one of the crew to assist.

“Put your laptop inside the second layer. It’ll stay warm enough there.” Brent nodded. “Here’s your third layer. It’s the hardest to get on.” After a few minutes he had all three layers on with openings sealed. The parachutes had already been attached to all the cargo. “They’ll be going out first”, said the aircraftsman, pointing to the cargo on nearly thirty pallets. "Then we'll go, OK?" Brent nodded. He could barely move in all the ECWCS. When he got on the ground would he be able to move, he wondered? Suddenly the rear of the plane began to open. Brent felt his ears pop as the pressure inside the plane equalized with conditions outside. The roar of the air flowing around the huge plane was deafening. Pallets began flying out through the huge opening and disappearing. Brent had seen this before. He never expected to be going with them, however. Everyone began moving toward the opening at the rear of the plane. "Not sure I can do this", Brent managed to say to no one. Chris had to shout for Brent to hear even though he was right behind him. He placed his hand on Brent's shoulder. "Ya got two choices, mate. Jump with the rest of us or go down with the plane. It's on automatic pilot but the fuel will run out when it's maybe 20 kilometres out over the sea. At this water's temperature ya'll live for about four minutes. Ya got 10 seconds to make up ya mind." With that, Chris gave Brent a shove and out he went.

Brent realized he hadn't asked anyone how to open his chute. Suddenly he felt a sharp jerk pulling his body upwards. He looked up and saw the white canopy opening above him. All he could see around him was a dense grey fog. Where would he land? Why couldn't he see anyone else? It was several minutes before he felt his feet slam into the ground. He knew to bend his knees. That saved him a broken leg. Now he was up to his waist in snow. He struggled to move, making very little progress. Several more minutes passed. "This is it. I'm going to freeze to death right here", he said, again to no one. Something pushed him forward. His face went into the snow. "Have to get on top of it, mate. Come on." He felt his feet being lifted until he was almost horizontal. Something was dragging him across the snow like an animal carcass. "You can stand up here", said a voice. Brent found his footing where the snow was only half a meter deep. "Lucky you landed in a snowbank", said a man standing next to him. "Some exposed rock about five meters over there.

Pick your feet up slowly and walk behind me." Brent did his best, but progress was slow. As he suspected all the ECWCS made it difficult to move. He wasn't cold, however. Just too much adrenaline in his system. Suddenly there was a metal cable in front of them. "Grab onto this and don't let go whatever you do", replied his escort. "The wind will be about 40 knots when we come out from behind this cliff. Just stay behind me. It shouldn't be that far." Brent's escort lied.

Gamma Ten

Brent was almost exhausted when a large shape appeared in front of them. Several men were outside a huge doorway ushering others inside.

It took a moment for Brent's eyes to adjust. The snow goggles were off, but his vision was blurry. "Ya have to give it time", said a familiar voice. Before Brent could answer, Group Captain Christopher had turned to the senior RAAF officer at the seed vault for a report of conditions in the vault.

"How many?" "194 sir, including you and your lot. We're only able to confirm 40,000 worldwide. No one knows for sure anymore." The wind howled outside. It was forty below. "Food, water?" "Maybe enough for sixteen months, if we're careful. That includes the stuff you dropped, when we can get to it." "Hunting party?" "Came back empty handed again. Just nothing out there…" "How 'bout heating, ventilation?" "No worries. It'll all still be running long after we've starved to death." "Radios?" "Both radios died last month. Just got one of them working an hour ago. Lucky you got through. Last message from back home was five weeks ago, sir." "Pearce?" "Yes sir. They weren't exactly sure how many were still there." A long broad tunnel in front of them disappeared into the mountain. "We heard from Alaska every two weeks until mid-September. Most everyone else has gone silent."

The Group Captain tugged at the outside glove on his left hand. Moisture had gotten between the outer and inner gloves when he fell in the snow and had already started to freeze. "How's the visibility out there?" "About three meters if you can keep the blowing snow off your goggles. I could see the main antenna was still up – it may not be for long in this wind. Probably doesn't matter now."

Flight Lieutenant Gibbs stared at the rough hardwood planks that had been pushed into place as a makeshift floor. He had been at Svalbard for three years. Under normal circumstances Gibbs would have retired from the RAAF on his 60th birthday five years ago. There was a good explanation for why he hadn't, which he steadfastly refused to discuss with anyone. "Your radio message was a surprise, sir. Last we heard you wouldn't be joining us until summer. Weren't sure you would make it, sir." Group Captain Christopher shook his head. "That was the plan. Plan changed. If anyone had lost their grip on the stainless-steel cable you rigged up around the perimeter, they would be dead by now." "So how will you get back?" "We won't."

Flight Lieutenant Gibbs shook his head. "We'll have to make some quarters for you and the rest. Any special requests?" "None", Chris replied. "There's space in Vault No. 3." "I'm sure that will do nicely." Rank didn't entitle anyone to anything under these circumstances. As the highest-ranking officer there Chris expected to rotate between the quarters in the seed vault and the structures outside just like everyone else. He liked it that way, except when it came to 'command and control'. That's when rank meant everything.

Life at Spitsbergen was harsh. Shelters outside the seed vault were insulated to a degree. Snow piled up against the exterior walls provided additional insulation and shielding from the relentless winds. Most of the shelters could be kept at a minimum temperature of 10 degrees Celsius. That was quite comfortable in winter when the outside temperature was between -40 and -20 degrees. Conditions in the latrine were slightly better. Brent agreed it was an improvement over the metal bucket on the Globemaster. Heating was provided by the twin wind turbines outside. There were days, especially in winter, when the wind turbines produced enough energy to supply all their needs and charge the batteries to full capacity. The batteries were rarely needed but would be essential if one of the wind turbines failed. No one would be coming from Emu Downs to repair it.

Inside the seed vault there were rows of bunks separated by partitions. There was only enough space for fifty occupants. Eight buildings outside were fitted in a similar fashion to house twenty in each. Vault occupants rotated on a weekly basis. Each spent one week inside the vault at a balmy 19 degrees, followed by three weeks in one of outside shelters at 10 degrees, regardless of rank. Summer temperatures provided a brief but welcome relief for everyone. Summer at Spitsbergen typically lasted six weeks. Nearly all the work outside had to be done in that short period of time. There was plumbing inside the vault for potable water from heated tanks. Water pipes for the kitchen and showers had to be routed through the thinner areas of rock near the vault entrance. All those at the seed vault had volunteered to be there except for the latest arrivals. Neither Brent nor any of Group Captain Christopher's crew had volunteered to stay at Svalbard. Brent had once thought about the idea but hadn't decided. Fate made the decision for all of them.

Group Captain Christopher and Brent found their height to be an annoying handicap. There were multiple locations in the seed vault where the height of the ceiling was only 180 centimetres. In a few places it was lower than that. Several of the new arrivals had rose coloured lumps on their foreheads as evidence. "Why are we the only ones", Brent asked? "Everyone else has been here a while. The problem will go away in a few months. Patience, mate." A majority of those who volunteered for Svalbard had previously served on missions involving isolation for long periods. Nearly three dozen had served on submarines that stayed submerged for up to six months at a time. Fourteen of these were women who were comfortable sharing close quarters and facilities with a mostly male crew aboard a submarine. Their reputations for adhering to miliary regulations preceded them. Nine also outranked 90% of the men at Svalbard.

Another failure of the second radio during the storm accentuated the isolation felt by everyone at the seed vault. They would be able to rob parts off the radios at Svalbard airport but that would have to wait until June. Attempting to reach the airfield in winter was simply too dangerous. The antenna had also fallen as Group Captain Christopher predicted. Five men had managed to get the antenna upright again. New anchors were drilled into the solid rock at its base. The wind turbines continued to operate even as wind speeds exceeded 50 knots. "They really know how to build them at Emu Downs", Group Captain Christopher remarked. The anchors for the wind turbines had been drilled over a meter into solid rock, a task that took nearly three weeks during a previous summer. There was one other thing everyone there had in common. No one at Svalbard left any family behind. Most had pictures of parents or siblings, even aunts and uncles – all deceased. Those who had lost children seemed to relish the isolation. Perhaps they believed they could escape their loss by falling off the edge of the earth.

"There's someone I want you to meet", Chris announced about two weeks after their arrival at Spitsbergen. He raised a hand, motioning to a fellow officer in a different uniform. Brent had noticed several different forms of dress in his short time there. As she approached, he also noticed her blonde hair in a bun and an extraordinarily attractive face wearing no makeup at all. "I'd like ya to meet Commander Stewart. Commander Stewart spent much of her career on nuclear boats including two six-month tours under the polar ice pack. Commander Stewart this is Flight Sergeant Thomas, one of the few people who seems to understand this moissanite thing that's causing so much trouble. "Very nice to meet you, sir", she replied with a smile. "Likewise", said Brent. "Is that an American or Canadian accent", she asked? "American." "Pilot?" "No, colourblind unfortunately." She nodded slowly. "Excuse me sir. I'm told there's a problem in Vault No. 3. Chris smiled and pointed down the entrance tunnel. "Please see to it, Commander." With a slight nod she disappeared down the tunnel.

Brent was staring at the wooden floorboards. "Ouch! Wonder what her third question would have been", he remarked? "Don't take it personal, mate", Chris replied. Brent nodded. "We have, excuse me, HAD this game in America called baseball." "I've heard of it", Chris replied with a nod. "In baseball if the batter gets three strikes he's out. I just got two strikes against me in less than a minute. The third strike was coming. I could feel it." Chris laughed. "Commander Stewart joined the Australian Navy right out of college. Her degree in mathematics is from University of Queensland, St. Lucia. When she joined the Navy, she used her mother's surname, Stewart. Her proper surname is Gibbs." Brent looked up suddenly. "You mean that's…" "Ya got it, mate. That's Gibbs' daughter. That information is 'Top Secret'. Nobody here knows. Both I and Flight Lieutenant Gibbs would appreciate it if ya didn't tell anyone." Brent nodded. "Understood." "One more thing. I would recommend against hitting on her. I don't need any more problems." "No sir", Brent replied.

Brent discovered quite a few people at Svalbard enjoyed a friendly game of chess. March and April offered little else to do. Playing against a live opponent was quite different from the chess program on his laptop. He managed to win a few games. Word got around quickly. Some declined to play him. The ones who would play won most of the time. "You learn a lot by playing a stronger opponent", said one fellow. Brent nodded politely. It didn't help his ego. His game did improve, however. The better his game the more people wanted to play him. "Curious game, chess", said Chris. "Happy to teach you", Brent replied.

Gamma Ten

Brent had decided on five books to include in the cargo being carried to Svalbard. All five were about the Victorian Era. They explained how things were done without machines, which weren't generally available back then. A possible exception was the steam engine. Not many individuals could afford one of those. Topics included not just gardening but many other skills including blacksmithing, sewing, hide tanning, smelting, carpentry and roof thatching, plumbing, and animal husbandry. There were also plans for building water wheels to drive flower mills, construction methods for erecting buildings, and a list of poisonous plants.

May 2057 brought warmer temperatures, occasionally climbing above freezing for a few hours each day. Longer days meant more opportunities to work outside. There was much to be done. Five of the eight outside structures needed repairs to their canvas exteriors. Interior insulation was also coming loose on four of them. Resecuring it required access to the outside of each building as well. Snow had to be shovelled from around the narrow wooden walkways that connected the outside structures to the vault entrance and to each other. Many areas outside these walkways were still difficult to traverse, being covered in snow up to one and half meters deep. There were ten pairs of snowshoes available at the seed vault. Experience had shown they were impractical when attempting to do work. They were useful when excursions outside the boundary of the compound were absolutely necessary.

Gamma Ten

It was early June when those at the seed vault were able to reach Svalbard airfield and cannibalize the radios for the parts they needed.

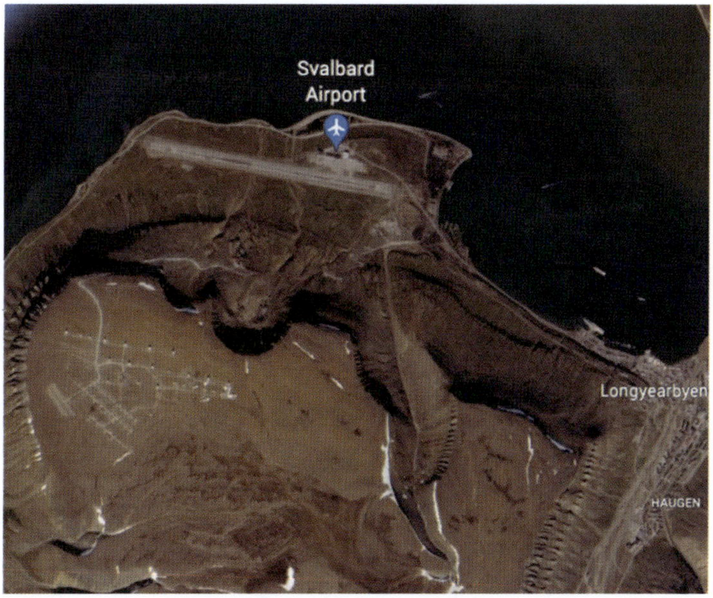

With both radios at the seed vault back in operation the highest priority was to get a status of surviving populations worldwide. A radio operator in Alaska confirmed nearly 1000 refugees were living with several Inuit groups. They appeared to be quite self-sufficient and didn't require help of any kind.

Group Captain Christopher was finally able to speak to a some of the RAAF personnel from Pearce who had settled in Kalgoorlie-Boulder. They had managed to find some needed parts and had one radio working again. Only a few people remembered how such things worked. There were no instructions or repair manuals for the radios or anything else electronic. For the past several decades none of that information was printed or supplied with the product. It was all online. Without the Internet there were no instructions or schematics for anything.

The population at Kalgoorlie-Boulder was estimated at 38,000. Other groups were believed to exist around the western third of the continent. The moissanite advance in western Australia seemed to have slowed significantly. Brent estimated any residual radioactivity in the moissanite had decayed to only 25%. The reports of it slowing made perfect sense. Brent requested information about Lydia, asking if she was at Kalgoorlie-Boulder. One of the RAAF aircraftmen reported seeing her and that she was alive and well.

"How much fuel is left at Pearce. Over", Chris asked? "Enough for two more missions to your area. Over." "One of those will have to be to Thule Airbase to refill the tanks there. Over", Chris replied. "That only leaves one flight to come get you lot. How many are there? Over." "Nearly 200. Over." "There's only one plane left at Pearce. It will take time to get it to Thule as a tanker, then get it back and reconfigured as a troop carrier. Looks like you're stuck up there for another year or so. Over." "Understood. We're not going anywhere. Over." Group Captain Christopher alerted those in Australia, Cairo and Johannesburg that there was no fuel at Thule. All agreed it was likely that large groups of refugees still existed in South America and Southern Africa, especially around Johannesburg and Cape Town. Their radios may have failed, or the batteries were dead. There might not be any electrical generating stations in operation there.

"Oxygen levels at the seed vault added to the difficult working conditions. Brent estimated oxygen levels might not fully recover for several decades, assuming there was regrowth of the plankton in the seas. Summer provided a brief window to assess the fish population in the Arctic around Spitsbergen. Several fishing parties reported larger catches compared to the previous summer. "Two data points don't a make a trend", Brent cautioned. The news was encouraging, however. Keeping the fish frozen wasn't a problem.

Chapter 21

It was mid-October 2057 when several members of Lydia's group arrived with startling news. About twenty kilometers north of Kalgoorlie-Boulder someone with the only radiation detector that still worked had measured radiation levels at the edge of the moissanite colony. Their readings were only a few percent above normal background. "Are you sure the detector was working", someone immediately asked? "Yes. They tested it with the source that came with it. It was working properly. But that isn't the best part. The moissanite has stopped moving. Last week someone placed a stick in the ground right in front of it. It's still there. The leading edge hasn't moved. Tiny green shoots are appearing where small cracks have formed in the moissanite. Stuff is growing up through the cracks!"

Workmen found they could fracture the moissanite into grey sand by pounding it with wooden mallets and other wooden tools where it was less than ten centimeters thick. The result looked like the material found on the beaches in Perth, Carnarvon and Geraldton. "It will take a lot of work, but we may be able to reclaim some of the land. Once we pound it down and mix it with the soil we can grow crops there with proper irrigation." "Maybe someone has a plough we could use", remarked an old man standing in the doorway. "Not if it's metal. Stuff's too abrasive. It'll destroy anything made of metal in no time. We must use wooden tools and do it the hard way." Hands went up across the crowd. Many were eager to get started.

Similar things were happening to the moissanite at a few locations in South Carolina, California and other locations around the world. There just was no one there to see it. ^{137}Cs and ^{90}Sr in the moissanite had decayed down to 25% - even less in some locations depending on the original source. Lydia recalled Professor Schareshiem having a theory about the long-term stability of the moissanite crystals. Because they replicated so rapidly in the presence of gamma radiation, they might also become unstable over some length of time in the absence of that radiation. He couldn't say how long. "It might be decades or even longer", he suggested. Nevertheless, the chemical bonds holding the crystals together might begin to fail if no radioactivity was present to keep them growing, however slowly. "A structure that forms so quickly can become unstable", he proposed. "'Quickly' was an ambiguous term, of course."

Lydia found physical work quite satisfying. It took a few months to get over the soreness but there was no monthly fee for use of the local gym. Insomnia was no longer a concern either. Neither was high blood pressure or high blood sugar levels. Lydia had 'forgotten' to bring her blood pressure machine, or her glucose test strips and meter. No doctors were available to advise her about such things in any case. There was a social aspect of physical outdoor work as well. In a few months' time she struggled to remember what it was like spending eight hours a day behind a desk with a computer screen and a phone to answer.

Those among the original Kalgoorlie-Boulder residents with 19th Century skills were in high demand. They were willing to teach others if they put in the work required. Learning on the job was mandatory. There were no spectators in this ad-hoc society. No one got a free ride. Some thought it communistic. Others insisted it was too democratic. Many thought it was as good or better than the way they lived before. It almost seemed as if all the government bureaucracy considered necessary over the past century was in fact quite unnecessary! "It will never last", said one lady in her sixties.

"Someone will take things over and make it all about them. Then the corruption will start. It always works out that way."

In time everyone in the 'new' Kalgoorlie-Boulder community began to accept the fact there was no Internet, no mobile phones, no news about what was happening anywhere else in the world, no Amazon online offering to deliver any item the world could produce, and no rapid or convenient transportation to 'somewhere else'. Lydia found it a rather peaceful lifestyle. "This must have been how it was in the 19th Century. It's so quiet. No cars or trains rushing by. No factories with loud machinery grinding away all the time. No planes flying overhead. No wonder everyone sleeps so well." "Don't you want things back the way they were", someone asked? "No", replied five people who had been quietly listening. One man couldn't resist the opportunity to disagree. Afterall his was the generation that would have to rebuild all that had been lost. "Do we really want to give up all the technological achievements of the last hundred years? Instead of putting fuel in our cars we're having to feed the horses and mules and other livestock. Isn't that a step backwards?" A gentleman with white hair and beard offered an answer. "Have you fed any of the livestock yourself", he asked? "No. Don't know anything about that", the younger man replied. "Then you'd better start learning. You'll be wanting to eat that pig you haven't fed long before Amazon is back online to deliver a fatted one to your door."

Lydia learned that Brent was at the Svalbard seed vault on Spitsbergen Island. She wondered if he and the others would make it back from the opposite side of the planet. It seemed almost impossible. The world was so much larger than it used to be. Having experienced a global consciousness via mobile phones, video calls and the Internet, Lydia realized the loneliness and isolation she felt at Kalgoorlie-Boulder was different from what those in the 19th Century experienced. They didn't miss what they never had. She lamented the lack of 21st Century technology, while being apprehensive about going back to it. If it was a simple matter of 'taking a bus back to the city', the anxiety she felt would have been trivial. Recreating 21st Century technology would require an extraordinary effort managed by huge bureaucracies spending enormous sums of money. How much more damage could the natural world withstand after barely surviving invasion by an alien material? How would organic life on earth react after being pushed to the precipice of extinction? Should the human species rethink its place on this planet and how we've treated it? Did it really matter what she thought? It wouldn't be up to her…

The mood at Svalbard was euphoric when they heard the news from Kalgoorlie-Boulder. Only a few had accepted the possibility they might be marooned there to starve in the icy wilderness. The rest remained in denial. "I like to think there's always hope", Flight Lieutenant Gibbs was fond of saying. Brent's chess game had improved so much he was getting compliments. Boredom continued to be a problem, especially during the long mouths of winter when the sun never seemed able to climb above the horizon for more than an hour or two. On a rare day when it wasn't snowing, either vertically or sideways, hunting parties were able to kill a few seals. Fishing would have to wait until summer. Attempting to reach the coast at Longyearbyen in winter was suicide even on a clear day. That blue sky could transform into a blizzard with five-meter visibility in less than an hour. It was still better than being on a Globemaster for three days. Flight Sergeant Thomas suddenly winced at the prospect. It was the only way for any of them to get home again.

Lydia picked up a wooden post more than a meter long and dropped it once again onto the edge of the moissanite, crushing it into fine granules. Another person working behind her would turn the soil over and mix the moissanite granules into it. She had reclaimed nearly 20 square meters that morning. They would do another 20 square meters before dark. Lydia had imagined better ways to spend her 59th birthday. Hundreds of others were doing the same, converting several acres per day back into fertile farmland. There were other groups like the one at Kalgoorlie-Boulder at other locations in Western Australia, all reclaiming land and digging irrigation ditches in the same manner. None were aware their efforts were being duplicated on other continents. The world was a very large place again, like in the 1500's. Progress was slow. It would take many years to reclaim enough land to support large populations like those that once thrived in major cities. It was a chance to start over. What would humanity make of it?

Lydia's shoulders and arms had become quite muscular. Her hands were rough and calloused. There was no longer any trace of the pale green nail polish she used to so carefully apply twice a week while sitting at her desk outside Professor Schareshiem's office waiting for the phone to ring. One day each week she taught the children how to tie poles together to support the beans when they sprouted, how to milk cows and goats, even the proper way to hold a sheep for shearing. When she was finished with that, she cooked an evening meal for fourteen. Perhaps this life was only a dream. Perhaps she would wake up suddenly with the Professor rapping his knuckles on her desk to get her attention. Strangely, she hoped not. She was happier in this world than she had ever been in the previous one.

"Flight Sergeant Thomas, there's a radio message for you, sir." The radio operator motioned for Brent to follow him into a partitioned area near the entrance to the tunnel in the seed vault. "Where are you? Over?" "You first. Over", Brent replied. "Johannesburg. Over." "End of the world. Over." "I suspected. This is Liza. I lost the dress when we had to leave the south of France. Still have the ring though. You still interested? Over." Brent sat down in the radio operator's chair. He took a deep breath and let it out slowly. "You still there? Over." "I wasn't sure you survived. Over." "Sailed from Marseille to Cape Town in January 2040. Long trip. How far is it from the 'end of the world' to Johannesburg? Over." "About thirty-eight hours, I think. Might be a year before I can make the trip though. Over."

"You've kept me waiting for twenty-five years. I suppose I can wait one more. Over." "Can you find another dress? Over." "No dressmakers here. I'll have to make it myself. Lots of bright colors. Maybe some beads and things. Is that OK? Over." "I'm sure it will be beautiful. Over." "You'll have to work on our farm, you know. Everybody works here. Farm's twenty kilometres west of Pretoria on the north shore of Hartbeespoort Reservoir. Part of the farm used to be a golf course. No one's played golf here for twenty years. Ploughed it all up to grow tomatoes, peppers, cumbers, beans, spinach, and sweet potatoes. Two hundred head of cattle. Some goats. Nearly two square kilometres, between the lake and Platinum Highway N4." Brent was shaking his head.

"Do you ride? Over", she asked? "Ride what? Over?" "A horse of course. It's about two days ride from the Johannesburg airstrip to our farm. We only make that trip about once a year. Over." "I suppose I could learn. Over." "Have to rough sleep the one night. Over." "No problem. Always wanted to be a farmer. Over." "Liar. Over." "You can teach me. Over." "Now there's a challenge… Over." "I'll let you know when I can travel. Over." "Radio the Johannesburg airfield when you have a date. There might not be anyone there to answer for several days so keep trying until you get through. I'll do my best to meet you on the day. Of course I might be busy that week… Over."

"This fellow's trying to get me off his radio. We'll set a date once I'm sure of things. Over." "You might have to remind me. Out." Flight Sergeant Thomas handed the mic back to the radio operator. As he stood up, he bumped his head on the beam above. "DAMN", he shouted, with a broad smile!

Printed in Great Britain
by Amazon

43884886R00149